Rachael English

The Night of
the Party

HACHETTE
BOOKS
IRELAND

First published in Ireland in 2018 by Hachette Books Ireland
First published in paperback in 2019

Cataloguing in Publication Data is available from the British Library.

ISBN 978 1 47365 378 8

Typeset in Garamond by www.redrattledesign.com
Printed and bound in Great Britain by Clays Ltd, Elcograf, S.p.A

Hachette Books Ireland policy is to use papers that are natural, renewable and
recyclable products and made from wood grown in sustainable forests. The logging
and manufacturing processes are expected to conform to the environmental
regulations of the country of origin.

Hachette Books Ireland
8 Castlecourt Centre
Castleknock
Dublin 15, Ireland

A division of Hachette UK Ltd.
Carmelite House
50 Victoria Embankment
London EC4Y 0DZ

www.hachettebooksireland.ie

For the Englishes,
a family of great storytellers

Part One

1982

Chapter I

County Clare, January 1982

They had never seen anything like it.

The first snowflakes arrived on Thursday afternoon. Before long, the flurries blurred into a steady fall, the snow folding itself around Kilmitten until everything was white. People took to the streets, beaming at the wonder of it all. 'Look at that sky,' they said. 'It's not finished yet, you know.' Children shrieked with delight, and adults turned into children. Snowballs went zinging through the air, while kids on makeshift sleds – here a coal sack, there a tea tray – zoomed down Toomey's Hill.

By Friday morning, the entire country was covered. On the radio, the newsreader warned against unnecessary journeys. Dublin was at a standstill, he said, and Wicklow was cut off.

Best of all, there was no school.

Tom Crossan sat at the kitchen table, swirling a spoon around his Ready Brek and listening to his parents have one of those conversations that was actually two separate speeches.

'I still say we're making a mistake,' said his mam. 'Nobody's going to come out in this weather. We'll be wasting good money on food and drink.'

'The front room looks like something out of a tenement,' said his dad. 'Could you not dry those clothes elsewhere?'

'You'd swear we had money to waste.'

'Why don't you bring them in here?'

'And have you seen the state of the roads? Seriously, if you think I'm driving into Templemorris, you'd want to think again. I could end up in a ditch. I suppose I'll have to buy the drink locally, and you know how much that costs.'

'It's a shame we had to take down the Christmas decorations. They brightened the place up. Could we string up a few lights, do you think?'

Tom zoned out. For as long as he could remember (which was eight years' worth of memories – he couldn't recall much before the age of four), his parents had held a party in early January. It's such a miserable month, they'd say. People need cheering up. He'd worried that this year the weather would put them off. He should have known better. The snow could be roof-high, and still his dad wouldn't cancel a get-together. He liked to boast that no one was turned away from his house: no matter how snooty, no matter how hard-up, everyone was welcome.

Tom had heard that there were places where people went an entire year without clogging up each other's houses, where there were no rowdy gatherings of red-faced men and overly perfumed women, no card games in the kitchen or ballad-singing in the front room, no morning-after gossip.

What a pain that would be. Everybody in Kilmitten liked a party, and while their parents were busy making fools of themselves, the village's youngsters got to experience some freedom. Tonight, Tom planned on making the most of it.

'You're quiet, Tommo,' said his dad, as he poked a knife at the concrete-hard butter. 'Are you not looking forward to a day in the white stuff?'

'I'm going to call up to Conor in a second.'

'Well, be careful not to fall over or do anything stupid,' said his mam, who was an expert in things going wrong. 'And don't forget I'll want you back here good and early. There'll be work to do. Oh, and eat up that breakfast, would you?'

Tom returned to his cereal. His mother was always baffled when teachers complained about him being too talkative. 'There's barely a word out of him at home,' she'd say. 'I can't imagine what he goes on about at school.' What she didn't understand was that, for most of Tom's life, there hadn't been any space for talking. If his sisters and their friends weren't yap-yap-yapping at each other, his parents were arguing or storytelling. Now that his sisters were gone, there were more opportunities for him to have his say, but what was the point in speaking when nobody listened?

'Ah, Cora,' said his dad. 'Don't spoil the lad's fun. Sure how often do we get a fall of snow like this?'

'Don't "Ah, Cora" me, Haulie. The last thing I need is a child with a broken leg or a head full of stitches.' She rose from her chair and began piling dishes into the sink. 'Anyway, shouldn't you be getting off to work?'

'I can't see there being much business today.' He leaned back and smiled. 'Throw us on another piece of toast there, pet.'

'Throw it on yourself. And if you're not going down to the pumps, you can wash these cups.' She patted her cloud of red hair. 'I've a hairdresser to see.'

There was chaos on Toomey's Hill with everybody skittering around at different speeds. One of the O'Grady brothers was shoving fistfuls of snow down the back of the girls' coats, or at least he was until Liesl Talty (her mam was obsessed with *The Sound of Music*) gave him a slap across the face. Tom was impressed. He wouldn't dare hit an O'Grady. Two other brothers whizzed past on election posters belonging to their uncle Paddy, who represented the county in Dublin. Majella Sexton slid by on a wooden pallet. A fourth O'Grady said she'd get splinters in her backside but he'd help her to remove them. Majella told him he'd never get that lucky. Some of the little kids from the new houses near the creamery were building a monster of a snowman. In the middle of it all, a stray dog ran around in circles, barking like he might have rabies.

Toomey's wasn't much of a hill, but it was the best Kilmitten had to offer. For miles around, the land was flat. Great farming land, the adults said. They also said there was no money in farming, these days, and that soon enough everybody would be living in Dublin or London. Or New York, like Tom's sisters.

Tom and Conor's progress had been slow. Conor had insisted on stopping every few steps and sticking out his tongue until a snowflake settled there. Tom's best friend was a long skinnymalinks of a fellow with grey eyes and sandy hair. At the front, one bright red tuft stood up, as though it belonged on someone else's head. Almost everybody liked Conor, but even if they didn't, they had to be nice because his mother was dead. His father, Flan Varley, was the local sergeant. Tom's dad maintained that this was the easiest job in Ireland: the last time there'd been a proper crime in the village, Queen Victoria had been in charge.

On Main Street, they'd passed Father Galvin, who was wearing a huge furry hat, like a Russian on the TV news. 'Morning, boys,' he'd called. 'How's the day off school treating you?'

'Great, Father,' said Tom. 'Did you get a day off Mass as well?'

Conor gave him a look that suggested this was a dumb question, but Father Galvin laughed. 'That's a good one,' he replied. 'No, I'm afraid the Lord's work has got to continue. I'll be seeing you later, though. I hope your mam's not going to too much trouble.'

Father Galvin always came to the Crossans' parties and he always brought the same gift: a bag of Lucky Numbers and a box of Maltesers. He liked to drink a small Paddy with a dash of water and no ice. (Tom tried to remember everybody's favourite drink. This made it more likely that they'd slip him fifty pence – or even a pound.) As priests went, Father Galvin was okay. His Masses were short, and he handed out hardly any penance, just a Hail Mary or two and a warning to behave yourself in future. The year before, there'd been a visiting mission and the priest had given Tom two decades of the rosary. Two decades! Tom wouldn't have minded but he hadn't confessed all of his sins. He'd left out the part about looking at his dad's dirty magazines.

The two might have stayed talking to the priest, only they saw Noel O'Grady coming. Father of the dreaded brothers, Mr O'Grady was a total bore. Tom's dad said he always looked like he was one fried breakfast away from a heart attack.

They were at the top of the hill, laying out the fertiliser bag they'd taken from Conor's shed, when a familiar voice rose up behind them.

'Are we still on for tonight, boys?'

It was Tess Fortune, smothered in a massive grey overcoat, a pink woolly hat pulled low over her green eyes. Tess was even thinner than Conor, so thin that one of the lads at school had called her a Cambodian. Without missing a beat, she'd given him a dirty look and said, 'It's Kampuchea now, you ignoramus.' Tess was tough. She had to be. She had no dad, and people gossiped about her mam, saying she spent too much time in Pilkington's Lounge. Her mam was younger than most parents. Oh, and she was beautiful. Not as beautiful, mind, as Tess's best friend, Nina Minogue, who was the best-looking girl in Kilmitten.

'Yep, we're definitely on,' said Tom, as he glanced around for Nina. No sign. What if she didn't like the snow and decided to stay at home tonight? He'd bet his life that the Minogues' house was good and warm. He couldn't imagine Nina seeing her breath when she got up in the morning or having to wipe the ice from the bedroom window with the sleeve of her pyjamas. Nina's father was a doctor, so he probably knew all about the importance of central heating. Of course, the Minogues were loaded, which must help with heating and such.

'You will be able to get away, won't you?' continued Tess. 'I mean, won't your mam and dad want you to take people's coats and fetch drinks and that?'

She was wearing long silvery earrings and the reflection from the snow made it look like they were shimmering and dancing against her face. She had a really small face.

'It'll be fine,' said Tom, with a wave of one hand. He wished he'd taken off his gloves. You wouldn't catch the O'Gradys wearing gloves. Gloves were soft. 'I'll have to hang around for a while. But once they've had a couple of drinks, I'll be able to escape. Don't worry.'

'And I'll get out the window, no bother,' said Conor, digging his hands deep into the pockets of his Christmas anorak. It was a genuine Lord Anthony with thick grey fur around the hood, not an imitation, like Tom's.

'Cool,' said Tess, as she twirled away. 'I guess I'll see you then.'

'And—'

She turned back, a grin splitting her face. 'Don't panic, Tom. Nina's coming too.'

*

The Crossans' house was big. Big and ugly, according to Tom's mother, who was always talking about selling up and getting a nice modern bungalow with fitted wardrobes and wall-to-wall carpet. Tom's dad had spent all his life in the grey detached house and wouldn't hear of moving. If you were being kind, you might describe it as in need of some work. If you were being honest, you'd say it was dilapidated. Tom didn't care. True, the ceilings sagged, water streamed down the walls and wind whistled through the windows. True, there were so many rooms that as soon as one was fixed up, another was calling out for repair. But how many people were lucky enough to live in a house where it was possible to hide? Where you could dodge interfering parents and annoying sisters for hours on end?

The back garden, too, was untamed. For large parts of the year, the grass came up to Tom's waist. If he lay on the ground, no one could see him. Every now and then, his dad would be overcome by a fit of busyness, and they'd all have to go out the back and hack down the grass and weeds and briars. When they'd finished, his dad would hold out his arms and say, 'Isn't it a fine old place all the same?' In no time, the garden would be as wild as ever.

At the bottom, beside the hedge, there was a wooden shed packed with years – no, *decades* – of rubbish. Tins of paint jostled for space with damp rolls of carpet and prehistoric tools. It smelt of creosote and mould. That was where Tom and Conor were now, sitting on two overturned tea chests, their only light provided by an old torch. Their shadows looped and flickered against the walls, making the shed feel like the opening of *Tales of the Unexpected*. Two brown bottles of Harp stood on the floor. Tom's pockets held three John Player Blue, a box of matches and a bottle-opener.

'Maybe they're not going to come after all,' said Conor.

'They'll be here,' Tom reassured him, although his knees were doing a nervous jiggle. He, too, was starting to have doubts. Tess's mam and Nina's parents were at the party, and both girls should have been able to escape. So why weren't they here? Come to think of it, what had he been doing, inviting them over for a drink and a smoke? They probably got scores of invitations. There was every chance that at this very minute they were somewhere else, having a laugh at him.

Despite the snow, almost everybody on his parents' invitation list had turned up. A few who weren't on the list had arrived too. Before the doorbell began to ring, Tom's father, who'd put on his multi-coloured sports jacket, had got into a tizzy about the house being too cold. He'd made Tom place two pages of *The Irish Field* in front of the fireplace until the flames roared up the chimney. 'Will you stop that, Haulie?' his mother had said. 'You'll set the chimney on fire, and then what'll we do?'

'We'll enjoy the heat, that's what,' he'd replied.

Tom's mother, who was wearing her best blue dress, the one with fake diamonds on the belt, laughed. This made him suspect that she'd already started on the Cinzano.

It was that kind of night. To begin with, there was the usual phoney politeness. 'Just a small G&T for me, Cora. I had far too much over the Christmas,' and 'Go easy with that brandy, Haulie. I've milking in the morning.' As the numbers multiplied, Tom was called into action, filling drinks, finding ashtrays and carrying extra chairs from the back kitchen. He handed around sandwiches, cocktail sausages and little pieces of cheese on sticks. The noise rose from a low mumble to a babble to an all-out roar, like a class with no teacher. Party-goers asked Tom about the snow, what he'd got for Christmas and how he was getting on at secondary school. Then they asked if he had a girlfriend. Finally, they forgot he was there at all. For a short while, he listened in, in case he might learn something important. One woman had the big C, apparently. 'Riddled with it,' according to Mercedes Talty. Somebody else was in the family way ('and not a boyfriend in sight') while another neighbour was 'inside, drying out'. Noel O'Grady told a story about New Year's night when he'd driven home from Pilkington's with a hand over one eye to stop himself seeing double.

'You'll know all about it if Flan Varley catches you,' said Tom's dad. 'The guards are taking the drink-driving very seriously, these days.'

'Leave Flan to me,' replied Mr O'Grady, in a way that suggested he had few worries about the law.

Conor's father was beside the window with Tess's mother and Father Galvin. What they found to talk about, Tom didn't know. Save for the fact that all three were on their own, they didn't have much in common. He wondered if Mr Varley would ever find a new wife. Not that he'd say it to Conor. Even though he rarely mentioned her, it was obvious that Conor missed his mother. One day in religion, Miss Casey had been boring on about what happens when someone dies, and Conor had turned the colour of watery rice pudding, then barged out of the room. Seánie O'Grady said Conor was acting like a poof, but Seánie was a moron who stuck out his tongue when he read, so nobody took any notice of him.

When Tess and Nina did arrive, it was with a rat-tat-tat on the door, a burst of freezing air and a rush of apologies. Nina said it was her fault they were late. Her parents had hired a babysitter for her younger brother, and the sitter had insisted on watching Nina too.

'I hope you haven't started without us,' said Tess, who was still wearing the gigantic grey coat. Her pink hat had been replaced with something that could have doubled as a tea cosy. Perhaps it *was* a tea cosy. There were snowflakes in Nina's long chocolaty hair and on the shoulders of her duffel coat. Tom had to stop himself brushing them away. She looked like she belonged in *Dr Zhivago* or one of those films that made his mam cry.

'We're only here five minutes ourselves,' he lied. 'There's a seat over there for you.' He pointed towards a mildewed two-seater sofa he'd covered with sacks.

'Do you hang out here all the time?' asked Nina, as they sat down.

'Yes,' said Tom.

'No,' said Conor, their answers colliding.

'What are the pair of you like?' said Tess, pulling off her tea cosy. She looked around. 'It's a bit of a kip, isn't it?'

'I think it's fab,' said Nina. 'If I had a place like this at home, I wouldn't ever want to leave.'

It turned out that Tess was the most experienced smoker. While Tom had had the occasional puff, he wasn't sure he could inhale. Conor was a wheezing amateur, and Nina wasn't much better. But Tess was a pro. Not only did she inhale, she knew how to blow actual smoke rings.

'I take my mam's smokes all the time,' she said, in her most casual voice. 'Believe it or not, she never seems to notice.'

Smoking, it turned out, came with a rule book. Tess took charge, showing them how to light one cigarette from the butt of another and instructing them not to slobber on the filter. This was known as a 'duck's arse' and was a very bad thing. She also knew the best way to remove the smell from your breath. Silvermints were handy, but a handful of grass was better. 'Just chew it,' she said, with an earnest nod.

'Like a cow?' asked Conor.

'Like a cow.'

Drinking beer was a lot simpler, but no matter how often Tom tried – and he often stole sips from his dad's glass – he couldn't get used to it. Why couldn't the beer people make it taste better? Still, it warmed you up and made words easier to find.

Tom didn't know what to talk about. Most of his girl conversations had been with his sisters or with the girls in his class at school. Those chats were simple: 'Isn't Mr Lillis a complete tool?' somebody would ask, or 'Do you think Miss McBride is having it off with Mr Noonan?' Luckily, as they passed around the first bottle, Tess did most of the talking. She nattered on about the snow and about school and about who was rumoured to be getting off with whom. Tom,

Conor and Tess went to St Ursula's in nearby Templemorris. Nina was at boarding school. She didn't say much, but Tom could tell she didn't like it. You had to queue for your meals, and when you got your food, it was cold or horrible or both. Some of the girls were right bitches, who teased Nina for sounding like a culchie. This was stupid because she had the nicest voice in Kilmitten – she could have read the news or anything. Tom was surprised to realise he'd said this out loud. Conor laughed, and Tess went, 'Woooh', but Nina smiled and her brown eyes crinkled, like she was genuinely grateful.

During their second bottle of beer, which tasted much better than the first, they talked about music and how sad it was that people bought records by Shakin' Stevens and Bucks Fizz when there were lots of brilliant groups like The Human League and The Jam. They agreed that this was a great time for music and that the old bands, like The Beatles, sounded very basic now.

'Primitive,' said Tess, and they all nodded.

They skipped onto a discussion about the challenges of being a teenager.

'Did you ever notice,' said Tess, 'that we're always either too old or too young?'

'Oh, yeah,' agreed Nina. 'Those are my dad's favourite words. One minute I'm too young for stuff, like getting my ears pierced or wearing lip gloss. Then, five minutes later, he's all, "Stop fighting with your brother. You're too old for that now." Honestly, it's such a drag.'

To Tom's relief, the girls seemed to have forgotten that he

wouldn't be thirteen until March. At one point, he worried Conor was about to say something. He sent his fiercest look in his friend's direction. The last thing he wanted was Nina dismissing him as a kid.

He was telling them about the gossip he'd picked up at the party when the beer ran out.

'It's a shame we don't have another bottle,' said Nina.

'There's no chance you could get one more, is there?' asked Tess.

Tom didn't want them to go. Not yet. He glanced from one to the other, at Tess's 'Go on, I dare you' face and Nina's look of expectation. Luckily, his parents stored most of the party drink, and all the food, in the back kitchen, which wasn't really a kitchen at all, just a ramshackle room at the rear of the house. Even better, the room had a door that led directly onto the garden. That was how he'd got out. By now, the party-goers would be drunk. If he was careful, nobody would spot him.

'I'd better go up and get another one, so.'

'Yay,' said Tess, rubbing her palms together. 'Now we're talking. Do you want me to come with you?'

'Nope, it's better if I go on my own. I'll see you in a tick.'

Tom moved slowly up the path. Sometimes he squelched; sometimes he slithered; mostly he sank. What he needed was a pair of those snowshoes they wore in the films, the ones that looked like tennis racquets for your feet. Around him the snow continued to fall. The air was clean as peppermint. He thought of his parents. They would assume he'd slunk off to bed, but in the morning, they might notice the footsteps between the shed and the house. He'd have to come up with a story. As he edged closer, he heard a dull thump. They were playing music, old-timer records from the sixties and seventies. That was good. It meant there was less chance of somebody hearing him. He'd sneak in, take a bottle, no, two bottles, and sneak out again.

As he reached the corner of the building, a lightheaded feeling came over him, an enjoyable sort of lightheaded, like speeding over a humpback bridge. The door was inches away now. The light was on, but that made sense: people had to go in and fetch more drink or sandwiches. He peeped in and, through the snowflakes, saw what looked like a familiar figure leaving the room. Well, it was only a blur, really. All the same, he decided to stay out of sight for another few seconds. Only then did it occur to him that his parents might have locked the door. He counted to twenty before pressing down on the handle and giving a gentle push. He was in luck.

Almost immediately Tom saw the leg. It was sticking out as though whoever it belonged to was having a sleep on the floor. He gave another tiny push. There was a second leg. Of course there was a second leg. *Jesus*, thought Tom, *am I drunk? Am I seeing things that aren't there?* The owner of the legs was slumped against a cupboard. Finally, he saw the head. He couldn't see the face, but that didn't matter. He knew the black curly hair. He'd know it anywhere. It was Father Galvin. The priest's head lolled, as if he wasn't just asleep. As if he was hurt or worse. *Oh, hell.* There was definitely something wrong. What had happened to Father Galvin? Tom didn't want to see any more. Quickly, he pulled the door shut and, falling over himself like the maddest drunk ever, scrambled to the side of the house and leaned against the wall. Salty liquid climbed up his throat. He swallowed.

Father Galvin. There was an odd sound in Tom's head, like being underwater in the swimming pool. He breathed in. And again. And again. The gulps of cold air hit his lungs and made his chest hurt. The person he'd seen leaving the room, surely they'd gone for help. That must be it. They'd gone to fetch somebody else. *Shit.* When they came back, they'd spot him. He didn't want his folks to see him. Out here. Half jarred. In search of more beer. With Conor and the two girls in the shed and Father Galvin on the floor.

He took another breath and told himself to calm down. As long as neither his mam nor his dad went upstairs to check on him, he'd be okay. He'd have to get back into the house later but he'd wait until the fuss – there was bound to be fuss – had died down. In the meantime, he'd return to the others. He wouldn't tell them what he'd seen. There'd be too many questions; questions he couldn't answer. They'd all want to know what Father Galvin looked like, and the girls might get upset. No, he'd say the door was locked and leave it at that.

First, he needed to stop shaking.

Chapter 2

Tess took a couple of minutes to adjust to the light. It glittered through the curtains, as if this was high summer rather than the depths of January. Then she remembered the snow. The snow made everything shine. She stretched out her legs until her feet reached the bottom of the bed. The sheets were freezing. Quickly, she curled back into a comma and thought about the night before.

Although she hadn't been sure about hanging out with Tom and Conor, especially in a poxy old shed, she'd ended up enjoying herself. They weren't the most popular guys at school but they weren't the saddest either. You wouldn't be embarrassed to say you'd had a drink and a smoke with them. Tess and Conor were two of a kind. Both had only one parent. The difference was, Conor remembered his mam. He'd been ten when the cancer took her away. Tess had never had a father. Or, to be more accurate, she'd never known him. He'd run away before she was born. When she asked about him, her mam waved her hands and said he wasn't worth thinking about.

She'd expected that Tom and Conor would want to play spin the bottle or some such, but when the beer ran out and Tom couldn't get any more, he'd said they should head home. 'You don't want to get grief from your folks,' he'd argued. They'd hidden the empty bottles at the back of the shed and buried the cigarette butts in the snow. The boys had insisted on walking with them, which was sweet, if unnecessary. This was Kilmitten where nothing ever happened.

In her head, Tess had an alternative life where she was from somewhere far more exciting, a place where nobody gave a hoot how many parents she had. In this fantasy land, her mam had a large detached house, not a two-up two-down in a crumbling terrace. They never ran out of money before payday. They never had to eat cheese on crackers for dinner or share bathwater or wear ratty clothes. Tess always groaned when adults claimed that money wasn't important. *Oh, yeah?* she'd think. *Believe me, if you don't have any, it's very important.*

All evening, she'd noticed Tom throwing gooey-eyed looks at Nina. Then again, everybody loved Nina: boys, parents . . . even teachers were mad about her. Tess and Nina had been friends since second class when their teacher had told them to share a desk. Mrs Nagle must have figured they wouldn't have much to say to each other. Oh, the innocence of that poor teacher! Before the end of the day, they were giggling like eight-year-old maniacs. They discovered that they liked the same cartoons (*Yogi Bear* and *Scooby-Doo*), the same comics (*Tammy* and *Bunty*) and the same sweets (the three-for-a-penny chews that welded your teeth together). When Nina was sent to boarding school, Tess worried that she'd fall in with the pony-owning types and ignore her old friends. She was wrong. Nina said her new school was a dump and she wished she could go to St Ursula's with everybody else. Tess thought she was crazy. She would happily have taken her chances at the posh school.

There was another reason she valued Nina's friendship. It didn't matter how cheap Tess's clothes were or how loopy her mam could be, being tight with Nina gave her a special pass. It was like people said, 'Well, if she's good enough for the doctor's daughter, she must be okay.' Of course, Tess never came out and said this. She didn't want Nina thinking she was a user.

From downstairs, she heard voices. Strange. Although her watch was out of reach, she thought it was fairly early. She could hear her mother and at least two other women: her friends, Mags and Mercedes. In Tess's view, Mags and Mercedes were a pair of witches, as likely to gossip about her mam as with her. So far, she'd managed to stop herself saying this out loud.

Mags had a rasp of a voice, like she'd starting chain-smoking in her cot, and it powered above the others. Even so, Tess could make out only the occasional word. She caught 'gardaí', 'fright', 'panic' and 'upside-down'. What her mam and Mercedes said in return, she didn't know. One thing was obvious: this was no time to be hanging about in bed. She peeled back the covers and hopped around in search of something to wear. Glad for once that she didn't need a bra, she pulled her jeans and red sweatshirt over her pyjamas.

Then she took her fisherman's socks from the drawer, ran a hand through her pale brown hair and wound a scarf around her neck. The morning was too cold for vanity.

Tess's mother, Ginny, was sitting at the kitchen table with Mags and Mercedes. In front of them were a pot of tea, three mugs, a plate of toast crusts and an overflowing ashtray. Once upon a time, somebody had told Tess's mam that in the right light she was Kilmitten's answer to Debbie Harry. Maybe this was true, but just then she looked crumpled, the remains of her party make-up clinging to her face, her blonde hair all mussed up.

'You're up and about early,' said Tess.

'Is it any surprise?' replied Mercedes.

Tess's mam intervened with a stare that said, *I'll handle this*. 'There's been some bad news, love. Get yourself a bowl of cereal and you can sit down and join us.'

All the bowls were in the sink, so Tess poured Rice Krispies into a mug and splashed on some milk. 'What do you mean "bad news"?'

Her mam pulled on her cigarette before replying. 'It's Father Galvin.'

'What about him?'

'He's dead,' said Mercedes, subtle as a steamroller.

'Like in an accident or something?'

'Not quite,' said her mother. 'Leave this to me, Mercedes, will you?'

'It's almost ten o'clock,' rasped Mags. 'We'd better get the news. Switch on the radio there, Tess, like a good girl.'

Tess was confused but did as she was told. As soon as the

transistor crackled to life, the news music rang out and a man with a rumbly voice began speaking about Kilmitten: 'Gardaí are treating as suspicious the death of a priest in County Clare. The priest, Father Leo Galvin, had been attending a party in the village of Kilmitten in the east of the county. From there, our Mid-Western correspondent, Séamus Toland reports . . .'

'Holy macaroni,' said Tess.

'Shush,' said Mags.

'An ambulance was called to the house on the edge of Kilmitten late last night following the discovery of the parish priest's body. Along with at least fifty other guests, Father Leo Galvin had been attending a party at the home of Haulie and Cora Crossan. Gardaí were quickly at the scene. Indeed, I understand the local sergeant was among those at the gathering. While officers initially believed this may have been a tragic accident, sources now say there are reasons to suspect that foul play was involved.'

'What reasons?' said Mercedes.

'Shush,' repeated Mags. 'We're missing it.'

'. . . has been sealed off pending a forensic examination. Originally from north Clare, Father Galvin had been based in this small village for fifteen years. Shocked locals described him as a popular and decent man. One woman, Lourda Ryan, said the tight-knit community was devastated. Mrs Ryan, who was at the party, said she was still coming to terms with Father Galvin's death. "We're not safe in our beds any more," she added.'

'Ah, please,' said Mercedes. 'What would—'

'I won't warn you again,' said Mags, giving her friend a sour look.

' . . . Catholic bishop, Dr Edward Clohessy, said he was numbed by the tragedy and asked why anybody would kill a man of God. He urged people to pray for Father Galvin. The state pathologist is due to examine the body. However, it's understood the snow has hampered his journey and it may be this afternoon before he reaches Kilmitten. Gardaí say they are following a number of lines of inquiry, but have appealed to anyone with information to come forward. They can be contacted on . . .'

Mercedes had heard enough. 'What I was trying to say was, imagine asking Lourda Ryan about anything. The woman's half simple.'

'Ah, Mercedes,' said Tess's mam. 'Would you let it rest? She was trying to help.'

'Don't get uppity on me, Ginny. I'm only saying what everyone else will be thinking.' She lit another cigarette.

'I'd say Lourda's upset,' added Mags. 'Everybody knows she was sweet on Father Galvin.'

Mercedes spluttered out a plume of smoke. 'You can't go around the village saying that. Then again, if I was married to Johnny Ryan, my eye would wander too.'

Tess's head was churning. *Woah*, she wanted to say, *it can't be true*. Father Galvin was killed at the party, when all the while she'd been in the shed, drinking and smoking and talking about bands? Should she have seen something? Should she have heard something? What about the others? Had they seen anything? She wondered how she'd find out.

Beside her, the newsreader was rumbling on about the snow. She switched off the radio and sat down, a move that seemed to remind the others of her presence.

Her mam reached over and squeezed her hand. 'Are you all right, Tessy? I didn't mean for you to hear the news like that.'

'Why didn't you tell me last night when you came in from the party?'

'It was very late, so I thought I'd leave you be. There was an awful commotion up in the house, and Cora was in a desperate state. We all were. But Cora . . . she found the body. The poor woman, she was hysterical. She screamed until Emmet Minogue heard her. There was pandemonium after that.'

Tess noticed that her mother's words were hesitant, like she was more shocked than she was letting on. 'But whoever killed Father Galvin is still out there.'

'Chances are he's long gone. Don't worry about that.'

'Mind you,' said Mercedes, 'whoever did it might have been at the party.'

'What gives you that idea?' said Mags. 'I'd bet the house on it being a tramp or a criminal down from Dublin. Isn't that what usually happens?'

'It doesn't make any sense. Why would a criminal from Dublin kill Leo Galvin?'

'Because Father Galvin, the Lord have mercy on him, must have disturbed the fellow while he was trying to rob the place.' Mags put on a special tone, like the one teachers used with kids who couldn't read properly.

Fresh thoughts whirred around Tess's head. Had Tom gone to bed by the time the cops arrived, or had he been caught up in the mayhem? Now that she thought about it, he'd probably had to leave. The guards wouldn't allow people to sleep in the same place as a dead body, would they? If the house had a telephone, she'd call Nina. Nina would know what was happening. But Tess's mother thought phones were an expensive nuisance. 'Answer me this,' she'd say, 'who'd be ringing here?'

'Friends?' Tess would offer.

'No,' her mam would say. 'All we'd get would be bad news and people wanting something.'

Mags continued her speech about the dangers posed by Dubliners. Tess reckoned she was enjoying herself. Mercedes, too, had an excessively shiny look about her. Alone among them, her mam appeared . . . well, upset might be stretching it, but she did have the decency to look shaken.

'Will the guards be calling here?' Tess asked.

'I'll have to give a statement,' said her mam, 'either to Flan Varley or to another chap. We all will.'

'The place is crawling with guards,' chipped in Mags. 'And no doubt there'd be even more if it wasn't for the snow.'

'To be fair,' said Mercedes, 'it is a big deal. I mean, people don't kill priests. It just doesn't happen.'

'There are lots of things happening now that never happened before.'

'I'm off out,' said Tess, rising from the table.

Her mother pulled a cigarette from the box. 'Where are you going?'

'I've people to see.'

Usually, Tess bombed around the village on her bicycle, but the snow made this impossible. There was another snag: her legs had grown too long for her bike. She hoped she'd stop growing soon. Not that she wanted to be a midget, but she didn't like being a freak either. Normal would be good.

Although the snow was no longer falling, the sky suggested it would start again soon. The streets were quiet, a special sort of quiet as if everybody had been warned to stay indoors. Perhaps they had. Perhaps she was the only person who hadn't been given the message.

A meaty-looking guard, his face blotchy from the cold, was standing at the gate to Tom's house. For a moment, they stared at each other.

'What is it you want?' he said eventually.

'Is Tom about?'

On the other side of the gate, Tess could see more policemen. One was wearing a white suit, like a gangly snowman. In front of the house, there were two squad cars.

'You'll get nobody here today,' replied the guard. 'Why don't you run along before you get in the way?'

Tess was tempted to point out that running was almost impossible in the snow but thought better of it. 'Do you know where Tom is?'

'I'm afraid I'm not at liberty to divulge his whereabouts.'

She considered his words. Sometimes when an adult

used a funny word Tess went to the school library and took down the dictionary. She'd looked up *paranoid*, *inebriated*, *heterosexual* and *repressed*. With the policeman, it wasn't that she didn't understand his words, more that they sounded silly, like he didn't want her to understand.

'Tom's not in the station, is he?' she asked. 'With Sergeant Varley and all the others?'

'No, but you'll be in trouble yourself if you don't get moving.'

Even though Tess didn't think this was likely, she decided not to take the risk. She crunched on towards Conor's house. The Varleys lived in Kennedy Crescent, in a bungalow with a teak door and white blinds. She was trying to figure out what she'd say if somebody other than Conor answered that door, when she heard a shout.

It was Tom and Conor, dragging their empty fertiliser bag behind them.

'You've heard the news?' said Tom.

Tess pulled at her hair. 'Mam told me. Were you there?'

'No,' said Tom. 'After we left you, I went round to Conor's house. His sister and her boyfriend were in the front room, so we climbed in the bedroom window.'

'I didn't want Paula to see us,' continued Conor, 'because she'd tell Dad I'd been out. We were talking, and then the phone rang. We thought that was strange because it was really late. But that sometimes happens in our house.'

Tess nodded. 'Because of your dad's job.'

'Mmm. Anyway, it was my dad on the phone, and he wanted to know if Tom was with me, and when I said he was, he didn't give out or anything; he just said, "Thank Christ," and told us not to go anywhere and to put Paula back on the phone.'

'So then Paula had this conversation with her dad,' added Tom, 'and she was going, "You're not serious" and "What'll I tell the boys?"'

'And then she told us,' said Conor.

'We had to go around checking the doors and windows in case anybody tried to break in. I wanted to see my mam and dad, but I wasn't allowed.' Tom hesitated, and Tess thought he might cry. 'They came over to Conor's house this morning. I thought they'd be worked up because I'd gone missing. Normally, Mam would eat the face off me, but she didn't.'

'She kept hugging him,' said Conor. 'They both did.'

Tom wriggled his shoulders, like he wished Conor hadn't said that part.

'Your poor folks,' said Tess. She noticed that the fertiliser bag was flapping down the street. 'Will I . . .'

'No, I'll get it,' said Tom. 'We're not in the mood for the hill, but Conor's sister said we had to go out.'

When Tom turned his back, Tess rounded her eyes at Conor.

'No,' he whispered. 'Nobody has a clue we were in the shed.'

'Good,' she whispered back. 'We'll keep it like that, so. There's no point in making trouble for ourselves. I'd better have a word with Nina.' She watched Tom trudging back up the street, his dark fringe flopping in his brown eyes, his shoulders drooping, like he was carrying a full bag of coal rather than an empty sack. 'Do you want to come with me?' she said.

Nina lived on the other side of the village. Although her house wasn't quite as big as Tom's, it was in far better shape. Her father's surgery was in a separate red-brick building to the side. As they walked, the snow returned, whirling and dancing around them, making it hard to see more than a few inches ahead. This was good. Tess didn't know how the Minogues would feel about all of them arriving on the doorstep. In this weather, though, nobody would turn them away. She told Tom and Conor about hearing the report on the radio. Conor said the radio guy had gone to the garda station. Other journalists were there too. From what he could gather, Father Galvin had died from a bang to the head. More than that, nobody would say.

'You'd swear we were kids,' he added.

For most of their walk, Tom said nothing. This was unusual, and Tess didn't know how to deal with the situation. She ended up chattering about what Mags and Mercedes had said. They passed the Crossans' petrol station, but it was closed.

Nina's mother answered the door, and if she was surprised to see them all, it didn't show. 'Come in out of that snow,' she said. 'You must be frozen.' Then she ran a hand through her hair. 'You'll have to forgive the state of me. I'm a little frazzled today.'

To Tess, Helen Minogue looked as beautiful as ever. She always wore the kind of plain clothes that cost an absolute mint. A while back, Tess had realised that the best way to look wealthy wasn't to wear lots of jewellery or flouncy gear. If you wanted to look rich, you had to dress in boring clothes. Mrs Minogue had gorgeous hair too. Ash-blonde, Tess supposed you'd call it. Nina said her mam had her hair cut and coloured in Limerick by a man who used to work in London. Most of the women in Kilmitten went to Mrs Grogan who insisted on doing a shampoo and set like it was 1962. You were lucky to escape without a blue rinse.

After they'd trooped in, Nina's mother was all fuss. She even gave Tom a hug and told him not to worry about anything. He went stiff, as if it hurt to be touched. *You'd better get used to it*, thought Tess. *There's going to be a lot of hugging and back-patting over the next few days.* By now, Nina had arrived, her eyes as big as dinner plates.

Mrs Minogue told them to go into the sitting room. 'You look to me,' she said, 'like a gang who could do with some hot chocolate.'

Tess wanted to kiss her.

The Minogues' sitting room had a green velvet suite and a huge TV in a wooden cabinet. It smelt of books and furniture polish. Near the TV, there was a large family photo taken a few years back by a proper photographer. With her velvet dress and ribbons, Nina was seriously cute. Her mother looked like a famous actress, and her dad still had hair. Her brother, Hugh, who'd been little more than a toddler, appeared confused. 'Mortifying,' was Nina's verdict on the picture, but it always made Tess smile.

To begin with, they all spoke in exaggerated whispers,

like they weren't sure how to behave. Nina said that after she'd left them she'd crept in the back door.

'Thankfully, the babysitter had the telly on full blast, and nuclear war wouldn't wake Hugh. By the time my parents got home, I must have been asleep.'

'So, when did you hear about Father Galvin?' asked Tess.

'This morning. My dad examined the body. He didn't want to talk about what happened, and when I asked, he got cross. Then five seconds later he was full of apologies. "You don't expect something like this in Kilmitten," he kept saying.'

'My dad was the same,' said Conor.

'Imagine, we were only yards away. Do you think . . .' Nina trailed off. Her mam was at the door with a tray of mugs. This time, her dad was there too.

Tess wished Dr Minogue had stayed away. It was funny how some people had to shout their opinions in thumping great letters while others, like Nina's father, didn't have to say a word. A twitch of the eye or a tightening of the mouth: that was all it took to let you know you weren't good enough. If he thought she was too young to notice, he was wrong. *I've got the measure of you*, she thought.

While Mrs Minogue handed out the drinks, her husband turned his attention to Tess. 'I see you're well layered up,' he said.

For a few seconds, she was puzzled. Then she noticed he was staring at her ankles. The pink fleece of her pyjamas was peeking out beneath the hem of her jeans. She slapped her cheek. 'Ah, I get you. It is kind of cold out there. Better safe than sorry.'

Dr Minogue gave her a smile that didn't travel as far as his eyes. 'I saw your mother earlier,' he said to Tom.

'She's not sick, is she?' asked Tom.

'No, no, she's fine. I gave her something to help her rest, that's all. She's gone to your aunt's house, I believe.'

It occurred to Tess that Dr Minogue must have heard more secrets than anybody in the village. More than Father Galvin had ever heard in the confession box. He knew about every pregnancy, every cancer, every dose of something nasty.

'And you, Conor,' said the doctor, 'your father's going to be very busy. You understand that, don't you? He'll need you to be on your best behaviour.'

'He knows that, Emmet,' said Nina's mother, with a smile. She was almost too smiley, as if stopping would cause her to get upset.

Tess sipped her hot chocolate. She was mulling over the spat between Mags and Mercedes. 'Do you think . . .' she said. 'Do you think that whoever did it was at the party?'

Immediately she regretted her question. Nina's dad gave her a stare, like she'd thrown up on the beige wool carpet. 'I doubt that,' he said. 'In fact, I have it on good authority that the police are looking elsewhere.'

'Oh?' said Mrs Minogue.

'I've been on the phone to a friend who knows about the investigation. Not Conor's dad, I should say. Flan has enough to be doing without me poking my nose in.' He paused. 'I wasn't going to say anything, but I reckon I should put your minds at rest. He told me that whoever killed Father Galvin came in from the back garden. Apparently, there's a lot of flattened snow around the shed, and there's a trail between the shed and the house. The guards suspect the killer must have hidden out there.'

'Really?' said Tom.

Tess's heart drummed in her ears. Not daring to look at the others, she studied her fingernails.

'There's a group of itinerants camped near the Templemorris Road. I'd say that's where the guards will start looking.' Dr Minogue squared his shoulders. 'Now, I've probably said more than I should, but I don't want any of you worrying that somebody from Kilmitten could have killed Father Galvin.'

'Thanks, Dad,' said Nina, in a small voice.

Chapter 3

'We've got to own up,' said Conor, as they walked back towards his house, cheeks stinging from the wind. Tess had stayed at Nina's place.

'You're kidding me,' said Tom. 'If we say anything about the shed, we'll be in big trouble.'

'It'll be even worse if we don't.'

'I don't see how. And can you imagine what it'd be like for the girls – or for Nina, at any rate? You saw her folks. Her dad would go ballistic if he thought she'd sneaked out of the house to go smoking and drinking with two lads. She'd be grounded for life.'

Conor kicked a clump of snow into the air and watched its powdery fall back to earth. True, he and Tess had agreed to stay quiet about the previous night, but the situation had changed. She'd understand, wouldn't she? 'I don't think you're getting this,' he said. 'My dad and the other guards think that whoever killed Father Galvin got into the house through the back door. You heard Nina's dad: they're going to arrest the Travellers when it wasn't them at all.'

'How do you know it wasn't?' said Tom, but he didn't sound convinced. 'Or maybe someone else crept in the back. Who knows?'

Conor was quiet for a moment. Although his thoughts were mangled, he knew something wasn't right. 'When you came back to the shed, you said the door was locked.'

'So?'

'So how could anyone have got in that way?'

'You know what my house is like. Everything's tricky, including the back door. I could've got it wrong. Perhaps it wasn't locked after all, just stuck.'

'Fair enough, but if somebody went in that way, we would've heard them.'

'Nah, we wouldn't. The shed's a long way from the house. Besides, what if they didn't arrive until after we'd left?'

'I still say we've got to tell the truth. It'll come out eventually, and then we'll get major grief.' Conor gave the snow another kick. 'It's not like we saw anything. And we don't have to mention the beer. Or the girls. We'll say it was just the two of us, sitting in the shed having a chat.'

'Don't be such a spa. Nobody will believe we were sitting in the shed having a chat. Why would we do that when it was freezing cold? We could've had a chat in the house.'

'I'm not the one being a spa. Do you want the guards to catch Father Galvin's killer, or don't you?'

Tom gave the fertiliser sack an angry rattle. 'Huh. That's

a stupid question. Of course I do. It happened in my house, remember?'

'You do know that not telling's a crime? When my dad works out what happened, we'll be sent to one of those homes full of hard-chaw joyriders and glue-sniffers, like the O'Grady brothers except a million times worse.'

'Lighten up, would you?' said Tom.

They walked the rest of the way in silence.

Although Conor didn't really believe they'd be sent to a home for rough lads, he was convinced they should come clean. He didn't like to think of his dad wasting time questioning people who'd had nothing to do with Father Galvin's death.

Most of the time, his father's job was pretty dull – and most of the people he dealt with were soft in the head. A large chunk of their stupidity was connected to drink. People either didn't know when to stop drinking, and his dad had to arrest them for being in the pub when it should have been closed, or else they got all violent and messy, and his dad had to calm them down. Then there were what his father called 'domestics'. He didn't like getting involved but sometimes he had to arrest fellows who'd hit their wives. Afterwards, he'd say he didn't know why he bothered, because in no time at all the wife would be calling around to the house claiming that her husband hadn't meant any harm and that he was a good man who'd taken to the drink on account of having no job.

Apart from dealing with alcoholics and idiots, his father's other main task was to keep an eye on what the TV news

called 'subversives': men – and women – who supported the
IRA. His dad said that most of them were only 'sneaking
regarders', who wouldn't know what to do with a gun,
not to mind a stick of gelignite. Others, like the Duggan
family, who lived next door to Tess, were more involved. Mr
Duggan hung around with men who'd been to prison for
being in the IRA. Not that long ago, Conor had watched
his father knocking on the Duggans' door. Mrs Duggan had
poked her head out of an upstairs window.

'What do you want now, Flan Varley?' she'd roared.

'A chat, that's all,' his dad had said.

'If you've got a search warrant, you can fuck off,' she'd
yelled back. 'But if you haven't, you can come in for a cup
of tea.'

Conor's sister perched on the kitchen counter, her face
glowing with insider knowledge. Paula was sixteen and she
wore her three extra years like a crown. While Tom and
Conor removed their scarves and anoraks, she told them
what she'd heard.

'Dad was here for a few minutes,' she said. 'An important
guy's after arriving from Dublin. He knows all about forensics
and evidence so he'll turn Tom's house inside out. Apart from
the guards, nobody's allowed in until he's finished.'

'What'll I do?' said Tom, the first words from his mouth in
ten minutes or more.

Paula fiddled with her leg warmers. (For once, Conor
could see a point to them. If it got any colder, he'd consider
wearing a pair himself.) 'You'll have to stay here for another

couple of days. You can have Conor's bed, and he can sleep on the old sun-lounger. If we put some blankets and sheets on it, it'll be grand.'

'I'm not taking anyone's bed,' said Tom. 'I'll be okay on the lounger yoke.'

'No,' said Paula. 'That wouldn't be right. You're a guest. The lounger's good enough for Conor.'

'What about my mam and dad?' asked Tom.

'They're still at your aunt's house, but the guards might want to talk to them again, so I'm not sure if you'll be able to see them tonight.' She gave a sorrowful shake of the head. 'You know the way it is.'

Actually, thought Conor, *we don't know the way it is. We haven't a clue how it is.* 'Did Dad say anything else?' he asked.

'Not a lot. Father Galvin's body's been taken to the hospital in Ennis. His brother was due to arrive, only Dad reckons he's been delayed by the snow. Apparently, some of the roads are blocked off entirely. Where have the two of you been?'

Conor told her, then realised he'd made a mistake.

Paula whistled. 'Fan-cee. The doctor's house, no less. Since when did you become such big buddies with Nina Minogue?'

'We're not really. It's just she's mates with Tess.' He toyed with the idea of telling her what Nina's father had said, but decided against. With Paula, it was always good to keep some information in reserve.

'Nina and Tess, now that's an odd pairing, if ever there was one,' she said, jumping down from the counter. 'Come on, you'd better help me get the tea. Dad'll be giving out if we don't feed Tom.'

*

Later, Tom came up with a plan.

'We'll write a letter,' he whispered, as he settled into Conor's bed.

Conor turned over on the lounger. 'I don't follow you.'

'We'll write to your dad. We won't put our names on the letter or anything, but we'll say he's looking in the wrong direction and that whoever killed Father Galvin definitely wasn't in the shed.'

'That's pure stupid. He'd know right away it was us. He'd recognise my writing and then he'd go balubas.'

'Ssh,' went Tom, 'Paula will hear us. I can do the letter, and there's no way he'd know my writing. You saw him on the news. He wants people to come forward with information. That's what we'd be doing.'

Father Galvin's death had been the main story on the news, bigger even than the snow in Dublin. Conor's dad had been interviewed. He'd looked startled. Then again, everybody on the telly looked like that. Conor had hardly been able to breathe, but there'd been no mention of how the killer had got into the house. According to his father, the guards didn't know why anybody would want to hurt Father Galvin. At the end, the reporter stood in front of Tom's house and, with the snow tumbling down around him, he said something about Kilmitten being a community living in fear. Paula went demented and made them recheck every window for fear Father Galvin's killer tried to attack them in their beds.

'I still say writing a letter's a dumb idea,' said Conor.

Tom snorted. 'I can't believe you're slagging off my ideas when you don't have any of your own.'

'I have a perfectly good idea. It's called telling the truth. I'm sorry now that we ever arranged to meet Nina and Tess.'

'When did you become such a pain in the arse?' said Tom, but he didn't seem to want an answer. Instead he turned over to face Conor's football wall.

Liverpool were Conor's team. He had posters of the most popular players, like Kenny Dalglish and Ian Rush, but his favourite was David Fairclough, the bionic carrot. Conor's mam had liked him. 'Are you sure he's not Irish?' she used to say. 'Look at the big mop of red hair on him.' When she'd been in hospital, propped up on four pillows, her face as yellow as a wizened apple, she'd promised they'd go to see Liverpool play. She must have known it was never going to happen.

For a while, Conor had worried that he'd killed his mother. He'd remembered how she used to say things like, 'Conor Varley, you'll be the death of me.' It had taken him ages to realise that her remarks hadn't meant anything. When she'd made those jokes, the cancer had been only a speck inside her, so tiny she hadn't known it was there. Even after she'd died, people hadn't used the word 'cancer'. 'The big C,' they called it. Or 'the bug'. It was as if saying the word would be enough to invite the disease into their own house.

Occasionally, Conor pretended his mam was still alive. He'd think he could smell her perfume or hear her singing along to the radio. Most mothers had shocking taste in music. Conor's mam had been different. She'd liked The Eagles and Meat Loaf and Bruce Springsteen. Not that she'd been much of a singer. He could hear her now, crucifying 'Born To Run' or 'Bat Out Of Hell'. Once upon a time, his dad used to talk about her. 'What would Caroline do?' he'd say, or 'It's a shame Caroline isn't here to see this.' These days, he rarely mentioned her. When he wasn't at work, he foostered about the house with a hammer or a screwdriver. He was always mending stuff.

Overhead, the water pipes gurgled and whined. In the bed, Tom's breathing was shallow and steady. He sounded like he was asleep, but Conor knew he was pretending. He couldn't sleep either. His brain was too busy.

It wasn't quite bright when Paula roused them for Mass.

'Wakey wakey, lads,' she said, her hands clapping time. 'If we don't leave soon, we won't get a decent seat.'

Like a fool, Conor had assumed this would be a Mass-free Sunday. The priest was lying in the morgue, after all. No such luck. Father Smith, the curate in Templemorris, had been called in.

Despite their early start, Conor's dad had already left for the station.

Half an hour later, the three were plodding up the street, the ground as slippery as margarine, the sky flat and milky. Ahead of them, Mags Moynihan took an almighty skid and ended up on her backside. If this had been a normal Sunday, Conor and Tom would have collapsed with laughter. But the village felt odd, as if a heavy blanket had been placed over it, and laughing would have been wrong. Tom was lost in his thoughts and didn't appear to notice Mags's somersault.

Tom wasn't usually this quiet. At school, he was full of games and schemes. That didn't stop him from doing well. He'd pretend he couldn't follow the hard stuff, like theorems or the *tuiseal ginideach*. Then a teacher would ask him a question, and he'd reel off the answer, no problem. Conor had to make more of an effort. Even after his mam had died, when he could have got away with skiving, he'd done most of his homework. He hadn't wanted anyone thinking he was thick.

The Church of the Holy Name stood in the centre of Kilmitten, its grey bulk making the surrounding buildings appear all the smaller. Groups of people milled around the entrance. There were reporters too. With their sheepskin coats, spiral notebooks and drawling Dublin accents, they stood out like donkeys in a field of cattle. Although most folks turned their backs or filed past with a tight-lipped glance, others, like Mercedes Talty, weren't so shy. There she was, in front of the scrum, her mouth working overtime, her hands slicing through the air. 'Heaven only knows what was going on,' Conor heard her say.

Inside the church, Paula shepherded Conor and Tom to the third row. The holy Joes occupied the front pew, with the well-to-do, like the Minogues, sitting directly behind. For once, there were no messers slouching down the back. Even the O'Gradys sat in a neat line, their eyes closed as if they were actually saying prayers, their faces so shiny their mam must have spat on a hankie and given them a polish. Nina was sitting in front of Conor. He touched her back. She swivelled around and looked at him with questioning eyebrows. Then her mother gave her a swift poke in the side, and she turned away again. Tess was on the other side of the aisle, on her own. It was strange how she went to Mass when her mam didn't bother. Tess was cool, though, and she could do whatever she liked. Conor recalled how, the previous summer, Philly O'Grady had thrown a dead rat in her direction. It had whizzed past her ear. Without making a sound, she'd picked the rat up by the tail and pelted it straight back. Her aim was much better, and it had hit him, *wham*, on the cheek. That had put a halt to his swagger.

Yeah, Tess was cool.

Father Galvin's Masses had been all right. He hadn't gone on about Hell the way some priests did. And unless it was Palm Sunday, when the Gospel was so long that women fainted, he'd rarely spoken for more than three-quarters of an hour. Father Smith, on the other hand, seemed determined to drone on for the rest of the day. He liked a lot of incense too. One of the altar boys, Paschal Ryan, was swinging the thurible like a lunatic. The smell made Conor feel sick.

In his sermon, the priest talked about evil being in their midst. Was it possible, Conor wondered, that the killer was sitting there, reciting prayers and acting like nothing had happened? He thought of Father Galvin. Had he been on the floor when Tom's mam found him? Had there been anyone to say the last rites – or had he needed the last rites? Were priests so holy that they bypassed Purgatory and went straight to Heaven? Conor tried to push these thoughts aside. There was enough bad stuff in his head as it was. He wished there was an easy way to do the right thing. He glanced at Tom, but his friend's face had a glazed look. Even when Nina turned around, hand thrust forward for the sign of peace, there was barely a stir out of him.

As the Mass meandered on, Conor realised that he was content to sit there and let Father Smith's voice wash over him. In the church, he didn't have to make a decision. He didn't have to talk to his dad or anybody else. For the first time, he could see why old people were so fond of Mass.

Afterwards, Tom's dad appeared. 'Your mam's having a rest,' he said, 'but she'd love to see you. You can get your dinner in your auntie Noreen's house.'

Tom practically skipped away, relieved, no doubt, to avoid any further talk about the shed. Conor would have liked to speak to the girls, but Nina was with her parents and Tess had disappeared.

After they'd answered a flood of questions about their dad ('Did the poor man get any sleep at all?') and ducked out of various invitations ('You're welcome to have your dinner with us. It's not a big chicken, mind, but there's plenty of veg'), Conor and Paula wandered towards home. Conor wanted to buy a newspaper except he didn't have enough money. Paula hummed and hawed and finally agreed. 'We can't read it on the street, though,' she said. 'We don't want to appear too nosy.' While this didn't make much sense to Conor, there was no point in arguing: she had the cash. He picked the *Sunday Herald* because there was an enormous picture of Father Galvin, and a smaller one of Tom's house, on the front. *Holy Murder* read the headline. *Gardaí Find*

Vital Clues. Paula threw her eyes up to Heaven, but Conor knew she was gasping to read it too.

Back home, he unfolded his paper and laid it out on the kitchen table. Paula hovered behind him.

'Oh,' he said. As he read, the lump that had been in his stomach since the day before became harder and rose up towards his throat.

Gardaí believe the killer of a County Clare priest may have left behind crucial evidence. Fr Leo Galvin died on Friday night in the isolated village of Kilmitten. He'd been attending a party at the home of a local businessman. The crime has sent shockwaves across the nation and united Church and political leaders in expressions of grief and condemnation.

A source close to the investigation has told the Herald that a cigarette butt and another item found close to the scene may provide vital clues. The source said that while nothing was being ruled out, it was likely that whoever killed the 44-year-old priest entered through the back door of the detached house which is home to Haulie Crossan, his wife Nora and their young son, Tom.

'Typical. They couldn't even get Cora Crossan's name right,' said Paula. 'And there's nothing isolated about Kilmitten.'

Conor ignored her. The lump was edging closer to his mouth.

Like the rest of the country, Kilmitten has seen heavy snowfall in recent days. The snow in the back garden is understood to have been disturbed, and several sets of footprints were detected.

'Up to four people may have been involved,' added the source.

Late last night, a post mortem was being carried out on the body of the slain cleric by the state pathologist, Professor Harry Burtenshaw. Local reports suggest that Fr Galvin may have suffered head injuries.

People in the close-knit community say they are in shock.

'I was at the party,' said Mercedes Talty (34). 'What is the country coming to when a Catholic priest isn't safe?'

'I'd say it's a long time since Mercedes Talty was thirty-four,' said Paula. 'Who does she think she's fooling?'

Conor tried to say something sensible, but all he managed was another high-pitched 'Oh.'

His sister gave him a puzzled look. They read on.

Noel O'Grady (42), who was also in the Crossans'

house at the time of the priest's death, warned that the people of Kilmitten wouldn't stand by and watch as their village was destroyed. 'There are lots of rumours about who might have been responsible,' he said. 'I hope the police make an arrest soon.'

The Herald's source expects an early breakthrough. 'An intensive search is being carried out,' they said. 'Every inch of the surrounding land is being examined. If whoever was responsible for this heinous crime was stupid enough to leave evidence behind, they'll be caught sooner rather than later.'

The paper promised further coverage on pages four to seven and twenty-three to twenty-five, plus an editorial called 'The End of Innocence'. It also boasted a ten-page special on what it called 'The Big Snow'.

'Do you think all of that's true?' asked Paula.

By now, Conor was shivering. Seeing the details in a newspaper made everything feel different. More serious. More scary.

Paula's eyes narrowed. 'Is something wrong?'

'I need to speak to Tom – and to Dad.'

'I'm very disappointed in you,' said Conor's father, as he patrolled the front room. 'Very disappointed in both of you.' He tipped his head in Tom's direction. Tom's dad was there too, his eyes baggy, his face grey. His clothes looked like he'd slept in them. Maybe he had. Usually Mr Crossan was all jokes and sport, and it was weird to see him like this. Tom's mam was still resting.

Awkward as it was, Conor hadn't wanted to tell the story without Tom. He didn't want anyone accusing him of being a snitch. In Conor's world, there were few people more despised than a snitch. After Tom had seen the paper, he'd reluctantly agreed to talk.

They'd given their fathers the full rundown: the beer, the cigarettes, Tess, Nina, everything. Tom had pleaded with the grown-ups not to say anything to Nina's parents. 'They'll get upset,' he'd pointed out. 'What good would that do?' Neither man had replied. Conor's dad had pulled a face, while Tom's had closed his eyes. Although Conor knew he'd have to warn the girls, he suspected that leaving the house wouldn't be easy.

The snow had returned and, even though it was barely two in the afternoon, the lights were on. His dad came to a halt beside the fireplace. 'To be clear about this,' he said, 'there was no funny business?'

'I don't—' began Tom.

'No,' said Conor. 'We were being friends. That's all.'

'Fine, but if I find out there was anything else . . .'

'I swear to God, Dad, we were only talking.' He hesitated. 'We haven't . . . we haven't messed up the investigation, have we?'

'No.' His father sighed. 'Now you've told the truth, you've . . . well, you've cleared up something that's been confusing us. It's a shame you didn't have the guts to come forward yesterday. You'd have saved us all a lot of hassle. I thought I'd raised you to be honest.'

'Sorry,' said Conor, for what might have been the thousandth time.

'And of course I'm going to feel like a total fool going back to the station and saying, "Guess what, lads? You know the butt and the bottle top we found in the snow? As chance would have it, they belong to my son and his friend. The young eejits were trying to impress two lassies."' Another sigh. 'That's going to go down well with the boys from Dublin, I can tell you.'

Conor stopped himself saying sorry again.

'So,' said his dad, 'are you sure you didn't see or hear anything?'

'I promise.'

'And what about you, Tom? When you went up to the door, did you spot anything unusual? Anything at all?'

'No,' said Tom, all the while staring at the carpet. 'Not a thing.'

'I've got to get back to work.' Conor's dad glanced around the room. 'A word to the wise: don't go thinking the papers know what's going on, because they don't.'

Conor looked at Tom, but his friend's eyes never left the floor.

Chapter 4

On Monday afternoon, the power went. Nina and Tess were in the Fortunes' sitting room, watching television, when the picture shrivelled to a dot and disappeared. Tess tried the lights, but nothing happened.

'My dad said there was something on the radio about power cuts in other parts of the country,' said Nina. 'The snow's brought down lots of the lines.'

'It might be a while before the electricity's back, so,' said Tess, giving the light switch another flick. 'We could go out, I suppose.'

'Maybe we should call over to Conor's house and see how the lads are getting on.'

'Mmm. Only what'll we do then?'

In the days since Father Galvin's death, going out had become increasingly complicated. A blend of mourning and fear had taken over the village, and anybody seen larking about could expect disapproval. Even Toomey's Hill was out of bounds. Tess said this was a waste of good snow, but Nina didn't mind. Her headmistress had called to say the weather was terrible in Kildare and the boarding school would remain closed for another week. A week without school felt like such a blessing that she didn't care how she spent it.

Tess's mother was at work in the chipboard factory in Templemorris, so they had the house to themselves. In all the years Nina had been visiting Tess's place, it hadn't changed. While her own home had been through countless renovations, the Fortunes' sitting room had the same mossy-brown sofa and chairs, the same shiny coffee table, the same smell of coal and cigarettes. The one photo was of a six-year-old Tess and her mother. It had been taken on a day trip to the seaside. Tess had more gaps than teeth and her mother's hair was in Farrah Fawcett wings. They both looked like they were having the best day of their lives.

Tess sat down again and wrapped her arms around her knees. 'It's not like there was anything worth watching on the telly, anyway. I wish we had all the channels – or a video recorder. The Moynihans rented one for Christmas. Mags had Mam's head wrecked from boasting about it.'

'We've got five channels at school,' said Nina. 'Because Kildare's so close to Dublin, we get the BBCs and ITV.'

'That must be magic.'

'Not really. Apart from the odd show, like *Top of the Pops*, we're not allowed to watch the British channels. And sometimes I don't even watch that.'

'Why not?'

'The Emers are always in the TV room.' The Emers weren't all called Emer, but three of them were, and Nina couldn't stand them. They were forever making fun of her, mocking what she said and the way she said it. They thought they were God's gift, asking crazy questions about Kilmitten. Did her house smell of cow dung? Had she ever plucked a chicken or killed a pig? All the while, they honked with laughter. No matter how many times she told them her parents weren't farmers, their act never changed.

'The witches,' said Tess. 'Why doesn't somebody stand up to them? It sounds to me like they're in need of a good slap.'

'It's not worth it. They'd only get their revenge later on. And their parents all have tons of money, so none of the teachers says boo to them. At least the weather means I haven't been able to go back. It's a shame the snow can't last until June.'

Tess tilted her head towards the window. 'The way it's going, it might. Those Emer girls ought to spend a few days in Kilmitten. We'd sort them out.'

Nina tried to imagine what the Emers – Dubliners all – would make of the real Kilmitten. What would they think of the old men who drove their tractors to the pub or the women who wore curlers in the street? How would they react when they learned that all phone calls had to be made through an operator? And that the operator listened in?

And what would they say about Father Galvin? Nina knew it was wrong, but when she'd seen some of the locals on the news – teeth crooked, caps skew-whiff, accents as thick as month-old milk – she'd prayed the Emers weren't watching.

Wasn't it strange, she thought, *how without trying you*

could be two different people? In Kilmitten, she felt like her real self. No, better than her real self. Okay, compared to Tess, she was a bit of an innocent, but so was everyone else. Tess understood dirty jokes; she knew how to smoke; she'd French-kissed two of the boys in her class. All things considered, though, in her home village, Nina was on the cool side of average. In Millmount Abbey, she was a thousand miles from cool. She was tongue-tied and dull, a second-rater who always said the wrong thing at the wrong time. There were days when just walking into a room and sitting down were difficult.

She hadn't wanted to go away to school. Her parents had insisted. For the first couple of weeks, Nina had tried her best. She'd thought about Malory Towers and St Clare's and done everything possible to fit in. But the truth was, her new school was awful, awful, awful. She missed her parents, her little brother and her friends. She missed the chancers and the characters who knocked about the village. She even missed silly things, like the giddy women boarding the Templemorris bingo bus and the way mist clung low to the grass on fine mornings.

Tess and Nina fell into another conversation about Father Galvin. Nina remained scared that her parents would find out what she'd been doing on the night of the party.

'You shouldn't worry,' said Tess. 'Everybody's got enough to be going on with. They won't be thinking about us.'

But Nina did worry. She was a bundle of worries. That somebody could be killed in Kilmitten frightened her.

Violence didn't belong here. It belonged in Dublin and Belfast where people killed each other over money or drugs or whether they were Irish or British. Okay, bad things happened for other reasons too: men killed their wives, and fathers their sons. But not in Kilmitten. She couldn't imagine why anyone would want to hurt Father Galvin. She hadn't read any of the papers because her father wouldn't allow them into the house. 'Bloody vultures,' he'd said, about the journalists who'd approached him on the street. Nina didn't think they looked like vultures at all. They were too well padded.

They were deciding what to do with the rest of the afternoon when the front door creaked open and Tess's mam came fizzing in. With her black leather jacket, glittery scarf and stretch denims, she didn't look like any other mother. To be fair, she was quite a lot younger than most mothers. She was thirty-two, which meant she was also younger than Debbie Harry and Olivia Newton-John. Tess said that when her mam got depressed, she lay in bed moaning that her best years were behind her. Then Tess would have to sit on the floor and list all the famous people who were older than her. Usually this helped to perk her up again.

'Hi, Mam,' said Tess. 'What has you home?'

'Uh, hi . . . Ginny,' said Nina. Addressing Tess's mother was awkward. Technically speaking she was Miss Fortune, but that made her sound like a teacher. Besides, she always insisted that Nina use her first name.

'No electricity, no work,' said Ginny, shaking off her jacket. 'The scabby so-and-sos don't have a generator, so they told us all to go home. I'm sorry now that I bothered going in at all. The roads are a fright. We couldn't even clock out because the machine had stopped, but they made us sign our cards. "I'm not losing half a day's money over something that's not my fault," I said to the supervisor. "You take as much as twenty pence out of my pay packet, and there'll be trouble." You should have seen the face on her. You'd think she was chewing thistles. Not, mind you, that there was a tap of work done today. All anybody wanted to do was talk about Father Galvin, and when I said I was at the party in Cora and Haulie's place, they had me plagued.' She knocked her knuckles against her forehead. 'Oh, listen to me – going off on a rant. Work does that to me. Sorry, Nina, pet. Your mam's never had to get a job, has she?'

'No. I mean, she worked in an office before she got married, and sometimes she helps my dad with the paperwork, but she says running the house keeps her busy.'

'Lucky her.' Ginny removed a box of cigarettes and a red lighter from her jacket pocket, lit up and took a long pull. 'How's your day been, girls?'

'Fine,' said Tess. 'Better than school, anyway. What were people saying about Father Galvin?'

'What weren't they saying? It seems the outsider theory's been abandoned, so everybody's convinced the killer must have been at the party.' She shivered. 'Which, when you think about it, is pretty scary.' Tess and Nina exchanged a glance, but Ginny didn't appear to notice. 'And of course they're all going on about why anyone would want to harm a priest.'

'Really?' said Tess.

'Yeah. I heard every kind of crackpot notion today. Some folks say he owed money, and others insist that, no, people owed money to him. More say he fell out with some men over a sermon he gave about violence against women, and another lad swore it was all part of a mad conspiracy connected to the Pope who died and . . .' She paused to look at Tess and Nina. 'Here, you won't say any of this to anybody, will you?'

'Don't worry,' said Tess.

'Seriously, it's all nonsense made up by people who've nothing better to be doing.'

'We won't say a word, honest,' said Nina, her mind doing cartwheels. Was it possible that any of this was true?

'Good girl. Anyway, the removal's been arranged for tomorrow. The funeral Mass will take place here, but he'll be buried up in Knockgreelish where his family lives.'

'Will everybody have to go?' asked Tess.

Ginny took a drag of her cigarette and exhaled a thin stream of smoke. 'You won't catch me there, that's for sure.'

'I know you're not a fan of Mass, but why not go to the funeral?'

'I'll be at work.'

'Not for the removal, you won't.'

'The reason I won't be there, Tessy, is because, unlike some people, I'm not a hypocrite.' With that, Ginny stubbed out her cigarette in a way that made it clear the subject was closed. 'So,' she said, 'we'd better find some candles.'

'They're in the cupboard under the sink,' said Tess,

'beside the gas stove we used when the electricity men were on strike.'

Ginny smiled at her daughter. 'Where would I be without you?'

'Lost. What about the food in the fridge? Will it go off, do you think?'

'Hopefully, the power won't be gone for too long.'

Nina had an idea. 'I know what you can do,' she said. 'You can bury the food in the snow. That way it'll stay frozen.'

'That's insane,' said Tess.

Ginny, however, greeted the suggestion with enthusiasm. 'You know what, Nina Minogue?' she said. 'You are a genius.' She picked up her jacket. 'Come on, girls. It's time to go burying.'

The afternoon sky was a hundred different colours. Nina had never seen so many shades of blue and grey and white and cream. As if that wasn't enough, the clouds were tinged with wisps of pink and orange. The wind had dropped, and the air had a lovely frosty tingle.

Tess's mam reckoned the small front garden was the best place for their task. There was a streetlight there, so when they went to retrieve the food, they'd be able to see what they were doing. 'It'll be dark before we know it,' she said, as she scooped out a hole in the snow, popped in a bag of peas and threw some snow back on top. 'Beats me why everybody isn't doing this.'

'Probably because they don't want to lose their dinner,' said Tess. 'How will you know where to find everything?'

'It's not exactly the Phoenix Park out here. There aren't many places to look. And we're only burying a few things.' At her feet were a bottle of milk, a box of fish fingers and half a pound of sausages. 'We'll put them all in a line and we'll have no bother finding them.'

'But those few things are all we've got.'

'Jesus, Tess, you're a right moaning Minnie today. Calm down, would you?'

Nina stepped in. 'What we could do is place a reminder on top, like – I don't know – a stone or something? Just so you know where the food is.'

'What did I say?' replied Ginny. 'The girl's a star. That fancy education's definitely not wasted on you, Nina, love.'

Nina wondered what the Emers would make of the scene. The thought made her smile.

And so they continued digging. While it wasn't a big job, the snow had become hard and icy and Nina's hands quickly turned purple and orange. She wished she was wearing her gloves, but neither Tess nor Ginny had theirs on and she didn't want to be different.

It was Tess who started the snow fight. She threw the first snowball at her mother, who threw one back, and then Nina joined in, and in no time they were flinging snow at each other, the crystals flying through the air, reflecting the light like diamonds. There was whooping and squealing and shrieking, and it was brilliant. The snow slipped down Nina's back and seeped into her mouth, but she couldn't remember when she'd laughed so much. Her chest hurt from laughing. So giddy was she that when the car drew up she barely noticed. The low sun glinted in her eyes, and a few seconds passed before she recognised her father.

'Hi, Dad,' she said, as Tess and Ginny stood beside her, panting and giggling from the fight.

'What's going on here?' he asked.

'We've been burying the fish fingers,' said Tess.

The sun ducked behind a cloud, and for the first time Nina saw her dad properly. The set of his face gave her an uneasy feeling.

'Is everything okay?' asked Ginny.

He hesitated before replying. 'No, it's not. Nina, I want you to come home with me.'

'Why?' she asked.

'You know why, so do as you're told and get into the car.'

Her father rarely got angry in public. Unlike some parents who became narky for no reason at all, he always thought everything through.

'I won't ask again,' he said.

Tess's mam tucked her hair behind her ears and squinted towards the sun, which had come sliding back out. 'I'm mystified here,' she said. 'I can't picture Nina doing anything wrong. She's a great girl, a credit to you.'

'Let me be the judge of that. And, by the way, if you have to mess about in the snow, could you not find somewhere more appropriate? The village is in mourning. People don't want to see this type of carry-on.'

'Ah, give over, Emmet. Where's the harm in the girls having some fun? They won't be young for ever.'

By now, Nina was trembling. *Please stop it*, she thought. *Please don't fall out here on the street.*

'I'm not going to make matters any worse than they already are,' said her dad. 'Now, for the last time, Nina, get into the car. We're going home.'

Nina sent a look of distress to her friend, then did as she was told.

'See you tomorrow,' Tess called after her.

As Nina climbed into the BMW, she heard Ginny asking her father what the problem was.

'I'll leave Tess to fill you in,' he said. 'She can tell you what their little gang was up to on Friday night.'

Nina watched the candlelight flicker across her parents' faces. The only other light came from the glow of logs in the grate. She was glad the electricity was off. By now, her own face must be a mottled mess. Tears ran down her cheeks, and her eyes felt sticky and raw.

Conor had told his dad about their evening in the shed, and Sergeant Varley had informed Nina's parents. 'And I'm glad he did,' said her father, a slight vibration in his voice, like he was trying to control his anger. 'Otherwise we would never have known what you and Tess were up to. Have you no sense?'

Plainly, this was one of those questions that didn't require an answer because he continued his lecture with warnings about what happened to young girls who were foolish enough to go smoking and drinking with boys. Very bad things, apparently. Things that led to shame and misery and ruined lives. Nina tried to explain that the evening had been harmless, but she stumbled over the words. Neither parent wanted to listen.

For ten minutes or more, she sobbed and whimpered while her dad reminded her of all the advantages she had in life. She didn't need a reminder: she knew she was lucky. Lucky to have two parents who loved her. Lucky to live in a big warm house. Lucky to wear expensive clothes.

All the while, her mam played with her gold chain. 'And think how fortunate you were to get into Millmount Abbey,' she said. 'One of the finest schools in Ireland.'

Nina couldn't let this pass. 'I'd prefer to be at home with you and Dad and Hugh. Why can't I go to St Ursula's with everybody else? There's no reason why I wouldn't do well there.'

'What's brought this on?' asked her dad.

'What do you mean?'

'I thought you were keen to go to Millmount. Don't all girls love boarding school?'

'I never wanted to go there, but now . . . now I hate it.'

'Oh, Nina,' said her mam, her voice softening, 'why didn't you mention this before?'

'Because I didn't know what to say.'

'I'm sorry to hear that.' She rubbed her necklace. 'I know it's hard for you to grasp, love, but Millmount will give you opportunities you'd never have here. You've got to give it time. When I was there, it took me a while to adjust, but when I did, I adored it. What is it that you hate?'

'They're mean to me.'

'Who's mean to you?'

'The other girls. Not all of them, obviously. But plenty of them.'

Her dad shifted in his chair. 'What is it that they do to you?'

Nina explained.

'If you ask me,' he said, 'they sound very foolish.' For the briefest of moments, Nina thought she was making progress. 'But,' he added, 'I doubt there's any real harm in them.'

'That's—'

'You mightn't like to hear this, Nina, but sometimes even the best of people behave like idiots. You'll have to stand your ground with the Emer girls. And if you do, I bet they'll leave you alone. They'll find someone else to tease.'

'We could have a word with the headmistress,' said her mother.

'No!' said Nina, with more force than she'd intended. 'You can't do that. I'd get nothing but hassle then. Please don't make me go back.'

'All right,' said her dad. 'If you don't want us to get involved, we won't. But your mother is right. You've got to give it more time.'

'We'll always be here for you,' said her mam, 'and Kilmitten isn't going anywhere.'

'But I don't want to go back. If I do, I'll . . .' The sentence fell away, lost in a stupid, teary quiver.

More than four hours had passed since the electricity had cut out. The room smelt of candle wax and, faintly, of perfume. Nina's mother wore Rive Gauche. Sometimes, she allowed Nina a spray or two. 'Remember to press lightly,' she'd say. 'Too much is worse than not enough.' For some time, they sat in silence. Nina sensed that more was to come. Sure enough, her father eventually swapped looks with her mother, coughed into his hand, and began again.

'One of the reasons we're keen for you to go away to school is... we'd prefer if you didn't see so much of Tess.'

'Why?'

'I think what happened the other night shows why she's not an appropriate friend for you.'

'I don't understand.' Nina did understand, but she wanted to hear her father say the words.

'Tess isn't a good influence. You don't want to get caught up in her world.'

'Tess's world is the same as mine.'

Her dad looked down, and her mam took over. 'It's not, though, is it? I know you're fond of Tess, but how much do you actually have in common?'

Nina tried to think of a clever answer, but the row had left her tired and the right words wouldn't come. If she was being honest, she knew her life was different. Tess had no dad, and her mam had no money. From time to time, this made Nina uncomfortable. She found herself being careful about what she said. The previous summer, the Minogues had gone to Portugal, and even though Tess had been full of questions, Nina hadn't wanted to talk about it. She'd been scared of appearing boastful. In Millmount, the girls were keen to let you know where they'd been and what their families owned. In Kilmitten, that wasn't the done thing. Having too much was frowned upon. Nina wished she could spool back to the days when she'd been unaware of the differences between her and Tess.

'We have lots and lots in common,' she said. 'We're interested in the same sort of stuff and we like the same bands and—'

'You see,' said her father, 'harsh as this might sound, in a few years' time, you'll be leading a very different life from Tess. She'll probably have a similar life to her mother – and that's not what we want for you.'

'I like Ginny. She's fun. Tess is fun.'

'Believe me, Nina, the older you get, the more you'll appreciate that fun's not enough. Now, if you're wise, you'll listen to what we're saying. We're not forbidding you from ever seeing Tess again, but we think you ought to spend a couple of months away from her. That will give you time to adapt to your new school. When you return to Kilmitten, you'll have a fresh perspective on the situation.'

A silly hiccuping sob escaped from Nina's mouth. 'I don't know why you're doing this.'

'We all feel the same when we're young,' said her dad. 'We're convinced our parents know nothing. I promise you, one day you'll look back on this and you'll understand.'

Chapter 5

After the funeral, Tom and his parents went home. Save for a brief trip to collect some clothes, it was the first time they'd returned since Father Galvin's death. Tom could see his breath in every room. There was frost on the inside of the windows and ice in the kitchen sink. The place was a mess too, with the remains of the party still scattered about. He'd heard neighbours offer to come and help with the clear-up, but his mam had said no. 'Another day,' she'd said. 'Another day.' He'd expected her to tear into the task, with him fetching and carrying. He'd been wrong. Instead, she'd walked around in a heavy-footed way before announcing that she needed a rest.

How could she still be tired?

Father Galvin's funeral had been a massive affair with the bishop and four other priests. Tom had sat six rows back, between his parents, who'd kept their eyes closed most of the time. The church was as packed as he'd ever seen it, so packed that some people had had to stand outside in the snow. On the way in, the Crossans had stopped for a word with Mercedes Talty.

'Here we are,' she'd said, 'a church full of suspects.'

'For pity's sake, Mercedes,' Tom's father had snapped, 'there's no call for that kind of talk.'

His parents hadn't gone mental over the shed business. Or maybe they had, but in unexpected ways. His dad told long stories about his own school days, while his mam just nodded. Her eyes were pink, and her cheeks were hollow, as if somebody had sucked all the air out of her. Although Tom wished Conor hadn't told his father, he wasn't surprised. That was Conor for you: he always had to do the right thing. It was like a disease.

During the funeral Tom had seen Nina on the other side of the church with her parents and brother. He tried – and failed – to catch her eye. Tess was down the back, on her own. Tom had heard that her mam was an atheist or a pagan or something, so that must be why she'd stayed away. Still, this wasn't a regular Mass. Even the simple people and the men who rarely left the farm were there, and he wondered how Tess felt about her mother's absence.

Tom's parents had rung his sisters in New York to tell them about Father Galvin. Dympna had offered to come home. Then Deirdre had pointed out that if she did, she'd be stuck in Ireland and might never get back to America again. 'It's a funny state of affairs,' she'd said, 'when a city like New York is safer than your own house.'

There was a weird atmosphere in the village. People huddled into small groups, exchanging titbits of information. Then, those same people would check themselves and start to act as if they hadn't said a word; as if they were too sad to gossip. It felt as though all the normal everyday noise had been drained away. The grown-ups spoke about 'appropriate behaviour', but how did they know what that was? It wasn't like they had any experience to fall back on. Nobody could say, 'Well, the last time the parish priest was killed . . .'

Some folks were moaning about Paddy O'Grady, the politician, who was trapped in the Canaries. His flight home had been cancelled because Dublin airport was buried in snow. 'If he wanted to be here, he'd make it,' Tom heard Mags Moynihan say. His dad said that if people were upset about Paddy O'Grady getting a few rays of sun in Lanzarote they had little enough to worry them.

Although most of the bars and shops were open, the petrol pumps remained idle. Normally, Tom's mother would have got worked up over this. At the moment, she didn't seem to care.

During the funeral, the bishop had spoken about what Father Galvin had done with his life. Apparently, he'd always wanted to go on the Missions and had been hoping to live in Africa one day. At this, several people sniffled, and one woman let out a long wail. Tom tried to imagine Father Galvin saying Mass in a mud hut, but the image was all wrong. He had belonged in Ireland where he could drink a small Paddy (dash of water, no ice) and go to the horse races. The bishop said he'd had two brothers and three sisters. Tom had been fascinated by the priest's parents, who looked really, really ancient. They might be ninety or more. For the first time, it struck him that Father Galvin had been a real person with a real family; that he might have fought with his sisters and bunked off school and had thoughts about girls.

Back home now, his father was making an effort to be cheerful. He pressed the buttons on the gas heater until it fired up with a loud whoosh.

'Are you okay with sleeping here?' he said to Tom. 'Because if you're not, you can stay with Conor.'

Tom wasn't looking forward to a night in his room, but neither did he want to stay with the Varleys. Paula was a bossy-boots, and Conor was trying too hard to be nice. He told himself that he didn't have to go near the back kitchen. He didn't want to go there ever again.

'I'm fine,' he said.

'Good man. Now, I reckon it's our job to get the dinner today. What do you fancy?'

'We have liver on Wednesdays.'

'We might give that one a miss. Why don't you go down to the butcher's and buy some steaks?'

'Mam always says steak's too expensive.'

'And most of the time she's right, but just this once I think steak is called for.' His dad reached into his trouser pocket, pulled out a five-pound note and handed it to Tom. 'You're looking very serious, Tommo. Is anything else on your mind?'

Tom thought again about what he'd seen – or what he thought he'd seen. Nobody knew that while Father Galvin had been lying on the floor, he'd been cowering outside. The problem was, if he said anything now, he'd be in trouble for not speaking sooner. And that wasn't all: for every reason to tell, there were two reasons not to. Telling might make everything worse, and life was difficult enough already. How he wished he could go back in time. A week would be enough. Imagine: a week ago his biggest concern had been impressing Nina. He tried to convince himself that what he knew didn't matter. Every night, he ran it all around his brain until he thought his head might burst open. Now they were back home, he'd be able to steal some of his mam's tablets.

School was due to open again in the morning, and he'd have to answer a zillion questions about Father Galvin. The Templemorris lads would probably be full of smart comments too. They were forever making fun of people who got the bus to school, calling them muckers and bog-trotters. The way they carried on, you'd swear Templemorris was the size of New York. Tom wasn't sure if he should brag about being in the shed with the girls or act like he knew nothing. He needed to talk to Conor and Tess.

'So?' said his dad.

'There's nothing to tell. Only . . . well, you know the way it is . . .'

His father patted his shoulder. 'Don't I just, son. Don't I just.'

Tom put the fiver in his pocket. 'I won't be long,' he said.

Chapter 6

This, Tess would have to admit, was not going well. She hadn't meant any harm. The letter had been so tedious she'd felt she was doing the boss a favour. He ought to know how others would respond. So, after she'd typed up his pompous nonsense, she'd added a short note. *You might,* she'd written, *want to lighten up a bit. After all, this is a PR company, not a funeral home. Also, starting with 'It has come to my attention'? Not a smart move. You sound like you're issuing a final warning on an electricity bill rather than trying to suck up to a client who's taken some of his business elsewhere. In fact, why write a letter at all? Why not lift the phone and have a chat?* Unfortunately, her suggestions hadn't been welcome, which was how she found herself receiving a severe talking-to from the office manager.

'Do you understand,' Harriet was saying, 'the role of a temporary typist?'

'Of course I do. I just reckoned Simon was making a

mistake. There's no point in being hoity-toity with people when you're looking for their money. I'm sure the client's a head-wrecker and everything, but I doubt—'

'Tess, how long have you been working here?'

'Um, a week and a half.'

'And how long do you think Mr Beaumont has been in the public relations business?'

'Gosh, I—'

'Allow me to give you the answer. Eighteen years. So, with the greatest of respect, I should imagine he knows rather more about client relations than a young girl who's just off the boat from Ireland.'

'Like I said, I was only trying to be helpful.'

Although her experience was narrow, it seemed to Tess that bosses were disappointingly similar to teachers. They felt the need to adopt a superior attitude and to use a limited number of phrases, all of which were aimed at keeping you in your place. Any indication you were questioning that place meant trouble. If that was the worst thing about work, one of the best parts of this particular temping job, Tess's fourth since her arrival in London, was studying her supervisor. From her blonde bouffant to her rope of pearls, from her lace collar to her clumpy court shoes, Harriet was a one-woman tribute to the style of Princess Diana. No bow was too floppy, no shoulder pad too wide. She was also an almighty cow.

'Anyway,' she was saying, 'I've called your agency to ask for a replacement. We'll pay you up until this evening, but Beaumont and Associates require a more responsible sort of girl.'

'You're not serious.'

'I'm afraid I am. I told the agency that your attitude was wrong for a consultancy like this. "Where these girls get their ideas from, I do not know," I said. "In fact, I'm not at all sure that office work is Tess's forte."'

Tess felt anger bubble inside her. How she'd love to put Lady Snooty in her place. The snag was, the women in the temping agency were decent types, and she didn't want to piss them off. Still, she thought, as she scooped up her handbag and rose from the hard office chair, she couldn't allow Harriet to escape unmarked.

'Before I go,' she said, 'a small style tip: your teeth are too yellow for orange lipstick. And blue mascara? Hid-e-ous. Even Lady Di wouldn't touch the stuff these days.'

Harriet looked at her as if she was unhinged, but before she could say anything, Tess was out the door and mingling with the bobbing crowds. She would have to return to the secretarial agency. Hopefully, her next job would be more interesting.

She had arrived in London six weeks earlier with Nina, Tom and a college friend of Tom's named Fergal. They'd managed to find a tiny flat in Shepherd's Bush. As dingy a place as had ever been built, it had two bedrooms, a living room, a minuscule kitchen, a mould-infested bathroom and a resident mouse. The rent had made Tess gasp. On the plus side, the flat was a short walk from the Tube and a few streets from the bar where Tom was working for the summer. In

September, he'd be returning to college in Dublin, as would Fergal and Nina. Tess couldn't say what she'd be doing.

Following a mediocre Leaving Cert, she'd drifted into a secretarial course at St Ursula's. Although she'd been able to discard her school uniform, the woman who ran the course, Miss Gallagher, had insisted that her girls wear office clothing. By this, she meant a skirt, a cardigan, preferably in shades of grey or beige, and sensible shoes. Miss Gallagher, who was as thin as a stalk of celery and about as much fun, handed out extra work to any girl who broke the rules. Tess delighted in stretching her diktat to its limits. Her shoes were either vertigo-inducing or more suited to a building site than a typing pool; her skirts swept the floor or barely covered her backside. She paid for her distinctive style with the one pound fifty an hour she earned from a part-time cleaning job at the supermarket in Templemorris. One squally April afternoon, following a disagreement about the best way to take office minutes, Miss Gallagher had asked if Tess wanted to continue with the secretarial course. 'Do you know what?' she'd replied. 'I don't think I do.'

At least she'd stayed long enough to become a moderate typist. Her shorthand was more of a work in progress, and her bookkeeping skills were non-existent.

Tess's departure for London had been hastened by her mother's latest boyfriend. Jim Duignan wasn't an out-and-out sleaze, but Tess couldn't warm to the guy. He hovered around the house, laughing at his own jokes and giving unasked-for advice. When she'd first spoken about moving, her mam's reaction had been muted. Indifferent, almost. On the eve of her departure, this had changed, and her mother had practically clung to her leg. 'What'll I do without you, Tessy?' she'd said. 'You're all I've got.'

'I'm not going far,' Tess had replied. 'These days London is as close as Dublin. You'll have to come for a visit.'

They both knew this wouldn't happen, and weeks later Tess still had guilty thoughts about her mother, stuck in Kilmitten with Jim Duignan, a man with all the charisma of a cement block. Adding to her guilt was a row they'd had about her father. She wanted to know who he was. Her mam said all she needed to know was that he hadn't been interested in either of them. Tess wheedled and cajoled until her mother began to cry, but she didn't get an answer. She considered the possibility that somebody in the village might be able to help. Mags or Mercedes, perhaps. But, no, they'd have been incapable of staying quiet. If they knew her father's identity, they'd have let it slip before now.

None of this meant she was in any hurry to go home. As much as she loved her mother, she would never want her life. Tess's mam spent forty hours a week in a cold, smelly factory. On Fridays, she received a small brown envelope containing enough money for a few groceries and a night out. If she complained, some sour-face or other would tell her she was lucky to have a job. Who would want that life?

As she'd moved through her teens, Tess had grown into her looks. She was still too thin, but there were worse afflictions. Plus, being two inches shy of six feet had its advantages. She could intimidate little scuts like the O'Grady brothers without even trying. She'd also had blonde highlights added to her light brown hair. Friends, and some teachers, had maintained that her looks should be an advantage. But how? She had no interest in the beauty contests that proliferated at home: the Queen of the Back End of Nowhere where all the contestants had fat red cheeks and bad perms, and the top prize was a hamper of cheese and your picture in the local paper.

She loved London. It had taken her all of ten sleepy minutes sitting in the concourse of Euston station to discover this. Fresh from the Holyhead train, a paper cup of coffee in hand, her rucksack at her feet, she'd looked at the rush of commuters and thought, *This is the place for me.* Every day brought something new to amuse or intrigue: the beauty of the Georgian terraces, the dusty tang of the Underground, the stalls that sold exotic fruits, like watermelon and cherries, wine at two pounds a bottle, women in saris and *salwar kameez* . . . and the heat. Why had nobody told her about the heat? She'd assumed, with England being so close to Ireland, that the weather would be similar. Yet even on damp days, the city had a gorgeous soupy warmth. And still people complained. It was too humid, they'd moan. Tess told them that a week in Kilmitten might change their minds. 'Where I'm from,' she'd say, 'it's always windy. Even on the best day of the year, a sudden gust could slice you in two.'

Londoners, she was discovering, were partial to a good moan. If it wasn't the weather, it was the Tube. If it wasn't Margaret Thatcher, it was the price of property. 'It's all great,' Tess liked to say. Her colleagues would sigh and give her a look that said, 'You'll learn.'

She'd always wanted to go to London. In her early teens, she'd spent hours in the Templemorris library, poring over old copies of the *NME*. It wasn't the music that interested her so much as the characters, the venues, the fashions. She would read about the Brixton Academy or the Hammersmith Palais, and dream that one day life would take her to such places.

So far, the city hadn't let her down. Even simple things, like walking down the street, watching the hordes streaming past and wondering at their stories, gave her joy. Nobody knew who she was or where she came from, and that suited her just fine. There was scant chance of anyone wrinkling their nose and saying, 'Kilmitten? Isn't that the place where . . ?'

 In the years since Father Galvin's death, they'd all grown used to it. 'Yes,' they'd say, 'that's where the priest was killed and, no, they never caught anyone.'

However awkward this was for Tess, it was miserable for Tom. At college, he said, everybody had asked, and eventually he'd told the truth: it had happened in his house. Some people were content to leave it at that; more were brazen enough to question him. Who do you think did it? they'd ask. In the end, he looked an interrogator in the eye and said, 'Professor Plum in the library with the lead piping.' After that, they left him in peace.

Most people in Kilmitten had a favourite theory about Father Galvin, some plausible, some ridiculous. At the same time, they tended to fall back on wishy-washy words. They'd refer to 'the trouble', 'the tragedy' or 'the night of the party', as if, in the entire history of the village, there'd only ever been one party. From time to time, Tess and the other three spoke about the priest's death. Conor always maintained that whoever was responsible would be tracked down in the end. Tess suspected that this view was shaped more by loyalty to his dad than anything else. She didn't reckon the killer would be caught. Neither did Nina. It was hard to know what Tom thought. He didn't appear to enjoy talking about Father Galvin, and it rarely took him long to steer the conversation in another direction.

Officially speaking, Tess, Tom and Nina weren't in London together. Nina's father remained sniffy about Tess. How he felt about Tom, she didn't know, but Tom was a man and Dr Minogue wouldn't approve of his daughter sharing a flat with a man. That the arrangement was entirely sex-free, that they were eighteen years old, and that this was 1987, not 1957, didn't matter. As far as the Minogues were aware, their daughter was in London with friends from her teacher-training college. When Nina called home, which she did twice a week, she had to invent stories about Cathy, Orla and Gráinne, her make-believe flatmates. Tess had warned her mam not to reveal the real story, especially not to gossip hounds like Mags and Mercedes. 'If anyone asks, I'm with a girl from Templemorris, and Nina's with a gang from St Pat's,' she'd said.

Tom was always making fun of St Pat's, describing it as 'the virgin megastore'. Nina pretended to get annoyed, but Tess knew from the twitch in her cheeks that she was only messing.

*

'Harriet Osborne-Webb called,' said Marjorie, as she gestured at Tess to sit down.

'Ah. She told me she'd been talking to you.'

'No, I mean she called again – in a total tizzy. She's going to use a different employment agency in future. She said you'd made a nasty comment about her . . . eyeliner, was it?'

'Mascara.' Tess gazed at the grey carpet tiles. Overhead, the strip lighting buzzed. 'Shit, Marjorie. I'm sorry. She's even more of a cow than I thought.' When she looked up, Marjorie was passing her large red-framed glasses from one hand to the other.

'You'll have to learn to think before you speak.'

'So people tell me.'

'Perhaps you should listen to them.'

It hadn't occurred to Tess that Harriet would punish the agency. Marjorie had been good to her, and she didn't deserve to lose business. Tess knew she wasn't a model worker. Two of her three previous placings hadn't been successful either. The first office had been so eye-crossingly dull that she'd fallen asleep; the third so much sport, she'd ended up getting plastered during her lunch break. (That was another revelation about London. Although the Irish had a reputation for boozing, the English were devils for lunchtime drinking.)

Marjorie took a long breath. 'I'm sorry, Tess, I can't give you any more work.'

'Oh, hell.' Call her naive, but Tess hadn't seen this coming. 'Listen, I genuinely am sorry about Harriet. I'll never speak out of turn again, I swear. And I can do the work. You know that, don't you?'

'I do, but that's not the issue here.'

'Please, Marjorie, I promise I'll behave. I'll keep my opinions to myself. I'll get a proper night's sleep. I'll stick to lemonade. I'll—'

'No. You're making me feel bad, but no. It's more than my job's worth. Remind me again, how old are you?'

'Eighteen.'

'That's your problem, isn't it?'

'I'm not with you.'

'You're too young. You've got to get some of that craziness out of your system. Go and do something else, and when you've calmed down, come back to me.'

'Will I come back in a couple of weeks?'

'A couple of years, more like.'

'You're having me on.'

'I truly am sorry, lovey,' said Marjorie, 'but I can't afford to lose clients.'

Tess felt tears gathering in her eyes. She would have to leave before she made a fool of herself.

'Fair play to you,' said Tom, as he passed the joint to Tess. 'That Harriet woman sounds like she needed putting in her place.'

'It was fun while it lasted, all right. For once, though, I should probably have kept my thoughts to myself. I can't afford to be without a job.'

Rain pecked against the sitting-room window, while the

sky made ominous grumbling sounds. That was something else they didn't get much of in Kilmitten: thunder and lightning. The bare bulb cast a dim light over the room. The dark purple sofa, which might have been fashionable twenty years earlier, added to the gloom. Fergal was at work. Tom had a rare evening off.

Tess took a hit of the joint. With her other hand she played with the soft material of her skirt. An ankle-grazing number in swirls of blue, she'd bought it from a stall in Camden Market. It was her current favourite. What she would do now, she didn't know. For all that she moaned about secretarial work, it was moderately well paid. It allowed her to meet the rent and have a life. She could apply for full-time office jobs, but how long might that take? She'd need a reference, and Marjorie was unlikely to supply one. She could scrounge off Nina and Tom, but only for a week or two. They were saving money for their second year at college.

'I'll start looking again in the morning,' she said, giving the joint back to Tom. One of his work colleagues had a sideline as a hash dealer. Tess wondered if he made much money. 'I'll have to try another agency and hope they don't want a reference.'

'There's always bar work,' said Tom.

'I suppose, except I don't have any experience. Besides, I like having the evenings free. Sure we hardly see you – or Fergal.'

'I don't know how the pair of you cope without us.'

Nina rolled her eyes and took a sip of her wine. While

not a smoker, she was fond of cheap sauvignon. They all were. So far, their summer had been fuelled by Moroccan hash and dry white wine. 'I'll ask in our place tomorrow,' she said, 'but I don't think there's anything left.'

Nina had a strange job in the City. She spent her days processing cheques and application forms from people who wanted to buy shares in Britain's airports, which were about to be privatised.

'Who owns the airports now?' Tom had asked.

'Everybody,' Nina had replied.

'So they're selling them to themselves?'

'That's about the size of it.'

'You'd have to love this country,' he'd said. 'They've so much money, they're buying what they already own.'

They were a conundrum, Nina and Tom. It was obvious that Tom fancied her, and that she liked him back. Tess had imagined that sharing a flat for the summer would bring them together. Instead, they'd fallen into a pattern where Tom pretended to make fun of Nina, and she pretended to take offence. Tess thought of Tom as a fellow traveller. He was always up for a lark, for having a laugh today and worrying about the consequences tomorrow. Nina was more measured. She would veer only so far from the straight and narrow before her puritanical streak took over and dragged her back again. Still, there was a spark between them, Tess was sure of it. One of them had to make a move, though, and neither was showing any sign of doing so. Tom was surprisingly slow, and while Nina liked to talk about women taking control of their lives, she could be very old-fashioned.

'I've the job for you, Tessy,' said Tom, through a cloud of smoke.

'Go on.'

'Did you ever consider becoming a nightclub hostess? A lovely-looking girl like you should have no bother. I'd say any of those places around Leicester Square would snap you up.'

'Stop it, Tom,' said Nina. 'Next we know, you'll be suggesting that Tess puts a tart card in a phone box: "Long-legged Irish girl available for light caning".'

'Needs must,' said Tess. 'I can see myself serving cocktails in a bikini, feathers in my hair.'

'That's the attitude,' said Tom. 'You'd be in your element, coming home with fistfuls of fivers.'

'All of them shoved inside my bra by grateful patrons.'

'You're joking,' said Nina.

Tess laughed. 'I am. Although I read a piece in the *Evening Standard* the other day about marrying for money – so the guy can get a work visa, you know? – and I must admit, it's starting to sound attractive.'

The sky was at full snap, crackle, pop now, the rain drumming against the glass. In London, even the rain was loud.

'Seriously, Tess,' said Nina, 'you'll get a new job. You might even find something you like. And if you don't, you can always go home again. That wouldn't be the end of the world, would it?'

'It mightn't be far off. The thought of another year in Kilmitten makes me feel ill. No, I've escaped, and I'm not going back.' She signalled to Tom for the joint.

'It doesn't have to be Kilmitten. What's wrong with Dublin?'

'Nothing, except I prefer it here. Anyway, I'm sure you're right. London's a big old place. There has to be a job with my name on it.'

Lightning whipped across the sky, filling the room with white light. Tess realised that sadness was creeping over her. More than this, she felt out of sync with the others. She'd hoped the summer would cement their friendship. Instead, it was emphasising their differences. She remembered Conor saying they'd always be bound together by the night of the party. Maybe so, but it was an uncomfortable connection.

It was easy for Nina and Tom. Here they were, having an adventure. Soon enough, they'd be heading home, their lives stretching out in front of them, opportunities waiting. Conor also had plans. He'd told Tess about them before she'd left Kilmitten, then sworn her to secrecy. She was different. With no particular talent or ambition, she was fumbling along, aiming to get through the day with as little grief as possible. In her darker moments, she pictured herself alone in some rancid bedsit, doing a job no more satisfying than her mother's, stumbling from pay cheque to pay cheque, a magnet for losers and users. She couldn't say any of this out loud. Nina would give her an intense look before explaining why she was wrong. Tom would urge her not to be daft.

Tess took a pull on the joint, then returned it to Tom. She told herself to grow up, to act like the adult she wanted to be. Try as she might, though, she couldn't shake off her fears.

Chapter 7

Kilmitten

The miracle was that he'd got this far without his father's knowledge. Conor had assumed the news would filter down or that his dad's intuition would point him in the right direction. Yet, as far as he knew, his secret was intact. There was no method to this secrecy, no grand plan. He was nervous, simple as that. No matter that the news was good – well, most people would consider it good – he couldn't be sure how his dad would react.

They were at the kitchen table, the remains of their pork chops in front of them. It had been Conor's turn to cook. Once or twice a week, Paula still made dinner, but she had a life of her own now with an office job in Templemorris and a husband. Two months previously she'd married the eldest O'Grady brother, Marty. They'd been going out for three years, and marrying had been the logical step. If they were in Dublin, they would probably have lived together, but in Kilmitten that wasn't an option. If you were young and wanted regular sex, you did the decent thing and got married.

Conor, too, was working in Templemorris. While he'd had the points for college, he hadn't been able to find a course that appealed to him. When a position as a trainee car mechanic had become available, he'd decided he'd better take it. All the while, he'd shied away from saying what he actually wanted to do. He'd been biding his time, waiting for the right advertisement to appear in the papers. Part of him envied Tom, living it up in UCD, an entire city of women to charm, nobody to monitor his behaviour. Although Tom continued to lust after Nina, this hadn't prevented him pursuing a stream of others. 'I don't want to get tied down,' he'd claim. Conor suspected he was scared of being knocked back. If there was one thing he could say for sure about his friend, it was that he was more complicated than he liked people to think.

'So,' said his father, 'what's the story?'

'What do you mean?'

'Something's going on with you.'

'Ah.' His old man wasn't so dozy after all. 'I was about to tell you.' He got up and went to the cupboard beside the door, the one where they kept the bills and whatnot. He removed a brown envelope from the pile, then sat down again. 'This came today.' He passed the letter to his dad, who unfolded the A4 sheet and read.

'Well, now,' he said, his face hard to decipher. 'Why didn't you tell me what you were doing?'

'I didn't know if they'd have me.'

'You never said. About wanting to be a guard, I mean.'

'I didn't know how you'd feel, so I thought I'd apply and see how I got on.'

For the longest five seconds, his father said nothing. Conor sat motionless, paralysed by doubt. Why had he insisted on keeping it to himself? What was wrong with him that he couldn't be upfront? What if his dad thought he was making a mistake, that he wasn't suited to the force?

Finally, his father stuck out his hand. His grip was firm, enthusiastic. 'If it's what you want, it's great news. The best news. When do you start?'

'The training begins in September.'

His father's lips curved into a smile. When he spoke again, there was amusement in his voice. 'It's true what the fella says: you learn something new every day. There I am, the man who's supposed to know what's happening around these parts, and I don't even know what's going on under my own roof.' It was his dad's turn to rise from the table. He returned with a bottle of Jameson and two tumblers. 'If anything ever called for a drink,' he said, 'this is it.'

Conor's father had never been given to drinking, but in recent years, he'd had even less time for alcohol. And far less tolerance for drunkenness. Like so much else, Conor traced the change back to the killing of Father Galvin. If the first major upheaval in their lives had come with the death of his mother, the second had been prompted by the death of the parish priest. It seemed too simplistic to say that his dad had never been the same, but it was true. While the crime hung over all of them, his father relived it every day.

For a few months afterwards, the village had throbbed with activity. Opinions had been canvassed, statements taken, leads pursued. Gradually, most of the investigating gardaí had been called back to Dublin or Limerick, leaving Conor's dad to work on the case alone. Every now and again, there was a spurt of activity. Somebody would come forward with a new theory or what they claimed as a fresh piece of information. For a short while, his dad would be filled with purpose and vigour. He'd be up early, out late, making calls, interviewing witnesses. But every time the hope would wither away. To all intents and purposes, the investigation had failed.

In the intervening years, Conor had heard more about what had happened that night. Excluding his father, there had been fifty-four people at the party. Fifty-four suspects. Or should that be fifty-five? There were those who argued that Flan Varley should have had no role in the investigation. He'd been at the party. He'd been seen talking to Leo Galvin. How could he conduct a fair and thorough inquiry? Although Conor's father had attempted to brush aside these claims and insinuations, it was clear they'd left their mark. 'We talked about the snow,' he'd say. 'Nothing else.'

From the start, the investigation had been hampered by the number of people in the house and by the fact that most of them were drunk. It had been dark. The music had been loud. People had wandered from room to room. So many possible killers, so many conflicting stories. One person would say, 'What about X? He disappeared for ages.' Somebody else would say, 'No, I saw him on the stairs with

Y.' The guards suspected that some witnesses were trying to settle old scores. More were plain confused, addled by alcohol and shock. Then there were those who questioned whether a crime had been committed at all. Suppose the priest was the worse for drink, they'd say. Suppose he fell. The guards, including Conor's father, said this didn't tally with the evidence. According to the post-mortem, Father Galvin had had less to drink than most. The angle at which he'd fallen, the way he'd hit his head, suggested he'd been pushed with considerable force. Someone else had been in the room, and if they hadn't meant to hurt him, why hadn't they raised the alarm? They'd left the discovery to poor Cora Crossan, who hadn't been right for months afterwards.

And there was the glass. The priest's whiskey glass had been smashed against the far wall, shattering into so many pieces that lifting reliable fingerprints had proved almost impossible. The fragments had contained Cora's prints, but she had poured the drink, so that told them nothing. Had Father Galvin thrown the glass himself? If so, why? Or was it more likely that his killer had been responsible? Although some would disagree, Conor's father always referred to what had happened as murder. 'I don't give a toss whether they set out to kill him,' he'd say, 'whoever hurt the unfortunate fellow walked away. That's as bad as murder in my book.'

Conor had garnered information over the years, from snatches of overheard conversation, from chats with his dad and, occasionally, from reports in the papers. There was one fact on which everyone agreed: whoever had attacked Leo Galvin was no career criminal. There had been no repeat offence, and the village had returned to being as quiet a spot as you could find. Two stolen bicycles amounted to a crime wave.

The interview board had been careful not to mention Kilmitten, and in his answers, Conor had been equally reserved. He liked to think he'd given honest reasons for his application. He wanted to be a guard because he reckoned it was something he could do. His ambitions lay in tackling serious crime, he told them, not arresting lads for broken headlights or women for stealing a loaf of bread. He'd have to begin with the basics, they warned, and he might never get any further. He said he'd take his chances. He was, of course, nervous about letting people know that he'd be following his father into the police. It seemed so unimaginative. Still, he was confident that his career would be different.

'You know you can't be stationed around here,' said his dad, as he poured them another measure of whiskey. 'There are rules about that class of thing.'

'So I gather.'

'They'll probably send you to Dublin. The city's crying out for guards. Or the border. They're always looking for men there.'

'True, but I might get somewhere closer. There's Limerick. Limerick's busy.'

'That wouldn't be too bad.'

For the first time, it occurred to Conor that his father might miss him. Although his old man had gone out with a couple of women, he remained unattached. As it was, the two of them rattled around the bungalow. There was definitely too much space for a man on his own. 'Who'd have me now?' he'd say, when Paula nagged him about being single.

'Plenty, Dad,' she'd reply. 'Plenty.'

He was forty-five. Old, certainly. But not decrepit. Not beyond all hope.

'Your mam would have been pleased,' he said.

Conor swallowed a mouthful of whiskey. He was more of a beer drinker, and the spirit burned and tickled all the way down. His eyes watered. 'Thanks,' he said. 'That's a good thought.'

'Have you been talking to them at work?'

'Not yet. They'll let me go straight away, I'd say. There'll be no shortage of lads looking for the job.'

'What'll you do with yourself between now and September?'

'I was thinking of heading over to London for a few days, to see Tom. And Liverpool are playing at Arsenal next month, so . . .'

'Aren't you the crafty lad? You have it all figured out.'

'I wish.'

His father ran a finger down the side of his glass. 'The reason you were reluctant to tell me about the application . . . would it have anything to do with the Father Galvin business? With you thinking that, maybe, it's jaundiced my view of the job?'

Conor floundered for a response. No plausible lie came and, tongue loosened by whiskey, he told the truth. 'To be honest, yes. With the way everything panned out and all the hassle you had to put up with, I wouldn't blame you for thinking, *What does he want to do that for? Why doesn't he find something easier?*

'You're assuming I've given up.'

Something flashed across his father's face. Irritation? No, Conor decided, it was closer to disappointment. Him and his big mouth. 'I'm sorry. I didn't mean it to sound like that.'

'Well, I haven't. You're right, though. It's not an easy job. It's not like the films where everything comes together in the end, and where it all makes sense. Sometimes nothing makes sense.'

'I don't—'

'Do you remember how people used to ask, "Why would anyone kill a priest?" Over and over again, I heard that question. But why wouldn't someone kill a priest? Why should that be harder to understand than any other violent crime? Don't get me wrong, I'm not certain that whoever attacked Leo Galvin went out that night with the intention of killing him, but they obviously felt they had a reason to assault him. That reason might sound deluded to you or me, yet they must have thought it had some sort of logic.'

He paused to take a drink.

Realising his dad wanted to talk, Conor did his best not to make a sound. He didn't want to break the flow. He was conscious of something else too: maybe this was a one-off, but there'd been a subtle shift in his father's attitude, as if he recognised Conor as a fellow adult.

'That's one lesson I've learned,' he continued. 'People

don't always behave in ways the rest of us would consider logical. And still they manage to justify their actions to themselves. How often have I heard, "Sure I didn't mean any harm, Sergeant"? As though that excuses everything.'

'People can be fairly thick, right enough.'

'It's more than that. Why do otherwise smart people make bad decisions and keep on making them? Take your friend Tess. Her mother lets idiots – and worse – take advantage of her again and again. She gets rid of one gobshite, if you'll pardon the expression, then replaces him with another. And Ginny's not a stupid woman, so why does she behave like that?'

Outside, the shadows were lengthening, the sun slowly dipping. Conor's dad took a slug of his whiskey. 'What I'm trying to say is that sometimes people are hard to fathom.'

Conor wanted to nudge the conversation back towards Father Galvin. 'Did you ever settle on a motive?' he asked.

'A motive? Like I told you, the problem wasn't that we couldn't find one. It was that we found too many.'

'How so?'

'Listen, Conor, I can't trawl through every possible reason why somebody might have fallen out with Leo Galvin. I don't want you going around suspecting half of the village. But . . .' he hesitated, as if grappling for the right words '. . . to give you an idea of how complicated it all became, it took us a little while to learn that several people owed him money. You might say that any one of them had the motive to hurt him, but I don't think that any of them was to blame.'

Conor was intrigued as to who might have been in the

priest's debt, but was wary of asking. 'How come, ahm . . . how come people owed him money?'

'Gambling debts, mainly. He was a useful poker player, was Leo Galvin. And then he lent money to a few others, like . . .' His father pinched the bridge of his nose. 'What I'm saying to you is to go no further than this room.'

'Okay.'

'Two or three people in the village were in a bit of difficulty, and they borrowed money from him, money they couldn't pay back.' Shock must have registered on Conor's face for his father quickly added, 'Now, I don't for a moment believe that any of them was involved in his death. But that's the reason I'm telling you this: so you can see how easy it would be to jump to conclusions, and how wrong you'd be.'

'I understand.'

'Not a word to anyone, now. You promise?'

'Promise,' said Conor, who paused, then asked another question. 'After all this time, do you really think you'll get to the truth?'

His father drained his glass. 'I do.'

Chapter 8

'What do you make of Conor?' asked Nina, as she swept the brush across her toenails. She wasn't convinced that bright red – or, to use its actual name, Acapulco Sunset – was her colour. Tess had insisted otherwise. That was Tess for you: hardly a penny to her name, yet she'd come home swinging a shopping bag full of make-up, half of which she'd given to Nina. 'Imagine if we had this many colours in Ireland,' she'd said. 'Wouldn't life be so much better?' Nina didn't know whether to be worried about her friend's spending or embarrassed by her generosity.

'I think he's made the right choice,' said Tess, from the other side of the sitting room where she was painting her fingernails a metallic blue. 'And not because of his dad. You know Conor, he's so determined. So . . . what's the word? Dogged. That's it. I reckon he'll make a great guard. Tom didn't look impressed, mind.'

'I wanted to give him a dig. He could have made more of an effort to look pleased. What's his problem, do you think?'

'Who knows? Although, if I had to guess, I'd say it's not Conor's choice that bothers him. What gets to him is the notion of his best friend having a "career".' Tess made air quotes with her fingers. 'Tom can be a restless character, and he hates the idea of his friends becoming settled. He wants everybody to be a drifter. Like me,' she added, her voice low.

After she'd lost her secretarial work, Tess had resolved to take the first job she came across. The following morning she'd spotted a 'help wanted' sign in the window of a nearby burger place. That evening, she'd started work. 'It's just to tide me over,' she'd said. Nina worried that she wasn't showing any interest in moving on. Yes, she was having a great time at Wonder Burger – 'Basic wage, maximum crack,' as she put it – but, in less than a month, the rest of them would be returning to Dublin. She needed to secure something better. She also needed to find new flatmates; people who were able to afford the rent, not come-day-go-day types who were happy to bed down but unable or unwilling to pay the bills. Nina had tried saying all of this. She'd been met with a dismissive wave of the hand. 'Tomorrow,' Tess had said, like a Kilmitten Scarlett O'Hara.

All the same, there were times when Nina envied her friend. More often than not, Tess fizzed with enthusiasm. Even the tiniest thing, like the fabric shops near Shepherd's Bush Market, made her beam with pleasure. Nina would find herself thinking, *Where does that joy come from?* It wasn't that she didn't like London, more that she found herself noticing its fissures and joins. Every morning, she got the tube to work. She studied her fellow passengers, the dreadlocked boys and big-haired girls, the cut-off Levi's and boxy suits. She inhaled the patchwork of scents, the Dewberry and Old Spice and sweat. And she tried to feel part of it. Before long, though, she'd be distracted by the graffiti and grime. She'd be struck by the ugliness of a tower block or she'd find herself gazing at the men who lived in cardboard boxes, too many of them Irish.

It's a wonderful city, she'd think, *but it's not for me.*

Conor and Tom were at a soccer match. Fergal, bored with Kilmitten stories, had abandoned them for his girlfriend's flat. A Roscommon-born nurse, she was trying to persuade him to leave college and stay in London. Later they were all going to a party. 'Some Irish guys living near Goldhawk Road. That's as much as I know,' Tom had said.

Tess put aside her nail polish and lit a cigarette. 'I wonder what your old man would say if he could see us now.'

Nina didn't like to be reminded of her father's lofty attitude towards Tess. Nor did she like to dwell on his mistaken belief that she was sharing a flat with three friends from college. 'I hear you,' she said. 'I know I'm a coward, but I wanted to get away without any trouble.'

'Relax, I'm only playing with you. It can't be much fun for you either. Are you not running out of stories about the three Marys or whatever they're called?'

'Orla, Cathy and Gráinne,' said Nina, with a laugh. 'And, no, I'm fine at the moment.'

'Lovely girls, no doubt.'

'Oh, the loveliest.'

The two rarely discussed how Nina's father had treated

Tess. They followed the long tradition of saying everything apart from what ought to be said. Sometimes, however, it hung between them, heavy as lead. Nina was well aware that she ought to take a stand. It was time she told her parents that she was old enough to choose her own friends. This was what she'd tell anyone else to do, and she wasn't proud of her hypocrisy.

'Does my dad's behaviour still get to you?' she asked.

'Yeah, it does,' said Tess, who then stopped, like she was thinking through what had happened. 'I'll never forget calling to your door and being told to vamoose. I remember standing there, the snow tipping down around me, thinking, *What do I do now?* I didn't want to tell Mam because I figured she'd storm up to your father and chew the ear off him . . . or else she'd get upset. I'd had to talk to her about being in the shed, so she was already mad with me. Not for the smoking – that didn't surprise her – but for messing up the investigation. She's always had a soft spot for Conor's dad.' Tess blew a twist of smoke towards the ceiling. 'Of course I had to tell her eventually because she kept asking why we didn't see you any more.'

'What did she say?'

'Not a lot. She went to her room. After an hour or so, she came back down with an inch of make-up on her. At first, I thought she was going out on the town. Then I realised she'd been crying. I didn't know what to say so I told her I was sorry, and then she got upset all over again.'

'You should have told me before now.'

'To be fair, how did you think she'd react? The way your

father behaved, it was like I had a disease. Like I was dirty. Besides, say I had told you back then, what difference would it have made? You were away at St Snotty's Academy for Respectable Young Ladies, or whatever it's called, so you weren't around much anyway. I asked Conor what I should do, and he advised me to let it rest. He said Mam wouldn't want people knowing how upset she'd been. And he was right. If she knew I was telling you now, she'd give me a clatter.'

Nina's thoughts flicked back to Millmount Abbey. Although the Emers had moved on to a fresh target, those early months had stuck to her like tar. She'd never been part of the in-crowd and she'd made no lasting friends. The irony was, her exam results had been little better than average. She would probably have achieved the same grades at the community school in Templemorris. Still, as she liked to say, she'd met a better class of bully. Oh, and she'd learned that no child of hers would ever be sent to boarding school.

While Nina's mother had welcomed her choice of primary-school teaching, her father had done nothing to hide his disappointment. He'd presumed she would follow him into medicine. Failing that, he would have tolerated pharmacy, dentistry or law, something that would have given her letters after her name and a permanent place in the world of the well-to-do. Teaching four-year-olds to share their toys wasn't on his list. People as clever as her dad couldn't understand the struggles of others. It had been impossible to explain that, while she was smart, she wasn't *that* smart. If she'd spent every waking hour with her head in a book, she still wouldn't have secured the points for one of his preferred courses. No matter how often she told herself that what she'd chosen was worthwhile, she couldn't shrug off the sense of failure. *Not quite good enough*: that was her.

She walked over and squeezed Tess's cigarette-free hand. 'I really am sorry. What my dad . . . what both my parents did . . . was wrong, and I should have stood up to them. When I call them this evening, I'll tell them the truth about my flatmates.' She gave the bony hand another squeeze.

'Careful,' said Tess, 'or you'll damage my beautiful nails.'

'You're something else,' said Nina.

'I hope you remember that when I'm down on my luck and looking for help.'

'As you mention it—'

'No,' said Tess. 'No nagging. Not today. I want to enjoy myself today.' She stubbed out her cigarette.

Nina went back to the sofa and sifted through their new make-up. For a few minutes they sat in silence, one dabbing on foundation, the other plucking her eyebrows. Something Nina's father had said before she left for London was on her mind. Her mother had referred to Tess's departure from Kilmitten. 'There's not a lot keeping her here,' she'd said.

'Shame her father never got involved in her life,' Nina's dad had replied.

'Indeed,' said her mother, her voice implying that the conversation shouldn't go any further.

It wasn't so much her dad's words that had resonated with Nina as his tone. That and the way her mam had shut down the discussion. *You know*, she'd thought. *You know who he is.* Later, she'd re-evaluated what she'd heard and concluded she was reading too much into it. She thought about saying something to Tess, but what? Tess's interest in her father had grown over the years. This might send her into a frenzy, and Nina couldn't be sure her parents did know the truth. No, she'd remain quiet for now and do some more digging when she got home.

'I've been meaning to ask you,' said Tess. 'What's up with yourself and Tom?'

'What do you mean?'

'Now, Nina, don't go acting all dumb on me. Are you ever going to get moving?'

Nina was surprised to feel warmth in her cheeks. She hoped it wasn't obvious. Her hope was in vain.

'Woooh,' said Tess, like a ten-year-old in the playground. 'Look at the face on you.'

Nina smiled.

Tess clapped her fingertips. 'You must know how much he likes you. He's been mooning after you since we were in primary school. And Fergal and myself have had to spend the summer watching the two of you playacting. When are you going to get it together?'

'I don't know,' said Nina, passing an eyeshadow from one hand to the other. 'Maybe we've known each other for too long. Maybe we're better off as friends.'

'Friends, my eye. Why can't you admit you like the guy?'

'What's this? An interrogation?'

'Nope. I'm taking a kindly interest, that's all. I mean, by any standards, he's a good-looking fellow. By Kilmitten standards, he's an absolute ride.'

'You sound like you fancy him yourself.'

'I'd be wasting my time. Anyway, I didn't come to London to go out with lads from home.'

'Okay,' said Nina. 'Yes, I do like him.' How could a straight, sane woman not like Tom? He was intelligent and entertaining. He was attractive. You could warm your hands on his smile. And yet . . .

'And?' asked Tess.

'And, like I said, I'm not sure.'

Nina had assumed that when they moved to Dublin she would hook up with Tom, but the situation had proved far from straightforward. He was living on the southside with four UCD classmates. She was in northside digs, her host family so strait-laced they made the Waltons look like the soul of debauchery. She had fallen into a relationship with an engineering student called Derek McNulty. While Derek wasn't the brightest bulb in the circuit, he was a nice guy, and she'd lost her virginity in a dusty bedsit on the Drumcondra Road, the experience neither as joyful nor as painful as anticipated. Derek had gone to Cape Cod for the summer, and Nina had no particular interest in rekindling their romance.

So, if there was no reason not to have a fling with Tom, what was holding her back? What she'd said to Tess about them knowing each other for too long was part of the story, but only part of it. Nina often found him difficult to understand. There was your regular Tom: witty, mischievous, engaged. And then, in a finger click, there was someone else. Someone evasive, distant, hard to decode. Someone who could give a harsh response to the most innocent of comments. A couple of weeks back, Tess had joked about the smell in the bathroom being so rank that there must be a dead body under the bath. Tom had snapped at her, saying it really was time she learned to think before opening her mouth. While they'd all been affected by the death of Father Galvin, Nina guessed the impact on Tom had been especially deep.

She couldn't be certain he was still keen on her. If he was, why hadn't he made a serious move? That this went against everything she believed in was beside the point. While Nina wanted women to be free to ask men out, it wasn't a freedom she intended to exploit. Not with Tom, at any rate.

'If you ask me, you're a hopeless pair,' Tess was saying. 'Now, pass me those tweezers while you still have some eyebrow left.'

'What? Oh, yeah, will do.' Nina got to her feet. 'I'd better do something with my hair. The humidity has made it go wild. I'd take an iron to it only . . .'

'. . . we don't have an iron. Honest to God, Nina, the nonsense you worry about. I'd give anything to have hair as thick as yours.' Tess lifted a hank of her own hair. She might have meant to emphasise how thin it was but succeeded only in highlighting its shine.

'It's true what they say, you never want what you've got.'

'Is that about hair or life in general?'

'Both,' said Nina.

Later, as they strolled towards the bar where they'd arranged to meet Tom and Conor, Nina decided she'd better keep her promise. She pulled her phone card from her bag. 'I'll give my parents a shout.'

'Ah,' said Tess, with a knowing smile. 'Good luck with that. Give my love to your dad.'

The early evening was warm, the sun covered by a gauze of cloud. The phone box stank of disinfectant and hot metal, and as she tapped out the number, sweat collected along Nina's spine. She breathed in and told herself to relax. She'd be casual about the truth and then she'd say goodbye, give them time to think it through.

Her brother answered the phone. 'Hi, Hugh, is Mam there?' she asked. She didn't want to get waylaid by chatter about football or some such.

'Wait until you hear—' he started, then surrendered the phone to their mother.

'I take it you haven't heard the news?' she said.

Five minutes later Nina rejoined Tess.

'What did you say to them?' Tess asked, rocking on her heels with anticipation.

'Ahm, there was a bit of a problem. I didn't get to the flat issue.'

'Why so?'

'Because they did most of the talking. There's big news at home. Noel O'Grady drove his car into a ditch.'

'There's a shock. Was he hurt?'

'He was killed. Conor's dad called an ambulance, but it was too late.'

'Oh, crap,' said Tess, linking arms with Nina. 'We'd better go and tell the lads.'

Chapter 9

'I take it he was drunk,' said Conor, who was wedged into the corner of the Eagle and Serpent, a cloudy pint in front of him.

'Mouldy,' said Nina. 'He'd been in Pilkington's all night.'

'What a fool. He'd have walked home in twenty minutes.'

Tess pushed her hair back from her face. 'We're definitely in the wrong place tonight. I'd say the hullabaloo in the village is something else. Mags, Mercedes and the gang must be up to ninety.'

Tom was becoming annoyed. It wasn't as if he'd liked Noel O'Grady. With his Brillo-pad hair, corned-beef face and shapeless brown suits, the guy was everything you didn't want to be when you grew up. Then there was his braying voice and his six sons, each dumber than the next. But the man was lying in the morgue. A bit of respect was called for. 'Come on, Tess,' he said. 'A guy – a neighbour of ours – is dead.'

'Fair enough, but what's it to you? Do we have to act like we're old people and every death affects us, whether we liked the person or not?'

'He is . . . was . . . an in-law of Conor's.'

'He wasn't really,' said Conor. 'He was Paula's father-in-law, but I don't think that made him anything to me. Besides, I've nothing against Marty, but I doubt Paula would've married him if she'd ever travelled further afield. Let's face it, the pool in Kilmitten is pretty shallow.'

Nina spat out her cider. Whether from shock or laughter, Tom wasn't sure.

'In fairness,' said Tess, 'Marty's the pick of the litter.'

'Yeah, but what a miserable litter,' added Nina.

'Seriously, girls,' said Tom, 'you're going too far now.'

'Ah, please,' said Tess, her voice tart. 'Having respect for a dead man is one thing. Having to pretend we give a monkey's about the O'Grady brothers is another. When I was a kid, Philly and Seánie were forever giving me stick about not having a father. Noel junior was worse. He used to claim that Father Galvin was my dad, only it had all been hushed up by the Catholic Church and that his death was some big conspiracy. If I said anything, I was accused of not being able to take a joke. Can you imagine how that made me feel?'

'All right, they're a shower of wasters, but that doesn't mean this is the right time to slag them off.'

'Believe me, Tom, there's never a wrong time to slag off the O'Gradys. And they're more than a shower of wasters. Except for Marty, they're a collection of scumbags. You know what your problem is? You're so—'

Conor, ever the peacemaker, intervened with a gentle cough. 'Lads, can we cool it? People are staring at us.'

'Okay, Garda Varley,' said Tess. 'I'll tone it down, but only because you asked nicely.'

'Thanks. When I've finished my pint, I'll go out and ring home. It's not Paula who worries me so much as Dad. He'll have had to look after the scene – and inform Breege O'Grady. It's not easy work.'

Tom couldn't stop himself. 'And it's all ahead of you.'

'On that cheery note,' said Tess, 'I'm going to the bar.'

Tom had brought them to the Eagle and Serpent because he'd wanted a night away from the pub where he worked. The Sheaf of Wheat was a grand spot, but you had to be in the humour for it. It was glued together by decades of nicotine and grease, and the head barman insisted on playing The Wolfe Tones and other Irish ballad groups on a scratchy loop. The customers were glassy-eyed, mossy-teethed Irish men. Many of them were obsessed with home, a place that was an hour away and a million miles away. Although younger Irish guys sometimes came in for a drink, there was something uncomfortable about their presence. In jarring voices, they spoke about their office jobs, their English girlfriends and their Ryanair flights from Luton to Dublin. 'Fine, we get it,' Tom wanted to say. 'You're not like the old lads.' No doubt the same guys spent their Saturday nights in the National Ballroom in Kilburn where they got legless and sang along to 'Four Country Roads', all the while telling themselves they were behaving in an ironic way.

That being said, the punters in the Eagle were annoying Tom too. And what was with the music? Was it possible to find a pub in London where your words weren't drowned out by the pounding of the sound system? If he never heard Rick Astley again, it would be too soon. Why didn't Londoners understand that bars were for drinking and talking, not for putting up with someone else's taste in music?

He knew he was being ratty, but he couldn't help himself. Conor's announcement had plunged him into bad form. They were young. They weren't like their parents. They could go anywhere. Be anyone. They could try on different lives to see what suited them. And what did Conor do? He joined the cops, like his father before him. What had he to look forward to now? He'd be stationed in some kip of a village or in a godforsaken Dublin suburb where kids in stolen cars would try to run him down and junkies would threaten him with syringes of infected blood. Oh, Tom knew he was exaggerating. He knew he wasn't being fair. But fairness would have to wait for another day.

They'd spent the afternoon in the sweltering heat at Highbury, watching Liverpool beat Arsenal, Conor as upbeat as Tom had ever seen him. He'd tried to be pleased for his friend. He just didn't have it in him.

Say what you like about Tess, she had the right attitude. She knew how to be young. As crazy as he was about Nina, she was so damn cautious. Take the way she fretted about Tess. 'She needs to get a proper job,' Nina would say. 'She needs a plan.' They were eighteen. What did any of them want with a plan?

His father had always tried to do the right thing and what good had it done him? There he was, marooned in the house of horrors, with neither the money nor the energy to tackle its dilapidation. He'd finally come around to the idea of selling the place. But who would buy a house where a priest had been killed? Major bad voodoo, as one of the lads at college had put it. In the two years it had been on the market, his parents had welcomed a trail of rubberneckers but hadn't received one serious bid. Tom had advised Nina to leave Tess alone, and she'd got narky with him. 'Tess ought to think more of herself,' she'd said. If you asked Tom, Nina still felt guilty about the way her old man had behaved. He told himself to stay quiet. Despite everything, Nina was close to her parents, and he didn't want to upset her.

Nina. He'd convinced himself that this was their summer, yet somehow he'd made no progress. They sparred and they flirted. They danced around each other, but for one reason or another, he always drew back. Imagine if he did make an advance and was rejected? How humiliating would that be? As it was, he found it hard to be close to her. Thankfully, she was slightly more buttoned up than Tess, who was given to wafting around the flat with half of her clothes missing.

If asked, he would find it difficult to explain why he liked Nina so much. She was very pretty, but so were lots of girls. It was possible that Tess was even prettier, and he didn't fancy her. The best answer he could come up with was that she was like him – and not like him. She was similar enough for him to relax in her company, different enough to provide a challenge. He'd gone out with several girls at college. Variations on a theme, they'd been blonde, Benetton-wearing and full of talk. He'd enjoyed a good deal of fumbling, and sometimes more, on sagging sofas in shared houses in Rathmines and Ranelagh. None of the UCD girls had captivated him the way Nina did. There was another complicating factor. Nina, bless her innocence, thought that he was like her, that he was all fired up by college. In truth, Tom hated his course. Nina was under the impression that he'd got a two-one in his first year commerce exams. In fact, he'd scraped a pass. Fergal knew the real story, and Tom had had to buy his silence with a ten spot of hash and a night of free beer. In a way, failing would have been preferable. Once his parents had got over their disappointment, he would have been free. Free to do what, he couldn't say. But he would have found something. Instead, he was facing into another soul-sapping year at UCD where the concrete merged with the sky and eighteen-year-olds thought their opinions were all that mattered.

Commerce had been the wrong choice. He'd picked it to please his parents, who'd wanted him to do something useful. His career-guidance teacher had been the same. 'Choose a course that will get you a job,' she'd said. Tom's reply, that he'd prefer to study something that would make a difference, had been met by a condescending smile. No doubt, she'd heard the same line a thousand times before.

There were days when he envied the certainty of Nina and Conor. They made life sound so clear-cut. Tom knew that no decision was straightforward. Every day, without fail, he thought of the decision he'd made on the night of his parents' party. And every day he questioned it. He saw that night with frightening clarity: the snow, the scene in the back kitchen, the way he'd acted like nothing was wrong.

He thought, too, of the days afterwards when he'd had opportunities to speak but had chosen not to. More than once, he'd asked himself if it was too late to say something now. He could talk to Conor, see what he thought. Then he'd changed his mind. He would have to stick by his decision.

He glanced at Nina. Her hands were stretched out on the table, her fingers taut with tension. He wanted to reach out and touch one of those hands. He wanted to stroke her long fingers, with their shiny red nails. And yet he sat there, his head filled with irritations and grievances. When Tess returned from the bar, there was every danger their bickering would resume. It was funny, he thought, people spoke about the difficulty of understanding others. Half of the time, Tom didn't even understand himself.

There was a pattern to the parties that summer. Hordes of young Irish people gathered in houses with English beer and American music and tried to be smarter, funnier and wilder than they'd been at home. Half of them were students, playing at being grown-ups for a month or two. Others had made a permanent move. For many, going to London was an ambition and achievement in itself; how they made their living was irrelevant. They told stories about friends who'd moved into a squat in Peckham. They talked about buzzing on speed and tripping on acid, about the play they wanted to write or the band they were going to form. And, as they spoke, almost every word was exaggerated. '*Heeey*,' they'd say. '*How arrre yooou?*'

The party near Goldhawk Road was no different. Tom

was several beers in and feeling mellow. He was at one with the universe, a man enjoying his Saturday night. The alcohol had helped, as had a reminder from Nina that this was Conor's weekend away. 'He deserves to have a good time,' she'd said.

Tom sat on the floor of the front room, watching the dancing. Tess, Nina and Conor were flinging their arms around and swaying their hips. Tess managed to smoke while she moved. Conor looked slightly earnest, like he always did. Nina sang along to the music. One of the thin straps on her top kept slipping from her shoulder. The drums and bass thrummed, the guitar jangled, and everything felt better.

When the pubs closed, more people arrived. Some had been invited, others had got the word from a friend of a friend, more heard the noise and wandered in.

In the kitchen, a crowd was singing. Tom liked how singing stripped away all the *faux*-sophistication. At the start of the evening, everybody had been poised and cool. Now they were pink-faced and beer-stained, roaring out the only songs they knew: 'The Black Velvet Band' and 'Spancil Hill', 'The Rocky Road to Dublin' and the first verse of 'Dirty Old Town'. They mightn't like to admit it, but they weren't that different from the old lads who drank in The Sheaf of Wheat.

Conor and Tess had disappeared. Nina was talking to one of the guys who lived in the house. A Trinity student, as far as Tom knew. Philosophy or psychology or some such. Despite the heat, he was wearing a PLO scarf and a fisherman's jumper.

Tom realised he had reached the right level of drunkenness. If he went any further, his brain would cloud over and he'd become incoherent. Right then, he was at the point where the distractions had receded and he was able to focus on what he wanted. He was sharp – and he was determined.

'Hey there,' he said to Nina, doing his best to crowd out Trinity Philosophy Guy.

'My flatmate,' explained Nina, but Mr Trinity was already moving on. 'I was making progress there,' she said to Tom, but there was laughter in her voice.

'That's what worried me.'

He took a step closer. Her strap had slipped again, and he had to resist the urge to ease it back up her arm. She had beautiful arms, not too fat, not too scrawny.

'Tess gave me a talking-to,' she said.

'Need I ask about what?' Tom took another half-step. He was close enough now to notice her breathing, how shallow it was.

'I think you can guess.'

He smiled. 'She had a word with me too.'

'Ah. Well, you know what she's like.'

He looked into Nina's face. In the grainy light, her eyes appeared even larger than usual. 'Perhaps we should listen to her.'

'Perhaps,' she said.

Chapter 10

There was a chance that Tess's brain had come loose, that it was banging around her skull doing irreversible damage to itself. At least, that was what it felt like. Her stomach was no better. Every time she moved, she was hit by a sensation like she'd just stepped down from a chair-o-plane. The sun was relentless, scorching her skin through her polyester uniform. This was no morning to be picking up rubbish outside Wonder Burger but, as her punishment for being late, that was what she was doing.

She'd spent an age in the fuzzy borderland between waking and sleeping, debating whether or not to bother with work. In the next bed, Conor had been snoring up a storm. She would happily have smothered him. Reluctantly, she'd got up, and after a carton of milk, a glass of water, five Anadin and a cigarette, she'd decided to give work a try. It hadn't been a wise choice. Now, as she removed the Saturday-night debris from the pavement, all she could think of was returning to bed.

Well, that wasn't quite all . . .

Tess and Conor were home by the time Tom and Nina returned. It was clear that they were together. Properly together. Nina turned as red as a rash while Tom couldn't stop smiling. They held hands in a loose way, as if they were scared to make their connection obvious. For once, Tess behaved with tact. She finished her beer in one swallow and announced that she was going to bed. Then she yanked Conor by the arm and ushered him towards the girls' bedroom. 'You can have Nina's bed,' she said, in her most emphatic voice. She didn't want him getting the wrong idea. Conor was like the brother Tess didn't have, and that was the way she wanted it to stay.

She'd been wrong to question her friendship with the others. Even when they were falling out, they were in sync in ways that outsiders would never understand. Tess would never like the O'Grady brothers, but she could appreciate why Tom bristled at jokes about sudden death.

Before she'd left for Wonder Burger, she'd scribbled a note for Nina: *I've gone to call your father to fill him in on your shameful behaviour. I expect he'll be over on the next flight. See you later. Your clean-living, hard-working friend, Tess.*

She hoped that Nina and Tom were properly together now and that, for once, something might work out the way she wanted it to.

A wave of nausea slammed into her. Would it be possible, she wondered, to slink over to the green and have a short nap under a tree? She decided against. If caught, she'd be sacked, and she couldn't afford to lose another job. She told herself that if she could survive the next few hours, she'd be able to go somewhere with Conor and get a proper dinner. She had an overwhelming desire for roast chicken and mashed potato. Oh, and a can of Fanta. She'd sell her soul for a fizzy orange.

Tess was wiping her forehead and cursing her sweaty brown uniform when she noticed a woman staring at her. With her wavy blonde hair, sinewy figure, small black dress and silver sandals, she looked like money. Tess felt as if she was being measured, not in a general sense but actually measured.

'Can I help you?' she said.

The woman smiled. She had surprisingly unruly teeth. 'Do you work here?' she asked.

'No, I get my kicks from wearing this manky uniform and picking up burger wrappers.' Tess winked.

'You're Irish.'

'Afraid so.'

The woman put out her hand. 'My name's Estelle Lonsdale,' she said, as she gave Tess a business card.

Chapter 11

Why was it, Nina wondered, that the most trivial issues could spark the loudest arguments? It wasn't as if Tom's change of plan was that big a deal. Okay, she'd been looking forward to the weekend in Kilmitten. Tess was due home for the first time in ages. Conor would be there too, and they rarely saw him any more either. But there was nothing to stop her making the journey on her own. Still, here she was, tingling with anger. She liked everything to be orderly, and when it wasn't, she couldn't mask her annoyance.

For the past two years, Tom and Nina had shared a rented cottage in Ringsend. They were lucky to live in such a fantastic location: close to the city centre, even closer to the sea. The place was decorated in shades of landlord brown and purple, and some of the furniture appeared to have been stolen from a hospital. The bedroom had two iron lockers, while one of the kitchen chairs was actually a commode. Then there was the heating, which worked only in fits and starts, and the neighbour who liked to play his Black Sabbath records at two in the morning. But all of that was fine. The problem was the cottage's size: it was so suffocatingly small that when they fell out there was nowhere to hide.

'I don't know why you're in such a strop,' Tom was saying, as he paced the sitting room. 'I'm the one who's losing out.'

'I'm not in a strop. I'm just surprised you didn't say no. Why didn't you tell Val you had plans for the weekend?'

'Because that wouldn't have been fair. He's stuck.'

Nina smoothed back a wayward lock of hair. 'There must be someone else who can give him a dig-out.'

'If there was, he wouldn't have asked me.'

'Well, I'm going anyway.'

'I wouldn't expect you to stay here.' Tom sat down in one of their creaking armchairs. 'I wish I'd had more notice, but Val's brother's in a bad way. He's worried the poor fellow won't last the weekend and he can't afford to close the shop.'

'I don't see why not. It's not as though . . .' She allowed her voice to taper off, but it was too late.

'It's not as though a rickety old corner shop really matters. That's what you were going to say, isn't it?' Tom was on his feet again, striding up and down. There wasn't much space for striding. 'Now, if it was your job, or anyone else's job, that would be a different matter.'

'Don't twist my words.'

'I'm not twisting anything.' He paused. 'You know what, Nina, I happen to enjoy what I do, and I happen to like the guy I work for. He reminds me of my old man: no badness in him.'

Nina felt another surge of anger. 'What's that supposed to mean?'

Tom said nothing, just lifted a shoulder.

'It's a dig at my dad, isn't it?'

'If that's what you want to believe . . .'

'Oh, for God's sake,' she said. 'This is stupid.'

'My thoughts entirely,' said Tom, returning to his chair. 'I'm genuinely sorry about this. I don't like letting you down, but it's not like there won't be other weekends.'

'That's true, only . . . I thought this would be a great weekend, the four of us together – like old times, you know? Besides, I want to find out what the story is with this documentary. Every time I talk to them at home, they're giving out about it.'

'My own pair are the same. "What's the point in dredging up the past?" Dad keeps saying.'

'It must be especially grim for them, all right.'

'And you can be sure the TV people will make everybody look like they've crawled out of the bog.'

Earlier in the year, a television researcher had arrived in Kilmitten. She was from an independent production company, she'd said. They were making a programme about the killing of Father Leo Galvin and how the crime remained unsolved. For a week or two, she'd knocked on doors, taken notes and generally made a nuisance of herself. Now she'd returned – with a camera crew and director in tow. The documentary would be aired the following January to coincide with the tenth anniversary of Father Galvin's death. 'Ten years,' people kept saying. 'How can it be that long?' To Nina, it did feel like a long time. The intervening years had distorted her memory, amplifying some events, dimming others. She remembered being in the shed, the cigarette smoke burning her throat. She remembered her father humiliating her. And she remembered the snow. She didn't expect they'd ever see snow like that again.

In Kilmitten, some people still spoke about Father Galvin. In Dublin, as elsewhere, the conversation had moved on. His was just another name on the long list of unsolved crimes. All the same, Nina had the feeling that a TV programme would rekindle interest in his death. While this didn't bother her, others, including Tom, weren't so relaxed. According to her mother, most locals had closed ranks against the TV crew, but some had an open mind, and a few were co-operating.

She allowed herself a smile. 'Don't worry,' she said to Tom. 'I won't go giving them an interview: "My night in the shed. How I didn't see what happened".'

'Seriously, Nina, there's nothing to joke about.'

'I know, I know.' She sighed. 'I'd better go and pack.'

'Grand,' he said, stepping forward and putting his arms around her. 'I'll miss you.'

'I'll only be gone a couple of days.'

'I'll still miss you. Tell everyone I said hello, and I'll be down soon. I promise.'

By the time Nina set off for Kilmitten, the worst of the Friday-evening traffic had cleared. She loved driving west at this time of year when, even as the sky darkened in the east, it remained bright up ahead. Buoyed as she was by the prospect of seeing Tess and Conor, she was disappointed with herself for falling out with Tom. She was more disappointed with him for not getting his life in order. No doubt his story about Val's brother was true, but it seemed to Nina that he always had an excuse for avoiding home. He was busy, or he was going out with the lads, or he wasn't feeling well. Not that long ago, she'd challenged him. His response had been cagey. 'We're not all sentimental about where we came from,' he'd said, and changed the subject.

If you asked her, he was reluctant to visit Kilmitten because he didn't like the village's nosier residents asking about his job. 'And you with one of the best Leaving Certs in the school, not to mention two years of college,' Mags Moynihan had said. 'Could you not find something in an office?' Tom had tried to explain that dropping out of college mid-way was the same as never having been at all, but Mags hadn't wanted to hear. She'd wittered on about Nina's 'lovely job' as a teacher and Conor's 'important work' as a guard. And then there was Tess. 'Answer me this,' Mags had said, 'could any of us have guessed that Tess Fortune would go and become famous?'

Nina believed that if Tom really wanted to find something else he would. The fact was, and this baffled her, he loved what he did. Invariably, he came home from Val's For Value, an inner-city grocery shop, with a string of stories about local characters and their complicated lives. 'Some crack today,' he'd say, or 'Wait until I tell you what I heard.' The wages were pitifully low, and he frequently worked overtime for no reward, but to Tom, Val's was like a vocation. Nina reminded herself that she'd also fretted over Tess's future. What a waste of time that had been. Still, she wished Tom would move on from Val and his fascinating customers.

He did have ambitions. They just didn't tally with hers. He wanted to see the world. 'India,' he'd say. 'Afghanistan, Vietnam.'

'Not yet,' Nina would reply. 'It's too soon.' After a year as a substitute, she'd secured a permanent position in St Fachtna's National School on Dublin's southside. Although she'd been there only twelve months, she was entitled to apply for leave of absence. Tom had pounced upon this. 'Some other young teacher would be thrilled to get the gig for a year,' he'd said. 'And then you can walk right back, no questions asked. You'd be mad not to go for it.'

'It wouldn't feel right,' she'd replied.

This had prompted a lot of muttering about them only being young once, but Nina wouldn't be moved. While Tom accused her of not taking his job seriously, couldn't the same accusation be levelled at him? In Tom's mind, teachers were interchangeable. One could waltz out, another could waltz in, and the children would barely notice. This rankled with Nina. What was more important than teaching small people how to read and write?

When they'd started going out, her parents had been amused. 'Are there no boys in Dublin?' her dad had asked. The longer they stayed together, the more perplexed her parents became. When Tom failed his second-year exams, he chose not to repeat. It was for the best, he told his disappointed parents. Commerce hadn't been for him (true) and he'd find another opportunity (not so true). Nina's mother and father weren't impressed. 'What's he going to do with himself?' her dad said, before delivering a speech about the importance of university education. Nina attempted to fob them off with stories about night classes and training schemes, but back then, she wasn't too bothered about Tom's career. She trusted that everything would come right in the end. They were having such a wonderful time that practical matters were irrelevant. Conversations, sex, nights out, days at home: everything felt fresh. They lived as if they were part of a two-person conspiracy, as if they alone saw everything as it really was. They needed no one but themselves.

Despite this, Tom remained prone to bouts of darkness. He might begin the day in high good humour and end it listless and withdrawn. Something small would tip him into silence. He would slide into another world, where he was impossible to reach. When Nina enquired about the root causes of this unhappiness, he would give a vague answer or ask her to leave him alone. Later he would apologise and claim he didn't know what was wrong. For a long time, she'd convinced herself that he'd grow out of these episodes. Now she worried they were becoming more frequent.

Moving in together was tricky. It was also unusual. Most of her college friends remained in shared houses. They ate takeaways, drank in Bad Bob's and spent any spare money on clothes and cassettes. For once, her father was vocal in his anger, his dark warnings about reputation and respectability slamming against the walls. Her mother talked him round, with soothing words about the ways of the modern world. 'Twenty-year-olds don't get married, these days,' she said.

'Fathers still worry about their daughters,' he replied.

Fortunately, that very week, Tess appeared on *The Late Late Show*. She was chat-show catnip: witty, articulate – and gorgeous. She charmed the audience with her well-practised anecdote about being discovered while picking up litter outside a London burger bar. And she sidestepped the inevitable 'Kilmitten, isn't that the place where . . .?' question with a careful answer about how young she'd been at the time. Chastened by Tess's success, Nina's dad responded with a muted 'Who would have thought?' He was subdued for some time afterwards.

Tess. How come none of them had seen what was in front of them? Presumably that was why Estelle Lonsdale was an internationally renowned model agent – a star in her own right – and the rest of them led more humdrum lives. Even Estelle must have been stunned by the speed and scale of Tess's success, and by the way that success appeared to polish and enhance her natural beauty. Two months after signing with Platinum Model Management, she was tearing down the catwalk at London Fashion Week. Before long, she was in the style pages of *The Face* and *i-D*. Then she was on the cover. Other covers followed. She was in Milan, New York, Paris, Rio. She rarely returned to Ireland but did make occasional calls to fill them in on her adventures. And, of course, they could see her in countless magazines. 'Here she is again,' Tom would say, when he returned from work with a monthly glossy. Nina would gaze at the familiar heart-shaped face and wide green eyes with mystification, pride and – let's be honest – not a little envy.

When they were children, Nina had been considered the pretty one. At primary school, she'd been the girl the others had gravitated towards. She supposed that when you were young you had one definition of beauty. Charlie's Angels were beautiful, as were the bouncy-haired women on *Dynasty* and *Falcon Crest*. Beauty was tanned and big-toothed and Californian. Then you grew up and appreciated that beauty could be different. It could be pale and snaggle-toothed and Irish. It could be Tess.

Nina had never expected to be eclipsed by her friend and she often thought about their contrasting fortunes. She told herself that this was petty, that she was no better than the girls who still talked about their debs night when they were in third year at college. 'Get over it,' she said to herself. But knowing that your thinking is corrosive doesn't make those thoughts go away.

If most people in Kilmitten were impressed by Tess's fame, there was sniping too. She was thin because she hadn't been fed properly as a child or because she existed on cigarettes and black coffee or because she threw up after every meal. Her looks were the kind that wouldn't last. It was a desperate shame she had no father. And why, in the name of God, if she was doing so well was her mother still clocking in at the chipboard factory? Ginny Fortune had put the doubters straight. 'I'm forty-one years old,' she'd been heard to say. 'What am I meant to do? Sit at home watching repeats of *Murder, She Wrote*?' This was followed by some suggestions as to what the begrudgers might do with themselves.

Tess said that, while she was able to help her mother, Ginny was determined to maintain her independence. 'The thing is,' she said, 'Mam won't ask for anything. I've given her money and clothes, and we've gone on holiday, but if I try to do too much she gets all thick on me.'

As Nina got closer to Kilmitten, she was struck again by the beauty of the narrow roads. In some places, the trees formed an arch; in others, the hedges were laced with honeysuckle and whitethorn blooms. Ten minutes and she'd be home. First, she needed to pop in to the local shop to buy a toothbrush. Packing straight after a row with Tom hadn't been a wise idea. The words continued to echo through her head, a reminder of the strains between them.

Once, she'd wondered if they would return to live in the village. Despite some lean years, the Crossans' filling station remained open. Nina had pictured Tom running the business while she taught in the primary school. Not that she'd ever said this out loud. Talking about the future made him anxious. More recently, she'd come to accept that he would never go back. The way he spoke about school friends who remained, his pitying tone and mournful headshake, made this clear.

Like so much in Kilmitten, Mangan's grocery shop belonged to another era. Tinned peaches and boxes of corn flakes were arranged in the front window, a handful of dead bluebottles completing the display. When they were growing up, the staff had wrapped tampons in brown paper before placing the parcel in a carrier bag. Tess had made a point of declining both paper and bag. 'Wouldn't it be worse if I didn't need them?' she'd asked, waving the box at Jimmy Mangan. His face had turned the colour of dirty dishwater.

Tonight, Liesl Talty, Mercedes' daughter, was behind the counter. Liesl had inherited her father's prominent nose and her mother's thirst for gossip. She was no fool, though, and Nina reckoned she'd ask her about the documentary.

Liesl got in first. 'Nina Minogue,' she said, in an overly chirpy voice. 'The very woman. You'll be able to help.'

It was then that Nina noticed a tall guy in a leather jacket and black denims lolling at the end of the counter. She raised an eyebrow at Liesl. 'Help with what?'

The stranger turned around. He had dark blond hair and blue eyes. He wasn't especially good-looking, but there was something appealing about him. He knew it too. He thrust out a hand. 'Julian Heaney.'

'Eh, right . . .' said Nina, as they shook.

'Julian's making a TV programme,' Liesl explained, 'about what happened to poor Father Galvin.'

'I've heard about you,' said Nina.

He smiled, revealing a slight gap between his front teeth. 'I've a feeling that's not good.'

'I've been trying to explain,' said Liesl, 'why not everybody likes to be reminded of what went on.'

'That's one way of putting it,' said Nina.

'Julian was asking about Tess. I told him that we hardly see her these days, but that if anybody knew where she was, it'd be you.'

Nina turned to the documentary-maker. 'What do you want with Tess? We were only kids when Father Galvin was killed.'

'I know, but I think a lot of viewers would be interested in what she remembers. To be blunt about it, this part of the world doesn't have many famous citizens.'

She decided to play with him. 'You'd want to mind yourself. Paddy O'Grady wouldn't like to hear you saying that.'

'He's the politician whose brother was killed a few years back, right?'

'Noel O'Grady, yeah. You've been doing your homework.'

'A couple of people have mentioned him. He was at the party.'

'Lots of people were at the party. My parents were there. Liesl's parents too. It'd be harder to find somebody who wasn't.'

'Noel liked a drink,' offered Liesl.

Julian scratched his neck. 'I did approach your father,' he said to Nina.

'I'm guessing he didn't say much.'

'He said plenty. Just nothing I could use.'

'I'd say you're getting a lot of that.'

'Some people have been helpful. And we do appreciate why others haven't been so forthcoming. Not everybody likes the spotlight on their village.'

'It's more than that,' said Nina. 'There are people who can't . . .' Why she was tripping over the words, she wasn't sure. She had offered similar explanations a million times before. She gathered her thoughts. 'There are people who went through a painful time. There's a danger you'll remind them of months they'd rather forget. Unless you've had a similar experience, it's not something you can understand.'

Liesl nodded slowly. 'Nina's going out with Tom Crossan, whose mam found the body. Actually, aren't you living together up in Dublin?'

Marvelling at how Liesl was able to make living together sound like a crime, Nina ignored the question. 'What I'm saying is you've got to remember people's feelings.'

'Believe it or not,' said Julian, digging the toe of his desert boot into a crack in the red lino, 'I don't want to go around stirring up trouble. I like it here. It's . . . interesting.'

'That's what I think. Not everybody would agree with that description, mind. Some folks might find it condescending.'

'Point taken. I'm enjoying the countryside as well. It really is lovely, especially in this weather.'

Nina was surprised to find herself thawing. 'Have you been over to the woods near Toomey's Hill? They're beautiful in the spring when all the bluebells are out, but they're pretty special at this time of year too.' She knocked the side of her head. 'Oh, listen to me. You're not here for the scenery. You were asking about Tess?'

'Uh-huh. Are you still in touch with her, by any chance?'

This wasn't the first time Nina had encountered the assumption that Tess must have abandoned her old friends, that they weren't sufficiently sophisticated or glamorous for someone like her. 'We talk all the time. But, I've got to tell you, it's unlikely she'll do an interview.'

'All I can do is ask. Do you have her number in London?'

'She's not in London.' Nina was being ground down. She could faff around for the next hour, but the chances were that if she didn't tell Julian about Tess's impending arrival, he would come across her anyway. Hiding wasn't easy in Kilmitten, especially when you looked like Tess. Also, to be fair to the guy, he was trying to understand how people felt about Father Galvin's death. Tom would be suspicious, but Tom wasn't always right.

'So, do you know where Tess is?' asked Julian.

'Right at this minute, no. But you'll probably find she's not far away.'

He stopped to consider the information. 'And Tom? Is he around?'

'Nope. You're out of luck there.'

'What about you? Would you talk to us?'

'I think,' said Nina, who couldn't help but smile, 'you should quit while you're ahead.'

Chapter 12

'What's the story with the luggage?' asked Conor, as he heaved two suitcases into the back of the car. 'I don't know if you've forgotten what Kilmitten is like, but there's not much call for finery. We're a fairly basic people.'

'Gosh, you're on top form this evening,' said Tess, folding herself into the front seat of his Ford Escort. 'I'm going to New York on Monday and then on to Buenos Aires for a shoot. It's winter down there, so I've got to be prepared.'

'It's well for some. You'd better make sure Cora Crossan doesn't hear about your New York trip or she'll be asking you to take a parcel of sausages over to Dympna. And put on your seatbelt there, would you?'

Tess did as she was told. She was grateful for the lift and delighted to see Conor, her brilliant, uncomplicated friend. Her antidote to all the London madness. No, that wasn't fair: he was too intelligent for that. But when you spent most of your time with people who were all artifice and show, it was great to have a friend who was so straightforward. Who had no agenda. It helped that Conor didn't have any sexual interest in her. Tess had considered the possibility that he was gay. He had a girlfriend in Cork, though, so it seemed the planet contained at least one straight man who didn't fancy her. No, make that two. Tom had only ever been interested in Nina. For a moment, she tried to imagine Conor in London. It occurred to her that he was more likely to arrest than befriend some of the people she hung about with. The thought made her smile.

Since she'd become well known, she'd dated a series of minor-league actors and singers. Most of them had turned out to be major-league idiots. Her last boyfriend, Striker Gibson, a singer of little note (and fewer notes), had left her for another model called India Tufton Black. India was famed for her willingness to let men snort cocaine from her – almost non-existent – breasts. While Striker was no loss, Tess feared she'd inherited her mother's talent for attracting losers. Thankfully, Jim Duignan was gone from the scene, as was his equally repellent successor, Lar McBride. Now that she thought about it, an age had passed since she'd heard mention of a man.

They were driving away from Shannon airport now, past the factories and the housing estates. When asked about home, Tess found it hard to come up with an adequate description. In her circles, people tended to have a toora-loora-loora, pigs-in-the-kitchen view of the west of Ireland. They thought it was all donkeys and drunks, nuns and the IRA. The month before, she'd met a designer who'd been genuinely amazed that she'd grown up with electricity and running water. It was hard to give people a sense of the real place, to say, 'Well, it's more complex than you think.'

'So, how are the police treating you?' she asked Conor, whose driving was as erratic as his temperament was steady.

'Guards, Tess. We're called guards. You're back in Ireland now.'

'Very funny. How are you getting on?'

'Okay. I can't pretend I love spending my days talking to women who've been mugged, and looking for young lads who might have done the mugging, but somebody has to do it.'

Conor was stationed in Termonbeg on the outskirts of Cork City. A suburb tacked onto a suburb, it sounded bleak.

'One day you'll be the boss,' said Tess, 'and you'll look back on this as good training.'

'Says the woman who gets paid a fortune to traipse up and down a ramp. Something big's up with you, though, isn't it? You haven't stopped grinning since you got off the flight.'

'I'm happy to be home.'

'You may well be, but there's something else.'

'Now I can see why you're the guard and I'm a humble model. You're right, I've had some news. Some great news. I'm going to be on the cover of British *Vogue*.'

'You're on lots of covers,' said Conor, his brow crinkling, the way it always did when he was confused.

'This is different. I'm sure most of the village would be more impressed if I was on the cover of the *Sacred Heart Messenger*, but in my world, this is a big deal.'

'Don't you have to be a saint to make it to the *Messenger*?'

'Damn. I guess that one's not going to happen, then.'

'Congratulations,' he said.

'Cheers. By the way, not a word at home. I don't want folks thinking I'm boasting.'

'I don't know where that girl got her notions from,' said Conor, in a raspy imitation of Mags Moynihan.

Tess giggled. 'Mam'll be pleased, though.'

Over the past couple of years, she had honed her nonchalant act. If she said so herself, she performed a decent 'little old me' routine. Don't change. Remember where you came from. That was her mantra. She didn't want anyone in Kilmitten claiming she'd lost the run of herself. At the same time, she had to ensure that they understood her success, that they knew she was making advances on a stage far bigger than their own. The tightrope was a slippery one.

There were days when Tess went to a quiet place and punched the air with joy. And there were other days when she couldn't keep a lid on her delight. At the start, even minor changes to her life had provided a thrill. She remembered the first time she'd been able to afford the flight home rather than having to squeeze onto the train and ferry. No more jostling for space with the women who'd spent their life savings at Argos. She'd savoured new experiences, no matter how small, no matter how offbeat. She'd called Nina from a bar in Berlin with the news that there was a condom vending machine in the ladies' toilets. 'A condom machine?' Nina had laughed. 'What sort of brazen hussies drink there?' Then, her stories had become more exciting, the developments more dramatic. A few months back, she'd woken Nina and Tom with the news that she'd met River Phoenix at a party in New York. Surprisingly, Tom had been the more impressed of the two. 'It's the middle of the night,' Nina had moaned, before handing over the phone.

If Tess was being honest, there were also times when her new world felt darker than dark. When she saw and heard things that made her think, *Now, hold on a minute*. She'd thought she had demons yet, compared to some of the stories she'd been told, her life was a chapter from Enid Blyton. Take her friend Marla, who'd been raped by her 'uncle' and beaten by her mother. Or another of the popular girls, Avery, who hid her heroin habit by injecting between her toes. Or Tia, who ate cotton wool to take the edge off her hunger.

There was relentless pressure to remain thin, thin, thin. This came easily to Tess: a day or two on a Granny-Smiths-and-Marlboro-Lights diet and she was as narrow as a coat hanger. Come to think of it, that was what she was: a walking, pouting coat hanger. But what if that changed? What if she became one of the gobble-it-down-and-throw-it-up girls, measuring out calories in vodka shots and celery sticks?

And, always, nestling at the back of her head, were the other questions: if her father saw her, would he know who she was? If he did know, would her success be enough to coax him out of hiding?

As if he guessed Tess's thoughts, and sometimes she suspected that he did, Conor asked how her mother was doing.

'Do you know,' she said, 'I'm not sure. She's gone quiet on me. Have you seen her lately?'

'No, but I haven't been home in a couple of months. I drove straight up from Cork this evening. She's not het up about this documentary, is she? Everybody else is.'

Tess twirled a lock of hair around her finger. 'What documentary?'

'I'm amazed you haven't heard about it.'

As they zipped through Templemorris and swung left for Kilmitten, Conor filled her in.

'Holy shit,' said Tess, 'I'd say they're all agog. It's a wonder Mam didn't say something.'

'I gather some people are loving the attention. Dad hates it, and the worst thing is, he's got to co-operate. The fellows in Headquarters reckon they can use the programme to appeal for fresh information.'

'Good luck to them with that. With all due respect to everybody involved, I'd say the chances of getting to the truth are slim. If whoever did it has managed to keep their mouth shut for almost ten years, they're unlikely to open up now.'

'I'm with you on that. I mean, I used to think a breakthrough was possible, but crimes like that are either solved quickly or they're not solved at all. Not that I'd say that at home. Dad's still convinced they'll get him – or her – in the end.'

Tess had found that, as she'd got older, her interest in the Father Galvin case had grown. She was surprised by how often it crept into her head. She'd be thinking of something else, and then – *whoosh* – there it would be. It was disturbing to think that a harmless man had been killed and nobody knew why or by whom. This didn't mean she liked the idea of a gang of outsiders in the village, poking and prying. Who knew what they'd ask?

'Imagine,' she said, 'it's ten years since we were in that shed with our smokes and bottles of Harp. Which reminds me – do you think we'll get a wedding soon?'

'Tom and Nina? Nah, they're too young.'

'Are they, though? They've been together for four years and they've known each other for ever. The village is full of couples who were married at twenty-two. What age was Paula?'

'Twenty-one but, like you say, she lives in Kilmitten. There wasn't much else for her to do.'

'Fair point. I take it Tom and Nina will be around over the weekend?'

'Yes and no.' Conor explained the situation.

Tess reached into her bag. 'I'll give Nina a ring, so. Will we meet up later?'

'Sounds good.' His eyes slid in her direction. 'What's that?'

'You know well what it is,' she said, flipping open the cover of her new phone. 'Mark my words, the day will come when everyone in the village has one of these. Even our parents.'

'Dream on,' said Conor.

Tess winked. 'I do love calling the Minogues now that Emmet's decided I'm worth talking to. Sometimes I reckon I can actually hear him squirm.' Meeting Nina's father also gave her a delicious buzz. The last time she'd been home, she'd made a point of calling up to the house. Surprise, surprise, she was no longer barred.

While she spoke to Nina, Conor pulled into Kilmitten.

The sky was streaked with neon, the pinks and oranges a sign of another fine day ahead. A sliver of moon, like the top of a fingernail, hung over Toomey's Hill. They stopped outside the Fortunes' house on Pearse Terrace. Tess noticed that the façade had developed a new crack. Before long, she should have enough money to buy her mother a house. Nothing flash. She'd recently bought an apartment in London and couldn't afford flash. But solid would be good, solid and comfortable. She pictured somewhere with white walls, double-glazed windows and a modern bathroom. Somewhere like Conor's house, she supposed.

There was something different about her mother. It wasn't so much how she looked as the way she carried herself. Her movements were jittery, her voice too high. Tess counted the months since they'd last seen each other. She was taken aback to realise she hadn't been home since Christmas.

'You're looking well, Tessy,' her mam said. 'You're too skinny, but I suppose that's part of the job. Mind you, I hope you didn't pay much for that frock. There's not a lot of material in it.'

Tess laughed. Her mother always made her laugh. Then she pulled at the skirt of her tiny floral dress. 'You can relax. It was a present from the designer. In fairness, you're no stranger to a short skirt yourself.'

'Those days are behind me now.'

'Stop it, Mam. You've the best legs in the village.'

'The competition isn't hectic.'

'How are Mags and Mercedes?'

'Fine, as far as I know. I haven't seen much of them lately.'

Tess wanted to talk about her big cover, but now didn't feel like the right time. Something was up. Was her mother ill? Was she anxious about the documentary? Was there trouble at work? While Tess had been bouncing around the globe, had something awful happened? She allowed these thoughts to circle around her. Then she had an idea.

'I told Conor and Nina I'd meet them in Pilkington's,' she said. 'Why don't you come along? We can have a drink or two and a natter. We've plenty of catching up to do.'

'I've no intention of cramping your style.

'Honestly, Mam, you wouldn't be—'

'Sit yourself down there,' said her mother. 'I need to talk to you.'

Chapter 13

Conor sensed that something was wrong. Paula's presence added to his unease. His sister kept touching her hair, a sign she was on edge. She'd left her two children at home with Marty. His first instinct was to blame the TV programme. Then again, perhaps someone was ill. His dad was nearly fifty. Not ancient, but who knew better than Conor that bad health could strike at any time? His mother had been only thirty-five when she died. When he'd been a kid it hadn't seemed particularly young. Now, he appreciated the full tragedy of her death.

'You'll have a cup of tea,' said Paula, her voice making it clear that this was an order, not an offer.

'Well, now,' said his father, from one end of the sofa, 'it's a good while since the three of us were together.'

'It is indeed,' replied Paula, who was sitting beside him, hands clasped, like an old woman at prayer.

For the next few minutes, they sipped their tea and swapped bland small talk. From his chair on the other side of the sitting room, Conor scrutinised his dad for signs of illness, for sunken cheeks or twitches of pain, but he couldn't spot anything. Finally, he decided to put an end to the shilly-shallying.

'I'd better get moving. I'm meeting Tess and Nina.'

'Ah,' said his dad. 'Tess. She's doing very well.'

'She is,' said Conor.

'So . . . what I've been meaning to tell you is that Tess's mother and I have been seeing each other. Nothing serious at first. But the way it is . . . it's got more serious. I like Ginny a lot. She's a smashing woman. And we've agreed that it's time we let people know we're a couple. We're too old to be mooching around like teenagers.'

Conor tried to stop himself appearing shocked. 'Aren't you the dark horse? I knew you were fond of Ginny, but I'd never pictured you together.'

His dad gave a self-conscious smile. 'She's a calmer woman than she was a few years ago. Not that there was anything wrong with her then either. She hasn't had an easy life.'

'Yeah, I—'

'Raising a child on her own, that took courage. Lots of women do it now. But back in those days there were plenty around here who would've preferred if she'd had Tess adopted. And look at what a top-class job she did. I was watching Tess on the telly a while back, and she was a star. A credit to her mother. Ginny's always worked hard too, you know. It's easy to forget that. She's very independent.'

His dad's words came tumbling out, as if he was reading from a prepared speech. As quickly as Conor's fears had gathered, they fell away. His father wasn't sick. He'd found a new woman.

Conor had never given much consideration to what life had been like for Ginny. He knew that Tess had borne the stigma of having an absent father. He remembered various morons taunting her and, while she'd pretended not to care, the words had hurt. He could still see the determined set of her small face, the look that said, 'These fools won't get the better of me.'

'Relax, Dad,' he said. 'Why would I be anything other than happy for you? Tess is one of my best friends.'

'You've no idea how pleased I am to hear that. Ginny brightens up my life, and that's the truth of it.'

Conor knew enough about his home village to realise that the swish of gossip would follow the new couple. His dad was the sergeant, a solid man in a uniform, whereas Ginny was . . . well, she was Ginny Fortune, the single mother with the spray-on jeans and red lipstick. The woman who didn't go to Mass and didn't give a damn what people thought. That both were more complex than these descriptions would suggest was irrelevant. The local busybodies weren't known for their charity.

He remembered four years previously, on the night he'd spoken about joining the force, how his father had talked about Tess's mother and the bad choices she'd made. He'd been thinking of her then. Going back even further, to the death of Father Galvin, Conor recalled his dad telling Ginny not to fret about the shed business, that there was no harm done. His old man was far more interesting than he'd suspected.

Conor finished his tea. He ought to get going. Presumably,

Ginny had told Tess by now. It was then that he noticed Paula's face. She still had an uncomfortable look about her. She squinted at their father, as if urging him to speak again.

'Right,' he said, 'that's not quite all.'

They waited for him to continue.

'Ahm . . . what it is . . . we recently discovered we're going to be parents. Ginny's expecting a baby. In December, all going well.'

Conor felt his mouth go slack.

His dad continued: 'To begin with, we were taken aback, but it's great news. Great news entirely. Now, I know you're thinking, *Aren't they too old for that?* But you've got to remember, Ginny's only forty-one. Loads of women have children at that age. She's been to see the doctor, and once she takes care of herself, she'll be grand.'

All the while, Paula stayed quiet. Her face was closed over now, making it impossible to gauge how she felt. All the implications and ramifications were charging around Conor's brain. His dad, a grandfather, was going to have a baby. With Tess's mam. He couldn't picture either of them with a child. Would they even remember what to do? Wouldn't they be worn out? And what would people say? While he felt bad for giving this last thought headspace, the fact remained: they were old folks behaving like youngsters. At the very least they could expect an outbreak of sniggering and unfunny jokes.

He was, he realised, expected to speak. 'Congratulations,' he squeaked. 'Yeah, congratulations. That's excellent news. Honest to God, excellent news.'

His dad smiled again, this version even more sheepish than before. 'Thanks, Conor. I know it's a lot to take on board. If you have any questions . . .'

Conor had a million questions. Every few seconds, up another one would pop. How long had his dad and Ginny been seeing each other? Would they live together? Would they get married? He fumbled for something else generous to say.

'Tess will be thrilled,' he said.

Paula looked at them both in a maternal sort of way. She'd always been older than her years, and with every month that passed this seemed more pronounced. 'That's good,' was all she said.

'And for fear you're wondering,' said his father, 'we do plan on getting married. We're thinking of next year, after the baby arrives.' He hesitated, then added something that made Conor abandon all his questions. 'Won't it be great to have a bit of noise around the house again?'

'I don't know what to make of them,' said Tess. 'Like, seriously, a child? At their ages? Are they insane? Mam kept giving me this dreamy-eyed look, and I had to tell her how delighted I was. And I *am* delighted about her hooking up with your old man. It's the first good decision she's made in years. But a baby! I mean, come on, she'll be forty-two by the time it's born, and I'll be twenty-three. I'm the one who should be thinking about reproducing. Not that I am. Because, unlike my mother, I'm not totally fucking mad.'

With that, she stopped and took a sharp gulp of her vodka and tonic.

'Why don't you climb down off the fence,' said Nina, 'and tell us what you really think?'

Despite himself, Conor laughed. 'I have to say I'm stunned too.'

'But you're okay with my mam?' asked Tess. 'Like, you don't—'

'Tess, stop it, would you? Your mam's the best. Dad's like a kid himself, he's so happy, but . . .'

'It's all topsy-turvy. Grandfathers shouldn't be having children.'

'That's about the size of it.'

From his seat in the far corner of Pilkington's Lounge, Conor could see people struggling to camouflage their interest in Tess. He spotted Brendan Talty in his summer shirt, lemon with short sleeves, and Timmy Moynihan in his Ireland soccer jersey, a legacy of the previous year's World Cup. They were pretending not to stare, but their conversations were too animated, their movements too jerky. If they had any inkling what she was talking about, they would slide from their stools in astonishment. They'd know soon enough. His father was already calling people. 'I want to get this over and done with,' he'd said, as though talking about clearing out the guttering or weeding the garden.

Fashions might come and go, but Pilkington's never changed. The walls were stained cigarette-smoke yellow, the seats sagged, and the carpet bore the marks of a thousand spilled pints. There was no television, no hot water, and the selection of beers was pitifully small. Yet even the slightest improvement – a new sign on the ladies' toilet, a mirror at the back of the bar – provoked complaints. The locals maintained everything was perfect as it was.

'So,' said Nina, 'you genuinely didn't know?'

'Not the foggiest,' said Tess.

'Not an iota,' added Conor.

Nina frowned. 'And nobody else seems to know either.'

'Amazing,' agreed Tess. 'It goes to show, you can keep secrets in this village, after all.'

'But haven't we always known that?' said Conor.

For a second or two, Tess and Nina appeared baffled. 'Ah, I get you,' said Nina, eventually. 'Speaking of which, I met the documentary guy earlier this evening.'

'And?' said Tess.

Nina drank the last of her cider. 'Hold that thought while I go to the bar. I'll tell you about him when I get back. You two can bond over your new family status. What will you be? Stepbrother and sister?'

'Yikes,' said Tess. 'I hadn't thought of that.'

'Me neither,' said Conor, who was still trying to absorb the enormity of his father's news. Although Tess had let rip about her mother, he had a notion that something significant remained unsaid.

'What's up?' he asked.

Her fingers ran along the top of her cigarettes. 'Where do I start? There I was earlier, talking about us getting a wedding. Little did I know that my own mother's was on the cards.'

'There's something else, though. I can tell.'

'I was . . . Oh, what the hell. I may as well come on out with it. It's been ages since I asked Mam about my father. I was thinking this might be the right time.'

'Or not.'

'I hear what you're saying. I don't want to hassle her, but I'm entitled to know. It's not like I want to be friends with the man. I'd just like to know who he is. Why that should be a problem is beyond me.'

Before Conor could reply, Nina returned, accompanied by a tall guy with an expensive leather jacket and an air of entitlement. They placed the drinks on the table. 'Ahm, this is Julian Heaney,' she said. 'As chance would have it, he was at the bar. He's—'

'I know who he is,' said Conor. At any time, his patience for this guy would be limited. Tonight it was non-existent. He was still grappling with his father's news. He didn't want to hear about the television programme and he definitely didn't want to be squeezed for information.

Tess raised her chin, as if to say, 'What's going on?'

'Julian's going to join us for a minute,' said Nina. 'He wants to talk about his project.'

'Join away,' said Tess to Julian, 'but I doubt any of us will be able to help you.'

He sat down and leaned in towards them. 'That's what I wanted to talk about. I gather some of you have this idea that we want to do a hatchet job on the village,' he glanced at Conor, 'or on the investigation. I promise you that's not our intention.'

'What are you doing, then?' asked Conor.

'In the main, we're focusing on Leo Galvin, on what type of man he was, and how his family misses him. One of his brothers has agreed to do an interview. As I understand it, the family have some theories of their own about what might have happened.'

'If they do, shouldn't they talk to the guards?'

'Who's to say they haven't?'

For some minutes, Julian gave his sales pitch. People all over the country still associated Kilmitten with an unsolved crime, he said. This irked Conor. The place was hardly Palermo: it didn't deserve to be stigmatised. As he listened, he was forced to admit that the guy was smooth. Infuriatingly so. He studied his friends' reactions. Nina was unexpectedly sympathetic, Tess less conciliatory.

'You don't look much older than us,' she said to Julian. 'You can't remember it that well.'

'I was eighteen, in my first year at Trinity, so I remember quite a lot. Because of the snow there were no classes for a couple of weeks, and the Father Galvin case was on every news bulletin.'

'Are you from Dublin?'

'Guilty as charged.'

'Let me guess, you thought we were like something out of *Deliverance*, a shower of murdering hicks.'

'Even if I did, I wouldn't own up to it. Besides, I doubt anybody could call an international supermodel a hick.'

Oh, puke, thought Conor.

'Plenty have tried,' said Tess, 'believe me.'

'Do you have your own theories?' asked Nina. 'About who did it, I mean?'

'We-ell, I . . .' He paused, as if waiting for a drumroll. 'No, I couldn't say that. That would be wrong. But the story is a fascinating one. What do you think yourselves?'

'We haven't a clue,' said Tess, 'and even if we had, we wouldn't talk about it here.' She peered around. Several eavesdroppers looked away. Craned necks drew back in, and men began staring into their pints as though they held the secrets of the universe. 'Anyway, what is it you want us to do?'

'I was hoping the two of you might talk to me,' he tipped his head towards Tess and Nina, 'about what it was like growing up in the village, your memories of Father Galvin, that type of thing. I'd ask Conor, only I've a feeling I'd be wasting my time.'

'Your feeling is spot on,' replied Conor. His eyes roamed the ceiling. He wished the guy would go away.

'Will you think about it?' asked Julian.

'Well—' started Nina.

Tess intervened. 'Gosh, I doubt it,' she said, a teasing tone in her voice. 'Not this weekend, at any rate. I'm busy and I'd say Nina is too.' She rooted in her bag and took out a business card. 'Here's my agent's number. I'll be away for the next fortnight. Give her a shout after that, and she'll let you know if I've changed my mind.'

'Could you not give me your phone number?'

'You've got to be kidding,' she said, like a queen dismissing a courtier. 'Now, if you'll excuse us, we've a lot to discuss.'

When Julian had left, Nina turned to Tess. 'Are you going to do an interview?'

'Not a chance, but I liked messing with his head. What about you?'

'I shouldn't think so.'

Conor reckoned Tess was as good as her word. About Nina, he was less sure.

Chapter 14

Tom stepped outside and inhaled the ripe smell of the city. Warm weather always gave him a freewheeling feeling. The shop had been busy earlier, but it was quiet now, and he expected it to stay that way. Many of the customers came directly from the nearby dole office, so the weekends were usually less lively.

When Tom had started working in Val's, he'd been wary of the locals. Scared, even. He'd realised that seventeen years in Kilmitten and two in UCD had left him ill-prepared for the north inner city. His nerves hadn't been helped by the lads who'd hung out on the next corner. A gang of teenagers with spiky hair and spikier attitudes, they'd revelled in shouting abuse at passers-by. Sometimes they'd smoked or kicked a ball or played with their crutches (there was always a lad on crutches), but mostly they'd got their kicks from firing stones and roaring 'Student', their highest grade of insult, at Tom. Eventually, he'd found the courage to yell back, and the stoning had stopped. Now, when he thought about those weeks, he was mortified by his immaturity. And his snobbery.

More often, he cursed the snobbery of others. There were days when he felt as if everybody was ganging up on him, conspiring to make him feel guilty about his life. Sometimes he succumbed. He'd look at Nina, Conor and Tess. There they were, finding their way: Tess a star, the other two with grown-up jobs. And what was he doing? Selling beer and cigarettes to teenagers, and lottery cards to pensioners.

It was funny, he thought, how even among friends nobody wanted to be the one left behind. At school, you longed to be the first name on the team, the first child invited to the party. Fast forward a few years, and while the situations might have changed, the competitive urge remained the same.

That being said, Tom was fond of the shop. There was something seductive about its rhythms and routines. He especially liked chatting to the young lads. He asked about school and home and what they wanted to do with their lives. None of this meant he was a creeping-Jesus, do-gooder type. He just enjoyed the banter. In lots of ways, working in Val's was like working in the petrol station at home. The customers were entertaining, cranky, brave, lazy, and a million other things besides.

He thought of his own early teens when Kilmitten's hierarchies had been almost as rigid as those in Dublin. Their gang had tried to sidestep the rules. He wondered how successful they'd been.

Back in the spring, he'd started helping a couple of the young guys with their homework. He might have flunked out of college, but he knew enough to give the boys extra tuition in English and maths. They were bright kids, both adamant they'd be staying on at school to do the Leaving Cert. They had an energy about them that Tom liked. And they made him laugh. He hadn't told Nina. She thought he'd been working extra hours in the shop. Oh, he knew he should have talked to her. She was a teacher, after all. An enthusiastic teacher. A good one. More than once, she'd accused him of not valuing her work. That was unfair. But Nina's school might as well have been on a different planet. In St Fachtna's, all the children had a nice safe home full of books and warm clothes. A slight sniffle and they were brought to the doctor. They never had to worry about money or food or whether their big brother was one stolen car away from jail or their little sister was playing in a park littered with dirty needles. Truth to tell, Tom was nervous about what Nina would make of his amateur teaching.

His thoughts turned to what she'd told him the night before. By now, the word about Flan and Ginny would be spreading through the village, fast as fire. When Nina had called, he'd thought she was joking. 'Go on,' he'd said, 'what have you been smoking?' In the end, he'd accepted that she was telling the truth. People certainly could surprise you.

But he knew that.

Nina had sounded preoccupied, and Tom feared that if it wasn't for the Flan and Ginny revelation she mightn't have rung at all. She'd let slip that she'd met the documentary producer in Mangan's shop. Although Tom pressed for more information, she was disappointingly offhand. He supposed she wasn't overly troubled by a television crew trawling the village and retracing the events of 1982. Her memories had dulled, and while that was good, he wished she understood that for some people forgetting wasn't an option. The night remained in his head. As did Leo Galvin. Tom pictured the priest, loping around the village, swapping wisecracks and enquiring after his parishioners' health. He couldn't say this to Nina, so he struggled on, hoping the day would come when he, too, could forget.

He presumed she was still annoyed with him for staying in Dublin. She reckoned he was using Val's as an excuse not to go home. He couldn't blame her: in the past, he had shied away from Kilmitten. This time, however, she was wrong. Earlier that month, after years of putting the house on and off the market, his parents had found a buyer: a guy who'd spent the last two decades in America and wasn't bothered by Father Galvin's death. Apparently, he spoke a lot about 'potential' and 'development', although his precise plans were unclear. Tom's parents were moving to Kennedy Crescent, a few doors down from Flan. He wanted to visit before they left.

After the phone call with Nina, Tom had lain awake, thinking about Conor's dad and Tess's mam. How long had they been seeing each other? Weeks? Months? Years? And was it possible that . . .? Nah, he told himself. He was overthinking.

He ought to ring Conor and offer his congratulations. He wouldn't get the chance this evening because he was going for a pint with his old college friend, Fergal. Tomorrow. He'd definitely do it tomorrow.

Looking down the street, Tom saw an elderly woman trudging towards him. Despite the afternoon heat, she was wearing a thick brown cardigan, a plaid skirt and the sort of tights that doubled as bandages. Mrs Kerrigan rarely bought much but she liked a natter. (Sample conversation: 'The politicians have the country ruined, Tom, ruined.' 'They do, Mrs Kerrigan, they do.' 'We should give the place back to the Brits and apologise for the state of it.' 'Ah, that might be going a bit far, Mrs Kerrigan.') He decided he'd better go inside and clear away his books and papers.

Tom was working on two projects. With every week that passed, he became more convinced he wanted to travel. He'd accumulated a library of Lonely Planets and a substantial file of routes and costings. Every penny he hadn't spent on rent, food or drink was collecting interest in a savings account. They'd begin their journey in Europe before crossing into Asia on the Trans-Siberian Railway. They'd go to India, China and Nepal. They might even make it as far as Australia. They could work there. He said 'they' because he knew Nina would come too. She was foot-dragging at the moment, but that would change. Besides, what would be the point in going without her? He pictured the adventures they would have: the two of them seeing the world, then returning to begin the next phase of their lives together.

That was where his second project came in. Tom had blundered into a college course. When it hadn't worked out, he'd taken the only job he could find. He'd batted away his parents' questions and Nina's concerns. He'd told himself that he didn't lack ambition. What he lacked was focus.

Finally, an idea had taken root at the back of his head. He was beginning to see what he might do with himself. Soon, when he had it all worked out, he'd talk to Nina.

Nina was on the patio in her parents' back garden, flicking through a novel and attempting to get a tan. Her thoughts kept switching back to the previous night. In particular, she thought about Tess. Tess and her tawny lipstick, her wrist of friendship bracelets and her Italian leather backpack. Tess and her haughty attitude towards Julian Heaney. The way she'd waved a hand and dismissed him from their company had made Nina uncomfortable. Admittedly, she'd just received some fairly shocking news but, still, the old Tess would have heard him out. And handing him her agent's card? Please! Who did she think she was? Cindy Crawford? Conor had also been cool towards him. But he had good reason to be cagey: his father's work was under scrutiny.

Nina found herself thinking about Tess's new apartment. Imagine: her old friend owning an apartment in London. 'It's not much,' she'd said. 'A glorified cupboard, really.' Her protestations weren't convincing. The apartment was in Kensington, after all. Kensington! Nina wondered if she'd ever get to see it. She wondered how much it had cost. No doubt Tess's *Vogue* cover would earn her a tidy sum. 'Obviously, I'm pleased,' she'd said, 'but, you know, it's just a stepping stone. If I make the cover of US *Vogue*, then we can all go mental.'

Nina was reminded of a saying favoured by one of her primary-school colleagues. When faced by a demanding pupil, Eddie Mason would shake his head and mutter, 'Much wants more.'

Stop it, she thought. *You're being unfair.* Tess had never been one for pretence. If she thought she could do better, she'd say so. If she didn't trust someone, she'd make her feelings plain. And yet something had altered. Step by step, she was pulling away. Nina supposed that everybody changed. Her own ideas were shifting. She didn't want to become one of those people for whom possessions were more important than ideas, but neither could she pretend that money was of no significance. Being good at her job wasn't enough. She wanted to be successful. These days, more women were becoming principals, and she reckoned this was something she should aim for.

She returned to her book, then quickly set it aside again. Martin Amis wasn't for her. Up ahead, a plane was scorching through the seamless blue sky. If anything, it was too hot, a rare complaint in Kilmitten. She was thinking about going for a walk when her mother arrived with two glasses of orange juice.

She handed one to Nina, then lowered herself into the other deckchair.

Nina rubbed the cold glass against her face. 'Thanks.'

'I gather,' said her mam, 'that you met the television fellow?'

'Your spies were out last night. Who told you that?'

'I bumped into Brendan Talty down the village. He said he saw you talking in Pilkington's. "The pair of them were having a great old natter," he said. You know Brendan, he's as bad as his wife for telling tales.'

Nina explained how she'd been introduced to Julian by Brendan's daughter, Liesl. 'I couldn't ignore the guy,' she said.

'Of course you couldn't, love. I'm playing with you. Don't mind your father. Granted, he's suspicious of the TV programme, but he'll calm down. He gets worked up and within minutes he's forgotten what it was that had him so annoyed.'

'I can't believe anybody had time to talk about me. I thought there'd only be one topic of conversation in the village today.'

Her mam laughed. 'Oh, there's plenty of that too. I spent an age in Mangan's listening to chatter about still waters running deep.'

Nina had told her parents about Flan and Ginny when she'd got back from the pub. Although he'd tried to pretend otherwise, her dad had been as stunned as everyone else. Initially, she'd been surprised by this. Shouldn't he have known about Ginny's pregnancy? Then she remembered how Tess's mam had transferred her custom to a doctor in Templemorris. Nina could understand. Why trust your health – or give your money – to a man who'd been mean to your daughter?

Nina listened while her mother ran through what she'd heard in the shop. According to Breege O'Grady, Flan had been seen earlier, sauntering up the street like nothing had happened. Lourda Ryan insisted she'd known that something was up with Ginny. 'Not a word of a lie,' she said. 'I just knew.' Liesl revealed that Tess had called in to buy a pint of low-fat milk and a bunch of bananas. She was delighted with the news, she'd said, and was looking forward to becoming a very big sister.

'I reckon she's less pleased than she's making out,' said Nina.

'Well, if you ask me, it's wonderful news,' replied her mother. 'Flan's spent more than enough time on his own. If he's happy, and Ginny's happy, that's all that matters.'

Nina recalled her efforts to uncover the truth about Tess's father. Every attempt had proved fruitless and, in the end, she'd given up. Despite this, she couldn't shake off the feeling that her mam and dad knew more than they were saying.

'It's a shame Tom couldn't come down for the weekend,' said her mother.

'He had to work . . . or so he said.'

'Are things all right between the two of you?'

Thrown off balance, Nina burbled a few lines about everything being fine. The honest answer was, she didn't know. She loved Tom, but increasingly she felt they were out of sync. Like he was holding back on her. She considered confiding in her mother, then decided against. Compared to many of her friends, Nina was quite open with her mam. This was different, though. She didn't want to stir up unnecessary worry.

She reflected on her parents' marriage. If they weren't obviously happy, they weren't obviously miserable either. They rubbed along. Maybe that was what you did. Her mother was nearly fifty now, and while she'd aged a little, her beauty remained intact. Ageing, she maintained, was a matter of choice. You could allow yourself to hide behind a

Crimplene tent or you could work at preserving what you had. Looking around the village, quite a few of her mam's contemporaries appeared content to crumble into middle age. Mags Moynihan's dark curls had morphed into a steel frizz while Breege O'Grady looked defeated, as if she'd never recovered from her husband's sudden death.

Nina sipped her orange juice and watched a bee swoop in towards the pansies in one of the patio tubs. Her parents' garden was always in perfect order. Her mother had a particular gift with flowers, not just growing them but arranging them too. She was often called upon to do arrangements for weddings and the like. It wasn't a talent she'd passed on. Nina couldn't tell a lobelia from a lobotomy.

Her mam put down her drink. 'How did you leave things with Julian Heaney?'

'What do you mean?'

'You're not going to do an interview, are you? That really would be a step too far for your father.'

'You can relax. I don't think Julian's that bothered about me, anyway. It's Tess who's the prize interviewee.'

This was true. Nina wouldn't be appearing on screen. All the same, she had a feeling she'd be seeing Julian again.

Down the street, Tess lay on an old bath towel. Around her the grass was so high she felt as if she was hiding in a jungle, as if at any moment Tarzan might come swinging in. Judging by the sounds floating overhead, everybody in Pearse Terrace was in their back garden. From one side, she heard Paudge Slattery making heavy work of cutting his lawn. On the other, the Duggans' grandchildren were screeching like monkeys. The sun danced across her nose. She would have to go in shortly. Arriving in New York with a big red face wasn't a good idea. She was preparing herself for a talk with her mother. *Five more minutes*, she thought. *Then I'll be ready.*

Later, they were going to Conor's house for dinner. 'Just the four of us,' her mam had said. It would be the first time Tess had seen her mother and Flan together, and she didn't know whether to be thrilled or apprehensive. Earlier, she'd risked a visit to the shop. Liesl Talty had offered her congratulations. 'Mam told me,' she'd said. 'She was beside herself with excitement. Between you, me and the wall, she was kind of ticked off too. "How many years have I been friends with Ginny Fortune?" she said. "And then she goes and does something like this without telling me."'

'But she did tell her. Didn't she ring her last night?'

'Yeah, only the word was everywhere by then. Mags Moynihan was at the door. I thought she'd explode she was so worked up. It must be the biggest thing to happen in Kilmitten since the death of Father Galvin.'

Tess had pointed out that this was an odd comparison.

'Ah, you know what I mean,' Liesl had replied.

Realising her five minutes were up, Tess pulled down her halter top, picked up her towel and Walkman and went inside. If she didn't do this now, her resolve would falter and she'd let another opportunity pass her by.

Her mother was at the kitchen counter making what looked like a cheesecake. 'Dessert,' she explained, 'for this evening.'

Tess had to smile. 'When did you become so domesticated?'

'Aren't you the cheeky young pup! I'm doing my best to be respectable.'

'Don't go overboard on the respectability. It doesn't suit you.'

'We both know there's no fear of that.'

'So,' said Tess, as she sat down on one of their old kitchen chairs, 'what I've been meaning to ask you . . .' She hesitated. 'What it is . . . ahm . . .' She pulled at the frayed hem of her shorts, appalled by her inability to come on out and ask the question. *They're only words*, she thought. *You've got to put one in front of the other, and then it'll all be done.*

'Come on, Tessy,' said her mam. 'Spit it out.'

When, at last, the words came, they flew out in a great rush, like pennies spilling from a slot machine. 'What it is is this. I know you're reluctant to talk about my father, and I understand that. And I've tried not to be a pain, but I'm an adult now, and I'd like to know who he is. You needn't worry that I'll go making a nuisance of myself. I'm not even sure I want to meet him. I'd just like to know something about him. Does he even know I exist? And, if he does, is there a chance he'd like to meet me? So, like I say, I get that this is difficult for you. Honestly, I do. But, please, Mam, I have to know who he is.'

Her mother sighed, a long, heavy sigh. She looked briefly

at Tess before returning her gaze to the floor. 'I'd a feeling this would come up. Listen, if I thought any good would come of you knowing his identity, I'd have told you years ago. I don't know why you can't trust me.'

'I do trust you, but I feel like part of me is missing. Like I don't have the whole picture. What if I have brothers and sisters? What if there are others in the family who'd like to know about me?'

'Plenty of people grow up without a father. You're not that special.' Her mam immediately thought better of what she'd said. 'Sorry, pet, that sounded tougher than I'd intended.'

Tess felt a swelling in her throat. This was even trickier than she'd feared. She'd come this far, though, and she had to continue. 'Okay, I'm reluctant to raise this, but here goes: for most of my life I've been friendly with Conor. He's always been like the brother I didn't have. In some ways, he's my best mate. And, last night, after you told me about Flan and the baby, I started wondering . . . do I feel that way because Conor *is* my brother? Is Flan my father? If that's the case, I can see why you wouldn't want to tell anyone. He was married to someone else, and then she died, and it was really tragic and . . .'

Her mam pressed her fingers against her temples. When she spoke, her voice was soft as a baby's sneeze. 'No. I swear to you there was nothing between Flan and myself until a few months back. You've got to take my word on that.'

'If not Flan, who?'

'Please, Tess, don't do this to me. Not now. Not when, for once in my life, everything's going well. You're not being fair.'

'But you're not being fair either. Can't you see that? To me – or to him.'

Her mother's voice became louder, more urgent. 'Just leave it, would you?'

'No,' she said. Tess thought of her new brother or sister and the fantastic childhood that lay ahead of them. A childhood with two parents. No questions. No rumours. No sideways looks or pitying comments. Growing up, that had been her lot. Yet she'd shunted it all aside and made something of herself. All she was seeking now was the truth. She wanted to know who she was. 'What if my father reads about me, or sees me in a magazine or on the telly? What then?'

'That isn't going to happen.'

'Why not?'

Her mother was quiet while she thought about her answer. Tess noticed that her hands were shaking.

'The reason it's not going to happen, Tess, is because your father is dead.'

Chapter 15

While Tom had many talents, cooking wasn't among them. His dinners were slapdash efforts, usually incinerated, occasionally semi-raw. Despite this, Nina was pleased that, when she got back to Dublin, he was attempting to make a chicken casserole. She saw it as a peace offering of sorts. That was good. She couldn't have handled another row.

Before leaving Kilmitten, she'd gone for a walk with Conor and Tess. It hadn't been a success. While both had claimed to be pleased by their parents' news, neither was in great form. Conor took aim at half of the village. They were stupid or mean-spirited or worse. This crabbiness was unlike him, and Nina assumed Lourda Ryan and Mercedes Talty were proxies for whatever had actually upset him. Tess was in unusually lacklustre humour, her only responses a feeble 'Yeah' or 'Why not?' Her thoughts were elsewhere. In New York or London, presumably.

'Sit yourself down there,' said Tom, then gave Nina a deep, enthusiastic kiss. He handed her a glass of red wine. 'I want all the news.'

While they ate, she gave a carefully edited account of the weekend. In the main, they spoke about Flan and Ginny. She mentioned Julian Heaney, but did her best to skip lightly over the documentary. Tom was in entertaining mode. Several of his questions were asked in the style of Kilmitten's more notable gossips. He imagined Mags and Mercedes, bubbling with anger at their failure to spot Flan and Ginny's courtship. ('I swear to you, Mags, I'm never giving that woman my *Beaches* video again.' 'Too right, Mercedes, and if she wants to borrow the good jacket I got in Todd's, she can think on.') Then he did a turn as the current parish priest. Father Cleary was a charmless character, whose homilies were strong on sin and weak on forgiveness. Tom captured him perfectly. Sometimes Nina forgot how funny he could be.

Relaxed by wine and laughter, they had sex. Afterwards, Tom slept in a satisfied curl. Nina lay there, listening to the snuffling sound he sometimes made, confusion coursing through her.

Julian rang on Wednesday afternoon.

'We've wrapped up in Kilmitten for now,' he said. 'We'll be going back later in the year. In the meantime, I'm in Dublin so I thought I'd give you a call.'

'I'd a feeling I'd hear from you,' said Nina.

'Even though you didn't give me your number?'

'I'm in the book – as you no doubt discovered.'

Nina hoped her casual words masked her nerves. Thankfully, she was on her own. Val's brother was clinging to life, and Tom's hours had become even longer than usual.

They arranged to meet in the Palace Bar. When she arrived, he was down the back, drinking a pint of Guinness. While he went to fetch her gin and tonic, she had a momentary wobble. What was she doing? If Tom knew she was meeting Julian, there would be trouble. Oh, let's be honest, if any of her friends or family knew, there'd be trouble. But there was no reason for them to find out. And if they did? She'd say she was on a mission. She was a double agent trying to discover what the TV people knew about Father Galvin – and what they were likely to say about Kilmitten. She instructed herself to play it cool, like she had on the evening they'd first met. She tried to arrange her face and body so that she appeared poised, sophisticated, the person she wanted to be. This was easier said than done.

They spoke about Kilmitten. People were strange, he said. They claimed they didn't like to dwell on the priest's death, yet when they started talking there was no stopping them. Others seemed to resent the man for having the nerve to get killed in their village.

'I assume you've heard most of the theories,' he said. 'At first, everybody was convinced the killer had to be an outsider. Then it became clear that whoever did it must have been at the party. That still left the guards with a long list of suspects.'

Nina reached for her glass, nodded, but said nothing. She didn't know him well enough to confess her part in the initial mess.

'So somebody must have had a reason to hurt Father Galvin, even though by all accounts he was a decent guy.

Pretty much everybody we've spoken to says the same thing: he was involved in the community, worked hard, liked a night out, was fond of a drink but not too fond.'

'That's how I remember him. For a priest he wasn't overly holy, if you know what I mean.'

'Yeah, I do. In fact, I began to ask myself if he had some dark secret, something so warped that even the most outspoken people either didn't know about it or were scared to mention it.'

'Like what?'

Julian steepled his fingers. 'You must have heard about the rumours elsewhere? The talk there's been about some priests interfering with children?'

'I have. I work with children, so I'm extra-conscious of what can happen. But Father Galvin? I'd be stunned.' Nina stopped to take a drink. The G&T was going straight to her head. It had been too long since she'd had a drink in the afternoon. Too long since she'd been in the Palace. She told herself to focus. 'You don't have any particular reason to suspect him, do you?'

'Not at all. Like I say, though, if it happened elsewhere . . .'

'Straight up, I don't see it. Not Father Galvin. He wasn't at all creepy. Also, if there'd been even a whisper of him abusing a child, the word would have got around. Somebody would have said something to the guards.'

'I suppose. Only I can't help but be suspicious. Killing a priest is very unusual.'

'You'll be going on about black Masses and satanic rituals in a minute.'

'Actually, I did speak to two or three people who thought the whole thing was part of some conspiracy or other.'

'There are a few grassy-knollers in Kilmitten, but I wouldn't pay any heed to them. What else have you heard?'

Julian laughed. He had a pleasing, tickly laugh. Oh, and there was a languor about his voice, as though he knew that what he was saying was worth waiting for. 'I thought I'd be getting information from you,' he said, 'but you're determined to turn the tables.'

'Ah, well,' said Nina, raising her palms to the glass ceiling, 'there has to be a bit of give and take in every relationship.'

'I get the feeling you won't be doing an interview. Am I right?'

'Gosh, Julian, not on camera. I couldn't. I hope you understand. Between my dad and . . . Tom and Conor and everybody, it . . . it wouldn't—'

'Hmm. I thought a woman like you would make up her own mind.'

'I would. Normally, I would, but—'

He touched her wrist. 'It's all right, Nina. I'm well aware how difficult it would be for you. Truth to tell, I didn't come here to twist your arm. I wanted to see you again. And if, by any chance, you come up with anything, any snippet of information that might help the programme, that would be brilliant.'

A tingling sensation rose from Nina's neck. It was, she assured herself, the alcohol at work. Nothing more. She hoped he didn't think her a fool, a compliant woman who meekly did what her father and her boyfriend asked.

'Thanks,' she said.

Julian slapped his knees. 'Time for another drink.'

'I'm not sure . . .' she started, but he was already halfway to the bar.

When he returned, they spoke about Tess. Was she always such hard work? he wanted to know. Nina was about to defend her friend, then chose to stay quiet. Tess was well able to speak for herself.

'Speaking of Tess,' he said, 'you know what I've been meaning to ask you?'

'I do, and the answer is no, I haven't a clue. The identity of Tess's father is Kilmitten's other great mystery.'

'She doesn't know herself?'

'Nope.'

He tilted forward, as if poised to say something, then drew back.

'Go on,' said Nina.

'Might the two mysteries be connected?'

'Might Father Galvin have been Tess's dad, do you mean? I remember how some of the young lads, like the O'Gradys, used to tease her about that, but I don't think it's likely.' She paused. 'Not impossible, though. Now that I think about it, Tess's mother didn't go to the funeral, which caused a stir.'

'For truth? In what way?'

'It was seen as disrespectful. But I can't remember any more than that. There was too much else going on. Plus, it wasn't as if anybody said anything to me. I was only thirteen, so I was relying on what I could overhear.'

'And now she's taken up with Conor's father, and there's a baby on the way. It's a lively spot, Kilmitten.'

'People outside Dublin are allowed to have sex too, you know.'

Julian laughed his throaty laugh. 'Ginny does sound like an interesting woman.'

'Haven't you met her?'

'Just briefly. I approached her for an interview. She told me she'd better things to be doing with herself, like – let me see if I've got this right – cleaning the oven or pulling out her fingernails with rusty pliers.'

'That'd be Ginny. She was quite a looker in her day.' Nina slapped her cheek. 'Sorry, I shouldn't describe her like that. She's still a very attractive woman. A nice one too. Although in her heyday she was too much fun for some people's tastes, if you get my drift.'

'Very diplomatically put.'

Gradually, the conversation moved on. She told him about teaching. He told her about his fascination with documentary-making. How he'd hawked himself around production companies, willing to work for nothing, until he'd begun to get regular gigs. His big break had come the previous year with a programme about young Irish people in London. She'd seen it, she said. It was good, really good. He thanked her and touched her arm again. A dart of excitement shot through her. She went to the bar and got another round because, let's face it, doing anything else would be stingy, and nobody wanted to be seen as stingy. She could have bought a 7 Up for herself but didn't. By now her thoughts were blurring at the edges. The bar gleamed in the late-afternoon sun. Everything felt dream-like. They had one for the road, and she made the mistake of looking at her watch. It wasn't late afternoon at all. It was seven thirty in the evening.

'Oh, hell,' said Nina, 'I'd better go.' She didn't have to add, 'Or my boyfriend will be sending out a search party.'

'Will I see you again?' he said.

And that was how it began.

Two days later, they went to his Ranelagh flat. They met twice the following week and three times the week after that. Nina felt a thrill as sweet as it was wrong. She was dizzy with sex and conversation and subterfuge. In the same way that all the best parties took place on Good Friday, it seemed that illicit sex was far more thrilling than the regular variety.

Obviously, their arrangement couldn't last. Julian was meant to be viewing the Father Galvin tapes; she was still on holidays. When he resumed filming, when she had to return to work, who knew what would happen?

Sometimes they went for coffee or a drink. She convinced herself that if they stuck to certain parts of the city, nobody would see them. They spoke about their ambitions. Julian wanted to make serious documentaries with international appeal, the sort of productions that got shown at film festivals and in art-house cinemas. If, in the meantime, he had to turn his hand to the occasional corporate video, so be it. 'I have no time for failure,' he said, and while Nina knew this would make some people gag, she found it refreshing. She didn't think she'd ever met somebody so sorted, so together.

Although she didn't risk meeting any of Julian's friends, she could tell that his circle was very different from hers. While most of them were a few years older than her, few had regular jobs. They seemed to spend their time putting together portfolios and talking about projects. Portfolios of what, Nina was never quite sure. Their lack of earnings didn't appear to be a problem. They drank in The Bailey and The Norseman. They went to Sides and the Pink Elephant and other places where Nina would have felt crushingly uncool.

Julian liked to say that Ireland was changing. 'Can't you feel it?' he'd ask.

Nina would make light of his claims. 'Oh, there's been big change in Kilmitten,' she'd say. 'We have the British TV channels now. And the Moynihans went to Santa Ponsa on their holidays. Oh, and Mangan's shop has started stocking vegetarian cheese and Greek yoghurt.' Despite her flippant words, she agreed. This wasn't the time to leave home.

Occasionally, they spoke about Father Galvin. Julian remained convinced that Ginny Fortune was part of the story. While Nina laughed and called him a conspiracy theorist, part of her wondered if there might be something in what he said.

Throughout August, they continued to meet. This was, she knew, the most reckless thing she'd ever done. Moving in with Tom might have irritated her father, but you could hardly call it reckless. They'd known each other since they were four years old. She told herself that hooking up with Julian was the type of thing that Tess would do. But that wasn't fair. As impulsive as Tess was, Nina had never known her to be unfaithful. The only person she ever hurt was herself.

She expected Tom to notice. Was there not something different about her? Did she not look like a woman who was sleeping with another man? Who was infatuated with another man? Why didn't he ask more questions about how she was filling her days? Why hadn't he spotted that she could barely eat? That she was irritable in his presence. Yet Tom went about life as usual. Once or twice, he appeared to be on the verge of saying or asking something but checked himself and pulled back. On another occasion, he enquired about the documentary. Had Nina heard any more? he asked. If he thought there was anything odd about her mumbled, evasive reply, he didn't say.

She came to realise that if you trusted someone, you didn't ask questions. Signs that might otherwise point to the truth went unnoticed. And Nina had never given Tom reason to distrust her. Until now.

Did she feel guilty? Of course. How could she talk to Tom, kiss him, go to bed with him, when her head was filled with thoughts of another man? She hadn't known she was capable of such deceit. The problem was, she felt so many other things too. When she was with Julian, she felt like a more exciting person. A grown-up. Corny as it might sound, she felt like this was what she'd been waiting for.

Chapter 16

In August, Ginny moved in with Flan, leaving behind the rented house where she'd spent most of her adult life. 'It makes sense,' said Conor's father. 'What's the point in waiting for the baby or a marriage certificate when this is what we want?' After some joking about the village not being able to cope with its sergeant living in sin, Conor agreed. He reckoned Tess's mother would breathe new life into the bungalow in Kennedy Crescent.

A couple of weeks later, he decided to use his day off to see how the pair were getting on. This wasn't the only reason for his trip. He wanted to talk to his father. Increasingly, Conor felt he'd made the wrong decision. He looked at people in Termonbeg and realised he knew nothing about their lives, about what motivated or scared them. Sometimes *he* was scared. He'd see the hostility in someone's face and want to turn on his heel and run. On other occasions, he felt out of his depth. Useless. Earlier that week he'd had to talk to a woman about her son, an acne-strewn seventeen-year-old whose low-level bad behaviour was in danger of tipping into all-out thuggery. She'd stared at him with disappointed eyes. 'Look, son,' she'd said, 'his father's an alcoholic, his brother's stoned out of his skull, and I'm worn out from cleaning up other people's filth. What is it you want me to do?' Then she began to cry, large tears slipping down her pinched face, her keening filling the room.

'I'm sorry,' Conor whispered. 'I'm sorry.' It was all he could say. When he left, she was still weeping. *I'm not any good at this*, he thought. *I shouldn't be doing it.*

How arrogant had he been when he'd maintained that the regular beat wasn't for him? In the four years since he'd joined the force, he'd learned that every young cop pictured themselves toppling drug lords and unmasking murderers. More often than not, they ended up directing traffic and looking for stolen pension books. That wasn't all: as much as he hated to admit it, he should have paid more heed to his father's advice. Who else had such a hard-won appreciation of how cruel the job could be?

Not that he'd say all of this. If he blurted everything out, and his dad didn't understand, he'd be making a bad situation worse. No, he'd have to talk around his problems and hope his father appreciated what he was saying. He'd considered confiding in a colleague, then concluded he couldn't take the risk. In the station, they were all bravado and bluster. They'd tell dark jokes about the people they arrested and the situations they encountered, yet there was a lack of honesty about their conversations. Nobody ever admitted to feeling down or unable to cope. They complained about lazy colleagues while skirting around the fact that some of their fellow guards were out-and-out gangsters, who got their kicks from stepping over the line. When locals were bullied and harassed, they looked the other way. Without a word being said, Conor had learned that loyalty to colleagues was prized above all else. Avoiding unnecessary hassle came next. Tackling crime was a long way down the list.

With his girlfriend, too, he kept up a front. Angela was a nurse in an Accident and Emergency ward, her job even more challenging than his. He wasn't in love – and he hoped she wasn't either – but they had a laugh together, and a laugh was what he needed.

He would have liked to speak to Tess, but she was so wrapped up in her new life, he didn't think she'd have time for his concerns.

Once, he would have spoken to Tom. Conor liked Tom; only an unreasonable person wouldn't. But after that weekend in London their friendship had never been the same. He suspected that Tom still hadn't forgiven him for joining the guards. They could go out on the beer or watch a match, but something had shifted.

Conor found his dad and Ginny in the sitting room, watching the news. The room was dark, the atmosphere sombre as a funeral home. Either they were seriously concerned about the coup in the Soviet Union or something was wrong. He told himself not to rush to conclusions. A few weeks previously, he'd worried that his dad was ill when, in fact, Flan had been priming himself to deliver good news. Still, Ginny appeared to have more than Mikhail Gorbachev on her mind. Obviously pregnant now, she looked about as far from blooming as he could imagine. Shrivelling would have been a more appropriate word.

'Hi . . . Conor,' she said, as though she had trouble recalling his name.

Neither did his father have many spare words. 'Journey okay?' He asked Conor to go out to the kitchen and put on a pot of tea.

'No tea for me, thanks,' said Ginny, rising from the sofa. 'I think I'll go for a lie-down.'

'Is—' started Conor, who was beginning to realise that his own issues would have to wait.

She gave a tight smile. 'Don't worry. I'm fine. A bit weary today, that's all.'

When she'd left the room, her footsteps heavy in the hall, Conor turned to his father.

'Ginny's a little off-key,' explained his dad. 'Like she said, though, there's nothing for you to get worked up about.'

She didn't look a little off-key. She looked rigid with misery. Conor was wary of asking questions. That wasn't what they did. His concern won out. 'What's wrong with her?'

'Oh, you know . . .'

'Jesus, Dad, if I knew, I wouldn't be asking. It's not the baby, is it?'

His father screwed his eyes shut, the wrinkles fanning out across his face. 'No,' he said, 'it's Tess.'

Chapter 17

Tess leaned back in the chair, closed her eyes and waited to be transformed. The studio smelt of lilies and coffee. On the stereo, Michael Stipe sang about 'Shiny Happy People'. As much as she loved REM, she would have preferred something more low-key. Something quieter. She'd got trashed the night before and every millimetre of her body was in revolt.

She shouldn't have gone out, not on the eve of a magazine shoot. According to Estelle, one of the big cosmetics companies was showing an interest in her. A cosmetics contract would take her career to another level, so a job like this, where the emphasis was on next season's trends in eyeshadow and Tess's face, was important. She'd been moping around the flat when her friend Zoë had called. 'Just one drink,' Tess had said, meaning at most two or three. Seven hours later, they'd swayed out of a Mayfair club. Next she knew, the alarm was wailing, and she was behind time, and . . . Oh, dear Lord, her head.

'A late one, was it?' asked Belinda, the make-up artist, as she dabbed on concealer.

'Is it that obvious?'

'Moisturiser is your friend, lovey,' replied Belinda, whose own face gleamed like she'd bathed in Castrol GTX. 'If you're going to go clubbing before a day's work, at least remember to take off your slap and put on some moisturiser. Your skin's like sandpaper.'

'Thanks,' said Tess, 'consider me told.' She reached for her coffee. It tasted like tar. 'Proper coffee', people called it. Give her an improper coffee any day of the week: a nice milky Nescafé with two spoons of sugar, the sort her mother made.

She was trying not to think about her mother. After Ginny had revealed that Tess's father was dead, she'd been reluctant to say much more. 'He wasn't from around here,' she'd said. 'I didn't know him that well.' What he'd been called and where he'd been from didn't matter, she maintained. 'He can't meet you, you can't meet him, so his name is irrelevant.'

'No, it's not,' said Tess. 'What about his family?'

'What about them? They're nothing to do with us.'

'When did he die . . . and how?'

'It doesn't matter,' said her mam, in a staccato voice. 'Now, I've said more than enough. Leave me be, okay?'

With that, she'd abandoned her half-made cheesecake and hurtled out of the kitchen like a sulky teenager. Three hours later, she'd reappeared, the filmy look in her eyes revealing that she'd been crying. Tess tried to say something, but her mam didn't want to listen. 'We've got to go to dinner,' she said. 'Please don't let me down.'

The evening was awkward. It might have been like that anyway. Twenty-four hours earlier, Conor and Tess hadn't known that their parents were seeing each other. Now, they were sitting around the dinner table, eating roast chicken and discussing baby names and wedding venues. They were going to move in together, they said. Conor teased them, then gushed about how delighted he was. Tess stayed quiet. He gave her a nudge.

'Fantastic,' she said. 'Just fantastic. I take no one minds if I smoke.' Although she could tell that Conor was annoyed with her, she didn't care. She didn't want to be there. She wanted to be alone so she could digest what her mam had told her.

Her father was gone. She would never meet him, let alone get to know him. He would never see her in a magazine or on the TV.

For the remainder of the weekend, barely a word passed between mother and daughter. Before she left for New York, Tess did make one further attempt to talk about her father. Her mam responded with a funny look, like she was chewing something sour, and Tess swallowed what she'd wanted to say.

Since then, they'd spoken only once. Her mother had rung to say she'd left Pearse Terrace. Tess's belongings – some clothes, a prehistoric cassette player and a box of assorted trash – were in Paula's old room. 'We're doing up Conor's for the baby,' she said. 'It's bigger and brighter, but there'll always be a bed here for you. You know that, don't you?'

'I'm likely to be busy over the next while,' Tess replied.

'Suit yourself. I've got to go. I don't want to be hogging the phone.'

Then her mother hung up without saying goodbye.

Belinda told Tess to look up so she could apply some eyeliner. A crescent of ooh-ers and ah-ers peered on, while the photographer, an overbearing character called Rik, adjusted the lighting. 'World class,' everybody said about Rik. 'A genius.' He was also a legendary name-dropper, and Tess knew she'd have to endure a stream of comments about what Christy, Cindy and Naomi were up to.

As usual, it took her a few seconds to realise that the trilling sound coming from her bag belonged to her phone. She presumed it was Estelle. Tess wasn't in the humour for work talk and allowed the phone to ring out. She would call back later. All she could think of was bed. She craved crisp cold sheets and at least ten hours of uninterrupted sleep.

When the phone rang for a third time, she decided she'd better answer it.

'Hi, Estelle,' she said. 'I'll—'

'Uh, howarya, Tess?' replied a familiar voice. 'What are you up to?'

'I'm about to do some pictures. It's an important . . .' She stopped. Conor wouldn't call unless something was wrong. *Shit*, she thought, *the baby*. 'What's up?'

'It's your mam. You've got to talk to her.'

While Belinda hovered, Conor explained that he'd gone home for the night and was taken aback by what he'd found. Tess's mother was in a bad way. After some probing, his dad revealed that she was upset because Tess wasn't speaking to her. 'Ginny's coming to the conclusion that she'll have to tell her about her father,' he said. 'Not that she'll find it easy to handle.'

'Did he say why?' asked Tess.

'Ah, here,' said Conor, his voice stiff with irritation. 'For once, will you think about your mother? She's five months pregnant and she looks wrecked. Haunted. And the old man's not much better. They don't know I'm ringing you, by the way. I'm in the callbox outside Pilkington's.'

'It's not all my fault, you know.'

'I'm not saying it is. But, if you want my advice, you should talk to your mam.'

'That won't be easy. She doesn't like phone calls, and, I guarantee you, the moment I ring she'll be all, "Everything's grand, Tessy. Don't you go fretting about me."'

'Then you should come home and have a word with her. No, not a word – a proper conversation. She can't go on like this.'

Tess didn't leave immediately. Belinda finished her first look, and Rik spent ten minutes taking test shots and whinging about the model's head being elsewhere. It was when he made a comment about the Irish being unreliable that she snapped.

'Right,' she said. 'I can't do this today. I'm off.'

'What do you mean you're off?' asked Rik, in his phoney south London drawl (everybody knew he was actually from some chi-chi spot in Surrey).

'I'm off home – to Ireland. I want to see my unreliable mother and her unreliable husband-to-be.'

Leaving Rik to grumble about ungrateful cows, and the ooh-ers and ah-ers to swap bemused glances, Tess picked up her handbag and denim jacket.

'Big mistake, lovey,' said Belinda. 'Big mistake.'

In her weariness, Tess couldn't think of a smart reply. She lifted a shoulder and walked out.

Within ten minutes, Estelle was on the phone. 'Where are you?' she said. 'And, more importantly, what are you playing at?'

'I'm in a cab on my way to Heathrow and I'm playing at nothing. I've got to go home. My mother's not well.'

'Is she on life support?'

'No.'

'Then you don't need to go running home. What you need to do is turn around and go back to that shoot. Your mother will still be there tomorrow.'

'I've got to see her today.'

Tess heard a quick breath. 'This is your moment,' said Estelle. 'Your *Vogue* cover will be out in a few months. The cosmetics people are very keen. You've got to be in New York again next week. It's all about to happen for you. And what do you do? You're at a major-league shoot and you do a runner. I promise you, if you screw this up, you'll regret it.'

Tess thought of her mam, pregnant and upset. She pictured Flan, pacing the house, not knowing what to do. She thought, too, about Conor's revelation: her mother was willing to tell the full story. By the end of the day, her questions might be answered. She reminded Estelle of how hard she worked; of how, compared to lots of girls, she was the definition of clean-living and responsible. She'd never arrived for a job coked-up or strung-out. She had no scars or bruises or track marks. Okay, from time to time she was slightly hung over, but she was young and she had to live. 'I'm sorry,' she said, 'but on this occasion, some slack will have to be cut.'

Then she clicked off her phone.

'Terminal One, please,' she said to the driver.

Flan opened the door. 'Tess?' he said, his voice heavy with confusion.

She grinned, affecting casualness, as if it was perfectly normal to turn up with no luggage and no prior warning. A light drizzle was falling, the sky marbled with grey.

'How did you . . . I mean, why didn't you . . .?' he asked. Then, as though suddenly noticing that she was standing in the rain, he ushered her in. 'Come on in, pet. You'll have to forgive me. I'm a bit . . .'

'. . . surprised to see me,' she said, then explained she'd got a taxi from Shannon. Driving wasn't a skill she'd managed to acquire.

'That must have cost you a few pounds,' he said. 'Why didn't you call me? I would have collected you.'

They were in the kitchen now. Tess's eyes swept over the man who would soon be her stepfather. He looked as drained as she felt. 'I didn't want to bother you. And, given the . . . eh, situation, I thought it might be better if I just arrived like this.' She handed him a Duty Free bag containing a bottle of whiskey.

'There was no need for that,' he said, placing the bag on the counter.

'Mam always told me it was bad form to arrive with one arm as long as the other.'

'Conor rang you,' he said, a statement rather than a question. 'He was here until a short while ago. He's had to go back to work.'

'He didn't know I was coming. I came straight from a job.'

'So that explains why you've no bag. And the . . .'

'. . . make-up. I tried to remove some of it in the aeroplane toilet, but I reckon I only made it worse.' Tess knew she looked like she'd escaped from the circus. Either that or a high-security hospital. She peered around.

'Your mother's having a rest.'

'I won't disturb her. I want to have a word, that's all.'

Flan pulled his left earlobe. 'You're not to give her any hassle. If you do, there'll be trouble.'

Tess wasn't stung by his warning; she'd expected worse. 'I swear to you there'll be no hassle.'

'Fine. Let her say what she has to say, and if that's not much this evening, so be it.'

Tess tried to imagine how the man in front of her really felt. His life had known no shortage of sadness, but otherwise it had been steady, undramatic. According to Conor, his family rarely fell out. Even a raised voice was unusual. What he did have was long experience of the dramas of others: the rows that became violent, the men who hit their wives, the children who went off the rails. The dead priest at the party.

'Come on, so,' he said. 'I'll say one thing, Tess. Nobody could ever accuse you of being predictable.'

'Like mother, like daughter,' she replied.

'Tessy! What are you doing here?' said her mam, who must have been feigning surprise for she'd surely heard her daughter's voice at the door. She was sitting up in bed, wearing what looked like a new nightdress. Tess suspected the room had also been given some fresh touches. The moss-green carpet looked to have come straight from the warehouse, while the bedside lockers had the gleam of showroom furniture. She recalled Conor complaining that the bungalow was like a time capsule. 'Homage to the 1970s,' he'd said. 'All that's missing is a hostess trolley and a lava lamp.' She guessed that was changing.

As if reading her mind, her mother nodded in the direction of the rose-pink curtains. 'Pretty bedroom, isn't it? Flan's been doing a spot of work.'

Conor's father shifted his weight from one foot to the other. 'I'll go and make us a cup of tea. If you want anything else, Ginny, give me a shout.'

Tess leaned in and kissed her mother. As she did, she could see the neat bump beneath the sheets. Her mother's face appeared bloodless, and there were dark shadows beneath her green eyes.

She switched on the bedside lamp and stared at Tess. 'If that's the latest trend, I don't think much of it.'

'Another one who doesn't like my make-up. Deranged clown is very autumn/winter 'ninety-one, I'll have you know.' Tess lowered herself onto a green-seated chair. The picture of the two of them at the beach was on the dressing table beside a box of tissues and a tangle of bracelets. 'My Farrah Fawcett photo,' her mam had always called it. Tess was glad it had made the journey from Pearse Terrace.

'I—' she began, but her mother interrupted.

'I don't want an argument. This pregnancy business is harder than I remembered, and I don't have the energy for a row.'

'I'm not much better myself,' said Tess. This was true. It felt like a week had passed since she'd been sitting in Rik's studio, drinking foul coffee and lamenting her night out. 'I'm not here for a row. I'm here to say sorry.' This, too, was true, but only part of the story. She had the feeling her mother knew that.

'And I'm sorry. I shouldn't have told you your father was dead.'

'You mean he isn't?' Tess fought, and failed, to keep the excitement from her voice.

Her mother gave a hurried shake of the head. 'No, that's not what I mean.' She paused. 'I mean it was wrong to give you some information and not the rest. And I shouldn't have lied.'

'I'm not with you.'

'When I said he wasn't from around here, and that I didn't know him . . . that part was a lie.'

Tess felt a fluttering high in her chest. 'I see.'

'If I'm being honest, I always knew this day would come. I just wanted to postpone it for as long as possible. But, like you told me the other week, you're an adult now and you're entitled to the truth. All the same, I've a feeling you won't like what you're going to hear.'

'You don't have to tell me.' Tess didn't mean this, but felt it was what she should say.

'We both know I do.'

Flan arrived with tea and a plate of toast. 'You look like you could do with something to eat,' he said to Tess.

'She always does,' said her mother. 'She's made a career out of it.' The three laughed. It struck Tess that, despite everything, her mother was happy with Conor's father. There was no artifice to her laughter. She realised how little thought she'd given to her mam's happiness. She disliked herself for that, but perhaps everyone was the same. Ordinarily, she'd have asked Nina, but the two hadn't spoken since the last time Tess was in Kilmitten. Although she'd tried calling, the phone was never answered.

When Flan left, the two fell into a tense silence. Despite the rain, three or four children were playing outside. That was Kilmitten: even in a hurricane somebody would feel the need to get out their football or skipping rope. A squeal crashed through the quiet.

'They're mad, those kids,' said Tess.

Her mam took a sip of tea. 'So,' she said, 'I suppose I'd better start talking.'

Chapter 18

'I was eighteen,' said her mother, 'and by today's standards, I was fairly tame. Still, I fancied myself as a lively young one. I had a million plans. I was going to move to Dublin and get a job and have an exciting life. I wanted parties and cool clothes and good-looking men, everything we didn't have in Kilmitten. Eventually I'd marry a rich guy and we'd live in a big house in Howth or Dalkey. We'd hang around with artists and musicians and interesting people. Oh, what I wasn't going to do! Mam and Dad said they didn't mind me going to Dublin. They just didn't want me leaving the country. They'd already lost three children to emigration, and they hated the thought of me joining them.'

Tess had always known that her mother was the youngest of four, but that the siblings weren't close. She had an uncle in San Diego, another in Brisbane and an aunt in Manchester. None kept in regular touch, and the only one Tess had met was her aunt Jacinta, a bossy woman with a scrubbed face and a husband who was 'something big in insurance'.

'One night,' said her mam, 'I was out in the village.

There was a gang of us, and some people were talking about thumbing a lift into Templemorris to go to a dance. I remember it was a shocking cold night. Well, I don't have to tell you what the wind is like around here. I'd had too much to drink and I wasn't sure about the dance. So, I got talking to one of the lads, and he said, "Listen, there's a place where we can go and continue the chat. It'll get us out of the wind." I didn't want to go home yet and I thought, *Well, why not?* It turned out he was thinking of the old barn, near where the Minogues live now.

'We were there for a short while, talking about this and that, making fun of some of the people in the village and . . . he kissed me. It wasn't what I wanted, but . . . I don't know . . . maybe I didn't make that clear enough. I probably just laughed or something. I wasn't interested, though. Really I wasn't.' Her mother stopped to drink some tea. Before resuming, she took a long breath. 'Next thing I knew, he'd knocked me onto my back and he was on top of me. Even in those days, he was a big man. "Strong" was the word people liked to use. I was as thin then as you are now. And I was drunk. In no time, my trousers were open. I tried to scream, but I couldn't. Not that it would have made any difference. It was late at night and nobody would have heard me. And then . . .' She hesitated. 'And then, he forced himself on me. Even though it was dark, I can still see his bloodshot eyes. I imagine that I can smell him too. He smelt sort of vinegary.' Another hesitation. 'You don't want me to go through everything, do you? You've got to understand . . . I've spent a long time trying not to remember. And I've come to believe that the mind does filter some things out. That otherwise we'd all go crazy.'

'No,' Tess heard herself say. Her reactions were delayed, as if her mother was at the end of a long-distance phone line rather than a few inches away. 'No, of course, I don't. But . . . this man . . . you haven't . . . you haven't mentioned his name.'

'Lord, Tess, I'm sorry. It was Noel O'Grady. That's who I'm talking about: Noel O'Grady. Afterwards, when he'd . . . when it was over . . . he told me he'd better be getting off home. He was a married man, after all, a respectable married man with a job and a car, Marty toddling around, Philly in the pram and another baby on the way. I remember lying there for an hour, maybe more, trying to make sense of what he'd done. But I couldn't. Of course I couldn't.'

So many thoughts were ripping through Tess's head that she was finding it hard to focus. Was her mam saying that Noel O'Grady was her father? Obnoxious Noel with the silent wife and the sons who'd made it their business to taunt and tease her. Noel O'Grady who'd got drunk and driven his car into a ditch. One thought won out. When finally she was able to speak, she said, 'That's rape. What he did to you, it was rape.'

'You can call it that, but it was what happened. There was nothing I could do to stop it or change it.'

'But didn't you tell anyone? Didn't you—'

'Oh, Tessy, you know what people are like. If I'd said anything, I'd have been the one in the wrong. I can hear them with their "So what were you doing with him to begin with? What did you think he wanted you for? To discuss the state of the nation? And how much did you have to drink? Weren't you leading the man on?" I started questioning myself, too. I thought that if I'd gone home, like Mam and Dad would have wanted, and if I hadn't had such grand notions about myself, well, it wouldn't have happened. I would have been safe. I blamed myself and my big ideas.'

'But he raped you,' said Tess, the tears at the back of her throat making her voice sound weedy and congested.

'Yes. Yes, he did. I couldn't say that then, but I can now. I'm sorry, I did warn you that you mightn't like what I had to say.' Her mother reached for her cup and took another careful sip of tea.

'Please, Mam. Don't say you're sorry. I understand why you couldn't tell me. O'Grady should've been behind bars, not strutting around the village.'

Her mam placed the cup back on the locker. A solitary tear ran down her left cheek. Fleetingly, Tess thought about the outside world. About London and Kilmitten. About the kids in the street and Flan down the hall. Nothing else mattered. Her whole world was in this room. She looked at her mother. 'You don't have to say anything else.'

'No, I've got this far. You deserve to hear the rest. You'll have other questions, and I want to deal with everything tonight.'

'Okay.'

'It was months before I told anyone I was pregnant. In the end, Mam guessed. She was devastated. I can still see her, sitting at the kitchen table, crying. No lie, I reckon that image was burned onto my brain – cut me open and you'll find it there. In those days, most parents would have sent me away. That was what you did. But Mam and Dad said I could stay and they'd decide what to do after the baby arrived. By then, it was obvious I was expecting. Nobody in the village said anything to my face, but I can imagine what they said behind my back. Let me tell you, it was a very lonely place to be. Finally, the parish priest came to the door and told my parents that the time had come to send me to a home for unmarried mothers.'

'Father Galvin did that?'

'No, Father Galvin was a young curate then. Father Keating was the man in charge, a right cranky old bastard if ever there was one. "There's a great home above in Carrigbrack," he said to Mam. "The nuns there know how to deal with girls who get themselves into trouble. And they'll deal with the baby too."'

'He made it sound like you got pregnant on your own.'

'That was the way people spoke.' She shook her head. 'Some still do. Anyway, he wouldn't let it rest. Two or three times he called to the house, telling Mam she'd regret her foolishness. "That girl is bringing shame on a good family," he said.'

'The old bollocks,' said Tess, her jaw trembling. *Noel O'Grady. Of all the men in the world, her father was Noel O'Grady.*

'You said it. I swore I'd never see the inside of that church again, and apart from Mam and Dad's funerals, and your own big days – christening, Communion and that – I've kept my word.'

'And there I was as a kid, trotting up to Mass on my own, wondering why you stayed at home.'

'Bless you, what a funny little thing you were. I could hardly stop you. You always had a mind of your own.' Her mother made a Tess-like face, big eyes peering out from beneath a long fringe, mouth in a determined line.

For a moment, they both laughed.

Tess touched her mother's hand. The skin felt paper-thin, but was warmer than she'd expected. 'Did your parents know about . . .?'

'I lied to them, told them your father was a guy I'd met in Ennis and that he'd gone to London. I shouldn't have lied, but I was scared. I wanted everything and everybody to go away. Besides, I didn't know how they'd react if I told the truth.'

'And did you tell Noel O'Grady that you were expecting his baby?'

'Mmm. He said, "I take it you'll be making sure the child gets given to a good home." Then he said he was sorry, but that keeping you would be a mistake. He gave me a right old sob story about how miserable life was with Breege and how he hadn't meant any harm and how I was a beautiful-looking girl and if I got over this I could have anything I wanted. "There's nothing for you here in Kilmitten," he said.'

'In other words, why don't you disappear?' *Noel O'Grady. Her father was Noel O'Grady.*

'That was about the size of it, yeah. After you were born, there were times when I thought leaving might be easier, only then sense took over and I accepted that, without Mam and Dad's support, I'd be sunk. I had to stay put. By then, I was determined to keep you. You were a lot of work, but I had plenty of energy, and you were a happy baby. Right from the start, you were alert and content. Mam and Dad were mad about you, and they agreed you should stay.

'Again, when you were older, after my parents had died, I toyed with the idea of leaving. But where would I go? Where would *we* go? You were getting on well in Kilmitten. I didn't have any skills. I was stuck.'

Tess's memories of her grandparents were hazy. Her grandfather had suffered a fatal heart attack when she was three. A couple of years later, her grandmother had died from breast cancer. Apart from mild sadness at their early deaths, she hadn't given them much thought. Now, she marvelled at their courage. They'd grown up during a time of unquestioning deference to the Church, yet they'd been gutsy enough to say, 'No, thank you very much. We'll decide what's best for our daughter and granddaughter.'

Three cheers for Nan and Granddad.

'Also,' her mother was saying, 'the more I thought about it, the more I knew I had to stay. I'd done nothing wrong, so why should I be forced out? When you went to school, I got a job. It mightn't have been a job I wanted, but it paid the rent. Until I moved in here, it still did.'

Another tear escaped. Tess rose and fetched the tissues from the dressing table. 'This sounds rough, but did I not remind you of him and of what he'd done to you?'

'Sometimes, yeah. Sometimes I'd watch you and it'd be

hard. But then you'd be all chatty and funny, and I'd think, *You can't take it out on her. She's her own person.* And you gave me so much happiness. For years, every moment of pure happiness I had came from you.'

Tess found this so touching that she couldn't think how to respond. In the end, she just said, 'Thanks.'

'It's the truth. Of all the regrets I've had, I never for one minute regretted keeping you.'

'When I was a baby, how did people treat you?'

'Most folks were all right, but some were thoughtless, and a few were deliberately cruel. There was one woman, Bernie Farragher was her name. You wouldn't remember her, she moved away years ago. Bernie thought I should be cast out of the village. I remember her looking at you and saying, bold as you like, "It's a shame that child has no father. She'll have a difficult life." It took me a few seconds to pull myself together, and, in the meantime, you gave the old witch your best gummy smile. "Her name is Tess," I said, "and she'll have everything she needs." Afterwards, I was devastated. I felt like I'd developed some sort of stain, like people thought I was dirty.'

'The cow. I hope wherever she went, she had a miserable life. Did he . . . Did O'Grady ever say anything about me? There I was, running around the village with the other kids. His daughter.'

Although she was managing to ask questions, Tess was trembling all over. Noel O'Grady was her father. Not some obscure figure. Not a film star or a millionaire. Not someone romantic or handsome, but Noel O'Grady, with the bloated face and the shiny suits. Noel O'Grady, who believed that, because his brother was a politician (a junior minister, no less), the rules didn't apply to him.

'He barely spoke to me,' said her mam, as she blotted her eyes. 'Even though I saw him all the time, we didn't really acknowledge each other.'

'That must have been grim.'

'Grim doesn't begin to cover it, but it's amazing what you can get used to. When you've no choice, you can endure almost anything. Did he ever talk to you or show any interest in you?'

Tess paused to think. Had he ever said anything, no matter how small, to suggest he might have an interest in her life? Nothing came to mind, and she shook her head. 'I don't know how you coped. Were you never tempted to tell anyone?'

'I did talk to one person. I didn't tell him how it happened, but I told him who your father was.' She hesitated. 'I told Emmet Minogue.' Tess must have looked shocked, because her mother immediately added, 'I know, I know. Of all the people I could've spoken to, I chose him. In my defence, it was a long time before all that carry-on over you and Nina and the lads. He was my doctor, and I had to unburden myself to someone who I felt wouldn't judge me. Oh, and I knew he couldn't spread the word.'

'Huh,' said Tess. 'Dr Judgemental himself.'

'Don't get me started on that man. Obviously, I've told Flan. I gave him the full story a few months back. I wanted to put all my cards on the table, so to speak. He was horrified.

For a week or so, he was in a daze. It's kind of messy because of Paula being married to Marty O'Grady.'

'Marty's the best of them. Everyone says that. As for the others? Jesus, what a shower.' Tess took another tissue from the box. 'I can't believe I'm related to the O'Gradys. They're my . . . brothers.'

'At least you don't look like them.'

'I look like you, thankfully. Imagine being as ugly as the O'Gradys.'

Her mother smiled, and a tear ran into her mouth.

'Were you never tempted to tell anyone else, like Mags or Mercedes? Or any of your other . . .' Tess didn't know what word to use. Boyfriends? Partners?

'I was. Sometimes, I'd think, *I can't keep quiet any longer.* Then I'd catch myself on. Nobody would be capable of keeping the information to themselves. The secret would be too much for them. So, I stuck to the tale I'd told my parents and embellished it along the way. His name was John, I said. He'd gone to London to look for work, and I wouldn't know how to find him even if I wanted to.'

'Do you reckon Breege O'Grady has any idea her husband was my father?'

'Honestly, no. She's a woman of relatively few words, but even so, I think that if she knew, she would have said something to somebody. At this stage, that's the way I'd like it to stay. There's nothing to be gained by telling her. I suppose, though . . .' Tess's mam ran a finger down her forehead. 'I have asked myself . . . if he did that to me, was he violent with her?'

'I hadn't thought of that.'

'I've had plenty of time for thinking.'

'I can't imagine how you did it. How you held it all together, I mean.'

'To be fair, I wasn't always the model mother. I was never going to win Housewife of the Year.'

'Thank God for that. I couldn't really see you up on that stage: "And here, with her sensational fairy cakes and her dee-licious tea brack, modelling a bee-yoo-ti-ful magenta suit and a pair of knickers she knitted from leftover wool, is Ginny Fortune."' Tess's silly voice – part newsreader, part circus ringmaster – forced another smile from her mam. 'And, by the way, you were a brilliant mother. You *are* a brilliant mother. I'm only sorry the men in your life didn't always appreciate you.'

'I certainly knew how to pick a loser. I don't know . . . maybe I convinced myself I didn't deserve any better. Or maybe that's too simplistic. I definitely got to the stage where I felt life was going to be difficult – difficult and unfair – no matter what I did.'

'You picked the right guy this time.'

'I think so too.'

By now it was dark outside, the rain tapping the window, the children gone home.

Tess considered what had been done to her mam. And how she'd reacted. She could have been swallowed by bitterness and self-pity. Instead she'd marched on, braver than a thousand soldiers. 'Thanks,' she said eventually. 'Thanks for telling me.'

She hoped that what she glimpsed in her mother's eyes was relief. They'd never been given to showy sentiment. Their relationship was long on banter, short on declarations of affection. Until tonight, the one exception had been when her mother had begged her not to go to London. Now Tess saw that plea in a different light. Her mam had been scared of losing the child she'd fought to keep.

She gave her mother another kiss. 'I'll let you get some sleep. I love you, Mam.'

'And I love you, Tessy.'

Walking down the hall, Tess realised how tired she was. Not that she expected to sleep. She'd spent the morning longing for her London bed. She would spend the night in Paula Varley's old room, allowing what she'd learned to percolate through her brain. Tomorrow she would have to return to London and grovel like she'd never grovelled before.

As she wriggled out of her clothes and climbed into bed, she recalled the mantras of her teenage years, how anxious people had been to see Father's Galvin's death as a one-off, an aberration. The phrases were lodged in her brain, as familiar as responses at Mass. What was Kilmitten? It was a close-knit community where neighbour looked out for neighbour and every door was open. What wasn't tolerated? Thuggery, thieving and bad behaviour. But if something bad did happen, who was to blame? Outsiders. Definitely outsiders. Meanwhile, there was her mother: a woman who'd spent more than twenty years afraid to talk about the crime that had scarred her life.

Tess wondered what else remained hidden.

Chapter 19

In early September, Fergal called to the shop and said he needed to talk. Tom, who'd been running the place singlehandedly since the death of Val's brother, asked if it could wait. Fergal's preoccupied face and the way he kept running a hand through his already rumpled hair suggested that it couldn't. They went into the stuffy back room, Tom staying beside the door so he could watch for customers.

'I'm not sure how to tell you this,' said Fergal, his knees jiggling.

Assuming something had happened to his friend, Tom tried to sound patient. 'I'm under a wee bit of pressure here,' he said. 'We're never quiet for long.'

'Grand, I hear you.' Fergal pummelled his cheeks with the knuckles of both hands. Then he came out with it. He'd seen Nina with another guy. They'd been in Rathmines, coming out of the Stella cinema. The man was tall and looked full of himself. 'You know the type.'

Tom stared at a box of Mars bars, reading and re-reading the advertising slogan. He instructed himself to concentrate on what Fergal was saying, but his brain was trying to shut down.

'Nina's at work,' he said. 'They started back on Monday. She's teaching second class this year. You couldn't have seen her in Rathmines.'

Fergal examined the blue lino floor. 'I saw them a week ago. I've been thinking about it ever since. Trying to figure out what to do, you know?'

'How can you be sure it was her?'

'We spent a summer in the same flat, Tom. It was definitely her.'

'And the guy, could he have been – oh, I don't know – a friend, a work colleague, somebody she'd bumped into?'

'He wasn't a friend.' Fergal's voice carried a world of information, and Tom decided he didn't want to hear any more. His initial impulse was to shut the shop, go back to the house and wait. Staying was easier. He did the job by rote, selling groceries, newspapers and cigarettes, exchanging insults with young lads, forecasting the weather with old women. At six, Val arrived and told him to get off home.

'And don't worry about opening up in the morning,' he said. 'I'll do that. The funeral was a week ago. It's about time I got back into my routine.'

Usually, Tom got the bus to Ringsend. Tonight he chose to walk; he needed to walk. He threaded his way along O'Connell Street, around the queue at the Savoy cinema, past the doughnut kiosk and over the bridge. He nodded at the man selling bootleg cassettes and gave a few coppers to a woman begging for change. At the end of Westmoreland

Street, he turned left, all the while running Fergal's words around his head. He tried pretending that his friend had got it wrong. That he was mistaken. Confused. Lying. But the more Tom reflected on what he'd heard, the more certain he became that Nina was seeing someone else.

He should have noticed the signs. There'd been nothing blatant. She hadn't come home smelling of another man. They hadn't stopped having sex. The one time they'd been apart, she'd definitely been in Kilmitten. There had, though, been small signals. The way she'd started pushing her food around her plate before announcing that she wasn't hungry. The way she'd shut down any talk about travelling. How, unusually for her, she'd seemed to relish an argument. How she'd failed to turn up for Val's brother's funeral. ('Terrible period pain,' she'd said.) *Christ*, thought Tom, *I'm stupid*.

By now, he was approaching home. A soft breeze rippled in from the Irish Sea. The sky was tinged with coral. It was a beautiful evening. Back-to-school weather, his father called it. Tom crossed the Dodder, his mind darting every which way. Part of him hoped that Nina wasn't there. He actually hoped that she was out with this man, whoever he was. A teaching colleague? The brother of a friend? A neighbour? He didn't know if he had the strength to confront her tonight. Another part of him clung to the possibility, however small, that there'd been a misunderstanding. That his girlfriend had a doppelganger, who spent her afternoons in suburban cinemas with confident-looking men.

She was there.

The smell of frying onions wafted from the kitchen. Her voice followed.

'With you in a sec,' she said. 'I bought wine. Would you like a glass?'

'Um, yeah,' he replied, as he lowered himself into an old brocade armchair.

A moment later she was in front of him, a glass of red wine in each hand. She was wearing his favourite top. White with a drawstring neckline – her mother had brought it back from a holiday in Santorini.

'I'm making dinner,' she said. 'It's nothing special, just bolognese, but I'm glad you're home in time for us to eat together.' She handed him a glass.

Although Tom thought he was wearing his deadpan face, Nina must have guessed that something was wrong. When it came to spotting trouble, her senses were more developed than his.

'Was there a problem at work?' she asked.

There was, he figured, no right way to go about this. No formula of words that would make it any less awful. He had to jump on in.

'I met Fergal today. He said he saw you last week.'

'Why didn't he say hello?'

'You weren't alone.'

'Oh.'

'Who is he?'

Blotches of colour rose in her face. 'I don't know what you mean.'

'Don't lie, Nina. Please.' Tom barely recognised his own voice. He sounded pathetic. He *was* pathetic.

She sat down. 'I met . . . I've been seeing someone. It only began recently, I promise.'

'Am I supposed to take comfort from that?'

'No, but I don't want you thinking it's been going on for a long time when it hasn't.'

'To be honest, I don't think the timeframe is the issue here. The issue is you sleeping with another man. Or, at least, I assume you do more than go to the cinema.'

'What—'

'Who is he?'

'I was going to tell you, honestly I was. I didn't want you to find out like this. I can't believe . . . I mean, Fergal . . .'

'Dublin's a small place.'

'I suppose.' The blotches deepened in colour.

'Who is he?' repeated Tom.

'Does it matter?'

'We've been together for four years. We share a house. I thought we'd go and see the world, and that one day we'd get married. So, yes, it matters.'

For the first time, Nina looked him in the eye. 'That's just it, isn't it, Tom? You have all those plans, but you made them without me. I don't want to go travelling. I want to concentrate on work. I've told you that a million times, but you've never listened. I've got to make my own choices. I don't want to wake up when I'm forty and think, *Well, I could have followed my own path but I kept my head down and did nothing.* Why can't you get that?'

'I asked you a question. Any fair person would say I deserve an answer.'

'You don't listen and you don't speak. You get into black moods and refuse to say what's wrong. You shut yourself off from me. Then, out on the street, you're all chatter. All "How's it going, lads?" and "Grand day, girls." But you're not the person you pretend to be. It's just a stupid bullshit image.'

That there was more than a splinter of truth in what she'd said was beside the point. She was trying to shift the ground. To turn him into the culprit. He couldn't allow that to happen. 'You can list my faults all day if you like, Nina, but at least I've never cheated on you. You'll have to tell me some time, so why not do it now? Who is he?'

'You're still not listening to me.' She shifted her gaze again. 'His name is Julian. Julian Heaney.'

Tom rose from his chair. Wine sloshed over the side of the glass and onto his T-shirt. 'You're joking, right?'

'It's not like you think. He's not like you think.'

'So much for all that guff about how fond you are of home.' Nina flinched, but he didn't care. 'You're sleeping with a guy who's trawling around Kilmitten for trashy stories about what happened in my parents' house. A guy who's looking to exploit people and put them on the telly for the rest of the country's entertainment. How's that for hypocrisy?'

'Stop it,' she said. 'You're not being fair. I know I'm in the wrong here, but I *am* fond of home, and Julian's not exploiting anybody. He's trying to tell a story, and if he uncovers new information, so much the better.'

Tom paused, took a drink of wine. Whatever he'd expected, it wasn't this. This was like walking through a door into an entirely different world. 'What new information?'

'Nothing major so far. But he's still got to interview Father Galvin's brother. And Conor's dad's going to talk to him too. He – Julian – has some interesting ideas.'

Tom listened while Nina spoke about Julian Heaney's theories. It was speculative stuff, nonsense mostly, not aided by her explanations being so garbled. Then she mentioned a particular name.

'Woah,' he said, 'go back a few fields, there. This character reckons Ginny Fortune might be mixed up in Father Galvin's death? I take it you put him straight.'

'That's not what I said. He doesn't think that at all. He just reckons it's odd that she won't tell Tess who her father is. You can't argue with that.'

'Cop yourself on, Nina. You claim this guy isn't interested in exploiting people. That's exactly what he's doing. And, by the sound of it, the person most likely to suffer is your best friend. Tess had nothing to do with Father Galvin. Dead or alive. He wants to drag her in because she's box office. That's all.'

'Please, Tom,' she said, 'I wouldn't blame you for being angry. But you're making everything sound worse than it is.'

Tears were showing in her eyes. Tom swallowed the rest of his wine. He found his denim jacket and pulled out his lighter and cigarettes. Nina didn't like him smoking in the house, but she couldn't object. His anger continuing to gather pace, he had another question to ask. 'What does your fancy man say, then? Who did kill Father Galvin?'

'Don't call him that, and he doesn't know.'

'He has a theory, though?'

'Yeah, only—'

'Go on.'

'Like I said to you a minute ago, Julian's heard that a few people owed money to Leo Galvin. Despite being a priest, he was a good poker player. Getting names has been tricky, but apparently one person owed quite a lot.'

Tom took a deep drag of his cigarette. 'Who?'

She dried her face with her sleeve. 'I probably shouldn't go into it.'

'Why not? This is hardly the time to take the high moral ground.'

More tears snaked down her face. 'It was Noel O'Grady.'

'Noel O'Grady didn't kill Father Galvin.'

'I don't think so either, but you can't be certain.'

'Yes, I can.' The words were out of his mouth, hanging in the air between them, before he appreciated what he'd said.

Nina's face clouded with confusion.

Tom was standing on a ledge. He could choose to jump. Or he could walk back. How sweet it would be to take control. To say, 'Here's why I know.' There was more. In that moment, he could almost understand why people chose violence. Why nothing else felt adequate. He took another pull of his cigarette and flicked the ash into the empty fireplace. Tom knew he couldn't hurt Nina. Neither could he tell her what he'd seen on the night of Father Galvin's death.

People kept secrets for all sorts of reasons. To protect themselves. To protect others. To avoid the consequences of telling the truth. After all this time, the consequences for him would be grave. Why hadn't he said anything before now? people would ask. 'I was twelve years old,' he would reply, 'and I couldn't be sure.' That wasn't enough, though, was it? Nobody would accept that.

Then there was the other question, the one that nagged and niggled: if he had raised the alarm, might it have been possible to save Father Galvin? What if, rather than slinking back to the shed, he had screamed and roared? What if he'd run into the house and fetched someone? Would the priest still be alive? But those questions were for him, not Nina.

He stepped back from the edge.

'I don't see O'Grady as a killer, that's all,' he said. 'Okay, he was a buffoon, a blowhard, but that doesn't make him a murderer. If he did have money troubles, his brother could've given him a dig-out. Besides, it's kind of convenient, isn't it? Blaming the dead man?' He put out his cigarette against the fireplace.

'Maybe.' Nina swiped at another tear. 'You've got to believe me, Tom. This isn't what I wanted.'

'And you can be sure it's not what I wanted. I still can't understand why you've done this to me.'

A different atmosphere had entered the room. He wouldn't call it calm, but some of the fury had gone. He asked himself: if she said sorry, if she suggested giving their relationship another try, would he agree? Sometimes, when Tom had a decision to make, he played 'What would Conor do?' The answer was always 'The right thing, of course.' This time, there was no right thing. He didn't want to break up with

Nina. He loved her. Even standing there, knowing she'd had sex with someone else, he loved her. But he had to leave. Compared to constant Conor, Tom had always been the flaky guy. Mr Inconsistent. His one certainty had been Nina. Now she was gone from him.

This wasn't the time for reflection. He had to get moving. He touched her arm. She recoiled.

'I'm going to pack some of my stuff,' he said. 'I can get the rest and sort out the bills and whatnot another day.'

'There's no reason to leave now,' said Nina, a spike of panic in her voice, as though she'd suddenly realised what was happening. 'Where will you sleep?'

'I can crash at Fergal's place. Or, if the worst comes to the worst, there's always the shop.'

'You can't sleep there.'

'I can do whatever I like,' he said, as he left the room.

He walked around the bedroom. He needed . . . He didn't know what he needed. He stuffed a couple of changes of underwear and some T-shirts into an old sports bag. Then he went to the bathroom and took his razor and toothbrush. He took Nina's brush and the toothpaste too, a tiny show of spite. It occurred to him that he didn't own very much. Almost everything in the house – from the bed linen to the TV – had been provided by Nina. He'd always believed in travelling light.

Back in the living room, she was crying, tears carving silvery tracks through her make-up. In the kitchen, something was burning.

'Don't go like this,' she said. 'Please.'

'It's for the best,' he replied.

Chapter 20

The village was aglow with the news. 'Did you hear?' people asked. 'Nina Minogue has left poor Tom Crossan and taken up with the documentary fellow. Julian Heaney, that's right. His people have money, apparently. His father's a builder, owns half of west Dublin. Emmet Minogue's in a right state. Helen's not much better. No, Nina hasn't been home since she broke the news. Not that I'd blame her. That sort of behaviour won't go down well around here, I can tell you.'

Tom didn't have to hear any of this to know it was being said. Wherever he went, curtains would twitch, conversations would stall, and meaningful looks would be exchanged. For the rest of his days, his name would be prefixed by the word 'poor'. Whatever they said to his face, some people would revel in the news: 'I always said Nina Minogue was too good for him. What was a woman like that doing with a lad like him? Sure he's a pleasant enough fellow, but what prospects has he?'

It had taken him more than a week to tell his parents. They didn't have to voice their disappointment. It was carved onto their faces, in his dad's strained mouth and his mam's empty stare. What was also clear was that they blamed him. Oh, they were too kind to say it, but he was sure that as soon as he left the house, the if-onlys would begin: if only he'd stayed at college, if only he knew what he wanted, if only he'd got a better job.

They weren't impressed with his plans to go away. 'You can't be serious,' his mother had said, her tone suggesting he'd expressed an interest in opening a brothel or selling heroin at the gates of St Ursula's. He did have sympathy for them. Their daughters were, to all intents and purposes, lost. Dympna remained in New York. Still illegal and married to another illegal, she hadn't been home in more than a decade. Deirdre had fared better, marrying an American, securing US citizenship and moving to California. While some emigrants became sentimental about Ireland, Deirdre had no such weakness. The last time they'd spoken, her contempt had oozed across the Atlantic. 'I don't know how you stick that place, Tom,' she'd said. 'You ought to come over here. There are plenty of opportunities for a guy like you.' Deirdre rarely called Kilmitten and wrote only at Christmas. Tom's parents had three grandchildren they'd never met: two in Queens, one in San Diego. Now the house had been sold, he'd expected them to make a trip to the United States. Surely they had the money for a holiday. He'd heard no mention of a visit, and he suspected that, after all these years, they were scared of meeting their girls again.

So, yes, he could understand why they didn't want him to leave. The night before, he'd done his best to explain that he wasn't emigrating, he was travelling. That was what young people did now; they saw how the rest of the world lived, and came home again. His parents chose not to listen, his mam lapsing into a sulk, his dad putting on the martyr act. 'I can see why people used to have such big families,' he said. 'That way they didn't grow old on their own.' Tom had no intention of giving in to their pressure. The thought of staying in Dublin without Nina didn't appeal to him, and he'd rather have his wisdom teeth removed without anaesthetic than return to Kilmitten. At the best of times, the village was cloying. The locals might have sympathy for him now, but in short order he'd be a figure of fun, the punchline of every joke.

Poor Tom Crossan.

That was how he found himself, on Saturday afternoon, in the kitchen, surrounded by a muddle of tea chests and boxes, helping his father to pack. This was likely to be his last weekend in the old house. He had to convince his dad that he was making the right decision. His mother, a lost cause, was at the petrol pumps. His father was reluctant to engage, choosing instead to reel off anecdotes about his childhood: 'Did I ever tell you about the time Frankie Stack brought a calf to school?' or 'Did you know your mother was so clever she was allowed to skip third class?' Tom continued his work, carefully wrapping glasses in newspaper. His mam insisted that every task be carried out like they were going to Australia rather than to a house barely five minutes' walk away.

In the end, he intervened: 'So,' he said, 'have you any

more questions about what I told you last night? About my travelling plans, I mean.'

'I do, but it sounds to me like your mind's made up. Am I right?'

'You are.'

'You'll have to go easy on your mam. You know what she's like. She tries to block out bad news. Give her time, and she'll get to grips with it.'

'Fine, only she doesn't have for ever. I've given Val my notice. I don't want to hang about.'

His father finished wrapping a plate and placed it in a box. 'You will meet someone else, you know. And maybe next time she'll be more like you.'

'More of a waster, you mean?' said Tom.

'Ah, now, that wasn't what I meant at all. Don't be getting maudlin on me. What I meant was, Nina sounds like a woman in a hurry, but we all move at different speeds. The two of you were very young when you started doing a line. Too young, if you ask me.'

'You weren't much older when you married Mam.'

'Different times, Tommo. Anyway, Cora and myself, we might have our arguments, but we've always agreed on the big things.'

They both knew this wasn't true. For as long as Tom could remember, his parents had squabbled. Mostly the arguments had been about money, but they'd also disagreed about selling the house. Still, he reckoned many people would consider them a happy couple. What that meant, he couldn't say. Did they share all their problems? Tell each other everything?

While he regretted not being more open with Nina, he wasn't convinced it would have made a difference. He wondered if she'd always been biding her time, waiting for someone like Julian Heaney, someone with showy ambition and a wealthy family, to glance her way.

'Like I say,' continued his dad, 'your mam's going to need some space, but, all things considered, she hasn't taken the news too badly.' He picked up another plate and, for a few seconds, stared at the pattern. 'What about you?' he asked. 'How are you bearing up? You've given us the bare bones, and I can see why you wouldn't want to dwell on it, but are you . . . are you all right?'

Tom looked at his dad, at his unruly fuzz of grey hair and fraying shirt collar. He couldn't give an honest answer. It was too personal a tale.

In truth, he felt like he was unravelling. The woman he still loved had humiliated him, and it hurt more than he'd thought possible. After he'd settled the bills and taken his remaining belongings from the cottage, he'd stood inches from the surging traffic and contemplated stepping into it. The following day he'd got wasted on neat Jameson and gone home with a dark-haired marketing student whose name he couldn't quite recall (hard times, he was discovering, brought out his clichéd side). He couldn't say any of this to his father.

Neither could he say that he'd tried having negative thoughts about Nina: how she got annoyed when he spent too long talking to people she didn't know; how she could be resentful of Tess's success; how squeamish she was about anybody who wasn't clean and well-kempt. These would sound like petty grievances, the cobbled-together complaints of a bitter man. The thought of Heaney touching her made him feel . . . oh, he didn't know how to describe it. A blackness came over him, a sorrow he found hard to shake off.

Tom couldn't admit to being in a constant state of irritation. Slow walkers angered him, as did dithering customers. He was annoyed by cheery people and whiny people, children and old folks. He wanted to shout at every last one of them.

Most of all, he couldn't admit how scared he was of Heaney's documentary. He was terrified of the memories it would resurrect and the questions it would raise. Even more than the split with Nina, the TV programme had prompted his decision to leave the country now.

He worried that if he said any of this he would cry and he couldn't allow that to happen. For the first time in his life, he wished he was a woman. Women were better at handling unhappiness.

'I'm fine,' he said. 'Well, I've been better, but what can I do?'

His dad smiled a tight, sad smile. 'You do know that Conor's around for the weekend? I met Flan earlier – or Flan Varley, Man of Mystery, as I've taken to calling him. He told me they were expecting Conor this afternoon.'

'I haven't been talking to him. I haven't really been talking to anyone.'

'Why don't you give the lad a ring?'

'A fluent spoofer,' said Conor, 'captain of the national team at the spoofing Olympics.'

'There must be more to him than that.'

'Not that I noticed. You know his sort, they're not like us. They grow up with so much self-belief, no amount of failure can put a dent in it.'

Tom took a mouthful of his pint. 'Why didn't we get any of that, huh?'

With his handkerchief-white skin and puffy eyes, Conor had never seen his friend look so rough. Or known him to be so miserable. Julian Heaney was his main topic of conversation, his only topic of conversation. Conor was doing his best to lighten the mood. It wasn't easy.

'Did you not spot anything when you met him?' asked Tom. 'Was he flirting with Nina? Making a play for her?'

'Seriously, man, no. He was friendly towards her but he was the same with Tess. There was nothing to spot.' What Conor didn't say was, even on that first night Nina had been unexpectedly warm towards Julian. Neither did he say that the guy looked the part: that he wore a pricey leather jacket and had a sharp haircut. Tom wore a flannel shirt, and his hair appeared to have been cut with pinking shears. There was no point in twisting the knife.

Pilkington's was brimming with customers. Lorraine Gilligan, who'd been the year behind them at St Ursula's, was holding her twenty-first in the function room. A band, Bobby Buckley and the Bandits, was setting up. Party-goers flitted about. A group of old lads congregated in one corner, huddled like sheep against a storm. A great night, complaining about young people, lay ahead of them.

Tom had been reluctant to meet in the village's most

popular bar. 'Can we not go somewhere quieter?' he'd asked. 'Like the graveyard?'

Conor had convinced him there was no reason to hide. As if to prove him wrong, four O'Gradys swaggered by. Conor got a grudging greeting, Tom a series of smirks and nudges.

'Is it true you're on the lookout for a new woman?' said Seánie.

'We heard the doctor's daughter came to her senses and gave you the shove,' added Philly.

Conor looked at Tom. 'Ignore him.'

Tom made a face but stayed quiet. After a few further jibes, the O'Gradys moved on. 'Have you been talking to Nina?' asked Tom.

'No. I wouldn't know what to say to her.' Conor had contemplated lifting the phone, but thought better of it.

Tess was livid. 'Nina keeps calling me,' she'd said, 'but if I answer, I won't be able to control my anger. I've got to calm down before we talk.'

'Grand. But if you do meet up with her, I won't mind. Like, she's your friend too.'

'People are on your side, you know. Timmy and Mags Moynihan were in the house this afternoon, and they were tearing into her. "She's only a stuck-up little strap." That's what Mags said.'

Tom drained his pint. 'I don't need people to take sides. It's not a football match.'

'I get you,' said Conor, convinced now that this would be a difficult night.

Tom rose to get another round. Next door, Bobby Buckley was performing a Neil Diamond medley, the music seeping into the bar in muffled waves.

Conor had been shocked by what Nina had done. He hadn't thought her capable of being so . . . callous: that was the word. Then again, he hadn't been looking. A while back, he'd heard someone claim that your taste in music at fourteen was your taste for life. Maybe your personality was settled quite early on too. Maybe Nina was more like her father than any of them had wanted to admit. Truth to tell, Conor had never understood why Tom was so obsessed with her. She was a pretty girl, but no prettier than many. Not the glittering prize of Tom's imagination.

Conor wondered if Nina felt guilty about how she'd treated Tom. He assumed not. Every day, he met people whose sins were far worse. People who hit their partner or abused a child or sold drugs. Few would admit to cruelty. They'd say they were provoked or they were weak or they, too, had been a victim. He remembered what his dad had said about Father Galvin's killer being able to rationalise what they'd done. The more he saw, the more sense that made.

A glance at the bar showed Tom having words with the O'Gradys. Conor was about to get up and intervene when Tom walked away.

'Do I have to ask?' he said, as his friend sat down again.

'Probably best if you don't.'

'So,' said Conor, 'I haven't had the chance to give you my own news. I'm being transferred to Mayo.'

'Town or country?'

'Village. A place called Aghaflesk.'

'Never heard of it.'

'Neither had I until a week ago. It's not much bigger than Kilmitten.'

'Fuck.'

'That's what I said. It's not that I'm mad about Termonbeg. It's a kip. But I was beginning to feel like it was my kip, if that makes sense. Oh, and I've split up with Angela too.'

'Ah, hell, man, why didn't you say? Here we are, two single men. We should be at the party trying to score with Lorraine Gilligan's friends.'

Conor must have looked uneasy, for Tom quickly added, 'I'm joking. I won't be going near a Kilmitten woman again, I can tell you that for nothing.'

At the twenty-first, the band was galloping through 'The Birdie Song'. 'They must be off their heads next door,' said Tom. 'There's something so naff about that song, it's almost sinister.' He took another gulp of his pint. 'What happened with Angela? Was there a Cork version of Julian Heaney involved?'

'Nah, it wasn't like that.' Conor explained how the break-up had been his decision. They'd had fun, but he couldn't picture himself travelling down from Mayo to see her.

They had another pint. And a whiskey. A conga of party-goers snaked through the bar before being shooed out again. Tom spoke about his plans. He'd been looking into becoming a youth worker. 'I want to make life easier for you guys,' he said, with a laugh. 'Give you fewer kids to arrest. The shame is, I never got around to telling Nina. I'd planned on sorting everything out before I spoke to her. And then it was too late.'

Conor could see the sense in Tom's plan. He'd always been good with people. Even as a child, there'd been no old fellow too crabby for him, no young girl too sulky. He had a way about him, all right. 'Would telling Nina have made any difference?'

Tom shrugged. 'I can't think about that now. I've done too much thinking as it is. Anyway, before I do anything else, I'm off on a trip. I'd planned to start in Europe, but it's too cold at the minute. So, first stop India, next stop – who knows where?'

'Oh.'

'Don't tell me you don't approve either.'

'I didn't say that.'

'That's good because you should hear them at home. You'd swear I was boarding a coffin ship.' He stood up. 'Time for another.' A grin took over his face. 'Here's a thought: why don't you come too? Leave work and everything else behind? Have a proper adventure?'

'I—'

'Don't say no straight away. Think about it.'

'Wonderful Tonight' spilled in from the function room. The walls of the bar were sweating. Conversations overlapped, the occasional shriek or bellow rising above the throng. Conor was tempted. He was annoyed about being transferred. For all that he'd felt out of his depth in Cork, at least he'd been learning. There would be no real policing work in Aghaflesk, just the same low-level bullshit his father had spent a lifetime coping with in Kilmitten. Same stupidity, different accent. He thought of what it would be like to feel free again, to have no obligations. Then he thought of how disappointed his father would be. In the end he'd decided against telling his dad about his disenchantment with the gardaí. The man had enough to handle.

'So what do you say?' asked Tom, on his return. 'I can change my ticket if needs be. I'd like to be gone before Christmas, mind.'

'I can't,' he said. 'I'm sorry but I can't.' He sighed. 'It's not work that's stopping me . . . but everything else. There's the baby and the wedding and . . . it's a sensitive time, you know.'

'That's a shame,' said Tom, his tone suggesting that was the answer he'd expected.

Conor wanted to say more, but couldn't. Two weeks previously, his dad and Ginny had told him about Tess's father. They'd asked him not to tell anyone, not even Paula. Especially not Paula. He'd spoken to Tess. She said she spent half her time peering into the mirror, trying to isolate her O'Grady genes. Her joking couldn't mask how affected she was. Every day, she said, she struggled with the fact that her father had been a rapist. For Conor, too, the truth was unsettling. He'd always seen the O'Gradys as cartoon baddies, big-mouthed but largely harmless. Now he'd been forced to reassess his view of Noel senior, he couldn't help but think about the rest of them. He worried about Paula. Then he told himself that this was unfair. Marty couldn't be held responsible for the crimes of his father.

Tongue loosened by beer, Conor began talking about the Father Galvin documentary. His father had to do an interview, he said. Tom reckoned he should lie. 'Why doesn't he spin Martin Scorsese a tale about ouija boards and devil worship at the ten o'clock youth Mass? Make a laughing stock of the whole thing?'

It was unlike Tom to joke about Father Galvin's death, and Conor was seized by laughter. The two of them laughed at everything and nothing until people began to stare. They had one for the road. And one more. They were plastered. Hammered. Polluted. They were every kind of drunk. They put Kilmitten to rights. Then they put the country to rights. It was like old times. Conor found himself becoming sentimental. He felt like the night marked the end of something. Their lives were changing, spinning off in different directions. Then he reminded himself that he was drunk.

At some point, the O'Gradys returned. Philly, Pat and Noel junior said little. Seánie, holding his cigarette between thumb and index finger, like the hard man he wanted to be, was more talkative.

'Some of the girls next door have had a fair few Malibu and pineapples,' he said to Tom. 'You never know, one of them might even be pissed enough to give you a go.'

At the party, they were singing the national anthem, raucous voices belting out the words as though their lives depended on it.

For a short while, Tom listened. 'You know what, Seánie,' he said eventually, 'there's something I've been meaning to do.' He stood, rolled his shoulders and, in one fluid motion, threw a punch that landed directly on his tormentor's chin. Perhaps the alcohol had given Tom extra power, or perhaps Seánie was so drunk that even the gentlest of pokes would have knocked him over. Either way, he stumbled back and hit the floor. His whiskey glass pirouetted through the air. He managed to hold on to his cigarette.

'Sacred Heart of Jesus,' said Mercedes Talty, who'd been walking past. Another woman screamed.

Noel junior and Philly darted forward to attack Tom, but Conor and several others jumped in to block them.

At the party, the crowd roared the last line of 'Amhran na bhFiann'.

And Tom? Tom grinned like a man who'd achieved a lifetime's ambition.

Chapter 21

At first, Nina was less than candid with her parents. She gave them an edited version of her story with just enough embroidery to place part of the blame with Tom. They'd grown apart, she said. She didn't mention Julian. Her father, adamant that the split must have been Tom's fault, kept asking questions. He assumed, as many would, that Tom had cheated. On and on he went until, feeling she ought to put him straight, Nina told the truth. A look passed between her parents while they absorbed her confession. There were no pyrotechnics. Her dad said he was disappointed. He reckoned that by hooking up with Julian she was trying to make a point. What point, he couldn't say.

'No,' she said, 'you're not getting this. I really like him. We're so well matched, you wouldn't believe it.'

After that, she struggled. All the lines she'd repeated to herself sounded wrong. Too embarrassing. Too juvenile. She couldn't say, 'We have amazing conversations, the best ever. A whole new world has come alive for me.' Her mother would be baffled, and her father would ask if she was taking drugs. In the end, she said simply, 'That's the way it is.' Then she returned to Dublin.

She was living on her own in Ringsend, the rent swallowing most of her wages. Her relationship with Julian wasn't at a level where they could consider moving in together. He'd been taken aback by her split with Tom. 'It's for the best,' she'd said. 'Now we can be a proper couple.'

For a few moments, he'd been quiet. Finally, he'd smiled his gap-toothed smile and agreed. 'You're right,' he said. 'No more skulking and hiding.' Then he kissed her, a long, warm kiss, and her apprehension melted away.

She left a message for Tess, explaining what had happened. That she didn't hear back didn't worry her. Tess was busy.

One evening, her mother called. Everybody in the village knew, she said. She recommended that Nina stay away for a while. 'It's not like we don't want to see you, love, but I don't think you'd enjoy the fuss.' Although Nina wouldn't admit it, a little part of her was amused. She'd never been the talk of Kilmitten before. Her mam also revealed that Tom had been in a fight with Seánie O'Grady. 'I don't know what it was about,' she added, her voice giving the lie to her words. 'The O'Gradys are in foul humour. They're going around telling everybody that Seánie was assaulted and that Flan Varley should arrest Tom. I met Noel junior, and he was ripping into Flan, saying the whole episode proved once and for all that the guards are corrupt. "We're getting Uncle Paddy to raise it in the Dáil," he said.'

'For real?' said Nina.

'Don't worry, even Paddy O'Grady's not that stupid.'

'What about Marty? His father-in-law's on one side, his family on the other. That can't be fun.'

'Apparently, he sided with his brother, and Paula's not talking to him. There's a lot of silliness around here at the moment. Touch wood, it'll die down soon. And, just so as you know, Tom's going to India next month. Cora Crossan's not happy.'

Great, thought Nina. No doubt she was getting the blame.

'But,' said her mother, 'if there's a silver lining, at least you won't have to worry about bumping into him.'

After they'd hung up, Nina thought about Tom. While his plans were no business of hers, she didn't like the idea of him going away on his own. She considered calling into Val's to wish him well. Then she came to her senses. Talking to Tom wouldn't be smart. Their parting had been hard, and she couldn't face treading that ground again. Her head was full of affectionate memories. She'd never doubted his love for her. That was the problem. His love had become a burden. It had swaddled her, like a scratchy blanket. Julian was more of a challenge. She worked at impressing him, something she'd never had to do with Tom. While she hadn't said that she loved him, she was convinced that she did. She wanted their relationship to evolve into something more serious, but held back for fear she'd scare him away.

In mid-October, Julian went to north Clare to interview Father Galvin's brother, Gregory. He returned elated, saying he had some first-rate material, part of it so strong he was going to pass it to a friend who worked for the *Sunday Herald*. To Nina, this didn't make sense. Why would he give his work away? Wouldn't that detract from the programme? Not at all, he explained. He needed to drum up interest in the documentary. Create a buzz. To her, what Julian had garnered sounded unremarkable. Gregory Galvin wasn't happy. Well, that was no surprise. His brother had been killed and no one had been charged, let alone convicted. How could he be anything other than unhappy?

On Saturday, they went into town for a drink. Usually they would go on to a club. That night, however, Julian was determined to get an early look at the next day's *Herald*. He bought the paper from the newsagent at the top of Grafton Street. Its lead story promised fresh revelations on the latest political skulduggery, while two other headlines focused on the war in the former Yugoslavia and a well-known actress's move to LA.

Nina was tickled by his enthusiasm. 'It mightn't be there,' she said. 'I don't know if you've noticed, but there's a lot going on in the world.'

'It'll be there,' replied Julian.

They stood at the door, the shop's glow providing just enough light for them to read. The night was bone cold, and she hoped the article was short. As she scanned the words, the city's bustle receded. Her ears filled with the sound of her own heart.

The family of a priest, who died in suspicious circumstances nearly a decade ago, have called for an independent inquiry into his death. Gregory Galvin, whose brother Fr Leo was brutally attacked at a party in the Co. Clare village of Kilmitten, says he's never been happy with how the gardaí conducted the investigation. Mr Galvin (60) was speaking to the producers of a forthcoming television documentary.

'The crime may have shocked the nation but, from the beginning, the investigation was a shambles,' said a still grieving Mr Galvin. 'How can it be right that one of the key men, Sergeant Flan Varley, was also at the party? If you ask me, he had a conflict of interest. He may well have been drinking with the person who killed my brother. That man should have had nothing to do with the investigation.'

In an interview conducted at his modest home in Knockgreelish, Mr Galvin said he was convinced that some in Kilmitten had chosen to shield the killer. 'I believe there are those who can help identify the person who murdered my brother. That's why I'm calling for a full independent inquiry into what happened. The inquiry also needs to look at how the gardaí failed to do their job. This family is entitled to justice.'

One of Nina's knees wobbled. Julian didn't appear to notice her unease. The piece was accompanied by two photographs.

The first was of Gregory Galvin, standing beside his brother's grave, his eyes hooded, his cheeks hollow. In the other picture, Father Leo Galvin beamed with life. He was wearing his Mass robes. The bishop was standing beside him. Nina recognised the shot. It had been taken on the day she and the others had made their Confirmation, less than a year before the priest's death. She continued to read.

> The local GP, Dr Emmet Minogue, was among those in attendance at the party, which took place in the home of Micheál, better known as Haulie, Crossan and his wife, Cora. Several sources have told the documentary makers that a large amount of alcohol was consumed by almost everybody at the gathering.
>
> The Sunday Herald sought a response from Sergeant Varley and from the Garda press office, but they failed to respond. Unholy Truth: Who Killed Fr Galvin? will be broadcast in January to mark the tenth anniversary of the priest's death.

In the taxi, Nina was quiet. Julian, transfixed by the newspaper, remained oblivious to her unhappiness. Tears formed at the back of her eyes.

When they got back to his flat, he folded himself into the brown leather sofa and studied the paper again. Compared to the motley assortment of junk in her place, the flat was beautifully furnished. At the start, she'd assumed he was renting. She'd even remarked on how lucky he was to have found such a fantastic place. He'd done nothing to put her straight until one night he'd let slip that his father owned the house. Julian lived on the upper floor rent-free. His family owned several similar houses. Investment properties, he called them.

'I might go home,' she said.

On a normal Saturday, they'd be all over each other by now. The previous weekend they'd had sex on the kitchen floor. She still had the bruises to show for it.

Belatedly, Julian realised that something was amiss. 'What is it?'

'Do you have to ask?'

He tilted his head to one side. 'I'm afraid I do.'

'The article – it's not what I expected.'

'How so?'

Nina walked around the room. Was he being deliberately obtuse? Or did he genuinely not appreciate how much hurt the report would cause? 'The piece makes it sound like Flan didn't want to catch the person who attacked Father Galvin, that the investigation was a screw-up because he was in cahoots with the killer.'

'It says nothing of the sort. Anything along those lines would be libellous. You must know that.'

'I do, but it looks to me like that's what Gregory Galvin wants people to think. He sounds like a right snake.' *Calm down*, she thought. *You've got to calm down*. Lately she'd been lurching from argument to argument and she didn't want to fall out with Julian.

'The man's brother was thrown up against a cupboard and left to die. Are you saying he doesn't have a right to be angry?'

'Of course I'm not, but the stuff about people in the village protecting a murderer. That's . . . that's not right. There's absolutely no reason to think that.'

'I don't know.' Julian scratched his neck. 'Is it really plausible that not one person has information about what happened? That no one suspects a loved one or a neighbour?'

'Some folks did come forward with suspicions, but none of them stacked up.' She stopped pacing and stared at him. 'This will be upsetting for people, for Flan and Conor in particular. And for Ginny and Tess. Oh, and was there any reason to mention my father?'

'I'm not setting out to upset anyone, least of all your friends. Why would I do that?'

She didn't answer.

'What matters most,' said Julian, 'is that someone gets to the truth. That's what you want too, isn't it?'

How could she disagree? 'Will the Galvins get their way? A public inquiry would be a big deal.'

Ridiculous as it might sound, images were floating through her head: men in grey wigs and black gowns striding into a public building; Kilmitten on the nine o'clock news; her father in the witness box. Nina had been there on the night of Father Galvin's death. She, above all people, should have a handle on this. Yet she felt as if everything had become too complicated, too slippery. For the first time, she wanted to shout, 'Stop.' She wished Julian wasn't making the documentary.

'You know what politicians are like,' he was saying. 'If any controversy gets knotty enough they tend to set up an inquiry. To be fair, though, I don't think that will happen here. Greg hopes that if he creates a stir, he'll give fresh impetus to the investigation. Give the guards a kick up the arse. Not that he'd use that type of language himself. He's a bit of a holy Joe.'

'Will Flan still talk to you? Take it from me, he's going to be raging when he reads that article.'

'He might be annoyed, but he'll have to talk. In fact, I'm hoping this will make him more forthcoming. That he'll want to fight back.' Julian patted the sofa. 'Come over here. I don't like you being angry with me.'

She frowned, then did as he asked. He looped an arm around her. 'You know what your problem is, Nina Minogue? You're too good.'

'Ah, please.'

'No, seriously. You're a good person, a sincere person, and you think everyone's the same.'

This didn't tally with how Nina saw herself but, right then, it was what she wanted to hear. 'Thanks,' she said. 'You're not the worst of them yourself.'

Several times over the next couple of weeks she tried to call Tess. She left messages galore, but not one call was returned. She knew she should ring Conor, but every time she lifted the receiver she became overwhelmed by nerves. The longer she delayed, the more difficult it became.

Her mother rang to say that some people in the village were upset by the newspaper article.

'What about Dad?' Nina hadn't spoken to her father since the day she'd broken the news about Tom and Julian. She had the feeling he didn't know her mother remained in touch. She had hoped he'd be swayed by Julian's family name. Compared to Tom, the Heaneys were very well connected. They weren't just comfortably off, they were properly rich. Her hopes had been misplaced.

'To tell the truth, your father's embarrassed. He worries what people will make of you being mixed up in all of this.'

'I'm not mixed up in anything,' Nina replied.

Her mother wasn't listening. She was telling a story about Hugh, a strained jollity to her voice. Nina's little brother was no longer so little. To her dad's delight, he'd secured a place to study medicine. Hugh's chosen college was less to his liking. He was in Galway, a city her dad dismissed as 'the capital of piss-artistry'. Nina was relieved to hear the focus shift to Hugh. For a few minutes, she muttered and clucked in agreement.

'See you soon, Mam,' she said.

In truth, she didn't know when she'd be able to face her family again.

In November, Julian returned to Kilmitten. That week, a letter with a French stamp arrived. The writing was instantly familiar. Nina had been reading it all her life. Slowly, she opened the envelope and removed the sheets of hotel notepaper.

Nina,

I gather you've been calling me. By now, you must have worked out that I don't want to talk to you. I wasn't sure whether to write, but we were friends for a long time, so in the end I decided I should let you know how I feel.

Unless you've become a completely different person, I think you'll understand why I'm so worked up. The way you treated Tom, lovely loyal Tom, was terrible. If you no longer loved him, you had to break up. But the way you did it baffles me. You, more than anyone else, know how Tom was affected by Fr Galvin's death. For the two of us, it's an unusual childhood memory. For him, it's much more. It changed his life. Despite this, you chose to take up with a guy who's determined to drag everybody in Kilmitten back to that time.

I haven't read the newspaper article – thankfully, the Sunday Herald doesn't travel as far as Paris or London – but Mam told me about it. She said that even though Flan tried to put a brave face on things, he was very upset. As you're aware, this should be a brilliant time for Mam and Flan. Both have had to endure more hardship and loneliness than you could ever imagine, and finally they've found happiness. I hope you appreciate the hurt that article caused. They're going ahead with their plan to get married in the spring. I'm thrilled for them. If I were you, I wouldn't expect an invitation.

This next part is difficult, so you'll have to forgive me if it's not too articulate. Your friendship has always been important to me. Even when my life was rough, and my mother was depressed, I used to believe that everything was all right because Nina Minogue was my pal. If Nina likes me, I'd think, I must be okay. Since I've become well known, I've been on the lookout for people claiming I've changed. In some ways, I have. But these past few weeks have taught me that the one who's changed most is you. Or perhaps I got you wrong. Perhaps you were always the spoilt little rich girl, and I didn't see it.

One other thing: I should let you know that Mam has told me everything about my father. Over the years the two of us spent so much time discussing who he might be, I could never have imagined not sharing the news with you. Hopefully, one day, we'll be able to discuss it, but right now I don't know when that day will be.

That's all I've got to say. Please don't try to contact me. I have no interest in talking to you.

Tess

Nina wanted never to read the letter again. Neither was she able to throw it away. She hid it at the back of a drawer. She tried to convince herself that Tess had written it in a moment of fury, yet in her heart she knew the letter was more considered than that. It sounded so formal. So cold. 'It doesn't matter,' she said. 'It doesn't matter.'

It mattered. For three, four hours she lay on the bed. She'd never been so cold. When the phone rang, she didn't answer. Strangely, she didn't cry.

She asked herself what would have happened if Fergal hadn't seen her that afternoon in Rathmines. Would her fling with Julian have fizzled out? Would she have stayed with Tom? Staying with him would have been easy. Easier than this, certainly. But would it have been right? 'Stop it,' she said. 'You can't turn back now.'

That evening, as the dark gathered around her and sleet rattled against the window, it struck Nina that she was cut off from Kilmitten.

When Julian returned, she didn't tell him about the letter. She feared he'd urge her to ignore Tess's instructions, to call and keep on calling, and she didn't want the pressure. She'd have to deal with it, but not now.

The encounter with Flan had gone surprisingly well. 'Oh, he was cranky,' said Julian. 'He gave me an earful. He also gave a good interview.' Even better was some off-the-record information that Julian described as fantastically useful: 'It brings everything on. This, Nina, is going to be a cracker.' His tone made her uncomfortable. He spoke about everything as if it were a game. Then she chastised herself for being unfair. She was discovering that Julian had a salesman's ability to adapt his personality to suit the occasion. He must have worked his magic on Flan.

Later that week, she decided to give the cottage a thorough clean. Julian was busy, busy, busy, and after two years living with Tom, she was unaccustomed to spending so much time on her own. Within an hour, she'd accumulated a large pile of rubbish, much of it belonging to Tom. She found books, papers, underwear, a tie. A tie! She couldn't recall him wearing it. She reminded herself that these were inanimate objects. Stuff. She wasn't going to get sentimental about stuff. Everything either went into a refuse sack or into the bag she'd set aside for the charity shop.

Next, she turned to an old shoebox containing bits and bobs, make-up, earrings and the Lord knows what else. Most of it she tipped straight into the sack. She picked up a bottle of nail varnish. Acapulco Sunset, not a colour she would ever have chosen herself. It was gloopy now. Unusable. She passed the bottle from one hand to the other and, as she did, she thought about the woman who had given it to her. *This won't last*, she thought. *Things change. People forgive.* There were too many threads connecting her to Tess, to Conor, and, yes, to Tom, for their friendship to be permanently severed.

She placed the bottle in the same drawer as the letter and returned to her task.

Chapter 22

Jaisalmer, India, January 1992

Tom waited for the crowd at the telephone office to clear. Ten days had passed since Father Galvin's anniversary, and he assumed the documentary had aired by now. He thought about it all the time. There were countless reasons not to call his parents, but he couldn't hide for ever.

It wasn't easy to contact Kilmitten from his temporary home in India's north-west. Until six weeks previously, he'd been only vaguely aware of Jaisalmer. In Jaipur, he'd fallen in with a gang of Australians: Stephanie, Craig, Ryan, Lachlan and Gail. Grand characters, too loud sometimes, but who was he to complain? They were heading to this crazy-sounding place, they said: a fort in the desert. Did he want to tag along? Two trains and fourteen hours later, they arrived. The city was more stunning than anything Tom could have imagined. An ornate fort of yellow sandstone, it shimmered in the desert sun. Clustered below, a colourful collection of houses and shops hummed with life. Beyond the fort was sand. Beyond the sand was Pakistan.

The telephone office was a tiny white room with a purple door. Its walls were decorated with washed-out photos of the treasures of Rajasthan. The manager, Mohan, chuckled when Tom complained about the heat. 'This is cold,' he said. 'In the summer, the temperature reaches the forties. Fifty, if we're unlucky.' Tom told him that in Ireland any temperature above the low twenties became the talk of the country. 'Anything beyond that, and it's headline news.' Mohan honked and wheezed with laughter until Tom joined in.

He liked Mohan. He liked India. Nearly a billion people, and not one of them knew anything about him or Kilmitten. You could arrive in an unknown city and discover that two million people lived there. How brilliant was that? All those stories. All those lives. Okay, there were days when the poverty and chaos ground him down. Mostly, though, he was in awe of Indians: their culture, their friendliness, their determination to get on with things.

He'd last called home at Christmas. The God-bless-all-here call, as his father had dubbed it. His mam had got tearful, but that was what she did at Christmas. As well as the expected fizz and crackle, the line had contained a lengthy delay. They'd ended up speaking over each other, hesitating, then colliding again. The most effective way around this had been to give a speech, then allow the other person to take over. In practice, this meant that Tom's dad had done ninety per cent of the talking. He hoped for something similar today.

After a series of clicks and whirrs, he heard the *brrring-brrring* of an Irish phone. Almost instantly, his dad was on the line.

'I've been waiting for you,' he said. His pro-forma questions followed.

How are you?

What's the food like?

Does it rain at all?

Have you met any Irish people?

Sweat collected on Tom's forehead, at the back of his neck and along his spine.

Finally, formalities out of the way, his father was off. 'I suppose you want to know about Kilmitten's hour on the telly,' he said. 'Well, it could have been worse. We were mentioned, but nobody pointed a finger in our direction. Mags Moynihan appeared and said we were decent people. I gave her a free fill of petrol to say thanks. Of course, there were a couple of snide references. "Haulie and Cora Crossan declined to appear on this programme," the announcer woman said. She'd one of those voices. You know the type, sounded like her throat needed clearing. Anyway, hand on heart, it wasn't that bad.'

'Right,' said Tom. 'So was—'

Before he could say anything else, his father had started up again. 'But you know what the big news is? The programme pinned it all on Noel O'Grady. I mean, they didn't actually

say he was guilty, but you'd have to be thick not to get what
they were driving at.'

'What do you mean?'

'They went on about how he owed a tidy sum of money
to Leo Galvin. As you know, back in those days they were
all demons for playing cards. On the morning of the party,
the two of them had had a row. Oh, and Noel O'Grady had
been telling people that Father Galvin needed "putting in
his place". I have to say, I'd heard all that before and I didn't
put too much store by it, but it seems the guards reckon it's
the most likely explanation for the poor man's death. On
the night itself, Noel had had a fair bit to drink – and he
disappeared for a while – so putting two and two together
. . .'

An echo appeared on the line followed by a burst of static.
Tom feared the connection had been lost but, no, there was
his father. 'Can you hear me, Tommo?' he was saying.

'I can, Dad, only—'

'Where was I?'

'You were saying that—'

'Yeah, Noel O'Grady. So, as you can imagine, his family
are on the warpath. Well, Breege isn't. The word is she's
taken to the bed. The lads claim they're not going to let it
rest. "We'll take this to the European Court," Noel junior
is telling anyone who'll listen. Your friend Seánie maintains
they're going to take the TV people to the cleaners. But, like
everyone says, they're wasting their breath: a dead man can't
sue. Paddy O'Grady's been in the papers giving out about
his brother's good name being blackened. He's calling for

the TV licence to be scrapped. Well, you know the way it is: he's probably worried he'll lose a few votes. We had the reporters back here for a few days too. Your mother hated it. I tried to keep the head down. Some folks were in their element, though. I swear it's what they live for.'

Tom ran a hand across his brow. Mohan sent him a look of concern.

'Are you there?' asked his father.

'I am. I am.' He thought of what Nina had said on the day he'd confronted her about Julian. She'd mentioned Noel O'Grady then, but that was just hearsay and innuendo. He couldn't believe it was possible to broadcast something that amounted to no more than gossip. When he managed to collect himself, he said as much.

'It's not as simple as that,' replied his dad. 'This stuff was clearly coming from the guards. What's that phrase? Informed sources. No lie, the cops were all over this one. You can be sure that they provided every last word. I asked Flan. "Remember," I said, "it happened in our house. I'm entitled to some information." But he clammed up on me.'

'If the guards reckoned O'Grady was to blame, why didn't they charge him?'

'Lack of evidence, Tommo. Same old, same old.'

His father sounded like a man untethered. He spoke like he'd been able to detach himself from the whole rotten mess, like Father Galvin had been killed in another house in a different village. Tom struggled for the right response. 'Um, any other news?' he asked.

'Bits and pieces. I told you at Christmas about Ginny

having a girl. Lauren Caroline, they've called her. She's a smashing little thing. Cute as a button. Even better-looking than her sister, according to Flan, but not quite as beautiful as her mother. The christening's next week and the wedding's in April, so Ginny will have to see the inside of a church again. There's no chance you'll be back, is there?'

It seemed his father didn't require an answer because, without pause for breath, he skipped on to the next phase of his monologue.

'Tess is in all the newsagents, on the cover of *Vogue*, no less. The February edition, except it came out in January. She looks gorgeous, sitting in a yellow New York taxi like a film star. If you ask me, she'd look even better with a bit more weight on her, but what do I know? Ginny's so proud she's grown six inches.'

The line wobbled.

'That's fantastic,' said Tom.

His dad was still talking: 'You know what else I meant to tell you? I bumped into Nina after Christmas. I think she was scared of me, so I made a point of marching over and saying hello. She was asking after you. She didn't look her best, I thought. Then again, who does at this time of year, huh?'

Tom had convinced himself that going away would make it easier to move on from Nina, yet there were days when he was ambushed by longing, when he wondered what she would make of a town or how she'd respond to a conversation. A dull sickness would come over him, and he'd want to crawl away and be on his own. Oh, he knew it made no sense. How, when the whole world was there for him, could he miss the woman who'd treated him so badly? But he did.

'If you're talking to Nina again,' he said, 'will you tell her I'm flying? Tell her everything's as great as I'd hoped.'

'Will do.'

'Listen, Dad. I'd better go. There are people—'

'Will you not have a word with your—'

He placed the phone back on the hook. Mohan asked if there was a problem. Tom did his best to smile, though what he forced out was probably closer to a grimace. Leaden-legged, he paid the bill and left.

Outside, he slumped against a wall. Not far away, two women were having an argument. Across the alleyway, a transistor was turned up to full volume. He nodded in time to the music's insistent beat. A man selling a rainbow of cloth raised an impressive eyebrow. Tom pretended not to notice.

He reflected on what his father had said and began to doubt himself. Was it the dry heat? The white light of the desert? The sounds and smells? He tried to picture what had happened ten years ago, on a night when the snowflakes had fallen large as petals. A night when he'd seen something he wasn't supposed to see. How many times over the years had the image invaded his head? Unbidden. Unwanted. Now his memories felt warped. Flimsy. As ephemeral as snow. He closed his eyes and pressed his fingers against them. The music thumped through his brain. A child laughed.

The night might never have happened.

Part Two

Twenty-four years later

Chapter 23

Dublin, March 2016

No matter that he had a hundred other things to do, Conor decided to call into the Avondhu Hotel. He'd heard a rumour that Warren Burke would be there, and while, officially speaking, Warren was free to go wherever he liked, Conor wanted him to know he was being watched. Plus, it was a fine afternoon for a walk, the watery sun offering the first hint that winter was coming to an end.

Warren wasn't the brightest criminal in town, but what he lacked in brains, he made up for in self-confidence. 'All foam, no beer,' according to one of Conor's colleagues. He spent much of the year in Málaga in a complex of houses owned by his father, Kenny. Burke senior liked to portray himself as an old-style villain when in fact he was a psychopathic thug who'd made his fortune selling heroin to the communities he claimed to love. Too cunning to risk coming home, he employed a network of couriers, street-sellers, enforcers and gunmen. A considerable number ended up in jail or dead, yet there was always someone greedy enough, or desperate enough, to take their place. Kenny's reluctance to visit Dublin wasn't based solely on his fear of the law (after all, he'd slithered out of the guards' grasp many times before), but on a falling-out with a rival gang. The McPartlands were even rougher than the Burkes. Liam McPartland would sell crack in a crèche if he could get away with it.

That didn't stop Warren making the occasional trip back to Dublin. He liked to throw his cash around the city's tackier nightclubs. And he loved to play poker.

The Avondhu was a dive of the old school: no Wi-Fi, no spa, the flock wallpaper encrusted with dirt, the carvery lunch offering fatty bacon and water-logged spuds. It was kept in business by tourists who didn't know any better and by poker tournaments.

The receptionist gave Conor a cool appraisal. He wasn't surprised. Everything from his tweed jacket to his sceptical squint shouted, 'Guard.' Lay him on the operating table, and you'd probably find the word was stamped right through him, like a stick of rock. The police weren't popular in this part of the inner city. Depending on who you asked, they were either too heavy-handed or not proactive enough.

He made his way down a narrow corridor, all threadbare carpet and photos of dead footballers, to the function room at the back. A poster of a bride and groom told him the hotel was available for weddings. God bless the couple who celebrated their big day in the Avondhu. As expected, there was a heavy on the door: Ray Tomelty, one of the Burkes' men. Conor had encountered plankton with a higher IQ, but Ray was loyal.

Conor lifted his chin, his way of saying, 'I know you. You know me. Let's not play around here.'

Ray pulled a face, then let him through.

After almost thirty years in the force, most of them in Dublin, Conor knew a lot of criminals. In some cases, he'd known their fathers before them. From time to time, he thought about moving on. But what else would he do? After the struggle of his initial postings – the grey hell of Termonbeg, the tedium of Aghaflesk – he'd secured a transfer to the capital. He'd never forgotten the grinding unhappiness of his early years in the force. It had given him a belief in perseverance that drove younger colleagues mad. 'Relax, old-timer,' one had said. 'The 1980s are over. We don't have to offer up our suffering for the holy souls in Purgatory.' That this was exactly what Conor had been urged to do at school didn't make the comment any more palatable. He was well aware that some of the youngsters in Drugs and Organised Crime considered him a relic. Forty-seven wasn't old. Was it? For years, he'd hardly thought about ageing. It hadn't seemed relevant and then – *boom* – he'd started feeling out of sync. He'd realised that all the truly old fellows had retired, leaving his generation in charge. Now, the old guys were playing golf in Wicklow – and watching their successors flounder.

He'd started to understand the seductive power of nostalgia. He'd hear a song he hadn't particularly liked as a teenager, something by Madonna or Bon Jovi, and find it had improved with age. He'd see an old photo and think, *We didn't look so bad, after all.*

A week or two back, he'd caught a few minutes of a soap opera. Sharon was a demon for them, the more ridiculous the better.

'I can't believe how old the actors have got,' he'd said.

'They might say the same about you,' his wife had replied.

Lauren was fond of telling him that everything had changed. 'My generation won't be slaves,' she said. 'Work doesn't define us.' But Conor's sister was twenty-four and still at college, so he wasn't going to take any lectures from her.

Speaking of the people in charge, it was Tom's birthday. No doubt he was at the negotiations. The papers were filled with them. One step forward, two steps back. As far as Conor could see, the country was managing fine without a government. He'd leave a message on Tom's phone. Or send a text. Or something. Tom had been hard to track down lately, and Conor suspected he'd been distracted by the whiff of power.

The function room was small and dimly lit. This was no modern casino with custom-built tables and uniformed staff. This was hard-core and grimy. And there wasn't a woman in the place. There were several wannabe Conor McGregors, guys with all the attitude and none of the talent. Despite the poor lighting, Burke was easy to spot. He was the only one with a tan and a full set of teeth.

Conor sidled over. 'How's tricks, Warren?'

Burke turned, giving Conor the sort of petulant stare

that most people grew out of in their teens. 'I don't know about you, lads,' he said, 'but I'm getting a shocking smell of bacon around here.'

'What has you back in Dublin?'

'I'm entitled to spend my Friday afternoons however I want, yeah?'

'I didn't say you weren't, only you don't need to get on a plane to play a few hands of cards.'

'What do you want?'

'There's no law against saying hello.'

'Do you make a point of harassing businessmen?'

'Just the ones who make their money from convincing kids to stick a needle in their arm. I saw a couple of your clients on my way in. *Night of the Living Dead*, I call them.'

The couple, who might have been anywhere between twenty and forty, had been rolling on the ground. They hadn't cared, or maybe hadn't noticed, that they'd attracted a crowd. Several onlookers had taken out their phones and were shooting videos for the entertainment of their Facebook friends. *Roll up, roll up. Your chance to see the fantastically awful addicts.* The two on the ground, with their scab-infested faces and filthy clothes, were repulsive, their audience even more so. 'Ah, come on, folks,' Conor had said to the crowd, 'have some decency.' To begin with, they were impassive. Only when he brought out his ID card, did they begin to scatter. He saw a uniformed guard with the wholesome look of a fellow who'd gone straight from Mammy and Daddy's house to the training college and onto the streets of the capital. He gestured towards the spaced-out couple. 'Sort that pair out, would you? They should be locked up for their own safety.' The young guard's mouth flapped open, but Conor was already on the move.

Now, as he watched Warren Burke pick up his cards, he noticed something twitchy about him. Perhaps he, too, was a user. Conor would have to find out. Extra information about the Burkes was always welcome.

'I've noticed a fair share of rough-looking kids myself,' said Warren. 'The poverty in this city is shocking. Maybe the new government will sort it out. What do you think, boys?' He winked at his playing partners.

They were getting annoyed. Good. 'I wouldn't worry about Warren, lads,' said Conor. 'His hand is terrible.'

He saw a flicker of impatience on one guy's face. Another, a fellow with ruddy cheeks and a bad comb-over, was more vocal in his irritation. 'Why don't you fuck off?' he said to Conor. 'And you can take your friends with you.'

'I don't follow you.'

Comb-over tilted his head towards the door.

Conor's first reaction was confusion. The two men striding into the room were wearing the dark uniform of the Garda Emergency Response Unit and carrying automatic weapons. The uniforms might have fooled the receptionist and Ray Tomelty. They'd obviously convinced Comb-over too. But Conor knew the men weren't guards. His mind tore through the possibilities.

'Jesus Christ,' shouted Burke, voice cutting through the air like a chainsaw. Slow as he was, he was trained to spot danger. He sent a look of panic in Conor's direction.

It took less than a second for the gamblers, Burke and Comb-over included, to clamber to their feet. A wave of fear rolled across the room.

'Get on the floor,' roared the taller of the two gunmen, his voice unexpectedly young.

'On the fucking floor,' parroted his accomplice.

Conor knew all the theory. He'd read every line of the manual. Been on every course. But, in that instant, he was frozen. As he reached for his own gun, he heard the first pop. The room filled with vivid colours. The smell, the sound, everything intensified. *Pop, pop, pop, pop, pop.* Burke crashed to the floor.

The shots were coming in quick succession. Then the stinging started. It was spreading from his arm, Conor thought. Or was it his shoulder? A sound, like a jet accelerating, filled his ears. The pain strengthened. He gulped for breath. He realised that he too was on the floor. Beside him, what remained of Warren Burke was trembling.

Chapter 24

Lincolnshire, England

'Mu-um,' said Daisy, from the back seat, 'may we have some music, please?'

How did I get such a polite child? thought Tess. At nine, she'd been a holy terror. 'In a few minutes,' she replied. 'I want to hear the news first. The man with the nice Scottish accent will be on in a sec.'

'We'll be home in a few minutes,' pointed out Daisy.

'Well, then you can listen to all the music you like.'

Tess slowed as she entered Willowthorpe-on-the-Hill. *Please Drive Carefully Through Our Village* read the sign. With its clusters of Clipsham stone cottages, Tudor-era pub, and rose-fronted vicarage, Willowthorpe was heart-stoppingly beautiful. Within weeks, the wisteria would come into bloom and the verges would fill with cow parsley, making it even more attractive. Tess liked to claim that her adopted home was the precise opposite of where she'd grown up. 'Here,' she'd say, 'the countryside is bland, but the villages are gorgeous.

In Ireland, the countryside is spectacular, but the villages look like Hurricane Charlie has passed through.' Strictly speaking, this was no longer true. In recent years, even Kilmitten had been spruced up. Gone were the days when the paint had been allowed to peel off the houses on Main Street and a pile of scrap metal had rusted away outside the abandoned creamery. These days, the grass was short and the houses were neat. That Tom had played a major role in this transformation tickled Tess. She could never have imagined him returning to Kilmitten, much less devoting his life to improving it.

One sharp pip and the Radio 4 news programme began. The man with the lovely voice said, 'It's five o'clock.' The main story was about the Brexit referendum. Then he said, 'Reports are coming in of a gun attack on a hotel in Dublin. Two men have been killed and a number of others, including a police officer, have been injured.'

Tess pulled the Range Rover into the car park of the Royal Oak.

'What's wrong?' asked Daisy. 'I thought we were—'

'Ssh, pet. I need to hear this.'

According to the reporter, details were sketchy. Two gunmen had opened fire on a poker tournament, he said. The attack was thought to be connected to a feud between Dublin criminal gangs. Why a policeman, a detective inspector, was in the room was unclear, but he was among those hurt. His injuries were believed to be serious.

Tess took out her phone and called Conor. No answer. He was probably busy. Of course he was busy. How many gardaí were there? Ten thousand? More? There was no reason to suspect that he'd been at a card game in some dive of a hotel. But the journalist had said the injured guard was a detective inspector. Like Conor. She'd better call home.

'I want to check that Uncle Conor's all right,' she explained to Daisy, who chewed her blonde hair and gave a solemn nod.

Before Tess got any further, her phone rang.

'Mam?'

Her voice must have given her away, for her mother immediately said, 'Oh, Tessy pet, I'd hoped to get to you before you heard the news. You've heard the news, haven't you?'

'I have. It was Conor, wasn't it?'

'I'm afraid so.'

'Is he okay?'

'I don't think they were aiming at him. He just happened to be there. Don't ask me why. You know what he's like. The man can't rest.'

Tess swallowed. Her mother hadn't answered the question she'd asked. 'Is he . . . He's not dead, is he? I mean, on the radio they said he was injured, but I thought they might be holding back information. "Until the family is informed". That's what they say, isn't it?' She was babbling. Pins and needles ran up and down her arms.

'Lord, no,' said her mother. 'He's in hospital.' She lowered her voice. 'Between you and me, he's not in great condition. He's in Intensive Care. Flan's in a state, though, and I don't want to make him any worse.' Her voice rose again. 'We're setting off shortly. We're waiting for Lauren. She's going to drive. If there's one thing both Flan and I hate, it's the traffic in Dublin.'

Tess became conscious of Daisy, sitting in the back, drinking this in. Her daughter was a sponge for information. 'Ahm, I'd better go, Mam. Call me as soon as you hear anything, will you? Miles is in London but, fingers crossed, I'll be able to get a flight to Dublin later tonight. Let me know if there's anything else I can do.'

'What about Daisy?'

'The Carters will be able to mind her until Miles gets back.' She turned to her daughter, who frowned. Tess's housekeeper and her husband adored Daisy, and she loved them back, but this didn't mean she'd want to be left behind.

After her mother had hung up, Tess rested her face in her palms. The clock whirred back. She was thirteen, leaning against the kitchen counter in Pearse Terrace, and the man on the radio was saying that Father Galvin was dead.

Chapter 25

Dublin

The reporters and photographers gathered around Tom in a messy semi-circle. The glimmer of camera flashes made him blink. He guessed they were more interested in Tess, but she wouldn't be arriving for another hour or more. In the meantime, a politician would have to do.

He paused by the hospital's main entrance and had a look to see if he recognised any of the scrum. While the photographers were familiar, the reporters were strangers. They were either grooved and grizzled crime correspondents or shiny-faced junior hacks. Heads upturned, mouths open, they reminded him of a nest of hungry chicks.

'Are you here to see Detective Inspector Varley?' one shouted.

'Yes,' said Tom, then recited the lines he'd prepared in the car. 'As you may know, Conor and I have been friends since childhood. I was shocked to hear about this afternoon's cowardly attack. Conor has served this country with distinction for the best part of three decades. My thoughts are with him, his wife Sharon and the rest of the family. I think it's fair to say that what happened today is a reminder of how some of our streets are no longer safe . . . and of the amazing work carried out on our behalf by the brave men and women of An Garda Síochána.'

'How is he, do you know?'

'You'll have to get the latest information from the hospital, but my understanding is that Conor – Detective Inspector Varley – has had emergency surgery. At least we know he's getting the very best treatment. Now, if you'll—'

'Minist—' began a reporter, then realising her mistake.

'Not yet,' said Tom, prompting a ripple of nervous laughter from the other journalists.

She smiled and started again. 'Does this mean the talks on government formation are on hold?'

'For the next few hours, my priority is here. We'll have to review the situation tomorrow. Now, if you'll excuse me, I can't say anything further.'

Five years after his first election, Tom was still shocked by his ability to sound like a politician. Unlike most of his peers in Leinster House, he hadn't spent his youth listening to stump speeches or knocking on doors for the greater glory of others. Neither had he spent his twenties perfecting a public face and preparing for office. He'd been to university twice – his unhappy period as a commerce student had been followed by a more successful stint doing social work – yet he'd avoided all the usual political and debating societies. His entry into politics had been haphazard. He had no family connections, no formal party affiliation. None of this mattered. Few parliamentarians could look and sound the part as well as Tom Crossan. He was skilled with the media too, adept at answering questions that hadn't been asked and ignoring the ones that had.

He'd been at a meeting when the news about Conor emerged. Since the previous month's general election, life had been an endless series of meetings, of grey coffee and curly-cornered sandwiches. This one had been with the man who might be justice minister in the next government and the woman who might be its deputy leader. They wanted to tie up a deal with Tom's collection of independent politicians. Without him, they didn't have the numbers to form a government. The reward would be a seat at the cabinet table for Tom, plus a couple of junior ministerial positions and a few additional sweeteners. Progress was slow to non-existent, and there were several obstacles in their path. St Patrick's Day was looming, and the following week would be eaten up by the Easter Rising commemorations.

So, when the future justice minister's phone began to throb, Tom assumed it was a ruse. A case of 'Look at me, I'm a busy man – I can't be fooling around with you guys for ever.' Within seconds, a flurry of civil servants arrived. Although the officials didn't know quite how close Tom was to the injured guard, they were aware of a connection. They moved to another room for the briefing, and nobody objected when Tom accompanied them. The boss, the caretaker taoiseach, was there, as were several other senior figures. While an official confirmed the details, a shiver travelled through the group, giving Tom his first real sense of what government would be like.

A criminal called Warren Burke and another man, Dessie Hartigan, were dead. Three more men, including Conor, were injured. One was unlikely to survive. The attack had been carried out by two gunmen who were thought to have been working for the Burke family's enemies, the McPartlands. The families were at war, principally over Dublin's drugs trade. But, as was so often the case, there was also a personal dimension: the McPartlands alleged that a member of the Burke gang had raped one of their daughters. The feud was squalid and brutal, and the guards were losing control. Kenny Burke, who hadn't been seen in Dublin for more than two years, would be going berserk in Spain. His retribution was likely to be swift. The gunmen had escaped through a rear door. Even as the briefing took place, key areas were flooding with guards and the usual suspects were being rounded up.

Tom had sat through all of this, his impatience threatening to break through. 'For crying out loud,' he'd wanted to say, 'nobody gives a rasher's about those spaced-out scumbags. They can all kill each other as far as I'm concerned. What's the story with my friend?' He kept his tirade to himself. This wasn't the time to sound like a caller to a low-end radio phone-in.

Finally, the official spoke about Conor. He'd been hit twice, once in the left arm and once in the shoulder. The bullets could easily have struck his head or neck. If the gunmen had shot from a slightly different angle, they could have entered his heart. He was lucky to be alive.

Tom cleared his throat. 'He will be all right, won't he?'

It was the first time he'd spoken, and he was conscious of heads swivelling to take a closer look at him. He explained how he and Conor were from the same few acres of land and had been friends all their lives.

'I hope you don't mind me asking,' said one man. 'Wasn't it Inspector Varley's father who led the investigation into the death of Father Leo Galvin?'

'It was, and as you probably know, it all happened at a party in my parents' house. Well, it's no longer their house. The place was knocked down years ago.' He realised he was rambling. 'Sorry, I reckon I'm in shock.'

'And the crime was never solved,' said the caretaker taoiseach.

'Not officially, at any rate,' replied a colleague.

Knowing smiles passed around the table.

'As I understand it, Inspector Varley's injuries aren't life-threatening,' said the civil servant.

At that point, the briefing had broken up. Statements had to be issued and reassuring words found. 'You can bet that the papers will say it's all our fecking fault,' said the future justice minister.

Now, as he dodged the trolleys in the hospital corridor, Tom tried to think of the right words for Sharon and the rest of the family. Dealing with real people was altogether more challenging than dealing with journalists. He didn't know if he'd be allowed to see Conor. What he did know was that he felt guilty. In recent months, he hadn't spent as much time with Conor and Sharon as he would have liked.

But, Lord, he'd been busy. There'd been the election, and then there was Vanessa and the boys and his parents and . . . There was just too much.

The first person he saw was Ginny. He hadn't met her in a few weeks, and she looked unexpectedly fragile. She was what? Sixty-six? Hardly ancient, but he figured that the older you got, the sharper the impact of bad news. Behind her came Flan. Although his corrugated hair had long ago turned white, he remained essentially the same. There was still a bounce to his walk and a gleam in his eye that suggested a clip around the ear would be yours if you gave any cheek. With them was Lauren, who shared Tess's other-worldly beauty – and almost nothing else. Lauren was as earnest as her elder sister had been giddy, as humourless as Tess was entertaining.

Ginny greeted him with a hug that gave the lie to her delicate appearance. Kilmitten people weren't given to showy sentiment. When they embraced you, they meant it, and he was touched.

'Thanks for coming,' she said. 'I know you're busy with the talks . . . and all of that.'

Flan shook his hand. 'They haven't killed the lad off this time, anyway.'

'Have you been in touch with Tess?' asked Lauren.

Tom nodded. They'd had a brief chat before she'd left Stansted. She'd managed to get the final flight of the evening. He enquired after Paula. She wouldn't be arriving until tomorrow, Flan said. Paula and Marty O'Grady had split up several years previously and, with their children grown, she'd felt no desire to stay in Kilmitten. She now lived in Italy.

The conversation moved back to Conor. Ginny said that Sharon was at his side.

'The doctors are with him too,' she added, 'so we should have more news in a little while. We're about to go for a cup of tea. You will join us, won't you?'

Their talk was stilted but, given the situation, he presumed this was normal. He hoped Tess arrived soon. No matter how long the gap between their meetings, they maintained an easy camaraderie. They might still have been eighteen years old, sharing a dank London flat. Or thirteen, sitting in a garden shed, drinking illicit bottles of Harp and discussing the latest bands.

'I will indeed,' he said. 'I'd better give Vanessa a call first and let her know what's happening.'

Tom had married Vanessa Broderick ten years earlier. Originally from County Limerick, she'd arrived in Kilmitten to spend a few days with an aunt. Tom had met her in Pilkington's Lounge and, although she was eleven years his junior, they'd become a couple almost immediately. Vanessa was tall and fair-haired with a sturdy seam of ambition. She had a degree in business studies and had been managing her mother's boutique in Limerick city. Against all of his plans and expectations, Tom had been working in Templemorris. What he'd expected to be a temporary job as a youth worker had become permanent.

Increasingly, he'd found himself getting involved in local campaigns. The biggest of these had centred on the closure of the garda station in Kilmitten. Personally, he hadn't felt it was any massive scandal. The new station in Templemorris was just a few miles away. But for many the decision was symbolic of a broader problem. 'We're seeing no boom here,' was the constant complaint. Again, Tom didn't necessarily agree. Eight-bedroom mansions were popping up like weeds, and his family's filling station had expanded to include a grocery shop and an off-licence. The site where the Crossans' house had once stood had become a small estate of starter homes. The local campaigns gave him something to do. He had more time on his hands – and more energy – than most Kilmittenites. Plus, he had Vanessa at his side. He might never have taken the final leap into politics if it hadn't been for her encouragement. During the depths of the recession, a number of business people approached him suggesting he run as an independent candidate. 'The area hasn't had a TD since the days of Paddy O'Grady,' they argued. 'Nobody in power is listening to us.'

Tom's initial impulse was to decline. 'I'm not ready,' he said.

'You're forty-one years old,' his wife replied. 'What are you hanging around for?'

His father liked to say that Tom had finally found his purpose. Privately, Tom felt that Vanessa had found it for him. He regularly reminded himself of his good fortune.

Following the birth of their third child, Vanessa had given up running the boutique. She ran their home, and Tom's life, instead. They had three sons: eight-year-old twins, Harry and Cormac, and Senan who was six. With their halos of blond hair and wide brown eyes, the three might well have been triplets. No wonder they were known in Kilmitten as Huey, Dewey and Louie.

Two years previously, they'd moved to a detached house on the outskirts of the village. With its five bedrooms, four bathrooms, oak floors and enormous garden, Tullaroe had cost Tom far more than he'd planned to spend. That was before he factored in the cost of heating, electricity, and the man who kept the enormous garden from reverting to the wild. He also had an apartment in Dublin for the days when the Dáil was sitting. Thankfully, it belonged to one of the businessmen who had encouraged him to enter politics, so the rent was low.

Frequently, Tom forgot that he was considerably older than Vanessa. She was, after all, the more driven, responsible spouse. Then up something would pop, and he'd be reminded of their age gap. The most striking example of this was Tess. Vanessa had been a teenager when Tess's career had been at its peak, and it was no exaggeration to say that she idolised Kilmitten's first and only supermodel. Tom remembered how on their first proper date, she'd peppered him with questions about his friend. He'd told the story about the night of Father Galvin's death (omitting one crucial detail, of course). Vanessa's first response had been to ask if Tess had been as beautiful back then.

After a few words with his wife ('Yes, Conor will live. No, Tess isn't here yet') and a quick goodnight to the sleepy-sounding boys, he checked the main news sites to see if he'd been mentioned. Every public figure did it. If they claimed otherwise, they were lying. Or stupid.

The video clip from outside the hospital was everywhere. He was disappointed by how drained he looked. There was much speculation about what would happen next in the feud between the McPartlands and Burkes. *Capital Braces For Bloody Revenge* read one headline. *Streets of Fear* roared another. As anticipated, the journalists were fascinated by the fact that the injured guard was the stepbrother of Tess Fortune. *Tess, one of the world's top models until her abrupt retirement, is understood to be very close to the stricken cop*, said one story. A second reminded readers that she was now married to the millionaire investor Miles Whittingdale, and was rarely seen in public. This image of Tess as a recluse didn't match Tom's perception of his friend. But, as he was well aware, image and reality didn't always coincide.

He was fitting his phone back into his pocket when it began to ring. At first he was surprised by the name. Then he recalled that they'd swapped numbers a few Christmases back.

'Hello, Nina,' he said.

'I'm sorry to bother you, Tom, only I saw on the news that you were at the hospital and I . . .' Her voice wavered. 'Will you tell everyone that I wish Conor all the best? And that I'm thinking of him.'

'No problem. Fingers crossed, we'll have some more information soon.'

Tom rubbed his throat. More than twenty years later,

how could this be so awkward? Surely there should be a statute of limitations on the impact of old relationships. Yet still they danced around each other, as if their awful break-up, and everything that had followed, had been months rather than decades ago.

'I don't know when he'll be having visitors,' she said, 'but if he wants anything, or if Flan and Ginny need a hand, well . . . I'm not far away. I only live in Ranelagh. I could be there in no time.'

'If you're around tomorrow afternoon, I'll be here again,' he said. *Why am I doing this?* he thought. 'You could drop in. If it suited you, I mean.'

'That would be great. I wouldn't stay long, and I'd call first to make sure.'

'Grand. I'd better . . .'

'Yes, you go and do what you have to do. Oh, and Tom?' said Nina.

'Yeah?'

'Happy birthday.'

Chapter 26

'I'll tell you one thing,' said Conor, who was propped up on a bank of pillows, 'morphine is a serious disappointment.'

'Is it not working?' asked Tom. 'If the pain is bad, can't they increase the dose? I'll give one of the nurses a shout.'

'No, you're fine. The pain has died down, right enough. The thing is, after years of watching addicts and thinking, *These lads must be on to something*, I finally get a good dose of opiates in my system, and what do they do for me? Nothing. You'd get more of a kick from a pint of shandy. Sorry, I tell a lie: I've got all the lousy side-effects. I feel sick, and every time I doze off, I get woeful nightmares.' He gave a weak smile. 'Chances are I would've had the nightmares anyway.'

Despite his jaunty words, Nina thought that Conor had a haunted look about him. In her experience, shock and injury made most people appear older, yet Conor looked like a frightened child. His face, pale at the best of times, was wan, while the red seemed to have leached from his hair. One arm and a shoulder were strapped up, and there was a gash on the side of his face.

They sat in an arc around the bed, Tess to the left, Tom to the right, Nina at its head. The room was tight on space, so everybody else – Sharon, Ginny, Flan, Paula and Lauren – had gone for a cup of tea. Nina hadn't expected them all to be allowed in like this, but Conor had insisted. She felt like an intruder, a feeling exacerbated by the gallows banter of the other three. They were trading bad-taste quips in the way that only close friends can.

'You do know that Tom was preparing his graveside oration?' said Tess.

'And that Tess had picked out her funeral frock?' added Tom.

'To be fair, I've always looked good in black.'

Nina remembered how Tom had found it difficult to joke about death. Plainly, this was one of the ways in which he'd changed. In recent years, it had been hard to reconcile the laid-back man she'd known with the polished character she saw on TV. 'His wife lit a fire under him,' Nina's father had said. While she accepted her dad's point, she also reckoned that Tom's transformation had begun while he'd been away. She remembered meeting him on his return, as stiff an encounter as she could ever recall, and he'd seemed different then. More focused. Less self-effacing. When it came to his appearance, the years had been kind. His dark hair was stippled with grey and there were creases beneath his brown eyes, but he was still good-looking. And still a charmer.

Tess, too, was a blend of the familiar and the new. She had the same laugh, the same sense of mischief. She also had the composed air of someone with impenetrable wealth. Even in jeans and a plain black blazer, her hair pulled back, she had a chiselled glamour that jarred with her surroundings. By comparison, Nina looked as if she'd already slipped into an older generation. Her hair needed cutting and her navy winter coat had lost its shape. She was ground down by work and family, and by a husband who looked at her in a way that said, 'I could have done better.' Her confidence had been eroded by a thousand minor slights and failures. The previous week, a waiter had flirted with her. She'd been disgustingly pleased. Then she'd realised he was angling for a bigger tip.

As youngsters, each of them had had their own strain of insecurity. She remembered marvelling that Julian had no such affliction. She'd never conquered her lack of self-confidence. The others had clearly been more successful. Nina took herself to task. This was no time to be measuring herself against her childhood friends. She was struck by how calm the room felt, how reassuring she found the smells of disinfectant and linen. Outside, the city was convulsed by the Avondhu shooting. Down the corridor, a third man had died from his injuries. In here felt like shelter.

'Apart from the pain, do you feel any different?' she asked.

'In what way?' said Conor.

'She means did you die and go to Heaven – even for a minute or two?' asked Tess. 'Did you bump into any angels?'

'Or maybe he went down below,' said Tom. He winked at Conor. 'Have you any suspicious burns?'

'I'm being serious,' said Nina. 'Whatever the papers say,

being shot is very unusual, so I was wondering if you had a moment of epiphany or anything like that?'

Conor dug his teeth into his lip. 'I'll have to come back to you when I've had more time to think. More than anything else, I feel relief that Tom gets to save his oration for another day.'

'And so say all of us. What happens now? Will you have to stay here for long?'

'Another few days. What comes after that, I don't know. A lot depends on how the arm and shoulder recover. I hope I can go back to doing the same job . . . but it's too early to say.'

Trouble passed across Conor's face, and Nina regretted asking the question.

Afterwards, when they'd been herded away by a nurse, the three went for coffee in the cramped hospital cafeteria. It had been a long time since they were together like this. Occasionally, Nina bumped into Tom in Kilmitten. Even more occasionally, she met Tess. She'd never been able to revive their friendship. She told herself that they might have drifted apart anyway. Still, that would have been preferable to years of enforced silence followed by a partial thaw followed by . . . whatever this was.

Tess was cutting sponge cake into fingers and pouring milk into Tom's Americano, the tell-tale signs of someone with a relatively young child. Nina had once done the same, but her two girls, Alannah and Bea, were on the cusp of adulthood, and she'd fallen out of practice.

They were surrounded by people in various states of ill-health, a mish-mash of voices pinging off the yellow walls. Even the visitors appeared gaunt, as if being close to so much sickness had stripped them of their vitality. At a corner table, a woman cried quietly. The girl beside her – a daughter, perhaps – looked embarrassed.

This being Dublin, most people cast a quick eye in their direction before looking away again. Admitting that they recognised Tess wouldn't be cool. Did they recognise Tom? The older ones probably did. With the younger ones, Nina couldn't be certain. As Alannah frequently pointed out, young people didn't watch the news. Everything important was online. As far as her elder daughter was concerned, 'everything' consisted of make-up lessons and pictures of people following their dream in Bali or living their best life in Koh Samui. In return, she posted sucked-cheek photos of herself to Instagram. 'In my day,' Nina had said, 'an entire year could pass without anyone feeling the need to take your photo. And taking one of yourself would have been weird.' But Alannah was only twenty-one. Nina was glad that both her daughters were less serious than she had been as a young woman. And she was delighted that being young no longer came with a side order of shame.

Tess asked her about work. Yes, she said, she was still in St Fachtna's. She'd been there for twenty-six years, more than half her life. She put on her brave face and lied about how much she enjoyed it. This wasn't the time to admit that her career had stagnated.

'And Julian?' asked Tess. 'What's he doing, these days?'

Tom stared at his phone.

'Working for his father,' said Nina.

'I thought . . .'

'That his old man lost everything in the crash? Not quite. The banks took a lot, but the family held onto a few properties, and Julian's managing those. As you know, the economy's improving and . . . well, we'll see what happens.' If ever there was a moment to be beamed up, this was it. Nina willed Tess to stop asking questions.

Tess ploughed on. 'So he's left the media business for good?'

'Mmm. It was too precarious. The income was so unreliable. Besides, there was always an expectation that he'd go into the family business eventually.'

Was that true? It hadn't been Nina's expectation. Then again, life had taught her not to expect too much. She was aware that to some people this would sound like self-pity. She thought of it as self-preservation.

Thankfully, she was rescued by a tiny woman with a latticework of wrinkles and a shock of white hair. The woman had seen both Tess and Tom on the news and wanted to pass on her good wishes. 'Those gangsters have Dublin ruined,' she said. Tom agreed, and Tess gave her most polite smile.

The conversation jumped on. Tom and Tess began talking about the last time they'd met: two months earlier at Breege O'Grady's funeral.

Nina looked at Tom. 'You went to Breege O'Grady's funeral? Since when were you friendly with the O'Gradys?'

'He's a politician,' said Tess. 'He goes to everybody's funeral whether he's wanted or not. Oh, and he drives around with spare wreaths in the boot of the car . . . for fear he comes across a hearse.'

'And what's wrong with that?' asked Tom. 'It's best to be

prepared. That's my motto. You never know when a tasteful wreath will come in handy.'

Nina found herself cringing at Tom's crassness. Surely he hadn't become one of *those* politicians. Then she noticed he was holding back laughter. 'Okay,' she said. 'Hands up, you got me.'

'Good and proper,' said Tom. 'I promise you, carrying around spare funeral wreaths is not something I do.'

'Yet,' said Tess.

'And, as far as the O'Gradys are concerned, my fight with Seánie was a long time ago. Not going to the funeral would have caused more offence than going. Besides, I'd no quarrel with Breege. The poor woman, what a life.'

'We probably shouldn't be joking about funerals in a place like this,' said Nina. 'What do you make of Conor?'

Tess fingered a sachet of sugar. 'I reckon he's fine once he's in here, surrounded by family and drugged up to the gills. But watching the person beside you being shot dead must have an impact. And imagine what goes through your head when you realise you've been shot yourself.'

'I know this sounds silly, but it made me think of Father Galvin. On the night of the party, we were only a few yards away from where he was killed.'

'I had the same reaction,' said Tess, pouring the sugar onto the table and running a nail through it. 'If you think about it, one of us could easily have stumbled upon the scene.'

Tom returned to his phone.

Nina considered what she was about to say. In her house, the words would be heresy. 'Do you know,' she said, 'I've always had trouble believing that Noel O'Grady was to blame.'

Chapter 27

Six weeks on from the shooting, and guilt was snapping at Conor's heels. It was there when he went to bed at night and when he woke in the morning. Could he have intervened? Could he have saved lives? Could he have stopped the gunmen escaping? Everybody reassured him that he'd no reason to beat himself up. He'd taken two bullets, for God's sake. He was a shoo-in for a bravery medal. Keep going to the counselling sessions, they said.

He remonstrated with himself, told himself he was like a dog chasing a car. That obsessing over the Avondhu wasn't just pointless, it was dangerous.

Yet the flashbacks kept crashing in. He saw the function room as it had been before the attack. He saw Warren Burke's tanned face and he saw Comb-over, whom he now knew had been called Dessie Hartigan. What followed – being shot, the ambulance, the first few hours in hospital – was less distinct. But it was still there.

The battle between the gangs continued. The Burkes had killed one of Liam McPartland's cousins. In return, the

McPartlands had targeted an associate of Kenny Burke. The attack had gone wrong, and they'd ended up murdering an innocent woman who'd been collecting her children from school. There was uproar, the new government promising emergency measures. The minister for rural and regional affairs made a speech in which he paid tribute to his lifelong friend, Detective Inspector Conor Varley. He also spoke about how, as a young man, he'd worked in a shop around the corner from the Avondhu. 'There are no better people in the country,' he said, 'than the people I met there.' He went on to explain how his experience in Dublin's inner city had been invaluable when he'd become a youth worker in Limerick and, later, in Templemorris. A listener would swear that Tom Crossan alone understood the blight of drugs and crime. The media lapped up his performance, with one tabloid anointing him the star of the new government, a genuine man of the people.

Conor read every news article about the feud and followed every radio report. He complained about the ignorance of journalists and the stupidity of politicians. When he started haranguing the television, even Sharon got fed up with him, and he'd never met anyone with a longer fuse than his wife.

The brass insisted he take more time off. Although he'd been doing physiotherapy, his arm still wasn't fully functional. Sharon urged him to make the most of the break. 'Haven't you been run ragged for years?' she said. 'Why not relax for a few weeks?' She was right, but then she was one of the most sensible people he'd ever met. In a world of fakery, Sharon was entirely herself.

They'd met when the bank where she worked had been held up by an armed robber. She'd been a dream witness: calm, thorough, reliable. It was rare for Conor to be overawed, but for Sharon Kirwan his brain had made an exception. A few weeks passed before he found the courage to ask her out. He discovered that, like him, she was forty-two and had all but given up on finding someone. Two months later, she put her apartment up for sale and moved into Conor's house in Phibsboro.

Sharon was one of the few people who hadn't asked if getting shot had been a transformative experience. Nowadays everything from cancer to a week's holiday was labelled transformative. True, his life had changed, but he couldn't quite nail down the changes. He couldn't say, 'This is how I'm different.'

One change he had noticed was how some thoughts and feelings had intensified. If he'd already been questioning his place in the force, those questions had become louder. He'd accepted that detective inspector was as high as he would rise. Sharon said he was too clean to reach the top, and while he'd like to believe that was true, it wasn't the full story. In his experience, most people saw themselves in a way that would surprise others. He was different. He knew that friends and colleagues considered him dogged, diligent, enthusiastic – but lacking in flair. He agreed. Oh, he could ham it up for guys like Warren Burke. He was a solid interrogator. The problem was, he lacked panache. He was missing the extra layer of guile that separated the regular detectives from the top tier. He was short on diplomacy too. When others were brown-nosing at retirement parties, he was with Sharon.

Once, he would have sneered at this defeatist attitude. Now, he saw the mid-forties as a cut-off point: if you weren't sprinkled in stardust by then, it wasn't going to happen.

Something else was pulling at Conor's thoughts. The death of Father Galvin was on the internet now. It popped up on lists like 'Eight Unsolved Irish Murders' and 'Ten Murders that Defined the 1980s' (with the passage of time, any nuance had been lost, and the crime was invariably referred to as murder). Every once in a while, the story was revisited on TV. It featured on an archive show about 1982, a year of two general elections, the Falklands War and the death of Princess Grace of Monaco. As snow tumbled down around him, Conor's father, looking scarily young, appealed for witnesses. The section on Kilmitten was at one with the rest of the programme. The Ireland of 1982 was thin, troubled and shrouded in a fog of cigarette smoke.

Officially the Leo Galvin case was unsolved, but if you asked anybody within a twenty-mile radius of Kilmitten, they would blame Noel O'Grady. Move slightly further afield and, while people mightn't have a name, they would probably say, 'Wasn't it a politician's brother who did that?'

To use a modern-day phrase, the accepted narrative was this: Noel O'Grady owed money to Leo Galvin. On the morning of the party, they were seen having an argument. That night, Noel O'Grady got drunk and, during another row, he hit the priest, causing him to lose his footing and bang his head. O'Grady then returned to the party, leaving Cora Crossan to find the body.

As Conor saw it, this version of events was overly convenient. He wanted to believe that O'Grady had been to blame. That was what bothered him. His father had wanted to believe it too. Questions were being asked about a failed investigation. His dad had needed a plausible suspect. And who was more fitting than the man who'd raped the woman he loved? A man who wasn't around to answer the charge. In Julian Heaney, his father identified a useful idiot, a guy who could be relied upon to help spread lies. A guy who thought he was getting a career-boosting scoop.

People in Kilmitten, and elsewhere, were willing to accept those lies. Most folks didn't have time to think a crime through. They were content to be nudged in a certain direction. It was like the phrase 'known to the gardaí'. How Conor hated that line. It told the public that the arrested man was guilty. Or, worse, it urged them not to waste their sympathy on the victim. It was shorthand for 'He had it coming.'

Until now, Conor had kept his doubts to himself. He decided to confide in Sharon. As she listened, she twirled a lock of dark hair around one finger.

'If it wasn't this Noel O'Grady character, and he does sound like a nasty piece of work, who did kill Father Galvin?' she asked.

'I haven't a clue.'

'So you can't be sure that your dad pinned it on O'Grady because of what he'd done to Ginny. For all you know, there might have been other evidence.'

'It's possible.'

She stroked his good arm. 'It seems quite likely to me. I

mean, when the TV programme was shown, your sister was married to Noel O'Grady's son. Wouldn't Flan have worried about Paula? It can't be much fun, everybody thinking your father-in-law killed the parish priest.'

'True, only Dad was under a huge amount of pressure. There'd been a really rough newspaper article about the Father Galvin investigation, Ginny was pregnant, Tess was giving her a hard time and . . . I can see him alighting upon O'Grady as the solution to his difficulties. If he thought the man was responsible, why didn't he question him when he was alive?'

'Perhaps he did. You were a child. Plenty could have happened without you knowing. Or perhaps O'Grady was already dead by the time evidence emerged?'

'Hmm, I suppose. I do remember him telling me that several people owed money to Leo Galvin, but he didn't think that any of them was the killer.'

'If it's bugging you so much, why don't you talk to your father? What harm can it do?'

That was Sharon. She came from one of those unusual families where they all spoke openly to each other. Oh, and she was a Dubliner. They were different.

He knew he was entering a diplomatic minefield. Still, he decided to take her advice.

Conor's father picked him up at the station in Templemorris. Ginny had come along for the drive. The afternoon was overcast, heavy battleship clouds filling the sky. The drabness of the day couldn't take from the beauty of the countryside.

In early summer, the land was at its greenest, the hedgerows at their most colourful. On the way to Kilmitten, the three chatted about Conor's injuries, about Sharon, Tess and Lauren, and about Tom's row with a fellow minister over money for the rejuvenation of provincial towns.

'Did you see him on the telly the other night?' asked Ginny, with a chuckle. 'I thought he'd eat the other lad.'

'He was hilarious,' said Conor's dad. 'I don't know where he gets the words from . . . but they're good ones.'

Watching them, Conor found it hard to believe there'd been a time when they hadn't been together.

Later, while Ginny made dinner, Flan and Conor went for a stroll. As they walked the lane beside Toomey's Hill, Conor explained what was on his mind.

For a while, his father remained quiet. 'Why are you bringing this up now?' he asked finally.

'It's always been at the back of my head, but I've never had the time to dwell on it.'

'After all these years, does it matter?'

'If whoever killed Leo Galvin is still walking around, yeah, it does.'

'It was almost thirty-five years ago. Chances are that the killer is dead.'

'Are you admitting that Noel O'Grady wasn't guilty?'

His father stopped. 'Hate isn't a word I use lightly, but I hated that man. He raped my wife and he got away with it. My only regret is that by the time Ginny told me, O'Grady was already in the cemetery.'

'By framing him, you were allowing whoever did kill Leo Galvin to get away.'

'As stitch-ups go, it wasn't exactly the Birmingham Six. The man was dead and he was a rapist.'

'Why did you do it?'

Shoulders in a tense line, his dad began walking again. 'Everything had come to a head. There was that poisonous newspaper article. Julian Heaney was hounding me. Headquarters were on my back. Ginny was in a desperate state over what to tell Tess . . . and then the O'Gradys started giving me grief over the fight in Pilkington's. They wanted Tom arrested. You were there – you know I couldn't have arrested the lad. He was provoked by Seánie. But they went on and on. At one stage, Paddy the politician came to see me. You should have seen the purple face on him while he bellyached about garda corruption. He had some neck. Everybody knew the same fellow was as bent as a U-nail.

'Anyway, the idea came to me, and I thought, *Why not?* So I told Heaney that the main suspect was dead. "I can't talk about it in front of the camera," I said. "What I can do is give you the background and show you a witness statement or two." I let him have a look at a few statements: one about the gambling debts, another about the argument on the morning of the party and a couple more from people who'd claimed that O'Grady had gone missing from the party. The young eejit thought that was enough.'

'And?' asked Conor.

'What I didn't tell him was that O'Grady had disappeared because he'd been upstairs with Lourda Ryan. You know what that old house was like – you were in it often enough. There were so many nooks and crannies, you could have hidden a football team upstairs.'

'You're joking me.' Conor pictured Lourda Ryan, a compact woman with red hair and teeth like a racehorse.

'Indeed and I'm not. Apparently, herself and O'Grady had a fling.'

They walked on, past the ruined cottage where, as children, Conor and Tom had made a den. Now the building was obscured by a thicket of brambles. In the near distance, the new wind turbines made a swishing sound.

'Why didn't Lourda come forward to say he was with her?' said Conor.

'She did. She told me. It's in her witness statement.'

'But, later, after the documentary, why didn't she make it public? She knew O'Grady had an alibi.'

'Come on, son, think of her husband. Johnny Ryan: best known for being handy with his fists.'

Conor stared at the rutted path. This being Kilmitten, everything had to be said through a layer of euphemism.

His father continued: 'Yes, Johnny hit her. Once, back before Father Galvin's death, she had the guts to come and make a complaint. I talked to him, he denied everything, and she changed her story. The Lord only knows what he would've done if he thought she'd been carrying on with Noel O'Grady. As you know, Lourda's dead now. As is Johnny.'

'So, back then, you took a gamble that she wouldn't come forward?'

'It wasn't much of a gamble.'

Conor shook his head. 'God bless her, she had terrible taste in men.'

He father gave a half-smile. 'Crazy as this might sound, she claimed O'Grady treated her well. "He makes me laugh," she said, "and everybody needs a laugh."'

'What about Paula and Marty?'

'There was no love lost between Paula and her father-in-law. She'd no difficulty believing that he was responsible for the priest's death. Not that she liked people talking about it. She said it was hard on the kids.'

'If it was hard on them, what must it have been like for Breege? She lived for nearly twenty-five years with people thinking her husband had killed a priest. All those nudges and winks and barbed comments. Did that not bother you?'

'Breege is my one regret. But let's face it, her husband was a bad bastard. There's no denying that. And she must have known it too.'

Conor wondered if O'Grady had ever attacked his wife. If so, there was little she could have done. In those days, marital rape hadn't been a crime.

'What I don't get,' he said, 'is why Headquarters didn't ask more questions. Surely the boys in the Park must have spotted that something wasn't right.'

'You don't need me to tell you how it works . . . or how it used to work. The case had been a monumental pain in the arse for everybody involved. It had been dragging on for ten years, with no sign of a resolution. Headquarters were only too happy to have a plausible explanation for what happened to Leo Galvin. Now, some people might call that corruption, but compared to a lot of what went on, it was nothing. I doubt it cost most people a second thought. To me, it felt like the closest thing to justice I could deliver.'

As the two headed back towards the village, a soft rain began to fall. They walked in silence. Whenever the guards were in trouble, people were quick to cry conspiracy. More often, chronic incompetence was to blame. This, thought Conor, was different. Noel O'Grady had been guilty of rape, but he hadn't been a killer.

'So who did kill Father Galvin?' he asked.

'I wish I knew.'

'You used to be convinced you'd find out.'

'I used to believe in that old phrase "The truth will out." But it's too late to get to the truth now. Half of the people at that party are dead. What we're talking about happened in another era. Another century. Short of the man rising from his grave, I don't think we'll ever know what went on.'

'Sometimes it does take decades for the truth to emerge.'

'Listen, Conor, I'm sure this isn't what you want to hear, but you've got to let it go. For my sake and, more importantly, for Ginny's sake, let it go.'

'I take it she knows you took matters into your own hands?'

'She does. And she supports me. He might never have been before a court, but most people are willing to accept that Noel O'Grady killed Leo Galvin.'

The rain was merging into a thin slick on Conor's jacket. He took in his father's pained expression, the pleading note in his voice. 'I hear you,' he said.

What he didn't say was that his mind was moving on. Maybe his father was right. Maybe it was too late to get to the truth. That wouldn't stop him trying.

Chapter 28

'Is that the end of them?' asked Tom.

Paige, who ran his constituency office, nodded. 'You'd quite a collection today. What was it that last fellow wanted?'

'Planning permission. His son's keen to build a house near the woods at Toomey's Hill. I did my best to tell him it wasn't possible, that you can't do that any more, only then he got thick with me. He claimed Paddy O'Grady would have fixed it. "Those days are gone," I said to him. "It doesn't matter if you own the land, you won't be allowed build on it."'

'And?' Paige was Liesl Talty's daughter. While Liesl owed her name to her mother's fondness for *The Sound of Music*, Paige had been named after a character in *Knots Landing*. The Taltys liked to stand out from the herd.

'He had an almighty rant, told me that if it was my own family I'd sort it out quickly enough. There was no point in arguing, so I sat there and soaked it up.'

'There's no talking to some people,' said Paige, as she picked up her bag and jacket.

'How right you are,' said Tom. 'Aren't voters great?'

Paige laughed her tinkling young laugh. 'I'll see you on Monday.'

'You will indeed. Have a good weekend.'

Tom's office was on Kilmitten's main street, between what had once been Mangan's shop (it was now a Spar) and the Cherry Tree café. There was a large photo of him in the front window, which he found embarrassing. 'I'm like Kim Jong-un staring down on the peasantry,' he'd complained to Vanessa.

'Not at all,' she'd argued. 'People have to be reminded of what you're doing for them.'

Tom knew that some Dublin-based politicians eschewed regular clinics. 'If a constituent is entitled to a grant or a handout, they'll get it without my help,' he'd heard them say. That attitude wouldn't be tolerated in Kilmitten, or anywhere else in the county. Tom also held clinics in Templemorris, Ennis, Shannon, Kilrush and Ennistymon. Saturday afternoons were reserved for Kilmitten, and more often than not, there was a queue out the door. Everybody was looking for something.

Given Vanessa's enthusiasm for political life, he'd once asked why she hadn't run for election. 'I wouldn't have the patience,' she'd replied. 'Every single person you meet has their hand out.' Even though this was true, Tom got a buzz from constituency work. Sometimes one phone call was all it took for him to secure what a person was seeking. He knew the system was wrong, but, while it was there, he was content to work within it. 'Give me a better system,' he'd say, 'and I'll operate that one instead.'

During his first term in Leinster House, critics had

complained that he was a glorified constituency secretary with no firm policies or positions. That he was a triumph of style over substance. This had rankled with Tom, who liked to see himself as being on the side of the regular man or woman. He took every issue on its merits.

Tess had teased him. 'So, essentially,' she'd said, 'you're in favour of good things and against bad things?'

'That's about it,' he'd replied.

He was fortunate that the local businessmen who'd suggested he run for election didn't interfere too much. During his first campaign, a couple of them had provided what was known as walking-around money. It had paid for election expenses: giving kids a few euro to distribute fliers, buying drinks for canvassers, that sort of stuff. In return, they'd expected him to speak up for the area and to lobby for the west in general. In his twenties, Tom would have been sceptical about the arrangement. He'd have seen it as borderline corrupt. But age made everything fuzzier. He told himself that he was not only helping Kilmitten, Templemorris and the rest of County Clare, he was giving a dig-out to towns and villages everywhere. Dublin got all the money; he was trying to redress the balance. From time to time, he questioned what he was doing. Mostly, however, he was able to push his doubts aside.

Tom's first five years went smoothly, and few were surprised when, next time out, he topped the poll.

A month since his elevation to the cabinet, he was still adjusting to the spotlight. As an opposition politician, he'd received a certain amount of attention. He'd grown used to local radio looking for his views on everything from the new hanging baskets in Templemorris to the future of the European Union. Now it felt as if everybody wanted his opinion on every matter imaginable. Sometimes he had no opinion to give. Following the shooting in the Avondhu Hotel, he'd been inundated with calls from journalists who wanted to write about his friendship with the injured guard and the guard's famous stepsister. TV and radio programmes had also put in requests. Although Tom was keen, he knew Conor wouldn't like the publicity. And Tess didn't do that sort of thing any more. Since she'd retired from modelling, she'd retreated from public life. 'Who wants to see me?' she'd say. 'Let the young ones have their time in the limelight.'

For the past week, Tom and another minister had been engaged in a noisy spat over spending. When he wasn't arguing with Simon Forrester, he was grappling with his other responsibilities. He had a huge office in his department's headquarters beside the Grand Canal. He also had a driver, a press officer, an adviser and a small army of civil servants. But every second of every day was accounted for. He had no time to think. And while many of the meetings and functions he was forced to attend were a waste of time, he was powerless to say no. If he didn't go, somebody would tell Twitter or Facebook that he was an arrogant opportunist who wouldn't listen to the plain people of Ireland. In no time, scores of others would pile in, adding him to their list of useless and corrupt politicians.

Opposition hadn't prepared him for the endless bile of online critics. As they saw it, entering government was a sell-out and he deserved to be reminded of this on an hourly basis. For some, no jibe was too low, no insult too snide. What had Tom done wrong? What *hadn't* he done wrong? Homeless children? Crooked banks? Hospital waiting lists? His fault. One or two would have blamed him for the weather if they could.

Not that these onslaughts caused him to question what he was doing. His doubts came from within.

Small wonder he was looking forward to a quiet pint with Conor. In recent weeks, they'd met just once, their chat truncated by a late vote in the House. Tom hoped Conor understood that his life was no longer his own.

His parents were revelling in his new job. They still lived near Flan and Ginny in Kennedy Crescent. After nearly thirty years in New York, Tom's sister, Dympna, and her husband, Eamon, had surprised everyone by returning home to run the filling station. Having two de-facto Americans in charge of the business had presented challenges. 'You've got to get it into your heads,' his father had said, 'gas is what heats the house. We sell petrol. People pay in euros. And if someone is old enough to drive a car, they're old enough to buy a bottle of wine. Don't go bothering them for ID.'

If you asked Tom, his mam and dad were enjoying the best years of their lives. Devoted users of their senior citizens travel passes, they were constantly on the road. It was strange, he thought, how much time was spent dissecting the lives of young people when the biggest change had been in the lives of the older generation. When Tom was a child, anyone over seventy had been left in the corner with a blanket thrown over their knees. At school, few kids had a full complement of grandparents. Nowadays, seventy was nothing. If called upon, both of Tom's parents were willing to do a turn at the petrol station. And while his son, Hugh, was the main GP in the village, Emmet Minogue continued to see patients. Age hadn't mellowed him.

On his way to the office, Tom had bumped into Helen Minogue. She was unusual in Kilmitten in that she tended not to speak unless she had something to say. For once, she'd been full of talk. Nina had told her about all of them being together in the hospital, she said. No matter that they were nearly fifty years old, Helen made it sound as if her daughter was grateful to be included in the childhood gang.

Conor sent a text to say that he was in Pilkington's snug. In twenty years, the place had barely changed. The owners were either indifferent to shifting fashions or too lazy to update the decor. Tom suspected the latter was closer to the truth. The best you could say about Pilkington's on a Saturday afternoon was that it was quiet.

'Here we are, like two old lads,' he said, as he lifted his pint.

'There's nothing wrong with that,' replied Conor. 'Donie and Seánie O'Grady are watching the racing in the bar. I thought you'd prefer the snug.'

'A wise decision. How are you?'

'Grand. A bit sore, but that's to be expected. I'm likely to be off work for another while, and the visitors have dried up. Once everyone was happy I wasn't going to die, they disappeared again.'

'That's probably no harm. You were never a man for fuss.'

'True. Although you know who did call in the other day? Nina. She rang to say she was in the area, so I invited her round.'

Tom thought of what Helen had said earlier. 'How was she?'

'Too cheery, like she was trying to convince me that everything was good. Or like she was trying to convince herself. She might be that way all the time. I don't see enough of her to know.' He paused for a mouthful of Guinness. 'It's mad to think that her daughters are grown-up. One's doing the Leaving Cert this year, and the other girl's at college. She said the elder girl, Alannah, was going to London for the summer.'

'You're bringing me back now. 1987: the year you joined the guards, Tess became a model and myself and Nina started going out. Those were the days.'

That's what Tom should have said to the journalists. 'Actually,' he should have said, 'there were four of us. There was me, Conor, Tess, and Nina Minogue. You can't forget Nina.'

He bought two more pints, and somehow Conor steered the conversation around to Father Galvin. It wasn't Tom's favourite subject, everybody knew that. When he'd first been elected, the priest's death had been raised again and again. He'd fallen back on his old line. 'I was only a child,' he'd said. 'There's not much I can tell you.'

Mostly, Tom allowed people to think what they wanted

to think. They'd needed someone to blame, and they'd alighted upon Noel O'Grady. Good luck to them.

'You don't reckon O'Grady did it, do you?' asked Conor.

'Sure what do I know?' he replied.

The honest answer was no. He didn't think O'Grady was to blame. He never would.

Tom's round-the-world trip had lasted for more than three years. After Asia, he'd spent twelve months working on a sheep station in New South Wales. Next, he'd moved on to Africa and then to America. Those had been wild, eye-opening years. They'd also been the years in which he'd come to terms with what he knew. He'd decided he couldn't allow one memory to scar his life. He couldn't recall if, back in the early nineties, people had used the word 'closure'. But the focus on Noel O'Grady had given him closure of sorts.

That didn't mean the memory had vanished. You could live so much, yet one decision, one night, would always be there.

Now, for the second time in a couple of months, one of his friends was suggesting that O'Grady mightn't have been the killer. Nina's doubts were one thing; Conor's had to be taken seriously.

'You should have heard my father,' Conor was saying. '"Half the people at the party are dead," he said. Only, when I thought about it, that's not true. Apart from a handful – Noel O'Grady obviously, Breege O'Grady, Johnny and Lourda Ryan, Willie Hehir, Bridie Sexton – most of them are still alive. Still living in the village too.'

Tom took a drink of his pint but said nothing.

'What I need,' said Conor, 'is to get my hands on the witness statements. I can't rely on the old man for help. And with the local garda station closed, who knows where the files ended up. Then again, I've always liked a challenge.'

There was acid in Tom's mouth. Unsure what to say, he went for the obvious: 'I can see why you're interested in what happened, but have you thought about the consequences?'

'What do you mean?'

'I mean, you could make life difficult for my parents. They're old. They could do without a load of hassle being tipped on top of them.'

Conor cupped his hands around his glass. 'I won't go charging into anything, you have my word on that. Besides, I probably won't get far. It's not as though this is official. It's just . . . after what happened in the Avondhu . . . it's all back in my head, you know. And, while I have time on my hands, I thought I'd make a few subtle enquiries.'

'I'm not sure it's the best idea you've ever had, but I can hardly stop you.'

Tom considered whether to have a third pint. Vanessa would be annoyed. He could hear her slightly nasal voice: 'You've mountains of work to do, and you choose to spend half the day in the pub. Sometimes I don't understand you, Tom Crossan.' He came down in favour of one more. Say what you like about Conor, when he got an idea, he followed it through. He had the perseverance of ten men.

That was the problem.

Chapter 29

Gregory Galvin sounded confused by Conor's call. 'Are you the boy who was shot?' he asked.

Smiling to himself, Conor confirmed that he was.

'And you're a son of the man who investigated my brother's murder?'

Again, Conor agreed.

'What is it you want?'

Conor spoke about his interest in the case. 'A few words,' he said. 'That's all. Nothing formal.'

They arranged to meet in the Galvins' home in Knockgreelish, the same house that had featured in the TV documentary almost a quarter of a century before.

Sharon warned him to be careful. 'If your father finds out, he'll be upset,' she said.

'Well, I'm not going to tell him,' he replied, 'and I doubt he has regular chats with the Galvins, so I think I'm on safe ground.'

Knockgreelish was in north Clare. Not an easy place to reach if, like Conor, you weren't in a position to drive. His arm and shoulder still weren't strong enough to risk taking the car. He took the train to Templemorris and caught the bus from there, an experience he found surprisingly enjoyable. The bus driver greeted everyone by name and made several unscheduled stops to allow the, mostly elderly, passengers to alight at their front gates. From time to time, the driver sang along with the country songs on the radio. Gradually, deep green fields framed by drystone walls gave way to the rocky landscape of the Burren.

Knockgreelish was a throwback to another decade. Grubby lace curtains hung on narrow windows, while the one shop had a forgotten look. Another shop had closed, leaving letters from the Revenue Commissioners pooled by the door. Conor passed two Polish men and felt a twinge of pity. Imagine leaving your home and ending up in a miserable spot like this. He expected that if he looked a particular way he'd see young fellows pushing a car, a group of kids hitching a lift in a trailer or some other scene from a bygone age.

The house where Gregory Galvin lived with his wife, Hannah, was at the edge of the village. Pebble-dashed on the outside, the inside was gloomy but immaculate. There was a Sacred Heart lamp in the narrow hall. In the sitting room, an old-style dresser was laden with family photos: here a graduation, there a wedding. The Galvins had a substantial family. Most poignantly, in the middle of the display there was a large picture of Father Leo.

This, Conor reckoned, was a house where they still said a daily rosary. He also sensed that they'd deliberated over whether to offer him tea. In the end, good manners won out, and Hannah said, 'You'll have a cup in your hand.' This, it seemed, was an order, not an offer. Some minutes later, she returned with a thick brew and a plate of fruit scones.

Conor had a visceral dislike of Gregory Galvin, dating back to the newspaper article in which he'd criticised the garda investigation and called for a public inquiry. As they spoke, this floated away.

'Now, this mightn't be easy for you to accept,' said Gregory, 'but my brother was let down. The entire family was let down. If the guards suspected Noel O'Grady, why didn't they arrest him before he drove into a ditch?'

Conor waltzed around the question. 'Maybe they didn't have enough information until after he'd died. I know how difficult it can be to assemble sufficient evidence.'

Hannah nodded.

Her husband was less conciliatory. 'Leo was a good man. You're too young to remember that.' Although his hands were swollen with age, he held his back as straight as a soldier on parade. He'd clearly given considerable thought to what he wanted to say. 'You know what I learned from our family's tragedy? Everybody forgets about the victim. The only reason people remember Leo's name is because he was a priest. That gave him novelty value. I guarantee you, other men and women were murdered that year and, apart from their families, nobody talks about them. People don't forget criminals, though. Take the three fellows who died the day you were shot. If you went out now and asked someone their names, they'd say "Warren Burke". They'd know him because his family are gangsters, and gangsters are interesting. I doubt anybody could give you the names of the other two.'

'Dessie Hartigan and Keith Fraser,' said Conor, in a quiet voice.

'My point is this: I always felt that people in Kilmitten were so wrapped up in themselves, and in which of their neighbours might have been responsible for Leo's death, that they forgot about the victim. I'm not saying my brother, the Lord have mercy on him, was a saint . . . I wish he hadn't been so fond of gambling . . . but he deserved better.'

Conor couldn't argue. He believed the impact of the priest's death had been blunted because he'd been viewed as an outsider. No matter that he'd lived in the village for more than a decade, in the eyes of some locals he wasn't really one of them.

Hannah tapped her husband's wrist. 'To be clear about what you're saying to us, Inspector Varley—'

'Conor, please. Like I told you, this isn't official business.'

'To be clear, you think Leo's killer might still be alive?'

'I don't know. And I don't want to make this any more difficult for you.'

She fixed him with her blue gaze. 'Not knowing exactly what happened to Gregory's brother, and why it happened, is a terrible burden. Over the years, we've come to accept that we'll never get the full story: that either Noel O'Grady took it to the grave . . . or that someone else was responsible and has managed to stay quiet. I've heard other guards say that crimes tend to be solved quickly or not at all. That doesn't give us much hope.'

Conor placed his cup on a lace coaster. 'If you don't mind me asking, do you have any idea why somebody might have wanted to harm Father Leo?'

'Money,' said Gregory, an edge to his voice. 'It's always the same, isn't it? Every blessed problem comes back to money. For a man who'd no particular interest in the high life, my brother loved to gamble. As I understand it, he played cards regularly with some of his neighbours – and he usually won.'

'My father once mentioned that others may have also been in his debt. That he lent money to people. Does that ring any bells?'

'We heard that too, but the guards wouldn't say any more. They claimed it was sensitive information. They were never very good at keeping us informed. Maybe you should ask your father.'

Conor explained that his mission didn't have his dad's backing.

'I'd help you if I could,' replied the priest's brother, 'but we've told you everything we know.'

Conor wrote down his number and handed it to Hannah. 'If you think of anything else, anything at all, give me a ring.'

As he left, she took his hand. 'Please do your best for us,' she said.

Chapter 30

Lincolnshire

Tess was worried about Conor. More specifically, she was worried about his attempts to reopen the file on Father Galvin.

'He's being completely irrational,' she said to Miles, who was staring at his laptop.

'I've never known you to place a premium on rationality.'

'Ah, Miles, I'm being serious.' She closed the drawing-room door to ensure that Daisy remained out of earshot. There were many episodes in her life she'd like to share with her daughter, but not yet. 'Remember I told you about what happened when we were teenagers? When the priest was killed, and everyone went crazy? Mam says Conor's become obsessed with it. He reckons he can get to the truth.'

Years before, Tess had told Miles about her mother's ordeal. She'd also explained how, with the unwitting connivance of a documentary-maker, her stepfather had pinned a different crime on Ginny's rapist. Conor, with his inconvenient ideas about right and wrong, hadn't been let in on the secret. Unfortunately, he'd figured it out for himself.

'If you ask me,' said Miles, 'you should leave Conor alone. The chap's had a difficult time. Before you know it, he'll be back at work, and he'll let this priest business rest.'

'Fine, except Mam's worked up, and I assume Flan is too. You know Conor – he means well, but once he gets an idea into his head he won't let go. I mean, he followed one of those gangsters around until he got himself shot. If I don't intervene, Mam will get more and more stressed.' Tess adopted her wheedling voice. A rarely employed weapon, she used it when she didn't believe that Miles was taking her concerns seriously. 'At this stage in their lives, they shouldn't have to fret about Conor stirring up bad memories.'

Finally, her husband looked up and pushed his pale brown hair back from his forehead. 'Why don't you invite Conor and Sharon over this way for a few days? Our treat. Conor can have a spot of R&R, and you can ask him to back off a little. But do tread gently.'

'Miles,' said Tess, rising to kiss his head, 'you're a superstar.'

Tess had never forgotten the advice she'd received from Marjorie in the employment agency. 'Calm down,' she'd said, 'and then come back to me.' Tess had been eighteen. When she was thirty-six, she'd calmed down. By then she was millions of pounds away from needing a secretarial job.

She'd ricocheted through her twenties and early thirties. She'd been in every magazine and on every catwalk She'd been to all the right parties and a lot of the wrong ones. She'd had all the sex and all the success, and she didn't regret a single minute. Well, okay, she did have a sprinkling of regrets. But she'd avoided so much tedium. She'd managed to skip the phase where people went to dinner parties and talked about tiling. She'd never been part of a conversation about clamping or school admission policies. She'd never visited a DIY store or a clothing outlet (even the name was horrific). Nowadays, she looked at young models and saw how the most successful girls treated it as a business. For her, it had been a lifestyle. And, for the most part, it had been wonderful.

And then she'd got tired. Caution had set in. That and self-preservation. Oh, and she'd met Miles.

After her first decade as a model, Tess had realised that to become internationally famous is to become fenced off. The only people who gain access to your enclosure tend to be equally well known. Or extremely wealthy. Miles Whittingdale fell into the latter category. Banker father, stay-at-home mother, lesser-known public school followed by Cambridge, career in hedge-fund management, one sister a barrister, the other a hospital consultant: there was little in Miles's life that suggested common ground with Tess. Although he protested that his family wasn't upper class ('We're more upper middle'), they were close enough to make Tess wary. Despite her gilded career, the English ruling class put her on edge. When faced by one of their number, she either ramped up her Irishness to Agnes Brown levels or became scared to open her mouth for fear every last vowel and consonant sounded wrong. She might have left Kilmitten, but she'd carried her accent around the globe. For her, it was 'nooze', not 'news', 'fabalas' rather than 'fabulous', and Prince 'Willum' was second in line to the throne.

When she'd first met Miles, at a gallery summer party, she'd expected him to have the indestructible self-assurance of his species. He did. But he was also interested in her. Properly interested. He didn't just ask about modelling or drop names or talk about money. He asked about where she was from and how it differed from where she lived now. He wanted to know what her family and childhood friends thought of her success. That she was impressed might sound pathetic to some, but his approach was unusual. As a rule, the men who chatted her up asked questions to which they already knew the answers. Then they talked about themselves.

Perhaps the most refreshing thing about Miles was that he didn't assume, as so many did, that she was incapable of talking about subjects other than clothes and make-up. Tess wouldn't have described him as spectacularly good-looking, but he had the type of slanting blue eyes that had always appealed to her. Plus, he was at least four inches taller than her. She liked that.

She soon learned that he'd been married twice before but, as he said himself, the first time didn't count. He'd been twenty-three, his brain muddled with drugs. Tess felt the same about her own first marriage, although it had been tequila rather than cocaine that had propelled her down the aisle. Thankfully, the wedding, to a long-forgotten singer called Aaron Grace, had taken place in Las Vegas, and once they'd sobered up neither bride nor groom had been keen to stay married. That was the nineties: you could do whatever you wanted without sending Twitter and the *Daily Mail* website into a frenzy. Miles's second marriage had been a rather more serious affair, lasting eight years and producing two children.

Initially, Tess had balked at the idea of getting married. Not because she wasn't in love with Miles or because she was unsure that he loved her back. She reckoned she'd finally found the right blend of comfort and desire, the thousand subtle cues that made her say, 'Yes, this is the one.' The problem was her. The high glare of her fame had dimmed, and she didn't know what to do next. Yes, she continued to get editorial work and, yes, her advertising contracts remained first division. But, with forty edging closer, her options were becoming more limited. Already she was too old to walk for the top designers. Pretty soon the ad campaigns would become less prestigious, the editors less keen. After that she'd be one ropy photo away from the cover of a downmarket magazine. She'd be Exhibit A in *Celebs lose the fight against cellulite* or *Barefaced cheek: the stars brave enough to go without make-up.* Even thinking about it made the energy drain from her body.

Oh, and she was bored. She'd posed through five – or was it six? – incarnations of the polka-dot trend. She'd been centre-stage for countless reruns of 'ladylike chic' and 'fashion's new laid-back aesthetic'. Navy had been the new black, as had white and red. Then black had been the new black. Images of Tess had told readers that fashion was all about fantasy. Six months later, her picture had assured them that fashion had got real.

That wasn't all. Her tolerance for bullshit had dipped to a dangerously low level. She read a glossy feature about a fellow model who 'kept fit by chasing the chickens around her idyllic country estate'. The woman in question was a major coke fiend who'd only ever chased her dealer and whose off-duty look was more hobo than boho. Another model was lauded for her devotion to extreme exercise. 'Tuh,' said Tess, 'devotion to liposuction and sticking her fingers down her throat, more like.' That she had benefited from similar dishonesty didn't make it any easier to take.

So, after talking to Miles, Tess decided to give up on modelling before it gave up on her. Estelle was bewildered. She enthused about all the geriatric models – she preferred the term 'mature' – fronting major campaigns. 'Everything's changing for the better,' she insisted. Tess reckoned that the only change was negative. 'Being young is what matters,' she said. 'It's what sells. And I don't feel young.'

At least she didn't have to worry about money. It had taken her several years to adjust to her multimillionaire status. Her fortune was based on sheer dumb luck: on the face and figure she'd inherited from her mother and the thick skin she'd grown in Kilmitten. She tried to be generous. She offered to buy her mam and Flan a grander house. They declined. Lauren wasn't so proud, and Tess was paying for her sister's – never-ending – education.

For the first year of their marriage, while Willowthorpe

Hall was renovated, Miles and Tess lived in London. Her friends were puzzled by their decision to move to rural Lincolnshire. 'It's where Miles was born,' she explained, 'and he's always wanted to return.' Her new husband's parents lived less than thirty miles away.

At the start, she found the countryside strange. Compared to the soft contours of home, it felt so angular, so efficient. She'd grown up surrounded by cattle and sheep. Here there wasn't an animal to be seen. Crops – wheat, barley, sugar beet and cabbages – formed the landscape. The hall itself was magnificent. A listed Georgian building in honey-coloured stone, it had ten bedrooms, six acres of garden, a stable block and a swimming pool. It even had its own lake with a resident kingfisher. When Daisy came along, an unexpectedly placid and self-contained little girl, Tess devoted herself to full-time motherhood with an energy she'd once reserved for three-day parties. She'd always been scared of children. She worried that she was too flighty, too selfish. Gradually, her concerns burned away. Willowthorpe became her cocoon, 'Don't look back' her mantra.

None of this meant her new life was perfect. Miles spent a large part of the week in London, and while Tess had made some local friends, she feared they held her at arm's length. There were days when she couldn't stop nostalgia washing over her. She missed her old lifestyle. She missed the hush when she walked into a room; the hubbub of the shows; the exhilaration of being able to go wherever she wanted whenever she wanted. Most of all, she missed her old self. For much of her life she'd had no internal editor. She definitely hadn't been fearless. She'd worried – pointlessly it had turned out – about a million things. Nevertheless, she'd always come on out and said what she'd thought. But what was charming at seventeen could sound nasty at thirty-seven. At forty-seven it would come across as unhinged or, worse, bitter. Tess struggled with this.

Anniversaries became more important to her. The thirtieth anniversary of meeting Estelle outside Wonder Burger was approaching, as were the twenty-fifth anniversaries of her first *Vogue* cover and big advertising contract.

A couple of weeks back, she'd been musing about all of this with Miles. She'd been part of so many different worlds, she'd said, thinking about them made her dizzy.

'But you're happy here?' he asked, concern in his voice.

'I am.'

'Did it ever occur to you that Willowthorpe is an English version of Kilmitten?'

'It did,' said Tess, 'and the scary part is I like it.'

Afterwards, she sifted through her thoughts.

In her head, she divided her life in two. Most people would guess the line fell at the point where she'd become famous. In fact, it marked her discovery of the truth about her father. Afterwards, she'd been more conscious of danger, more suspicious of men. She'd become less tolerant of sleazy banter and of the reptiles who took advantage of young models. She'd like to say she'd been extra-sensitive towards her mother. She hadn't. Tess knew that her wilder episodes had hurt Ginny and Flan. The older she got, the more she thought about her mam – and about others who'd suffered in the same way. As much as she loathed women gushing about how motherhood had changed their lives, Daisy had knocked something loose in her. While Tess wouldn't claim that getting older had made her a better person, it had made her a more equable one. She didn't want Conor tramping in and spreading disarray.

'Before I know it,' said Conor, 'you'll be eating cucumber sandwiches and drinking Pimm's.'

'Don't mock it till you've tried it,' said Tess, polishing her sunglasses with the skirt of her mint green dress. 'There's nothing wrong with a glass of Pimm's, especially in this weather.'

'What's next? Shooting pheasants? Entering your gooseberry jam in the village fete?'

'Conor, if you knew anything, you'd know it's the wrong time of year for shooting pheasants. I have eaten a few, though. Very tasty they were too.'

'If only they could hear you in Kilmitten. "Notions," they'd say.'

'I'm sure the notions police gave up on me a long time ago.'

Polishing complete, Tess put on her sunglasses. The June afternoon sparkled with the promise of early summer. The sky was an interrupted blue, the trees a pale shade of green. In the paddock, Daisy was displaying her pony-riding skills for Miles and Sharon. Tess and Conor were sitting at the rear of the house, banks of flowers in front of them, the air perfumed with lavender and rosemary.

Their talk shifted to Tom's latest exploits. The previous week, he'd given a long interview to a Sunday supplement. *The Accidental Minister*, the piece had been called. The photographs of the rising politician and his lovely family had been soft focus, the interview even softer.

'How does he do it?' asked Conor. 'All that nonsense about his passion for rural life. He ran out of Kilmitten when he was seventeen.'

'Didn't we all?' said Tess. 'I suppose he changed his mind . . . or had it changed for him.'

She admired the way Tom had confounded everybody. He insisted that, like so much else, his return to Kilmitten had been accidental, but Tess reckoned he'd underestimated the village's tidal pull. For years, she'd been an irregular visitor. She'd encouraged her mam, Flan and Lauren to come to England instead. Now, her trips to Ireland were more frequent. She wanted Daisy to have some feel for her background.

She'd read the interview online and had been tickled by the way Vanessa introduced her name. 'Our good friend, Tess Fortune,' she'd said. If Tess thought about Vanessa, she thought of her as generically pretty. Good skin, well-tended teeth, expensive hair. And she was thirsty. Thirsty for success and respect and the security that came with knowing her status was several notches above that of the neighbours. Tess wondered if, left to his own devices, Tom would have become a politician. Yet he'd twice persuaded a large number of people to vote for him, so he must have some aptitude for the job. He had a touch of the 'cute hoor' about him (one of several phrases in Tess's vocabulary that Miles could never grasp), but wasn't as unctuous as some of his colleagues. Most importantly, he was hard to dislike.

Conor stretched out his legs. Their blue-white colour reminded Tess of skimmed milk.

'Is this where you thought you'd be at forty-seven?' he asked.

'Gosh, when we were youngsters, I doubt my imagination stretched that far. Thirty was my outer limit. I remember at Mam's fortieth figuring her life was as good as over.'

'Little did you know how much was ahead of her.'

'True. All the good stuff was still to come.'

Conor picked an imaginary thread from his khaki shorts. 'When you met Nina in the hospital, how did you think she looked?'

'Old,' replied Tess, without pausing to think.

'That's not an answer.'

'She looked worse than you, and you'd just been shot.' While not a fan of obvious cosmetic surgery, Tess had no intention of sliding into middle age without a fight. Every year she visited a man on Harley Street for a few discreet tweaks. Nina would benefit from his expertise.

'Do you ever talk to her?' asked Conor.

'I talked to her then.'

'But other than that?'

This was awkward. Since inviting Conor to Willowthorpe, Tess had concentrated on promoting her own agenda. It hadn't occurred to her that he might also have plans.

'I rarely see her. It's not as if we have much to say to

each other. We spent the best part of a decade not talking at all, and after that our friendship never recovered. You'll probably say this sounds harsh, but when she took up with Julian Heaney, I lost interest in her.' Conor tried to speak. She swatted him away. 'And don't say I shouldn't have let a man come between us, because there was more to it than that, as well you know.'

Tess was keen to move on, Conor equally determined not to. 'That was a long time ago,' he said. 'Twenty-five years ago.'

'There's no law saying you have to remain friends with the people you knew as a kid.'

'You make it sound like you were casual acquaintances. For years, the two of you were inseparable.'

He was right. In their teens, Tess had felt a kinship with Nina, consulting her on every decision, no matter how small. Okay, Nina had had her annoying tendencies: her insecurity; her inability to stand up to her father; her kowtowing to authority figures in general. By comparison with these minor flaws, Tess's failings were many. But the autumn of '91 had changed everything. Nina and Tess had been wrenched apart, and it was too late to change that now.

She held up her hands in a mocking gesture of surrender. 'All right, you win. I'll give her a shout some time. But I've got to be straight with you, I've no time for phoney reunions. Miles is plagued by them. He usually goes and he's usually disappointed.'

'I'm not asking you to meet up with our entire primary-school class.'

'And you know what I always say to him? "There's a reason you don't keep in touch with some people, Miles. It's because you don't like them."'

Conor gave a slight shake of the head, his way of telling her she'd gone too far.

She decided to take charge. 'Can I ask you something?'

He smiled. 'Ask away.'

'It's not a question, more of a request. Mam's been telling me about your interest in Father Galvin.'

'Oh?'

'She says Flan's worried, and she'd like you to tone it down a bit – before people get hurt.'

His smile dissolved. 'I'm not doing anything wrong here. I'm simply taking another look at a case that's bugged me for years.'

'All right, it's not just Mam asking you to go easy. It's me. Your father did what he thought was right. And, remember, for a long time he wasn't alone on that investigation. A lot of guards worked on it, and they were moved on because they weren't getting anywhere.'

'You wanted to know about your father. Your mother asked you to let it go . . . and you didn't.'

'Oh, come on, that was different.'

'I'm not claiming it was exactly the same. It's . . .' Conor paused. 'You're viewing this through one lens, and I don't blame you. In your position, I might do the same. All I'm saying is, there are other ways of looking at it.'

It occurred to Tess that far from dissuading him, the more she spoke, the more entrenched his position became.

The funny part was, in their younger days, both Conor and Tom had been reluctant to talk about the night of the party. Nina had been the one with whom she'd traded theories.

'Just take it handy,' she said. 'Please.'

'There's no guarantee I'll get anywhere. And, even if I do, it's not an official investigation.'

Tess removed her sunglasses. 'It's not like the rest of us don't think about what happened that night, you know. In fact, we talked about it in the hospital. Nina brought it up.'

'Really? What did she say?'

'Nothing of any significance.'

'Go on, Tess.'

'I'm not sure why I'm telling you this, but . . . well, I was surprised by her vehemence. She said she'd never believed that Noel O'Grady was to blame.'

'Why would she say that when it was her own husband who promoted the theory in the first place?'

This wasn't going how Tess had planned. She was beginning to feel like she was in a police interview room. It was impossible to keep the tetchiness from her voice. 'Ah, Conor, I don't know. Why don't you ask her?'

Chapter 31

It was funny, thought Tom, how you could go months, *years*, without talking to someone. Then, for whatever reason, you kept on meeting.

He was leaving his Saturday clinic when he saw her coming out of the chemist, stuffing change into the pocket of her jeans.

'Nina,' he shouted, before he had a chance to think about what he was doing.

She waved, and they met halfway.

It was Hugh's birthday, she said, so she was home for the night. Tom got the impression that she was on her own. After a minute or two of awkward chit-chat about Conor, they decided to go for a coffee.

The lunchtime crowd was gone from the Cherry Tree café, and they slipped into a corner seat. Mercifully, none of the village's more dedicated rumour-merchants was there. You could never be too careful in Kilmitten. In no time, a casual coffee would become a red-hot affair.

Nina sipped her cappuccino and assessed their

surroundings. The Cherry Tree was decorated in shades of pink and red, its walls dotted with colourful photos of local landmarks. The coffee was served in large blue cups. 'When we were growing up,' she said, 'who would have thought that one day the village would have a proper café with a proper coffee machine?'

Tom laughed. 'You've got to remember that, back then, spending money on a non-alcoholic drink would have been viewed as borderline insane. It's a great place, right enough. Lorraine Daly's the owner. Well, she was Lorraine Gilligan in our day. She married one of the Dalys from Lacken's Mills.'

'Hold on a minute. Wasn't she the . . .' Nina stalled, as if the significance of what she was saying had only just occurred to her.

'. . . woman whose twenty-first was taking place the night I got rotten drunk and gave Seánie O'Grady a dig? She was indeed. It's a good job she's forgiven me for wrecking her party or we'd be out on the street.'

Appearing to recover her composure, Nina gave a quick glance towards the counter. 'Hmm. She looks stern. No wonder you had to leave the country afterwards.'

'Ah, Lorraine's not the worst of them. She has a café in Templemorris too. Irina's usually in charge here. She's from Moldova. Lovely girl. Ridiculously over-qualified, of course. I gather she has two degrees.'

'There's something else we could never have imagined,' said Nina. 'People actually moving *to* Ireland.'

As their chat continued, Tom was surprised to realise he had relaxed. No, it was more than that: he was enjoying himself.

He'd spent so long trying not to think about Nina that he'd forgotten how easy their conversation had once been. Her mannerisms hadn't changed. She still leaned forward when she wanted to emphasise a point. She still fiddled with her hair. The fundamentals were intact. Admittedly, she looked older. But she *was* older. Tom was suspicious of people whose appearance remained the same. In his book, this meant they either spent too much time beautifying themselves or their life was too easy.

Mindful of what Conor had said, he was tempted to ask if she was all right. Then he decided he'd only ruin a perfectly good afternoon. He wondered, too, if he should tell her about Conor's interest in the Father Galvin investigation. But, no, the fewer people who knew, the better. Besides, even without Conor's mission, the case was a sensitive subject. Once, it had drawn the four of them together. Later, it had pushed them apart. Despite the passage of time, there was still so much they couldn't say. He remembered what Nina had said in the hospital about not believing Noel O'Grady was to blame. He didn't want to give oxygen to her scepticism.

The day before, Tom had bumped into Ginny. She'd told him that Conor and Sharon were in England for the weekend. With any luck, Tess would knock some sense into him.

'Do they have you driven mad next door?' asked Nina.

'What do you mean?'

'I passed by earlier and saw the queue. All those people wanting something or complaining about something. I wouldn't be able to handle it.'

'Says the woman who handles a class of children five days a week.'

'But if they don't behave, I can call their parents.'

'To be honest with you, most people in Kilmitten are grand. Later on, I'm going to the official opening of the new community centre in Danganstown and, no lie, they're the worst moaners in the county. I'll be lucky to escape before midnight.' He sipped his coffee. 'Your father was in to me a couple of weeks back giving out about the state of the road near O'Rahilly's Cross. "Somebody's going to drown in those potholes," he said, "and it'll be too late to fix the problem then."'

'That sounds like Dad. I don't know how Mam puts up with his obsessions. I suppose she lets a lot go over her head. I hope you reminded him that you're not a county councillor.'

'I did not. I can't go throwing away votes. Anyway, believe it or not, I like that part of the job: talking to people, seeing what I can do to help them.' Tom stopped. 'Would you listen to me? I sound like I'm being interviewed for Miss Ireland.'

'But you're so good at the other stuff,' said Nina. 'I've seen a couple of your speeches, and you're far more convincing than most of the chancers in Leinster House.'

'Thanks, only sometimes that carry-on reminds me of a slightly more grown-up school debate.'

'Seriously?'

'Don't get me wrong, there's a certain thrill from being up on the stage, jousting with the big boys. But at the same time I always feel like I'd rather be down the back of the hall, hanging out with the gang. Does that sound daft?'

'Not at all,' she said.

It occurred to Tom that this wasn't a conversation he could have with Vanessa. She'd find it troubling. No, not just troubling. She'd find it impossible to understand. He couldn't explain that some days he felt as if he was winning a race he hadn't wanted to enter. It would sound ungrateful and, in his world, there was no sin as heinous as ingratitude. Slightly embarrassed by this burst of candour, he drained his coffee.

Nina took the hint. 'I'd better let you go. You wouldn't want to keep the voters of Danganstown waiting.'

'They'd never forgive me.'

They both got to their feet. Nina insisted on paying. Tom took one pace towards the door, then turned around. 'Sorry. I meant to say I enjoyed the chat.'

She smiled. How well he knew that smile. 'Me too, Tom,' she said. 'Me too.'

Chapter 32

It turned out that the Father Galvin files hadn't gone far. A couple of phone calls revealed that, as Conor had suspected, they'd been transferred to the new garda station in Templemorris. This was a stroke of luck. A friend from his training-school days, Sergeant Jennifer Leahy, was stationed there. He rang and, after the mandatory twenty questions about the Avondhu Hotel, explained what he was looking for.

'Not a word to anyone,' he said. 'As far as I know, all my father's buddies have retired, but I'd rather he didn't get word of what I'm up to.'

'Oo-kay,' replied Jennifer, caution in her voice.

'There's nothing sinister going on, I promise. I just want to have a look at a few statements, and I don't want to worry the old man.'

'Which statements?'

'There's the snag. I won't know until I see them.'

Eventually, they agreed that he'd call into the station the following evening. On a midweek night, there wouldn't be many people around to ask questions.

When Conor told Sharon of his plans, her face tightened. 'Are you sure you're not taking it all a bit far?'

'Maybe I am but . . .' he weighed up his words before speaking again, '. . . while I'm doing this, I'm not stressing about the Burkes and the McPartlands.'

'I don't know that obsessing over something that happened when you were thirteen is any healthier. Did it ever occur to you that you spend too much time thinking about criminals?'

'I'll only be gone a few hours. Now I'm back on the road, I can drive down, have a look, and be home again before you know it.'

'I can't stop you, but you've got to think it all through. You don't want to make things worse with your father and Ginny.'

Bruised as he was by his disagreement with Tess, Conor was determined to continue his task. Tess was so accustomed to everyone being in her thrall that she found any opposition, no matter how friendly, difficult to accept. To be fair, it was a miracle that she'd remained relatively sane. All those years of entitlement and adulation would have warped many beyond recognition.

To begin with, her appeal had been straightforward. She'd been young, tall, thin, pretty. Later, it had become more complex. There had been more beautiful women, yet somehow Conor's stepsister had managed to turn her entire life into a show. At one point, it had been hard to find a girl over the age of twelve or a woman under eighty who hadn't bought something or travelled somewhere in emulation of

Tess Fortune. He had witnessed grown men and women go mute in her presence.

As her career had blossomed, she'd done fewer and fewer interviews. When she did speak, it was usually in Ireland. At home, she was guaranteed the questions would be gentle, bordering on fawning. Elsewhere, she might get more of a grilling. Her blink-and-you'll-miss-it first marriage, her stint in rehab for 'exhaustion', aka prescription-drug addiction (he probably shouldn't have joked about morphine in her presence), her chaotic affair with a loutish footballer: these were not episodes Tess wished to discuss with strangers.

Each scandal had added a line to Ginny's forehead, not that she'd ever admit it. That was why Conor had found the 'Go easy on Mam' lecture hard to take. Although he rarely got annoyed with Tess, he was irritated with her attitude towards him now – and he was irritated with her attitude towards Nina. Yes, Nina's behaviour had been tacky, but she'd been little more than a kid. In Conor's view, she'd been the most immature of the four. Tess wasn't making any allowance for that.

The new garda station in Templemorris had been built at the height of the boom. A large white building with long windows, it was a monument to a time when the country had been devoured by notions. If you asked Conor, it looked more like a shopping centre than a place where people investigated crimes.

To reduce the risk of being seen, he parked his car at the

rear of the station. Jennifer met him at the back door and showed him to an upstairs meeting room. The table was covered with an assortment of folders, paperwork spilling from every one. There was also a box containing pieces of evidence. Nowadays, everything was computerised, but in 1982 computers belonged to science fiction films. In Kilmitten, typewriters had been considered high-tech.

The window looked out onto the town's main street, giving him a view of a betting shop and a hair salon. The room smelt faintly of sweat.

'You do know—' started Jennifer.

'That you shouldn't be doing this?' finished Conor. 'I do, and I really appreciate your help, Jen. Seriously I do. By the way, I've been meaning to ask: has there ever been any talk of the investigation being reopened?'

'Not that I've heard.'

A specialist team was re-examining unsolved cases, most of them dating from the 1980s. Like the death of Leo Galvin, some of the crimes had been highly controversial. In more than one, scientific developments, like DNA testing, had led to a breakthrough. With others, the passage of time had made it easier for witnesses to talk. In at least two more, a fresh pair of eyes had been enough. Up until recently, Conor had expected the priest's death to be on the list, but after the conversation with his father he was less sure. If ever a case had fallen behind a radiator, this was it.

Jennifer picked up one of the files. 'I remember as a kid watching the reports on the news. The poor fellow.' She stopped, as if reconsidering what she'd said. 'Was there ever a suggestion that he'd interfered with kids or anything like that?'

'I don't think so. Why do you ask?'

'No particular reason, except that in the old days, folks didn't talk about abuse. People like my parents wouldn't have considered it possible, not by a man of God at any rate. And even when children did come forward, everything was hushed up.'

'Have you come across any theories about his death?'

'Nope. The one time I heard it mentioned was when one of the older lads was talking about Tom Crossan and how it all happened in his house.' Jennifer put the file back on the table and looked at her watch. 'I'd better get going. You shouldn't be disturbed in here. Give me a buzz when you're finished, and I'll come and put everything away again.'

'Thanks.'

She shrugged. 'Fingers crossed you'll find whatever it is you're looking for.'

What *was* Conor looking for? The truth was, he didn't know. He hoped he'd find some detail, however small, that had been overlooked back in the eighties. Some nugget of information that meant more now than it had then.

He sorted through the paperwork, trying to keep an open mind. This was easier said than done. Almost every statement was from someone he knew. He was struck by how young they'd been. To Conor, people like Brendan and Mercedes Talty had always been old, but in 1982 they'd been in their early forties. Younger than he was now. Ginny had been thirty-two. At forty-eight, Haulie and Cora Crossan had been among the eldest.

He thought about how nervous many would have been. How some would have feared saying the wrong thing. How others would have berated themselves for not remembering more. He thought, too, of how at least one of the statements was a collection of lies. Some party-goers were impossibly vague: 'I'd had a fair bit to drink.' Others were pointed: 'There are bad people in this village, believe you me.'

As he read, Conor discovered the failings in his own memory. He would have guessed that Father Galvin's body had been found around midnight. In fact, Cora had made her grim discovery shortly before eleven o'clock. Her screams had alerted a number of people, including Emmet Minogue. The doctor had attempted to administer CPR, but it had been too late.

At other points during his trawl, he felt half-forgotten memories being exhumed. Along with Tom, Tess and Nina, he featured in the investigation. They were referred to as 'local children', who had disturbed the snow at the back of the house. A typed report said they'd been questioned but had provided no useful information.

Many of the documents were in his father's spiky handwriting. As expected, he discovered several references to Noel O'Grady. Two people had witnessed the row with the priest on the morning of the party. Three others highlighted O'Grady as somebody who'd disappeared for a while on the night. One statement claimed he'd looked 'as guilty as a cat with a mouthful of feathers'. Of course, he did, thought Conor. He'd been upstairs with Lourda Ryan.

Dan Duggan was mentioned by several people. The Duggans, Tess and Ginny's neighbours on Pearse Terrace, were well known for being excessively sound on the national question. The year before the party, during the H-Block hunger strike, Dan had hung a black flag from an upstairs window. The youngest Duggan, Brian, had been in Conor's class at school. On the morning of Bobby Sands' death, he'd arrived with a black armband over his jumper. Their teacher, Mrs Clune, had made him remove it. Brian had returned after lunch in head-to-toe black. He'd given Mrs Clune a letter saying he'd wear whatever his parents wanted him to wear. Dan Duggan had been at the party. When interviewed by one of the investigating officers, he'd pointed out that if the dead man had been a British soldier the questions might have had some legitimacy. 'What would I be killing a Catholic priest for?' he'd asked. After several hours, the guards concluded that Dan's only crime was being a complete bore.

The files also contained a handful of poison-pen letters. One blamed Travellers for the crime. Another, in the green ink beloved of cranks everywhere, maintained it was the work of a group of Limerick teenagers who were known to 'sniff glue and worship the devil'. A third was typed. It alleged that during his time at the seminary in Maynooth, Father Galvin had 'kept company' with a single mother and that this should be examined. A fourth spoke about the card games that had been a regular feature of life in the parochial house. *They owed him money*, it read, *more than they could ever repay*.

Conor took a photo. He did the same with a few of the witness statements and some of the other documents.

One statement was missing, that of Lourda Ryan. Conor suspected his father had removed it. He tried not to dwell on his dad and Ginny, but still they tugged at his conscience. So, too, did Gregory and Hannah Galvin. The Galvins had made more than one complaint about the investigation. In Conor's experience, this wasn't unusual. Indeed, compared to some families, their what-aboutery had been restrained.

He recalled what they'd said to him. Like most victims, it wasn't so much their words as the way they'd voiced them that had affected him. Their quiet sincerity had given those words their power. If you asked Conor, the old line about time being a great healer had been coined by someone who'd never suffered the impact of a violent crime. The pain might dull a little, but for the Galvins, and many others, it was always there, circling them like a thunderstorm.

He'd realised early on that most criminals bore no resemblance to the characters in books and films. He'd never encountered an ingenious serial killer. Most crimes were born of greed or desire, fear or jealousy. Some stemmed from desperation or plain bad luck. For every criminal with the low cunning of Kenny Burke or Liam McPartland, there were twenty who lived hand-to-mouth, dreaming that one of their inept con jobs would transform their lives. Some were twisted, pitiful figures, prepared to inflict pain or suffering for small gain. Others were delusional: 'She was asking for it'; 'He's no loss'; 'I was provoked.' Many managed to convince others of their respectability. For almost two decades, Noel O'Grady had paraded around Kilmitten without anyone suspecting him of a brutal crime. Conor wondered if he'd assaulted other women, and if they, too, had been afraid to talk.

He ploughed on through the documents, his shoulders becoming hunched, his eyes scratchy. Gregory Galvin had been convinced that money lay at the heart of the mystery, and there was ample evidence that this was what the police had thought too. The poker school had been interviewed. Some, like Timmy Moynihan, Batt Meaney and Arthur Sexton, had admitted to being in the priest's debt. The amounts were minor. Noel O'Grady had owed most: one hundred and forty pounds, a tidy sum in 1982. People had killed for less. But O'Grady had had an alibi.

As far as the poker debts were concerned, Leo Galvin's record-keeping had been haphazard. When it came to the money he'd lent, he'd been more thorough. He'd poured most of his winnings, and possibly some of the parish funds, into money-lending. While there was no evidence that he'd charged interest, he'd kept a tight rein on his debtors. The names and the sums owed were catalogued in a red notebook, its pages crisp with age. The parish priest had been a one-man credit union.

A farmer called Anthony O'Malley had owed two hundred pounds. He hadn't been at the party, however. He'd been in the County Hospital in Ennis being treated for pneumonia. A woman called Gertie MacMahon, whom

Conor recognised as Father Galvin's housekeeper, had owed fifty pounds. The idea of Gertie breaking a set of traffic lights, let alone killing her boss, was unthinkable. Also in the priest's debt was Timmy Moynihan. But in January 1982 Timmy couldn't have hurt anyone. A kick from a bull had broken his leg and left him on crutches. Apart from a trip to the bathroom, he'd spent the entire evening on the sofa in the Crossans' front room.

The final name on the list surprised Conor. He spent some time looking at it, considering it. The more he thought, the more the entry made sense. The investigating officers had acted on the information but, faced with trenchant denials, they'd taken it no further.

That didn't mean they'd been right.

Chapter 33

Tom was on the television, doing battle with a particularly pompous current affairs presenter. A daily newspaper had carried a series of stories about rural crime: an elderly couple tied up, their house ransacked; a bachelor farmer beaten over the head with a shovel, his attacker escaping with just twenty-five euros; a six-year-old girl abducted, then abandoned five miles away. The minister for rural and regional affairs had been put forward to promote the government line. There was no cause for complacency, he said, but no reason for alarm either. Unlike some politicians he didn't look sweaty or shifty under the studio lights. Nina remembered what he'd said about school debates. She thought he was doing well.

Julian didn't agree. 'Would you look at him?' he said. 'Trying to be on both sides of the argument. People aren't fooled by that any more.'

She hugged a cushion to her chest. 'What else can he say? If he accuses the paper of exaggerating, they'll stamp all over him. If he says the situation is out of control, he'll be in even more trouble.'

'You always defend him, don't you?'

'No. I'm telling you what I think. What's wrong with that?'

'What's wrong is that you haven't thought it through. You see, you have this . . .'

Nina zoned out while her husband put her straight. If she responded, they'd get enmeshed in one of those circular arguments that could last for days. She suspected that after twenty-three years of marriage most couples didn't listen to each other. Tom was an especially contentious subject. She hadn't mentioned their coffee in Kilmitten. It would only have given Julian an excuse to deliver one of his speeches about Tom's lack of credibility.

She rose from the sofa. 'I'm going to bed.'

At the door, she paused and looked at her husband's profile. He had a double chin like a baby. That was what she should say to her daughters: 'Girls, a word of advice. Don't marry a man with a weak chin. Or someone who bores you.' Would she throw in a line about avoiding men who have affairs? That might be going too far. Besides, she didn't feel qualified to give advice. Not when her own life had become a list of questions. Too often she found herself looking back at the past quarter-century and thinking, *Well, there I was, and here I am, and how did that happen?* She reflected on decisions she'd made, friendships she'd allowed to fizzle out, opportunities she'd spurned. *Was that when I blew it?* she would ask herself. *Was that when I blew it?*

Sometimes, she invented versions of herself. She pictured herself living in a big house in the country or with a large family of children or as a free spirit who'd travelled the world. Then she told herself to make the most of what she'd been given.

While Alannah was in London for the summer, poor Bea was in the middle of the Leaving Cert. Her chemistry exam was the next day. As Nina passed her daughter's bedroom, she heard a tinny sound. She eased open the door and saw Bea with the bedside light on, headphones clamped to her ears. Her daughter was a music obsessive, her favourite bands from the 1990s, the decade in which she'd been born.

'I'm going to sleep soon, I promise,' said Bea, taking off her headphones.

Nina sat at the end of the bed. 'What were you listening to?'

'Nirvana.'

'There's a blast from the past.'

'Did you know that just before they became mega-famous they played in Cork?'

'It does ring a bell. What year was that?'

Bea scrunched her nose. '1991. Those must have been amazing times.'

'The year I met your father.'

'You could have met Kurt Cobain instead.'

Nina laughed. 'I was too square for that.'

'I bet you weren't,' said Bea. 'You were best friends with Tess Fortune so you must have been a little bit cool. I'm sure you could've met Kurt, if you'd wanted.'

'I was never as cool as Tess.'

'One day, Mum, we'll get to hear some of your secrets. Even you were young once.'

'Thanks a million, Bea. You make me sound like a pensioner.' Nina got to her feet and flicked off the light. 'I forgot to tell you, I'll be slightly late tomorrow. I'm meeting my old friend Conor after work.'

'No problem. After tomorrow, I don't have another exam until Friday.'

'Good woman. Now go to sleep.'

Nina went to bed with Bea's words floating around her. She felt like she'd been too old for too long. What a great hurry she'd been in and, looking back, she didn't know why. She hadn't been alone. Many of her generation had grown up too quickly. Then, around the turn of the millennium, someone had flicked a switch. Kids went from growing up too fast to not growing up at all. (And, yes, she knew their lives contained a million challenges that her generation hadn't had to face. As Alannah often reminded her, the day of the permanent job was over, rents were ridiculously high, and they'd all be living at home until they were forty. 'Forty?' Nina liked to reply. 'You'll have me in the madhouse long before then.') Too frequently, she acted like an old woman. She'd see a tattooed youngster and hear herself saying, 'How are they ever going to get a job?' She'd read an article about a twenty-something's adventurous sex life and think, *That doesn't sound very wise.* Then she'd round on herself for being such a moan. If she was honest, she envied them. She'd never had the same sense of youthful infallibility.

Nina and Julian had married two years after they'd met. The wedding had taken place in Dublin. According to the official explanation, this had been the most sensible location.

Most of their friends had lived in the capital, as had Julian's family. In reality, Nina had feared being shunned by people in Kilmitten. For a while, her visits home had been brief. If she hadn't been ostracised, she hadn't been very popular either. She remembered some locals, like Haulie Crossan, being kind to her, and it had meant a lot.

After Alannah and Bea were born, she continued to work, struggling on through exhaustion, telling herself that others coped with far more. Bit by bit, Julian became disillusioned with film-making. The commissioning editors were narrow-minded idiots; the budgets were too small; the media industry was rotten with nepotism. Although Nina suspected her husband's complaints contained an element of truth, she also knew that his vision had withered. His ambition had been replaced by inertia. She was disappointed when he told her he was going to work for his father, but not surprised. There was more opportunity in the building game, he said. He'd be a fool not to take advantage of his family connections.

It was all about money, after all.

By the time the girls were in their early teens, Nina realised the magnitude of her mistake. More and more, she thought about Tom. She saw how one impulsive summer had changed both their lives. In her quest to be grown-up, she'd behaved like a child. She'd been dazzled by grand words and shiny promises. Apart from dropping the occasional hint to her mother, she said nothing. In the staff room, everybody complained about their partners, but it was tepid stuff. True unhappiness was quiet.

By way of compensation, she poured too much love into her daughters, trying to shield them from the worst effects of the recession. The property crash hit the Heaney family like a runaway truck. While Julian's father lost much of his property empire, he was devious enough to hold on to several flats. Previously, their management had been handled by an employee. When this was no longer feasible, Julian became a landlord, squeezing rent from hard-up tenants, fobbing off complaints and carrying out minor maintenance. Nina thanked the stars that she'd held onto her solid pensionable job.

Over the years, Julian hadn't always been faithful. When the girls were small, she'd tried to ignore his unexplained disappearances. It was only when the truth had surrounded her and was lapping at her feet that she'd acknowledged it. She said nothing, a silence based largely on guilt. She reflected on how she'd treated Tom and told herself that this was payback time.

A couple of months ago, around the time that Conor was shot, she'd begun to fear it was happening again. She didn't need a rogue credit card receipt or a lipstick-smeared shirt. She just knew. This time, she wanted to find out more. So, one evening, when Julian claimed to be fixing a leaky shower in Harold's Cross, she followed him. The surprise was that the other woman wasn't some free-as-a-bird twenty-three-year-old. She was a thirty-something blonde who lived on the next street and whose children went to St Fachtna's. Emer Dawson didn't just share a name with Nina's teenage tormentors, she had a similar air of entitlement. She was one of those women who keeps a separate wardrobe of clothes for sun holidays; a woman who talks about supper when everyone in Ireland knows it's either dinner or tea; a woman who says her children's names out loud – 'Coco! Noah!' – so bystanders can hear how tasteful they are. While those children were at school, Emer had sex with Julian.

Nina had always hated confrontation. She liked to lower her head and muddle on. Still, there was only so much that anyone could take.

The following afternoon, she met Conor in a café in Rathmines. Only a few weeks had passed since they'd last met, so why he wanted to see her again, she didn't know. She'd gone to extra trouble with her appearance, putting on her favourite red jacket and cream trousers. Ridiculous, of course, but she didn't want to become known as the frumpy one. If only she'd been better dressed on the day she'd met Tom. Vanessa was always perfectly groomed, like a receptionist in a pricey hair salon.

Nina and Conor sat across from each other, cappuccinos in front of them, 1980s soft rock drifting from the radio.

'They used to play this at the community hall disco in Temple-morris,' said Conor, 'as a respite from AC/DC and Motörhead.'

Nina told him about Bea and her love of nineties grunge. She thought her daughter's Leaving Cert was going well, she said, but it was hard to be certain. 'She keeps shifting the conversation. She seems fairly relaxed, though. I'm the one who gets in a lather about it all.' She explained how Bea was the more easy-going of her girls. 'I used to fret about her being bullied. Then I copped on and told myself I was being daft. Just because I'd had a bad experience at school, it didn't mean the same would happen to her.' She raised her palms to the ceiling. 'I'm a terrible worrier.'

'You always were,' said Conor.

'Alannah's at the other end of the spectrum. Hurricane Alannah, I call her. She's all go. Her latest ambition is to be a social media coordinator.'

'Whatever one of those is.'

'My sentiments entirely. Julian says we have to let her follow her dreams, only . . .'

'You'd prefer it if she wanted a good old-fashioned job – like teaching.'

'Or the gardaí,' said Nina, with a smile.

Deep down, she knew this wouldn't happen. Deeper still, she didn't care. She was proud of her daughters: one mercurial, the other a dreamer. For all that she'd got wrong, they'd turned out better than she could have hoped.

She asked about Conor's recovery. He'd be returning to work in the autumn, he said. He told her how in less than three years' time, when he reached fifty, he'd be eligible for retirement. 'Mad,' he said, 'but I'll have thirty years' service, and those are the rules.'

'And will you go?' asked Nina.

'I'm tempted . . . except what else would I do?'

'I know the feeling. I've been teaching fifth and sixth for so long, even if I left I'd still be doing the lessons in my head.'

The conversation moved on to Conor and Sharon's visit to England.

'Is Tess's house very grand?' asked Nina.

'It's not quite Downton Abbey, but it's not far off.' Conor drank some coffee. 'In all honesty, the place is far too big for three people. They're outnumbered by the staff. Miles spends most of the week in London, and Daisy's as good a child as you'll find. I'm not sure what Tess does with her time. It's a funny old life.'

Nina detected tension between Conor and his stepsister. She decided not to pry. 'I reckon I'd cope, all the same.'

'Me too. As I think of it, I passed on your number. She said she'd give you a call the next time she's home.'

For a minute or two, they kept up the polite pretence that this would happen. Despite being back on speaking terms with Tess, Nina didn't fool herself that they'd ever be friends again. Tess – passionate, spiky, brave Tess – had been the best friend she'd ever had. Maybe everybody said that about their childhood pal, but in her case it was true. They'd been friends at an age when Nina had needed a confidante. When she'd needed someone to make her better than she was. She'd relied on Tess, then she'd grown up and realised that relying on anyone was a mistake. No, that wasn't fair. Nina was the one who'd destroyed their friendship. Not by falling for Julian but by succumbing to envy. With the cruel clarity of hindsight, she saw how her envy of Tess's success had shaped her behaviour. She'd wanted everybody's attention. Her own share of the limelight. She hadn't paused to consider the consequences.

Her eyes watered.

Conor touched her hand. 'Hey, are you okay?'

'I'm fine, just a bit nostalgic. Foolish, I know.' Nina didn't want his pity. 'Listen, don't pay any heed to me. I always get tired at this time of year. Another few days and the school holidays will be here.' She sensed something else was on his mind. 'You didn't call me to talk about Tess, did you?'

'No. It's . . . it's kind of sensitive.' He explained what he was doing. 'Tess said you didn't think Noel O'Grady could have killed Father Galvin either, and I suppose I've been wondering why.'

'There's a question. I . . .'

Although Nina knew an honest answer might have implications for Tom, she would be happy to see the O'Grady theory debunked. To this day, Julian was proud of his documentary. How he loved puffing himself up and recalling his glory years when Irish television had been a 'serious medium run by serious people, before the light entertainment morons took over'. Oh, wouldn't it be sweet if his proudest achievement turned out to be flawed.

'Before I go any further,' she said, 'I've got to stress that I don't know anything for sure. I can't say, "Such and such a thing definitely happened." What I can say is this: I told Tom that Julian reckoned Noel O'Grady was a prime suspect, and he pooh-poohed the idea. He was adamant – vehement, even – that O'Grady wasn't the killer.'

'Did he say why he was so convinced?'

'No. We were in the middle of a row. He'd found out about me and Julian.' Nina felt her cheeks darken. 'We were shouting at each other. It was pretty nasty, not that I didn't deserve it. Anyway, what lodged in my head was Tom's absolute certainty. I said something like "You can't be sure." And he insisted that he was. When I pressed him, he drew back, said it wasn't O'Grady's style, that being a drunken idiot didn't make the guy a killer.' She ran a finger around her cup. 'It was only later, weeks later, after the story about the Galvins had been in the paper, that I thought it all through. I asked myself if Tom knew more than he was letting on.'

'You weren't tempted to ask?'

Nina had never voiced these thoughts before. Her throat felt gravel-rough. The words came slowly. 'How could I? I couldn't approach Tom. I'd done enough to the man. In other circumstances, I'd have spoken to Tess. But that wasn't possible. She'd written a letter, telling me that our friendship was over.'

'You didn't consider confiding in me?'

'That wouldn't have been a good idea. Tom was your best friend. How would you have reacted if I'd rolled up saying, "By the way, I think Tom knows something"? Like I told you, all I had was a suspicion, a hunch.'

'Fair enough.'

'By then, your father had told Julian that O'Grady was probably the guilty man.' She looked down at the table. 'Julian was gung-ho. There was a lot going on. Nobody in Kilmitten was talking to me. So I tried to put what Tom said to the back of my mind.'

Conor nodded. 'I understand.'

'I wouldn't blame you if you didn't. I mean, you're

probably asking yourself why I didn't talk about this before now. I've thought about it, and the best explanation I have is that violence doesn't feature in most of our lives. It happens elsewhere, to other people. And then, when you got shot – when I thought you might die – I started thinking about Father Galvin. The thoughts wouldn't go away. I hope that makes sense.'

'Actually, it does. If it hadn't been for the Avondhu, I probably wouldn't be asking these questions now.'

'There's something else too. I spent so many years rushing around the place, busy all the time. Now the girls are older, and I've got past that stage, it's like I paused and found my childhood there waiting for me. Some episodes – that night in particular – kept coming back to me.' She shook her head. 'Now, that probably does sound mad.'

'Not at all. Did you ever get the impression that one of Tom's parents might have said something to him?'

'Gosh, I don't know. I . . . Look, what I'm going to say is based on nothing. Absolutely nothing, you understand?'

'Uh-huh.'

Nina leaned forward on her elbows. Even though the subject matter was bleak, there was something comforting about talking to Conor; her friend, her ally. 'Like I say, I've been thinking about the night of the party, about the four of us in the shed. I don't know if you remember, but Tom went back to the house.'

'I remember it well. He wanted to get another beer, only the door was locked. When he came back and broke the news, we all went home.'

'Mmm, but he was gone for quite a while.'

'And?'

'Was there a chance that he saw something?' Nina ran a hand through her hair. 'I'm not claiming he deliberately lied to us. There's every chance that if he did spot anything, he didn't appreciate its significance. He was twelve years old, for God's sake. But what if, in later years, it all made more sense? What if he genuinely did know that Noel O'Grady couldn't have been the guilty man?'

No sooner had the words left her mouth than she wanted to reel them back in. She shouldn't have given voice to her half-baked hypothesis. The last person she wanted to hurt was Tom. Nina had heard it said that, even in the happiest marriages, people imagined what life would have been like with their first love. And her marriage was far from happy. Given how often she thought about Tom, she wondered if he ever thought about her. About them. When they'd had that coffee together, she'd got the feeling that he did. Then again, she was probably fooling herself. Tom was a married man with three gorgeous sons. Whatever his misgivings about politics, he'd made a success of his life. Oh, and he was a flatterer, adept at making people believe that he cared, that there was nowhere else he'd rather be.

'Lord,' she said, 'I'm rambling here. I shouldn't have . . . I've effectively accused Tom of hiding information about a serious crime and I've nothing to back it up. What sort of person am I? Please, Conor, forget I spoke.'

Again, he touched her hand. 'You've no reason to feel bad. What you said about the night of the party? I've been asking myself the same question.'

Chapter 34

If there was no good time for the next meeting in Tom's diary, this was definitely the worst possible day. The last thing he needed was Conor in full-on crusade mode, and he feared that was what he was going to get. Tess had warned him. 'He's gone mad,' she'd said. 'He won't listen to reason.' Her comments had been an addendum to their main conversation. She'd called to harangue him about a colleague, although what business it was of hers he didn't know. She didn't even live in the bloody country. 'It's all on the *Guardian* website,' she'd said, as if that was the definitive word on the matter.

'I don't give two hoots about the *Guardian* website,' Tom replied. That was true. It was the deluge of criticism at home that hurt. Even so, he was taken aback by Tess's angry tone. Normally she sounded so laid-back, you'd think she was calling from a hammock.

'Seriously, Tom,' she said, 'the days of coming out with that sort of shite are over. Or if they're not, they should be. You can't tell victims they've got to share the blame. I trust you're going to give him the sack.'

'Strictly speaking, it's not up to me. I'm not in charge of the government.'

'Pfft. He's an affront to women. And he's got to go. Today.'

Tess's call had been prompted by one of Tom's independent colleagues, a moon-faced Carlow publican named Cyril Dinan, or Cyril Dinosaur as the papers now called him. As a junior minister, Cyril's talents were limited. He was, though, blind to his own mediocrity, which was of enormous help. He was also frighteningly good at getting people to vote for him.

Cyril had been bumbling along until he'd agreed to do an interview with a current affairs magazine. The interviewer had asked about unemployment. Everything would be tip-top, said Cyril, if more married women were content to stay at home and mind their children. It was no surprise there were so many badly behaved kids when their mothers weren't there to discipline them.

It got worse. The minister of state for lifelong learning went on to claim that young women were drinking too much and wearing too little. 'And they're surprised when men won't leave them alone,' he said. 'You can't lead a man on, then claim you bear no responsibility for the consequences.'

Tom was appalled. As was just about every woman in the country. Given the nature of the controversy, most politicians would have said something about their quotes being taken out of context. Then they'd have offered a wishy-washy apology. Not Cyril. He was unrepentant. 'The real people of Ireland know I'm talking sense,' he said. He also pointed out that while he and Tom were part of the same alliance, he was an independent and wouldn't be bossed around. 'You're not my leader,' he said, like a seven-year-old in a school playground.

If the controversy simmered on the airwaves, it threatened to boil over online. Cyril's opponents said this was what happened when the country was run by pale, stale males. Like Tess, they wanted him sacked. Today. An equally vociferous group supported him, dismissing his critics as the perpetually offended. A decent man was being subjected to a witch-hunt, they said. Whether he wanted it or not, Cyril Dinan had become a mascot for troglodytes everywhere. Vitriol dripped from the screen. Not for the first time, Tom was amazed by what people could write and walk away from.

Something else was nagging at him. He had thought of himself as a relatively young man. This debate, played out on social media, made him feel old. Unfamiliar terms and insults were thrown around. People used phrases like 'identity politics' and 'virtue signalling' and 'woke' until, frankly, he was lost.

None of this would have mattered if the government had been gelling well. It was in disarray. Cabinet meetings had turned into lengthy whinge-fests with everyone blaming everyone else for their shortcomings. Already there was talk of an early clearout of non-performing ministers. There was a famous political maxim: the worst day in power is better than the best day in opposition. This government was setting out to disprove it.

Challenging as Cyril the Dinosaur was, Tom's main

concern was Conor. Through the Templemorris bush telegraph, he'd heard about his friend visiting the garda station to look at old files. What those files were, he didn't have to ask. In a few minutes, Conor would be here. Tom would have to flim and flam and do his best to wriggle away.

Behind him, the rain was walloping against the window. It was, as they'd say in Kilmitten, a day borrowed from the winter. The summer recess was only two weeks away, and Tom was looking forward to a holiday. He longed for some sun. Vanessa had other plans. 'Now you're a minister,' she said, 'you've got to make it clear that you haven't changed. A photo of the family enjoying a holiday in Kerry or Donegal would help. You don't want anyone claiming you've lost the run of yourself.' Tom didn't agree. 'The recession's over,' he said, 'and so are the days of pretending to like the rain.' His wife then gave the example of Paddy O'Grady and the infamous trip to the Canaries. 'Ah, here,' he replied, 'you don't remember Paddy O'Grady. Were you even born at the time?' Vanessa reminded him that people had long memories.

Tom didn't have much time for reflection, but sometimes at night, after he'd run the next day's tasks around his head, he thought about the myriad ways in which the office was sucking him in. He'd grown accustomed to his life being arranged for him. He'd noticed that even those who claimed to hate politicians were slightly deferential in his presence. Others were totally sycophantic: 'Yes, Minister. Right away, Minister.' Then again, there were days when he wondered what in God's name he was doing, when he found himself battling nostalgia for his time organising community football leagues and drugs awareness seminars. This was one of those days.

Conor was early. He bounded into the room, hair in damp spikes, like a sandy hedgehog. While he'd never carried much weight, he looked thinner than ever. Tom knew Conor better than he knew his own family. He was trying to act casual, but falling short. His mouth was too tight, his movements too stiff.

'Some place you've got here,' said Conor, struggling out of his sodden anorak. 'I've seen smaller football pitches.'

'It's a bit OTT all right.'

For a little while, they talked about Cyril Dinan.

'You have to cut him loose,' said Conor.

'That's the plan. I'm meeting him later. We've got to convince him to resign. Unfortunately, unless we're smart, he'll become a martyr. Poor oppressed Cyril.'

Conor rearranged himself on the deep blue sofa. 'So . . .'

'So,' echoed Tom.

'The last day we met, I got the feeling you weren't too keen on my looking at the Father Galvin case.'

'I don't reckon there's anything to be gained by it. Simple as that.'

'That's a shame. I met Leo Galvin's family. They're good people. They deserve the truth.'

Tom sensed that he was being softened up for a revelation – or a question. 'The truth, Conor, is that we'll never find out what happened.' He got up from behind his desk. 'You know as well as I do that a lot of time and effort has been put into improving Kilmitten. Dragging up the past will only harm the reputation of the village. Nobody would want that.'

Conor's grey eyes narrowed. 'Three men being shot dead probably didn't help the Avondhu's rating on TripAdvisor, but nobody suggested we hush it up.'

'There's no need to be smart.'

'I'm being straight with you.'

Tom perched on the other end of the sofa. 'You went to look at the files.'

'Who told you that?'

'I have my sources.'

'Yeah, I did. Another look never does any harm.' Conor ran his hands along his thighs, as if steadying himself for what was to come. 'Ahm . . . Listen, I don't know if you're aware of this, but your father was one of the people who borrowed money from Father Galvin. He owed three hundred pounds. Not a whole pile now, but in the early eighties . . .' His voice trailed away.

Tom went to speak, then wavered. While in one way the news surprised him, in others it had the ring of truth. His father had always been short of cash. In those days, the petrol station had been quiet, and the house had been a sponge for money. He wondered if his mother had known about the debt. 'This is all news to me,' he said, 'but I hope you're not suggesting—'

'I'm not suggesting anything. It got me thinking, that's all.'

'Why mention it, then?'

'Because I thought you deserved to know.'

Tom thought for a moment. He wasn't sure if Conor genuinely suspected his father, but he guessed that more was to come. He had to take back the initiative. A height advantage would help. He stood up and patrolled the room. 'I've every sympathy for you, Conor. God knows, you've been through a lot. But what you're doing now is self-indulgent. It's like a vanity project. You can't do anything about the Burkes and the McPartlands so you've returned to a crime your father couldn't solve.'

Conor's response was immediate. 'It's not just "a crime". A man was killed in our village. In your house. And nobody has had justice. Noel O'Grady definitely wasn't to blame, by the way.'

'Suppose it wasn't O'Grady. That doesn't—'

'You know it wasn't.'

'No, I don't.'

'Yes, you do,' said Conor. 'Anyway, he had an alibi.'

'I wasn't aware of that.'

'You didn't have to be.'

'What do you mean?' Almost instantly, Tom regretted the question. He didn't want to hear the answer. His head was thudding. 'Christ almighty, man, give it a rest, would you? You seem to have this notion, based on the shakiest of evidence, that my father had something to do with Leo Galvin's death.'

'That wasn't what I said.'

'You said everything but. Now, just so you're clear about this, let me say it again: I don't know anything about any loan, but I swear to you, my father didn't kill Leo Galvin.'

'Do you know who did, then?'

Conor started talking about Tom's return to the house on the night of the party. Had he seen someone? Had something been wrong?

This, Tom hadn't expected. He felt as if he was hovering above the room. He was so light he might fly away. He didn't dare ask a question. He might reveal too much. 'That's bullshit,' he heard himself say. 'You're deluded.' He tapped his head. 'Crazy.'

'Calm down,' said Conor. 'The way you're going, they'll hear you next door.'

His voice was sharp. He was accustomed to these scenes. He was schooled in forcing information from reluctant witnesses. What an idiot Tom had been to think he could read Conor. The nervy, bumbling behaviour had been an act. A ruse. The thudding in Tom's head turned into a swarm of wasps. While he'd been wasting time on Cyril Dinan, Conor had been plotting.

'If this is an interrogation, aren't you meant to caution me or something?'

'It's not an interrogation. It's not even an investigation. I'm asking questions, that's all.'

'I can't believe we're having this stupid discussion.'

'Well, we are.'

'Actually, no, we're not. I'm tired, I've a lot going on and I'm running late for a meeting. I've got to convince a man to resign, a man who's too stupid to realise he did anything wrong. You can sit here for the rest of the day, if you like.

I've done my best to talk sense to you. If you don't want to listen, that's your lookout.'

Tom returned to the desk and picked up his jacket. The buzzing in his head intensified. Persistent bastards, those wasps. He was at the door before he spoke again. 'You know what, Conor? We've been friends for more than forty years, and I don't want to fall out with you. Truly, I don't. Let me tell you, though: if you think my father had anything to do with Father Galvin's death, you're wrong. As wrong as you'll ever be.'

Chapter 35

'Do I have to ask what you were doing?' said Flan, his first words since Conor had confirmed his visit to the station in Templemorris.

'I'd say you can guess.'

'I asked you not to go interfering.'

Conor held the phone away from his ear, like a teenager trying to avoid a dressing-down. He didn't need to hear the precise words. The disappointed tone, coloured by intermittent flares of anger, was enough.

'How did you find out I was there?' he said eventually

'I still know a few people.'

Tom told you, thought Conor. But why? Because he was scared?

After his father had hung up, he leaned back against the sitting-room wall and slid down until he slumped onto the floor. Thankfully, Sharon was at work. He was bone weary, his body hurting, as if he'd run a marathon.

What a mess he'd made of the meeting with Tom. What a total, gold-plated fiasco. He'd screwed up, rushing in, piling one question on top of another, making stupid assumptions like a half-witted beginner. He should have been more restrained. Not only had he antagonised the guy, he'd allowed him to slip from his grasp. He recalled the scene: Tom standing over him, head jutting out like a meerkat's, face saying a thousand things and saying nothing.

Conor's connection to the crime had impaired his judgement. He couldn't decide whether Tom's father owing money to the priest was significant or not. He was pretty sure that Tom hadn't been aware of the debt. At the same time, he was more convinced than ever that his friend knew something about Father Galvin's death. But what? And how? Had someone – one of his parents? – revealed that information? Or, as Nina believed, had he noticed something when he went back to the house? Like she'd said, though, it was no more than a hunch. A hunch based on a conversation that had taken place twenty-five years earlier. It was flimsy stuff.

Conor didn't see Haulie – genial, entertaining Haulie – as a killer. Yet he also reckoned that, when pushed, most people were capable of anything. He'd met more than one charming murderer. He'd met mild-mannered rapists. God-fearing smack dealers. Many otherwise blameless lives contained one violent incident. One rogue night. How he wished he could view Tom and his family dispassionately. In other circumstances, he might have chewed it all over with his father, but that was out of the question.

He thought of Nina. If anything, she'd looked worse than the last time they'd met: dead-eyed, gaunt, all her lustre stripped away. She'd chatted about her daughters, her parents, her brother, her job. She hadn't mentioned Julian. You didn't have to be a detective to suspect he was the problem.

The time ticked by. Conor remained on the floor, sorting through his own memories of 1982. In the days after the priest's death, Tom had walked around in a trance. He'd gone from insisting that the back door was locked to saying that maybe it was just stiff. The two of them had fallen out over the best way to explain the trail in the snow. Had Tom behaved like that because of what he'd seen? Had he been hiding something?

Get a grip, thought Conor. *You're kidding yourself.* Here he was, trying to attach meaning to a child's behaviour. To twist and mould it to fit his own theory. A man had been killed in Tom's house. His mother had discovered the body. The village had been ablaze with rumour. Of course he'd been shocked and distracted.

Apart from Nina, no one from Kilmitten supported Conor's interest. Sharon was increasingly impatient. Perhaps Tom was right. Perhaps this was a vanity project, a way of soothing his conscience over what had happened in the Avondhu. He'd seen three men shot dead and been powerless to intervene. The feud between the Burkes and the McPartlands rumbled on. The night before, one of Liam McPartland's nephews had been shot and seriously injured. The crime had knocked Cyril Dinan from the front pages. Cyril had resigned or, as one of the papers put it, been dispatched to the dinosaur graveyard.

Whatever Conor's motivation, he'd reached a dead end. For all his theories, he had nothing tangible. He was reminded of a case he'd worked on many years earlier, when he'd been stationed in Aghaflesk. A young woman named Rena Courtney had gone missing. While the official version of events was that her disappearance remained a mystery, local people were adamant that her boyfriend was to blame. The guards agreed. Unfortunately, the boyfriend's mother had provided him with an alibi. On the sixth anniversary of Rena's disappearance, her sister took her own life. All that was needed to break the chain of lies was one person courageous enough to say what they knew. Appeals didn't work. Neither did threats. Conor thought of Rena and the Courtney family now. The Galvin investigation was essentially the same. Even if no one was willing to tell the full story, there must be someone who could tell part of it.

He still believed Tom was that person.

For an hour, maybe more, he sat there. He thought over the case, his mind swinging one way then the other. He'd been arrogant enough to think he could roll back the years. That he could march in and – hey presto! – Tom would crumble, and all would be revealed.

How wrong he'd been.

Chapter 36

Dublin, December 2016

What got to Nina was the half-arsed nature of Julian's deception. If you're pretending to go on a week's golfing break with your friends, you should at least bother to pack your clubs. It was as if he didn't respect her enough to tell a convincing lie.

He'd bought a new suitcase – black, four-wheeled, expensive – and was upstairs filling it with summer clothes. In a couple of hours, he'd be off to Fuerteventura with his mistress for some pre-Christmas sun and sex. How they'd glow in those seasonal photographs. 'Stop it,' Nina said to herself. 'You sound bitter.'

She *was* bitter.

Through the staff room grapevine, she'd learned that Emer Dawson's marriage had ended. Noah and Coco's teachers were on guard for any sign of withdrawn or disruptive behaviour. A week or two back, Nina had seen Emer at the school gates. Like many of the mothers, she'd been trussed up in black Lycra. Despite the winter chill, she'd been wearing a sleeveless top, all the better for showing off her toned arms. Her hair had been in the sort of messy topknot that takes ages to perfect. Oh, and she'd had her lips done. They stood out like two slugs on her otherwise thin face. The two women stared at each other but said nothing. It struck Nina that while she no longer wanted to be with Julian, she didn't want this smug witch to have him either.

Over the months, she'd come to accommodate the affair. Julian knew that she knew. His disappearances became more frequent. His excuses dried up. Neither could bring themselves to acknowledge the situation. They still shared a bed. How pathetic was it that, after twenty-three years of marriage, she wasn't brave enough to ask her husband why he was sleeping with another woman.

The only fireworks had come from Bea. When she'd discovered what was happening, she'd tackled Nina. 'You can't let him treat you like this,' she'd said, her face bright with youthful certainty.

'You're right,' Nina had replied. 'I'll sort it out.' She'd done nothing.

Bea had also confronted Julian. He'd told her that life was more complicated than she knew and that one day she'd understand this. She'd called him a useless condescending prick and charged out. She'd returned the following day but continued to say little to either parent.

Nina hated to see Bea burdened by adult worries. Normally so calm, she'd turned into a ball of tension. She'd just started at Trinity and was learning to make her way in life. She should be out having a good time, making friends and falling in love, not sitting at home, listening to old Pearl Jam songs and radiating resentment. When Bea announced she was off to London to see her sister, Nina didn't protest. Although she could picture the two fulminating about the general uselessness of their parents, she hoped some space would help them to adapt.

At the end of the summer, Alannah had revealed that she wasn't coming home. Not yet anyway. 'I'm not quitting college,' she'd insisted. 'I'm taking a year out to make the most of an opportunity.' She was working as a minimum-wage gofer in a PR company. 'Interning', she called it. If you asked Nina, the Americanism was a distraction. 'It was called exploitation in my day,' she said. Alannah's stay in London was facilitated by the generosity of a friend's aunt, who was charging her a very low rent, and by a substantial allowance from home. None of this sat well with Nina, who wanted her daughter to come back and complete her degree. 'London will still be there in a year's time,' she said. If she was being honest, her irritation was part-fuelled by envy. Who wouldn't want to be twenty-one and living it up in London, your story yet to be written? She wondered if there was something sinful about envying her daughter.

Nina would have to talk to her mother. Her parents needed to be prepared for the end of her marriage. Not yet, though. At the moment, she wouldn't be able to cope with her father's disappointment. What would she tell them? Obviously she would mention the affair. But the end of her marriage was more complicated than that. Everything Nina and Julian would ever have to say to each other had already been said.

She felt bad about her parents. In her twenties, she'd pictured herself as a conscientious, capable daughter; someone who would look after her mam and dad in their old age. Yet here she was, as useless and ill-at-ease as she'd been in her teens.

She wanted to confide in someone, but didn't know who. Everybody seemed disgustingly content. 'Are you looking forward to Christmas?' they asked. What would they do if she told the truth and said she was dreading it? She thought of Conor. He'd always provided a sympathetic ear. Their last proper chat had been during the summer when he'd been asking questions about Father Galvin. Since then, she'd heard no mention of the case. She assumed he'd abandoned his efforts. She'd been close to calling him, then changed her mind. She didn't want to come across as needy, the friend who was always looking for something.

Now, as she paced the sitting room, Nina realised that she couldn't allow Julian to saunter off on holidays without a word of protest. Her birthday was in two days' time. She would be forty-eight. She didn't want to be forty-bloody-eight. The mad part was, she'd spent many of those years urging people not to make a big deal of her birthday. No cake. No party. No surprises. Faced with spending the day alone, she appreciated her mistake. She would have liked some fuss, after all. Well, not fuss so much as . . . companionship, solidarity, affection. Human connection.

Over the course of her marriage, Nina had become skilled

at turning a blind eye. But everyone has a breaking point. It was, she thought, like water dripping onto rock. Given enough time, the rock will wear away.

She went upstairs to find Julian finishing his packing. Without saying anything, she plucked his washbag from the bed and began tossing its contents around the room. His toothbrush landed in one corner, his shaving foam in another. His nail clippers went slithering behind the head of the bed. A deodorant whizzed past his left ear. Tempted as she was to fling it straight at him, she didn't want to risk giving the louse a black eye.

'Hey!' he said. 'Stop it, will you? I was about to pack those. I'm running tight on time.'

She lobbed a box of antacids against the wardrobe. 'Why are you pretending that this holiday is with the lads? I know you're going with her.'

'Ah, come on,' said Julian, 'this is stupid. Give me the bag.'

A tube of toothpaste sailed over his head. 'I asked you a question.'

'Okay, I'm going for a short break with her . . . with Emer. Now, can you quit acting like a kid?'

Nina picked up the prize-winning novel he'd been pretending to read and aimed it at the chest of drawers. She scored a direct hit on their wedding photo. It landed on the floor with a satisfying clunk.

'Do you know how much I gave up for you?' She was appalled by how congested, how faltering, her voice sounded. She couldn't allow herself to cry.

Julian bristled. 'For God's sake, Nina, this isn't the time for a scene. Sure we've got to talk, but not like this.'

She sent a box of dental floss, her final missile, zinging across the room and threw the washbag back onto the bed. 'I lost my best friend. I hurt the man who loved me. I embarrassed my parents. To this day, there are people in Kilmitten who look at me like I'm not to be trusted.'

'That says more about them than it does about you.'

'I gave up a lot.'

Julian was retrieving his toiletries. 'You did what you wanted to do. You were bored out of your mind and ready to move on. I provided an escape. Don't paint yourself as some saintly innocent.'

'I wasn't bored. That's not true. And I never expected that you'd treat me like this.'

'You're overwrought,' he said, as he bent to collect the shaving foam. 'We can discuss everything when I get back.'

Nina rocked on her heels. 'Stop patronising me. I'm not "overwrought", I'm angry. I have every right to be.'

He placed the bag, minus a couple of lost items, in the case and zipped it up. 'I didn't want us to end up like this. I'd like to sort everything out with as little fuss as possible.'

'What's that supposed to mean?'

'We both know our marriage is over.'

'I see. You want us to separate, so you can live with Ms Lycra Pants. Is that what you're saying?'

Julian lifted the case from the bed. 'This isn't the time to get emotional. I know it isn't easy, but we can talk about it all next week. We'll have to include Bea and Alannah too.'

Nina closed her eyes. She urged herself to sound strong. She didn't want to be whiny. She didn't want to be a victim. A loser. The scorned woman.

She opened them again. 'Do me a favour and give your mistress a word of advice.'

'I'm sorry?'

'Her lips are horrendous. No lie, they're the worst I've seen. If you paid for them, you should ask for a refund.'

Julian's mouth swung open. He looked at her as if she was mad. Perhaps she was.

Nina turned towards the door. She didn't want him to see her face. Like he'd said, this wasn't the time to get emotional.

Chapter 37

The phone call had taken Conor by surprise. 'I don't want to make a nuisance of myself,' a quiet north Clare voice had said, 'but I'll be in Dublin for a couple of days, visiting my daughter, and I was hoping we could have a few words.' Conor had reassured Hannah Galvin that she wasn't a nuisance and arranged to meet in a city-centre café. Chances were that she wanted to know if he'd made any progress. If so, she wouldn't like what he had to say. All the same, he had to hope that she had something else in mind.

That was why he was striding down Dame Street when he should have been in Kilmitten, paying his last respects to Mercedes Talty. Poor Mercedes had suffered a stroke while out doing her Christmas shopping. Conor's father had wanted him to attend the funeral. 'It'll only take a couple of hours,' he'd argued. 'You'll be back in Dublin before anyone notices you're gone.' Conor had shuffled around the request, lying about how busy he was. He couldn't give the real reason for his absence.

The city was in the grip of pre-Christmas mania, the streets crammed with shoppers and party-goers. Girls in skyscraper heels, lads in flimsy jackets, beleaguered mothers, befuddled men: they didn't walk so much as ooze. Stalls appeared, laden with wrapping paper, cheap perfume and fake designer handbags. The homeless were knocked to the periphery, forced to huddle back into doorways and hope that someone remembered them. That was Dublin: beautiful and tawdry, glittering and sad, all at the same time.

After his confrontation with Tom, he'd effectively given up on the Galvin investigation. He'd had little choice. All he'd managed to do was stoke up bad feeling and alienate most of his family.

Five months on, relations with Tom were strained. How could they be anything else? Based on no more than an old piece of paper and some wild supposition, he'd practically accused his friend of aiding and abetting a killer. Even so, Tom's revenge had been petty. Conor's father hadn't forgiven him for looking through the files. Every time they spoke, his dad found an excuse to rail against sneaky behaviour and disloyal children.

The previous day, Conor had seen Tom in the papers. According to one report, 'speculation was intensifying' that he would be one of the main beneficiaries of the upcoming cabinet reshuffle. He was being tipped for a move to the Department of Justice, an enormous achievement for an independent politician without a legal background. Underneath the news report, an opinion writer weighed in:

With his heartfelt yet rigorous response to the Avondhu Hotel shootings, Tom Crossan showed himself to be one of the few politicians with an understanding of the cancer eating away at our towns and cities. He also appreciates the challenges being faced by rural Ireland, while his decisive handling of the Cyril Dinan controversy proved he's not afraid to take tough decisions. A reshuffle this early in a government's term is unusual, but the time has come for bold, imaginative moves. The justice minister doesn't have to be a solicitor or barrister. The post should be filled by someone with common sense. Promoting the minister for rural and regional affairs would send a message that the government is serious about tackling crime, reforming the gardaí and tackling the miasma of sleaze that threatens to engulf public life.

'For feck's sake,' Conor had said, 'why don't you canonise the guy while you're at it?' The question had prompted an alarmed look from the elderly man standing beside him in the newsagent's.

When he arrived at the café, Hannah was sitting in the corner with a pot of tea, her neat white hair and beige polo-neck at odds with the seasonal gaudiness of her surroundings. In a world full of people clamouring to be seen, women like Hannah were an anachronism. They slipped through life, attracting little attention. Often, they were deceptively tough. They'd had to be.

'I thought we'd hear from you,' she said, as Conor sat down and signalled for a coffee.

'I'm sorry, I should have called.'

'Are you still interested in what happened to Leo?'

'I am, only it hasn't been easy. I thought I was getting somewhere, and then I realised I wasn't. I'm back at work, so I haven't had a lot of time.' He considered giving her some of the detail, then decided it wouldn't be fair to anyone involved. He sighed. 'I wish I'd more to say.'

'That's all right,' she said. 'I understand.'

Conor's coffee arrived, its bitterness surprisingly welcome. They were surrounded by Christmas excess. At the next table, a woman with a whinnying voice was having a phone conversation about handbags: 'I told you, Gerard, that's how much they cost. I don't know what decade you're living in.' On the other side, two young guys were comparing hangovers: 'Honestly, man. The. Worst. Ever.' They segued into a discussion about their plans for later in the day: 'Fitzy's home from Australia. It'd be a crime not to go for a few beers.' Clearly, nothing said Christmas like alcohol poisoning.

Hannah sat bolt upright, one thumb rubbing against the other. She opened her mouth, then quickly closed it again.

'Is there something else?' asked Conor.

'It mightn't be of any use to you.'

'That's fine. If it's not, no harm done. If it is, that'd be brilliant.'

'Fair enough. It's . . . it's something that's been on my conscience. I'm eighty-four and my health isn't the best, so if I don't get this off my chest now, there's a danger I never will.' Her thumb-rubbing continued, to and fro, back and forth. 'Gregory doesn't know I'm meeting you. And what I'm about to say . . . he doesn't know anything about that either. I'd prefer if it stayed that way too. My husband's a good man but he's very traditional in his views. He always was, and that's unlikely to change.'

Hannah's voice was low, and Conor strained to hear her above the hiss and bang of the coffee machine and the babble of customers. He stayed quiet. One ill-timed word might put her off.

'You see, Inspec— Conor, Gregory's family were very religious. In those days, most families were devout, but the Galvins were something else altogether. They went to Mass every day and said the rosary every night. It's a miracle they hadn't holes worn in the lino, they spent so much time on their knees. No one drank or smoked, and every spare penny was given to the Church or the Missions. Now, don't get me wrong, they were kind people, only – how do I put this? – there weren't many laughs in that house. You're too young to remember those days, but take it from me, life was hard. Water came from the well, electricity was a novelty and frivolity was frowned upon.

'I was sixteen when I started doing a line with Gregory. We married the following year, and with hindsight I suspect he saw a wedding as the best way to avoid the priesthood.' Conor must have looked shocked, for she quickly added,

'Oh, we loved each other. Don't have any doubt about that. We were only children, though. We should have waited.

'As was the way back then, at least one son was expected to join the priesthood. All going well, one of the daughters would enter a convent. With Gregory out of the picture, the pressure was on the next eldest son. That was Martin. When he was eighteen, he entered Maynooth. Everybody was delighted.'

Hannah sipped her tea. 'Then the story went sour. After three years, Martin upped and left. He ran away to London and rarely came home. His parents were devastated. And, to make matters worse, none of the girls was showing any interest in becoming a nun. We're talking now about the late 1950s, and there was a growing sense that life didn't have to be quite so drab. Even in Knockgreelish, we heard about the high times being had in London – and in Dublin. One by one, the three girls left home. Gregory was married. Martin was in disgrace. So the Galvins' ambitions were pinned on Leo.'

She stopped for another sip. 'You're probably thinking, *What's this old woman on about?* Aren't you? Don't worry, I'm getting there.'

Conor gave what he hoped was an encouraging smile. 'No. I promise you, I'm not. I've plenty of time.'

'Poor Leo. God rest him, he was never given a choice. He was going to become a priest, and that was that. His mam and dad bamboozled him into believing he had a vocation.' She gave her head a gentle shake. 'He should never have been ordained. I'm not saying he wasn't a good person – he was a great fellow – but he loved life too much to be tied to the Church.'

'For what it's worth, people in Kilmitten thought he was fantastic at the job.'

'I don't doubt it. He was impossible to dislike, was Leo.

'Anyway, about a year before he was killed, he came to me and said he wanted to talk. I should explain that, even though I was a few years older, we'd always been friendly. In some ways we were what you'd call kindred spirits. We both had faith but we asked questions too. I don't think it ever occurred to most people that priests could get lonely. I can still see him sitting in the kitchen with a mug of tea.' Hannah winced at the memory. Her thumbs resumed their rubbing. 'He told me he'd met a woman and that he was in love with her. I'll never forget the tears in his eyes. He was distraught.'

'What did you say to him?' asked Conor.

'Whatever I said, it wasn't enough. I asked him if he was sure. Honestly, though, I didn't have to ask. His love for her was plain. It was there in how he spoke about her. "What are you going to do?" I said. He told me he didn't know. He wanted to be with her, but even thinking about it was tough.'

'From what you've said about his mother and father, I can imagine how they would've reacted.'

'They would have been shattered. In that family, anything to do with sex outside marriage was taboo. The very idea of Leo having relations with a woman would have killed his parents. They wouldn't have understood that he was a man like any other.'

Conor thought of one of the letters in the Father Galvin

file, the one claiming that, during his time in the seminary, he had been too close to a woman. A single mother, the writer had said, as though this made the transgression even harder to forgive.

He took out his notebook. He wanted to write down what Hannah was saying. Head humming, he urged himself not to get carried away. That was what he'd done before. But this was different. The files contained no mention of an affair. 'I hope you don't mind?' he said, glancing at the notebook.

'No, no. You're grand. Now, where was I?'

'You'd—'

'Yes. So a few months later, in the autumn of 1981, Leo spoke to me again. He was still seeing her, he said. Opportunities for them to be together were few and far between, but something had happened – I'm not sure what – to make life slightly easier. I got the impression he was considering leaving the priesthood. No, not considering. I was convinced that was what he wanted to do. I could barely sleep for worrying. I toyed with the idea of telling Gregory, then realised I couldn't. He wouldn't have understood. Besides, I didn't want to betray Leo.' She hesitated. 'And, then, before we ever got the chance to talk about it again . . .' She tapered off.

'He was dead,' said Conor.

Hannah looked towards the window. The dull winter sun revealed the tears in her eyes, her pain as raw as the night she'd first heard the news. 'That's right.'

Conor thought of all the interviews where he'd wanted to

wrong-foot people, discomfit them. This was the opposite. He needed to placate and cajole. He spoke slowly. 'I'm sure this is difficult for you. Like I said, take your time. I'm in no hurry.'

She nodded, and a tear ran down her face.

After a minute or so, he took a deep breath. 'Did Father Leo ever tell you who the woman was?'

'He never gave me her name. He was careful not to. All I know is that she was from Kilmitten.'

Conor tried to hide his disappointment. 'And after your brother-in-law was killed, did you ever—'

'Did I ever think I should say something? I did. Believe me, I did. But I was scared. And I told myself that all I would do was taint a fine man's memory. You've got to understand – in the grand scheme of things, 1982 isn't that long ago. In other ways, it may as well be a thousand years ago. People were very quick to judge. They still are, except in different ways. Leo's family would have been inconsolable. Many others, in Knockgreelish and Kilmitten, would have shown no mercy. There'd have been an almighty rumpus. And for what? The guards were talking about money and gambling debts, so I convinced myself that what I knew wasn't important.'

'I see.'

'I remember on the day of Leo's funeral, sitting in the front pew, thinking, *She must be here.* I had a notion I'd be able to spot her, that somehow she'd stand out. But I was fooling myself. At one point, the bishop said something about Leo wanting to go to Africa on the Missions. It was hard not to stand up and tell him he'd got it wrong. That the man he was eulogising had intended to leave the priesthood and be with the woman he loved.' She stopped to wipe away a tear with the heel of her hand. 'I'm sorry.'

'There's no reason to apologise.'

As Conor would have expected, Hannah's tears were quiet, dignified. This was not a woman who would bawl and wail.

She reached into her handbag and took out a tissue. 'Afterwards, when Gregory's parents had died, I almost told him. I should have told him. But again I was scared. I mean, can you imagine discovering that your wife was such a deceitful person? May God forgive me, but I haven't even been brave enough to talk about it in Confession.'

'You can't allow yourself to think like that.'

She patted her face. 'Nowadays, there'd be no reason not to open up. Two adults falling in love? Most folks wouldn't be shocked at all . . . especially after all the scandals and the way all those lovely children were treated.'

Conor felt for her, one of the faithful who'd been shaken to the core by the revelations of recent years. Her entire story was grim. For thirty-five years, she'd carried this burden. Father Leo Galvin had broken no law, but the unpalatable truth was that many in his community would have found law-breaking easier to forgive. Drink-driving? Tax evasion? No problem. Loving a woman? Shocking.

Hannah put down the tissue. 'I should have talked to someone. I'll always regret that I didn't.'

'Listen to me,' he said, in his most emphatic voice,

'you're not to beat yourself up over this. What you've told me mightn't be important. But, if it is, you're not to worry. I won't get you into trouble. What matters is that you've told me now.'

While he spoke, she tore the tissue into narrow strips. Rarely had Conor encountered such a nervous witness. He wasn't sure he'd be able to keep the pledge he'd just made, but that was a worry for another day.

'Thanks,' she said.

'Is there anything else you remember about this woman? Anything at all? For instance, do you know if she was married? Did she have children?'

'Well, I do recall one or two things.'

'That's good,' said Conor. 'Tell me what you can.'

Chapter 38

After the burial, they gathered in small groups, shuffling from one foot to the other and rubbing their hands together. A thin wind whipped around them. Of all the places Tess had been, few were as bleak as the graveyard in Kilmitten.

'In fairness to Mercedes,' said Tom, 'she wasn't the worst of them.'

Tess fought back a smile. In her adopted home, this would be seen as begrudging. Unkind, even. Here, it was high praise. She'd decided to come back for the funeral following a call from her mother. Although she'd tried to sound upbeat, her sorrow was clear. Tess still found it strange to see her mam inside a church. 'I've learned to see weddings and funerals as rituals,' she said. 'In my head, they've no connection to the man who wanted to take you away.' The Mass was an elaborate production with a soloist, a harpist and a long eulogy from Mercedes' daughter, Liesl. Tess had half expected a medley from the deceased's beloved *Sound of Music*, but the current parish priest didn't approve of such fripperies. The sombre atmosphere was interrupted only by an outbreak of competitive coughing and a baby who could have wailed for Ireland. By the time the soprano had finished 'You Raise Me Up' (surprisingly not on the banned list), she was wiping away tears.

It was easy to be snide about Mercedes and her sidekick, Mags Moynihan. Looking back, though, Tess saw they'd been good friends to her mother when she'd had little in her life, apart from worthless men and a daughter who asked too many questions.

'You're right,' she said to Tom. 'When I was a kid, Mercedes and Mags were always in the kitchen, chain-smoking Rothmans and gossiping up a storm. I thought they were a scourge. But, bless them, they were hardy women, the last of the species. It's Mags I feel sorry for. I'd say she'd rather have lost her husband than her best buddy.'

Vanessa, who was attached to Tom like lichen to a stone wall, nodded. 'Mercedes' granddaughter, Paige, works for us. She's a smashing girl.'

'Are you allowed to come for a drink?' asked Tess. 'Or does government business call?'

'We-ell—' started Tom.

'It'd be rude not to pop up to Pilkington's for a quick bite,' said Vanessa. 'You don't have any official engagements this afternoon.'

'Maybe I can set aside the challenging task of providing broadband to needy rural communities for an hour or so.'

'Spoken like a pro,' said Tess. 'Anyway, aren't they as well off without too much internet? Growing up with just the two TV channels never did us any harm.'

Vanessa sent a puzzled look in her direction.

'She's joking,' said Tom.

His wife smiled, as if she'd known that all along. 'Did you hear that Tom might be on the move?'

'So Mam told me,' said Tess. 'All joking apart, well done, Tommo. Minister for justice, no less.'

'Ah, now,' he replied, 'it's only speculation. It might never happen.'

'If it does, you'll want to stay on my good side. Otherwise, I might have to tell the papers about all the laws we broke in our youth.'

'What? Oh, very funny. I'd say they'd be fascinated by the news that I once stole a Twix from Mangan's. Not to mention that I went an entire winter without a light on my Chopper.'

Around them, the huddles were starting to disperse. People were drifting towards the function room in Pilkington's where refreshments were being served. As they walked, the atmosphere grew lighter. Affectionate memories were exchanged. Plumes of breath rose into the air as friends told stories about Mercedes.

'If you do become minister for justice, it'll be a big deal, won't it?' said Tess. 'Like, you'll have to handle some heavy-duty stuff, including the gangsters who shot Conor?'

'Don't remind me. I'm not sure I want the stress.'

'Come off it,' she replied. 'I bet you'll love every second of it.'

Almost as soon as Tess had voiced the words, it occurred to her that he might be telling the truth. Vanessa must also have sensed this because she quickly changed the subject.

'Will you be back for Christmas, Tess?' she asked.

'I won't, I'm afraid. We're going to St Barths.' Aware that this must sound horribly flash, she raised her palms to the sky. 'I know, I know. There's something wrong about spending Christmas in the sun. But Miles likes to get away at this time of year. Daisy's excited too. Will you get a break yourselves?'

'Vanessa doesn't approve of leaving the country,' said Tom.

His wife gave him a sideways glance. 'That's not true. All I said was, you don't want to be seen swanning around the globe. Voters resent that sort of behaviour. Someone has to think of these things.'

'My heart goes out to you, Vanessa,' said Tess. 'Being married to a big chancer like Tom can't be easy.'

Truth to tell, her sympathies were in the opposite direction.

In Pilkington's, Tess sat with her mother, Flan and Lauren. Although the Christmas decorations were already in place, nobody could accuse the bar of getting carried away. Apart from some weary tinsel and a few crêpe-paper streamers, the room was unadorned. The dinner was borderline inedible: fatty pork, gruel-like mash and mushy carrots. And the gravy? Tess half expected the waiter to ask if she wanted one lump or two. Her mother gave her a poke and whispered, 'You're at a funeral. Eat up your dinner and don't be a brat.' Tess was tempted to point out that she was forty-eight years old and could do as she pleased. She took another slug of white wine and thought better of it. The wine reminded her of petrol, but at least it was plentiful.

Time passed by, the swell of voices filling the room. Ginny and Flan were with a gang of old-timers, reminiscing about the days when Mercedes was in her pomp. ('Do you remember when she took up line dancing? Or the Christmas she put up so many lights there was a power cut on Pearse Terrace? And what about the time she told Father Cleary to lighten up on the Hell and damnation because people's lives were hard enough and they didn't need that sort of thing on a Sunday?') Mags Moynihan alternated between tears and laughter, as did Mercedes' husband, Brendan. Cora Crossan, hair starched into place, was at the edge of the group. Haulie, wearing a jacket so loud they could probably hear it in Dublin, was there too. If ever there was a day for regurgitating old stories and reliving past glories, this was it. Tess suspected that if you offered people in Kilmitten the choice between a party and a funeral, most would choose the funeral.

Tom had forgotten about the high-speed broadband crisis and was at peak hail-fellow-well-met. After a showy goodbye and an invitation to visit their house 'any time, any time at all', Vanessa went to collect the boys from school.

People kept telling Tess how great it was to see her and how kind she was to make the journey. They asked about Daisy and Miles. They looked at the photos on her phone without once appearing bored. She had another glass of wine. And another.

She floated back into Tom's orbit. 'Any word from Conor?'

she asked. 'I remember you saying he'd been pestering you as well. About Father Galvin, I mean.'

'No. I haven't heard from him in a while.'

'That's a relief. I kept telling him there was nothing to be gained by what he was doing.'

Not only was it a relief, it was a surprise. Tess knew how tenacious Conor could be. It was unlike him to let something drop. Back in the summer, her mother had phoned to say he'd been nosing around the garda station in Templemorris. In recent months, however, she'd heard nothing.

'I thought he'd be here today,' she said. 'Flan did too. He rang at the last minute to say he was busy. Money-laundering, or something.'

'Oh. I didn't know. Like I say, I haven't really been talking to him.'

'Here, you didn't fall out, did you?'

'No, no, nothing like that,' said Tom, his voice too brisk.

Once again, Tess sensed there was more going on than she knew. She was about to ask when Haulie arrived.

'How's Conor?' he said. 'I heard he's back at work.'

'Good, as far as I know. They're allowing him to take it fairly easy.'

'I hope he hasn't returned too soon.'

'He's well able to look after himself,' said Tom.

Haulie raised a substantial eyebrow. 'No offence, Tommo, but that's not true. If it was, the lad wouldn't have got himself shot.'

Late in the afternoon, Tess found herself beside Emmet and Helen Minogue. As was her way, she gave Emmet her best supermodel smile. After all these years, she should be indifferent towards the man who'd turned her away from his house. She should be too mature too care. But she wasn't. She wanted to say, 'You see this navy blazer, Emmet? It's Alexander McQueen. Now, that mightn't mean a lot to you. But it was very, very expensive. I store it in the dressing room of my listed mansion where I live with my multi-millionaire husband and my impeccably mannered daughter.' Thankfully, she wasn't quite drunk enough to come out with any of this. She reminded herself that Nina's mother had been complicit in Emmet's behaviour, yet for some hard-to-pin-down reason she was easier to forgive.

'It's a shame Nina isn't here,' said Helen, choosing to forget that a quarter of a century had passed since her daughter and Tess had been friends. 'She'd love to see you.'

Despite her promise to Conor, Tess hadn't contacted Nina. If asked, she had a convoy of excuses lined up and ready to go: she'd been too busy; Daisy had taken up all her time; she'd been involved in a project in the village; she'd lost the number. None of this was true. She had thought about making the call. What she'd said to him about not liking Nina wasn't true. She didn't even know her. Save for a few brief meetings, their encounter in the hospital included, they hadn't spoken in years. Call Tess a coward, but not lifting the phone was easier. Once they'd exhausted the basics – parents, children, Kilmitten – they mightn't have anything to say. The piece of paper containing Nina's number was gradually turning to lint at the bottom of her favourite handbag.

Helen was staring at her, expecting a reply.

'Ahm . . . Isn't it Nina's birthday this week?' she said.

'Yes, it's tomorrow. And the poor thing will be on her own. Julian's on a golfing trip, and Bea's gone to visit Alannah in London.' Helen twirled her wine glass. 'I do envy your memory. Imagine you remembering Nina's birthday.'

'The mad thing is, I can recite the birthdays of half of our primary-school class. Ask me for more recent dates, and I'm lost.'

Helen smiled. 'Daisy's not with you, is she?'

'No, she's at school. I was tempted to bring her, but a full-blown village funeral might have been too much. She'd be standing here now, saying, "Mummy, if a lady is dead, why are these people having such a good time?"'

'She sounds like a wise girl.'

'She frightens me she's so smart. As Mam says, "She's as sharp as a needle, that child."'

Helen asked about Conor. Tess gave her standard response about his life slowly getting back to normal. Then she mentioned his meddling in the Father Galvin case. 'I think he's got over it,' she said, 'but it was such a pain for Flan, which meant it was a pain for Mam too.'

She would have liked to continue the conversation. Unfortunately, Emmet appeared with his coat on one arm and Helen's on the other. 'It's time we made a move,' he said. 'Hugh and Gráinne want to drop down and pay their respects. They need us to watch the children.'

'Well, it was lovely to see you, Tess,' said Helen. 'I'll tell Nina we had a chat.'

'Do that, and, ahm . . . wish her a happy birthday from me, would you?'

By now, it was dark outside. Tess figured she'd probably had enough to drink. Everything was pleasantly blurry, the sound less distinct. She ought to find her mother and head home. She needed to call Daisy. And Miles. Then she did an about-turn: if ever there was an evening for more, this was it. She rarely had the opportunity to get drunk. Not like this, at any rate. Whatever their faults, at least Kilmitten people knew how to hold a funeral. Fond as she was of the English, they were terrible at funerals. Shocking. She could never understand why they waited a week, sometimes more. By then the momentum was gone. The ceremonies were limp affairs too: all meandering hymns and weak handshakes. No, when Tess's time came, she wanted a send-off like Mercedes'. Long Mass, lumpy gravy and lethal white wine included.

She was returning from the bar, where a man she hardly knew – Charlie Murray? Murphy? Molloy? – had insisted on buying her a brandy, when she met them. Two of them. The worst two: Seánie and Noel junior. A brace of O'Gradys. Age had given their ugliness an extra dimension. Seánie's suit trousers were at half-mast while Junior's face had turned the colour of smashed plums. They were as brash, as effortlessly obnoxious, as ever.

'There she is,' said Seánie, 'too stuck-up to say hello to her old school friends.'

Junior gave a joyless laugh. 'You'd think now she's knocking on a bit she'd lose the airs and graces.'

'I'm choosy about the company I keep,' said Tess.

'Is that a fact?' said Seánie. 'It didn't stop you from whoring around the globe for the best part of twenty years. There you were, in the papers with one fellow, then another. Your mam must have been mortified. Mind you, I've heard that, back in the day, old Ginny was good to go herself.'

Bile seeped into Tess's mouth. She shared a father with these men. They were her family. Her brothers. No, Conor was her brother. The only brother who mattered. She'd imagined that success had inoculated her against the O'Gradys. She'd been wrong. Sweat collected on the back of her neck. Her stomach tightened. In half an hour, her head might be full of caustic put-downs but, in that instant, all she wanted to do was tell the truth. She wanted to say, 'Your father raped my mother, and I'm ashamed to be related to you.'

A hand touched the small of her back. 'Is something up?'

She looked around and saw Tom. 'I . . .'

'Lads,' he said, 'do yourselves a favour and fuck off home. This is a select gathering. Mercedes always said you were a bunch of thugs. I doubt she'd want you here.'

'Thugs, is it?' said Noel junior. 'You're one to talk. Why don't you give one of us a dig, like you used to in the old days? That'd go down well with your pals above in Dublin. It'd put an end to your political notions, anyway. Uncle Paddy must be rolling in his grave, watching a scumbag like you get a job in the cabinet.'

'Come on, Tessy,' said Tom. 'We'd better leave them be. We don't want to attract an audience. They'd only get a kick out of that. It'd be the first time in years that anybody listened to them.'

'Thanks,' she said, turning away. 'I think you lost a couple of votes there.'

He placed an arm around her. 'Jesus, you're shaking. You shouldn't let them get to you. They're a pack of clowns. Nobody around here takes them seriously.'

'If only it was that simple.' Her voice wobbled.

Two stern lines appeared at the top of Tom's nose. 'I'm going outside for a smoke. Do you want to talk about it?'

Tess drained her brandy glass. 'Actually,' she said, 'I think I do.'

Chapter 39

Conor barely slept. Over and over again, he asked himself if Hannah Galvin's story was significant. If she'd come forward in 1982, would the information have made a difference? His every instinct told him that he needed to ask more questions.

He explained what he was doing to Sharon, who felt he should wait.

'Give it a week or two,' she said. 'What Hannah told you won't change.'

'In two weeks, Christmas will be here. And Tom will probably be the minister for justice.'

'So? This isn't about Tom. It's about Father Galvin and the woman, whoever she was.'

'It's still about Tom.'

It was also about his dad. Conor was scared of detonating another explosion. He would have to move with caution.

When he called in sick to work, there wasn't a word of complaint. His hero status remained intact, and he could probably coast for another year before anyone protested. That was the problem. He'd become a totem. A mascot, who looked good in the pictures but wasn't allowed to tog out for the team. Before the shooting, he'd got to see a bit of life, no matter how rancid that life could be. Now his superiors had him hemmed in behind a desk, shuffling paperwork and making pointless phone calls. He suspected his colleagues didn't trust his decision-making. They worried that he'd crack under pressure. Although the flashbacks had become less frequent, they hadn't gone away. For no reason, he would find his head back in the Avondhu. He couldn't quite see the room, but he could hear it all: the screams and the persistent *pop, pop, pop, pop, pop.*

By comparison, everything felt trivial. Well, almost everything.

He drove west under what Sharon liked to call a Turkish Delight sky: here a wash of lemon, there a streak of pink. On the road, he prepared a speech. He was conscious that Ginny was mourning the sudden loss of Mercedes. He also knew that his father wouldn't be around. Flan was in Limerick helping Lauren move into a new apartment. Conor's task would be altogether easier without the old man's presence.

Ginny's greeting was guarded. 'Is something wrong?' she said, before quickly adding, 'I'm sorry, Conor. I don't know where my head is. Come in, come in. It's good to see you.'

'Everything's grand,' he said, as he removed his coat and unwound his scarf. 'It's just . . . there's something I've got to talk about.'

'You do know your father's not here?'

'That's no bother. I can talk to him later, if needs be.'

'I was about to make a coffee. Do you—'

'Coffee would be brilliant,' he replied. 'Honestly, Ginny, there's no reason to fret.'

'It's unusual, though, you turning up in the middle of the week like this.'

'I would have called but . . . it's a long story. I've learned something new about Father Galvin and I want to run it by you.'

'It's as well your father isn't here, so,' she said, filling the kettle and spooning coffee into two flower-patterned mugs. In Kennedy Crescent, coffee was resolutely old-fashioned. There would never be a fancy machine in this house.

While Ginny cut thick slices of fruitcake, they talked about the funeral. And about Tess.

'I know she's a grown woman and can do whatever she wants,' said Ginny, 'but she had far too much to drink yesterday. I don't know what possessed her. Tom was the same. You'd think he'd have more sense. When we left Pilkington's, they were outside, smoking cigarettes like a pair of teenagers.'

Conor thought he detected envy as well as disapproval in her voice, but he let that pass. 'Do you know what they were talking about?'

'Something and nothing, I'm sure. If you'd been here, you could've joined them. I don't want to sound like an old woman, but you've got to take care of your friends. Mercedes would have said that.' Ginny paused. 'Actually, now that I think about it, she wouldn't have been so sentimental. She'd have said, "I may as well pal around with you because no one else will have either of us."'

'Poor Mercedes,' said Conor, his mind elsewhere. He worried that Tom and Tess had been talking about him.

'Then this morning,' said Ginny, thoughts still focused on her daughter, 'she announced that rather than flying home from Shannon, like she was supposed to, she wanted to go to Dublin. "I can get a lift into Limerick with Flan," she said, "and hire a car there." I told her to be sensible and get the train, but she claimed people would stare at her. "I guarantee you, Tessy," I said, "every last person on the train will have their head stuck to their phone. They're like zombies. The Queen of England could sit down beside them and they wouldn't notice."'

'What did she say to that?'

'She got narky with me, told me she knew what she was doing.' Ginny poured water into the mugs and gave a vigorous stir. 'I sometimes forget how famous she was.'

'She still is. I don't know if you can ever turn off that level of fame. Have you any idea why she wanted to go to Dublin?'

'I'm afraid I don't. You know how airy-fairy she can be. "Just something I've got to sort out," she said.'

Ginny splashed milk into the coffee and handed Conor a mug and a plate of cake. 'Dig in.'

Her words had become stilted. No doubt, she was trying to work out why exactly he was there.

He drank his coffee and looked out onto the back garden. Save for the grass, everything was brown. The sun was resting above the fence. At this time of year, it barely rose above the horizon before disappearing again, as though embarrassed by its own weakness. Thin streams of smoke rose from nearby chimneys. Outside, the air was laced with the smell of turf.

'So,' he said, 'I presume you're wondering what's brought me down this way. Like I mentioned, it's to do with Father Galvin.'

Ginny, who was leaning against the kitchen counter, tipped her head to one side. 'Given that you couldn't make it home for the funeral, we'd assumed you were very busy. Obviously, you still have time for a spot of unofficial work.'

Touché, thought Conor. 'In this case, the work came to me. Hannah Galvin rang me, so I met her yesterday.'

'What relation was she to Father Leo?'

'Sister-in-law. She's Gregory's wife.'

'Is that miserable old bastard still alive?' Ginny raised her hand, as if trying to stop traffic. 'And before you accuse me of being uncharitable, you've no idea how much trouble that man caused your father. Him and his "public inquiry". I'll never forget the interview he did with Nina Minogue's husband. I don't care how much he suffered, there was no call for that type of nastiness.'

Conor outlined what Hannah had told him. He'd thought he was well prepared, but Ginny was a step ahead, reading his words in a way he hadn't intended. Her expression hardened, and the network of fine lines around her eyes deepened.

'Hang on a minute,' she said. 'You're not suggesting that I'm the mystery woman, are you? Honest to God, Conor Varley, I can't believe you'd come into this house and—'

'Woah,' he said, 'relax, Ginny. Of course I'm not – (a) I would never have suspected you of being involved with Father Galvin, (b) even if I had, I wouldn't bring it up like this, and (c) the mystery woman, as you call her, was married.'

Ginny fidgeted with the hem of her navy sweatshirt. 'Ah, I see. That's all right, then. Forgive me, I spent too many years in this village being looked down on and treated like I was the root of all evil. You can't blame me for being paranoid.'

Not for the first time, Conor marvelled at his stepmother. He remembered how, as a child, he'd considered her very pretty. All the boys had. As they'd grown older, she'd had a starring role in many a teenage fantasy. In more recent years, Conor had seen photographs from her twenties and early thirties. It was no exaggeration to say she'd been every bit as dazzling as her elder daughter. And yet, according to Tess, Ginny had gone through periods of numbing depression. She'd lain in bed, too overcome by sadness to do anything with the day. It was only with hindsight, Tess said, that she appreciated the depths of her mother's trauma.

He wondered if Ginny had ever had counselling. Probably not. Back in the 1970s, anyone complaining of mental-health problems was in danger of being sent to the county psychiatric hospital where they'd be locked up and sedated. Had she sought help, her daughter might well have been taken away.

Ginny walked over and sat at the other end of the table. 'So, you reckon this may be important? That an angry husband might have had reason to attack Leo Galvin?'

'That's about it, yeah. As you know, I looked through the files. There was never any mention of an affair.'

'And you're certain Hannah Galvin's telling the truth?'

'Why would she lie? The easiest thing to do would be to keep on saying nothing.'

'I get why you'd want to discuss this with Flan, but why are you telling me?'

'At the moment, I'm not entirely sure what to do. Do I continue to pursue the case, or do I hand the information to the guards in Templemorris? One way or another, it might affect you – and Dad.'

'You mean, if the case is reopened, people will realise that O'Grady wasn't guilty?'

'Mmm.'

Ginny cradled her coffee mug while she thought. 'Answer me this,' she said eventually. 'Why do you think Hannah's come forward now? She could have broken her silence at any time, but she didn't.'

'The self-serving answer is that she seems to trust me. The more honest one is . . . she mentioned something about her health not being great, and I guess she's thinking of her mortality. She doesn't want to go to the grave with this on her conscience.'

Ginny grimaced, and Conor wanted to hide under the table. 'Forgive my lack of tact. I know you're upset about Mercedes.'

'When one of your friends dies, it's a fairly brutal reminder that life doesn't go on for ever. Up until recently, I'd never given much thought to death – just getting by took up most of my time.' She put down her mug. 'Your father's different. Well, of course, he would be, given how young your mother was when she died. That must have changed your outlook too.'

'I suppose. Mind you, I was probably too small to feel the full tragedy of it all. Paula had the more difficult time.'

This was only partly true. Although he'd been young, Conor hadn't forgotten the void left by his mother's death. She had died in the wrong way at the wrong time, and that was something you never got over. 'Anyway,' he said, 'Hannah's almost twenty years older than you. And Mercedes, she was a lot older too, wasn't she?'

'Ten years.'

'I guess what I'm trying to say is, I don't think of you as old.'

Ginny smiled. 'You're starting to redeem yourself.'

'Do you mind if I ask you something?'

'Go on.'

'Do you ever think about what you might have done with your life if it hadn't been for Noel O'Grady? I've seen the photos. You could have been every bit as famous as Tess.'

She looked down and made a small sound, softer than a full sigh. 'That's such a hard question to answer. When I was younger, I did think about what I could have been or where I might have travelled. Not that I'd have wanted Tess's life. Well, the money would have been nice. But not the fuss – I wouldn't have liked that. But, yes, there's every chance my life would have been different. I wouldn't have stayed in Kilmitten, for starters.'

When she looked up, Conor was taken aback to see that her eyes were wet. He thought again about how a life can twist on one night. One act of violence.

'Don't mind me,' she said. 'So many good things have happened too. Daft and all as she is, I wouldn't trade Tess for the world. Or your father. Or Lauren.' She brushed away a tear. 'Or even you.'

'I don't know what the old man would have done without you.'

'Me neither.'

They both laughed.

'So,' said Ginny, 'before I get all maudlin, did Hannah know anything else about this woman? The fact that she was married doesn't make the list of contenders much shorter. Apart from me, almost every woman over the age of twenty was either married or widowed.'

'She'd only one other piece of information. Father Leo got to know the woman because she did the flowers in the church.'

Ginny licked her lips in concentration. 'I'm afraid no one comes to mind. You're asking the wrong person. Other folks will know, though.'

'True, but I'll have to tread carefully. That's if I tread at all.'

They heard the front door open.

'Oh, hell,' whispered Ginny. 'I hope you're ready for this. I hadn't expected him for hours yet.'

From the hall, Conor's father roared, 'I'm back. Is that Conor's car outside?'

'It is,' she replied.

'What's going on?' he said, as he entered the room.

Ginny rose from her chair. 'Sit yourself down there, and I'll get you a coffee. How's Lauren's new flat?'

'I don't like the look of this. You're not here making a nuisance of yourself again, are you?' he asked Conor. 'You couldn't be bothered coming down for the funeral of one of our best friends, but you sneak in when I'm not around. If this is about what I think it is . . .'

Conor reminded himself that his father's temper, like his framing of Noel O'Grady, was based on his love for Ginny. 'Listen to me, Dad, there's no need to get worked up.'

Ginny patted her husband's arm. 'Please, pet, sit down and I'll make that coffee. I reckon you should hear what the lad's got to say.'

Chapter 40

The car smelt of new upholstery and Christmas tree air freshener. Neither was helping Tess's hangover. Once upon a time, her powers of recovery had been legendary. She'd been able to party all night and pose all day. Today, she felt wretched, like a squashed badger at the side of the road. Still, she'd made up her mind. She'd hired the car, changed her flight and called Willowthorpe to let them know what she was doing. She couldn't back out now.

She flicked on the radio. The guests on a news programme were having an aimless discussion about the expected cabinet reshuffle. 'Tom Crossan is definitely ready for promotion,' said a man with a voice so deep Tess could practically hear his jowls.

'Ha,' she said. 'Let me tell you, all he's ready for today is a fistful of Solpadeine and a litre of 7 Up.' She changed channels and caught the first few bars of 'Fairytale Of New York'. Nope. No Christmas songs this morning. Her poor head couldn't bear them. She remembered the year the song had been released. Still new to modelling, she'd been seeing an actor called Darren Hunter. Gorgeous as he was, poor Darren had been completely untalented. The last Tess had heard he was managing a DIY shop in Croydon. Another hop, and she arrived at one of those stations where every song is performed by a hyperventilating twenty-year-old. 'Get over yourself,' she said to the radio. And, yes, she did know she was talking to an inanimate object. She also knew that her twenty-year-old self would have been outraged at the suggestion she was too young for genuine pain.

Tess drove on in silence. She found the motorway strange. To her mind, roads like this belonged in England, Germany or America. She missed the villages with endearing names, community Lotto signs and slightly wonky Christmas decorations. On the plus side, the dreary towns and traffic bottlenecks were gone too. She'd be in Dublin before she knew it.

The funeral had been a reminder of all she loved and hated about home. She'd been hypnotised by the warmth, the stories and the men in stiff suit jackets who boasted about their age: 'I'm eighty-five myself, but you know Paddy Chambers? He's ninety-six. Ninety-six!' Then the other Kilmitten had slammed into her. The O'Gradys had provided a reminder of how shabby and bleak the place could be.

She'd told Tom everything about her mother and Noel O'Grady. He would never have guessed, he said. She explained how Flan had duped Julian Heaney and how, until recently, Conor hadn't known. Then she made him swear not to tell anyone, not even his wife. He said it wasn't the type of thing he'd discuss with Vanessa. He thanked her for trusting him. She said she should have told him years ago, that he was one of her closest friends and deserved to know. 'That's why you got so worked up about Cyril Dinan,' he said. 'Now I understand.' By then, they were crumpled from too much drink and too little food. They sat in the smoking area for another hour or more, the cold draping itself around them. From time to time, others came out, sent them a funny look, then walked away again.

She'd done most of the talking, and Tom had been a great listener. It was only now, with a slightly clearer head, that she realised she'd talked too much. Not that she regretted what she'd said, more that she'd missed her cues. On reflection, she saw that Tom had also wanted to speak and, blabbermouth that she was, Tess hadn't given him enough space.

On the outskirts of Dublin, she pulled into the car park of a small shopping centre, the kind of place that didn't contain any actual shops, just fast-food joints and bookmakers in boxes of concrete and plastic. The sky was quilted with white. She opened her bag and took out her phone.

Nina's hair had always been troublesome but in her forties it had become a total fright. She'd developed a cowlick on the left side to match the one on the right. Oh, and her roots needed doing.

'You're being ridiculous,' she said to the haggard woman in the mirror. 'It's only hair. What does it matter?'

Nina had been blindsided by Tess's call. She'd been on her lunch break and, not recognising the English number, had assumed one of the girls was ringing to wish her a happy birthday.

'Hello, love,' she'd said. 'How are things?'

'What a greeting,' Tess had replied. 'And things aren't great. I've got the hangover from hell. At least Mercedes went out in style.'

Nina had burbled something about the unknown number.

'I'm in Dublin,' Tess had continued. 'Your parents said you were on your own, so I thought I'd say hello. May I come visiting?'

What could she do but say yes?

It was six o'clock now, and Tess was due at any moment.

While Nina made another attempt at taming her hair, she urged herself not to stress. They'd have a drink. A chat. Nothing heavy. She wouldn't say anything about Julian. She'd make light of being on her own. 'I'm not a birthday person,' she'd say. 'Never have been. You know that.' Come to think of it, Tess hadn't mentioned her birthday. Well, she wouldn't have remembered. Why should she? That Nina remembered Tess's birthday – the ninth of November – was neither here nor there.

What else wouldn't she say? She definitely wouldn't reveal that she was in the middle of the worst bout of self-recrimination she'd ever experienced. She wouldn't say that she spent every blessed minute thinking about what she should have done differently. That she should have been more assertive, more engaged, more interesting.

The truth was, she'd always been dull. Her conversation

had always been pedestrian. As the years had passed, she'd lost her enthusiasm for sex. She wasn't good at intimacy of any sort. That was why she didn't have more friends. No wonder Julian had sought out other women.

She wouldn't say that she was barely holding it together. That controlling a class of twelve-year olds, never mind teaching them, took all of her strength. That she worried Bea and Alannah considered her a useless mother.

'Stop it,' she said. 'You're behaving like a fool.'

Of all weeks, why had Tess chosen this one?

Perhaps it wasn't too late to put her off. Nina could call back and say, 'No, sorry, I can't meet you after all. I've got a migraine, toothache, leprosy.' She could say, 'I've managed without your friendship for twenty-five years and I don't need it now.'

The doorbell rang.

Damn.

She ran the brush through her hair one last time.

Although Tess appeared tired, it didn't take away from her elegance. She was wearing a dark green coat, cashmere by the look of it, and a striped scarf. She was carrying a large black box and a bottle of champagne.

'Forty-eight, huh?' she said. 'Happy birthday.'

As she spoke, needles of icy rain started to fall.

Nina wanted to say, 'Thank you.' She wanted to say, 'Come in. Please, come in.' When she opened her mouth, all that came out was a silly little sound. *Glug.*

Then she began to cry.

*

'You see,' said Tess, 'in a way, the unorthodox welcome was kind of handy. Otherwise we would have spent ages doing the whole ice-breaking thing. Instead, here we are. I've seen you covered in snot. You've seen me gaping like a particularly dim fish. Oh, and I know all about your lowlife of a husband.'

'You were always good at accentuating the positive,' said Nina, her eyes like raspberries, her face shiny as a new coin.

Tess had sat and listened as Nina, heavy tears rolling down her face, had sobbed her way through the story of Julian and his mistress. What a pitiful sight she'd made, her shoulders shaking, her self-belief in smithereens.

Initially Tess had been embarrassed. She should have had more sense than to turn up with a bottle of champagne and a vulgar present, like Lady Bountiful spreading alms among the afflicted. She wanted to do a swift about-turn and run back to her hotel. She could have a long bath, a sound night's sleep and pretend this hadn't happened. Well, obviously, she would have to display a little more tact. She'd make her excuses and ask Nina to give her a call when she was feeling better. Then she realised that while her visit might not count as divine intervention, it was pretty close. She said as much to Nina, who apologised for making a fool of herself.

'I should have made dinner for you.' She sniffled.

'Relax,' said Tess, doing her best to sound like she knew what she was doing. 'This isn't the time to worry about trivia. Do you not have takeaways in Ranelagh?'

That was how they ended up at the kitchen table, eating prawns bhuna and drinking a bottle of Moët. Tess liked Nina's kitchen. It was warm and colourful. An old-style bulletin board was festooned with pictures of the girls. A dresser was laden with handmade pottery. If she was nit-picking, she'd say the room was too narrow, the pine cupboards old-fashioned and the appliances out of date. But this wasn't the time to be picky.

She swirled a piece of naan bread around her bowl. 'If you don't mind me saying so, Nina, Julian's got you so ground down that you can't see clearly. Your thinking's all wrong.'

'What do you mean?'

'First off, you can't allow him to stalk back in. You've got to change the locks.'

'I can't do that. What about Bea?'

'Tell her what you've done and give her a new key.'

'But what about—'

'Julian? Who gives a monkey's? Let him go and live with his fancy piece.' Tess took a swig of champagne. 'Or – didn't you say he was a landlord? – let him spend a few weeks in an unheated bedsit with a gang of noisy students next door and a drug dealer down the h all. Some mould. A rat or two.' An uncomfortable thought popped into her head. 'Here, you don't want him back, do you?'

'God, no. There are rules, though, Tess. This is his house too.'

'Rules, my eye. Jesus, woman, why do you have to be so bloody reasonable? Stop it. Lose the head a bit. Treat him like he deserves to be treated – like the cockroach he is. And, yeah, I know he's the girls' father, and you don't want to upset them, but girls these days are smart. A lot smarter than we were. They'll understand.'

'You're right about that,' said Nina, with a snuffle. 'I think Bea went to London because she was annoyed with me for being a doormat.'

'That's a shame. She'd be better off staying here to support you.' Tess pushed back her hair. 'I'm sorry, Nina. I'm hectoring you, and I shouldn't. You've got to make your own decisions. I'm trying to sound like I've got all the answers when I haven't.'

'Thanks,' said Nina, in a tiny voice. 'I feel so stupid. I remember how keen I was to organise other people's lives, including yours. And there I was, making a hames of my own.'

'We all do stupid things.'

'Some of us have a particular gift for it.'

'You want to hear about stupidity? I married a total idiot called Aaron Grace. Very pretty guy. American. Unfortunately, he was so thick he kept confusing Ireland with Iceland. He once asked me why I didn't look like Björk. Thankfully, the marriage only lasted five minutes.' Nina went to speak, but Tess batted her away. 'I once went AWOL when I was supposed to be filming a TV commercial. The perfume company said they'd never have anything to do with me again. I lost a fortune, as did my agent. I had a spell in rehab too. Did you know that? "Exhaustion" was the official explanation. The truth is, I was hooked on anti-anxiety drugs. I loved them so much I'd started hallucinating.' Tess picked up her glass. 'By the way, I'm being selective here. I've done plenty of things that were even dumber and sleazier.'

'All right, I'm not alone in my stupidity.'

'You loved Julian. You didn't love Tom. What could you do?'

'It wasn't as simple as that. I did love Tom. Looking back, it was as if being loved by someone from Kilmitten wasn't enough. I wanted an outsider to love me. To approve of me.'

'Beware the glamorous stranger,' said Tess, pouring some more champagne. The bottle was almost empty. 'Not that I ever followed that advice myself.'

'So much frightens me,' said Nina. 'Every day, no, every hour a new fear pops into my head. Most of them are practical. Will we have to sell the house? What'll my parents say? And then . . . then there are all the other fears. The mad, intangible ones. You know what I found myself wondering this morning? I wondered if I'll ever desire someone again. Or is that part of my life over?' She raised a hand. 'Don't worry, I don't expect an answer.'

For a short while, they ate in silence.

Eventually, Tess spoke. 'I almost forgot. I brought you a present.' She bent down and picked up the black box. Earlier, her choice had felt inspired. She was less confident now. Nina might not get the reference. She might find the gesture condescending.

Carefully, Nina removed the red ribbon and lifted the lid. The box was crammed with lipsticks, eyeshadows, contour kits, moisturisers, exfoliants, eye creams and every imaginable unguent.

Tess swallowed. 'Happy birthday. My way of saying . . .

Actually, I'm not sure what I'm saying. For some reason, I was thinking about—'

'London,' said Nina, picking out a nail polish and passing it from hand to hand. 'Shepherd's Bush, 1987. You and your bag of make-up.'

'I'm getting sentimental in my old age. I'll have to stop going to funerals.'

Nina returned the nail polish to the box. As she did, her face contorted and her sobs returned. Great heaves of unhappiness passed through her thin body. 'I'm sorry,' she kept saying.

'Stop it. Stop being sorry.' Tess removed a wad of tissues from the box on the counter, but they no longer seemed adequate. She had a quick look around and her eyes alighted on a clean tea towel, which she thrust in Nina's direction. Then she walked around to the other side of the table and kissed her friend's head. 'What are we like?' she said.

Presently Nina's tears eased. The tremors continued, though, and when she tried to eat, the fork clanged against the side of the bowl. She drank the last of her champagne. 'I don't have any more of this, I'm afraid, but there's a bottle of wine in the fridge.'

'That'll do nicely,' said Tess. 'I'll get it.'

She filled two glasses. Despite everything, she thought, there was still a distance between them. Like most people, she had romantic ideas about friendship. She believed that real friends would always find each other again. But normal friendships had an ebb and flow, not a twenty-five-year hiatus.

'This mightn't be the best night to raise this,' she said, 'and I know it was a long time ago, but you must have had questions about the way I reacted to your break-up with Tom.'

'I expected you to be annoyed,' said Nina. 'And, then, after the piece in the paper about Flan . . . well, I thought you might bawl me out of it. I wouldn't have blamed you for getting angry. I was angry myself. But, straight up, I didn't expect years of silence.' She gave a resigned shrug. 'At some point along the way, I accepted that we'd grown apart. It happens. After all, what did we have in common? I was a teacher with two small kids, changing manky nappies and watching *Teletubbies*. You were in New York, partying with movie stars. It would have been strange if we'd remained close.'

'Do you really think that? I still saw Conor and Tom.'

'Conor's part of your family.'

'Even so, there were times when keeping in touch did take a bit of effort.'

'I assumed I wasn't worth the effort.'

'That sounds awful. It was more complicated than that.'

Tess put down her glass and smoothed her fingers across her forehead. She wouldn't say the floodgates had opened. Out of deference to her mother, this would be the last time she spoke about it. But she'd told Tom, and Nina deserved to know too.

'When I wrote to you, I also told you that I'd discovered who my father was.'

'I remember,' said Nina. 'Julian was convinced it was Father Galvin.'

'If only.' For the second time in as many days, Tess began her mother's story.

Chapter 41

'If you'd known, what would you have done?'

His father had been asking questions for half an hour or more, so many questions voiced in such quick succession that it felt as if they were bouncing off the magnolia walls. This was the first time Conor had lobbed one back.

'I would have taken the information very seriously. The shame is that Hannah Galvin didn't come forward at the time.'

'So,' said Conor, 'you agree the affair might have given someone a motive?'

'I do, but that's a long way from proving that Father Leo was killed by a jilted husband.'

'Ah, Dad, give me some credit, would you?'

His father made a harrumphing sound. Ginny sat between them, lips slightly parted, the adjudicator in their tug of wills.

Conor started again. 'I'd stopped looking at the case. But when I heard Hannah's story, I had another think. And, yes, I'm well aware that this isn't easy for either of you. That's why I'm here. I didn't want to take it further without your blessing.'

His father's face was opaque. 'I won't deny that it's interesting. It's still one woman's version of what might have happened more than thirty years ago. That's all you've got.'

'Not quite all.'

'I don't follow you.'

Conor told them about Nina's conviction that Tom was holding something back. Then he gave a judiciously edited version of their meeting.

'Could you not have left well enough alone?' said his father. 'You went barging in on a hunch. Is that how you carry out enquiries, these days?'

Conor was about to give an abrasive response, but stopped himself in time. There had always been a danger that this would turn into a row about who was the better investigator. The trouble was, travelling that route would only deepen their disagreement – and take Conor further away from where he wanted to be. He changed direction. 'By any chance, do you remember who looked after the church flowers in the early eighties?'

'As a matter of fact, I do. It was Peggy McGoldrick.'

'Oh.' A vague memory of the late Mrs McGoldrick fluttered into Conor's head. He recalled a tight white perm, a black headscarf and a shuffling walk. He tried to suppress his disappointment.

'That's right,' said his dad. 'Peggy, a woman so old Haulie Crossan used to claim she could remember the Famine. She had chronic arthritis, she wasn't at the party, and she died twenty years ago.'

'At the risk of stating the obvious,' said Ginny, 'I can't

really picture poor Peggy having a mad, passionate affair with Father Galvin.'

Conor shifted in his chair. 'Was there anyone else? Anyone who might have deputised? Say she went on holidays, who did the flowers then?'

'Holidays?' said his father, his voice hitting the ceiling. 'The likes of Peggy McGoldrick wouldn't have known what a holiday was. If she got a day trip to Knock, it was the highlight of her year.'

He was right. Save for the wealthy few, proper holidays were almost unheard of until the 1990s. A weekend staying with cousins was as much as most people had hoped for.

'Did Peggy always do the flowers?' asked Ginny. 'What about weddings? Or christenings? Even in those days some folks liked to decorate the church for their big day. They might have wanted something more elaborate than Peggy would provide.'

'There's a question,' said Flan. 'I'm nearly sure the florist in Templemorris did the odd wedding and then . . .' He stopped. 'There was someone else. Helen. Helen Minogue did wedding arrangements.' His gaze shifted between Conor and Ginny. 'Don't go jumping to conclusions now. Please.'

'I won't,' said Conor. That was a lie. Already his mind was leaping, his heartbeat accelerating.

'Even if Helen did have some sort of relationship with Leo Galvin, that's no reason to get ahead of yourself and assume it led to his death.'

'Of course not.' *Another lie.*

'Helen always kept a beautiful garden,' said his dad. 'She still does.'

Conor nodded. 'Hannah Galvin mentioned something else. She said that in the autumn of 'eighty-one, the woman's circumstances seemed to change. After that, Leo was able to see her slightly more often.'

'And?'

'We started secondary school in the autumn of 'eighty-one. Nina went to boarding school. As I remember it, she hardly ever came home.'

'Hugh was at home, though. And Emmet didn't go anywhere.'

'But Emmet was very busy. In those days, doctors still did lots of house calls. He was here, there and everywhere. And Hugh was only a little boy. It would have been easy to pull the wool over his eyes. Nina would have been more likely to notice anything unusual.'

'I suppose.'

Conor looked at his dad and then at Ginny. For all that his father hadn't wanted the case reopened, he was too good a policeman, too good a person, to shut this down without thinking it through. 'Do either of you remember ever seeing Helen and Leo Galvin together?'

'No,' said Ginny, 'but that doesn't mean much. Just say I had seen them. Unless they'd been draped around each other, I wouldn't have considered it odd. It's a small village. Everybody talks to everybody else. There's not much choice.'

'Can we go back a step?' said Flan. 'If Tom Crossan did have information, important information, why didn't he say so?'

'If I knew that . . .' said Conor

'. . . you wouldn't be sitting here.'

'Precisely.'

'A few months ago, when he gave you the brush-off, what did you think? Honestly now, did you reckon he was keeping something from you?'

Detecting a thaw, Conor spoke softly. 'I did. And the more I thought about the night of the party, the more suspicious I became.'

'How well I remember the pair of you telling me about the carry-on in the shed. The small heads on you. You were petrified. And to prove what a funny old world it is, this time tomorrow, Tom will be the minister for justice.'

'The reshuffle isn't for a few days, surely.'

'No, I was listening to the radio on my way back from Limerick. They reckon it's been brought forward to tomorrow on account of there being so much speculation. It's all become a distraction apparently.'

'I see.'

His father stroked Ginny's hand. 'I'm surprised to hear myself say this, but I think you should ask some more questions.'

'I agree,' she said.

Relieved as he was to hear this, Conor didn't know how to proceed. There was no easy course of action. He could talk to Tom, but at what cost? He'd screwed it up the last time, why would he succeed now? This wasn't a game of Cluedo. He couldn't keep guessing until he got it right. The first time they'd spoken, he'd had surprise on his side. The next time, Tom would be prepared.

Conor considered talking to Helen Minogue. But what

would he say? 'Hello there, Helen. How's Nina? As I have you there, I heard a rumour you were involved with Leo Galvin. Did Emmet find out? Is that what happened?' If he wasn't careful, he would ignite a ferocious row. He thought of Nina. How would she react? What would she say? What would she want him to do?

The other option was to go to the guards in Templemorris and present them with what he knew. They could then pass the information on to the Serious Cases Review Team. While, strictly speaking, this would be the correct course of action, it might cause unnecessary trouble for his father. Why make it official, unless he had to?

Of course he could walk away. This had all become so fractious, so personal, that turning his back might be the best thing to do. But Hannah Galvin had come forward because she trusted him. He pictured her, so small and slight she looked as if a sudden gust could lift her up and deposit her down the street. She'd made a hard decision. She deserved his best effort.

Round and round the questions went, crowding out all other thought.

Outside, the light was dimming.

Conor attempted to strip away the nonsense. He reminded himself that what he wanted was the truth, simple as that. Oh, who was he fooling? There was nothing simple about getting to the truth. There never had been. But all he could do was ask.

'Right,' he said, 'if I'm going to have another chat with Tom, I'd better do it soon.'

Chapter 42

It had been a long day, far too long for someone whose head felt as if it was filled with porridge. Never had Tom been so glad to return to his Donnybrook apartment. He removed his shoes, loosened his tie and put on the kettle. His throat was flannel-dry, and he needed tea. A sturdy brew with plenty of milk, the type of tea he'd grown up with.

An early cabinet meeting meant he'd left home before six. The session had throbbed with a last-day-of-school air. Colleagues had swapped pointed jibes, and there'd been more than one bout of over-enthusiastic laughter. They all knew that change was on the way. The question was: how soon? A reporter had called Tom, claiming the dogs in the street knew the reshuffle would happen the next day. 'Haven't you noticed?' said Tom. 'There aren't any dogs on the street these days. They're all on leads and in kennels.' An hour later, the confirmation came. The taoiseach's private secretary asked if Tom could meet the boss at nine in the morning. An outsider might imagine that running the country would sate any man's desire for power, but the boss liked to control everything. If he could keep his ministers – and ambitious back-benchers – guessing for another few hours, he would.

Tom would be first in, which was how it should be. If the reshuffle wasn't to his liking, he could withdraw his men from government. He could sink the ship and precipitate a political crisis, maybe even an election. Not that this was likely: he'd already been sounded out about the Department of Justice. The taoiseach had raised it ten days earlier after a cabinet sub-committee meeting on Brexit. 'Hypothetically speaking,' he'd said, 'if I offered you Justice, would you be interested?'

Tom had paused before reciting some appropriate lines about enjoying the complexities of his current brief, then adding, 'If, however, an even greater challenge was to come my way, I could hardly turn it down.'

The boss boomed on about how Tom had seized the initiative on the Avondhu attack and on Cyril Dinan. Then he spoke about his background: 'Your own family being victims of crime,' he said, 'and your best friend getting shot while serving the state, you should make sure people don't forget about these things. Nowadays, it's all about empathy. Voters want to think you can relate to their suffering.'

Tom nodded. 'I get you.'

'And, of course, if you were to find yourself in Justice, you'd have to get tough with the gardaí. I don't know what they're doing, but too many serious crimes aren't being solved. Every day of the week, I have to listen to people complaining that the gangsters are getting away with it. We keep being told that witnesses are scared to give evidence. That has to stop.'

'Indeed,' said Tom, as the boss walked away.

A series of low-level arrests and a few well-publicised seizures of cash and drugs had drawn some of the sting from the feud, but the main players remained out of reach. Neither had there been any let-up in the supply of drugs. Paige had told him that, in Templemorris, buying a bag of heroin was no more difficult than buying a bag of potatoes. Without wishing to sound pompous, Tom thought of the Department of Justice as the natural culmination of everything he'd done. Okay, it did sound pompous, but that didn't make it untrue. When rivals had been warming their backsides in solicitors' offices or coining it in the courts, he'd been running community campaigns and persuading young guys to make something of themselves.

Eyebrows were being raised about the timing of the reshuffle, with critics inside and outside government claiming it was too soon. 'The current lot are only in their jobs five minutes,' went the complaint. 'They should be allowed a bit of time.' Tom didn't agree. An overhaul was needed. Doing it now meant that ministers with new portfolios would have the Christmas break to read themselves into the brief. He'd expected more of a fight from the current justice minister, but word had it that he was in line for a sinecure in Brussels.

So, that was great then. Everything was in place.

Except it wasn't.

Tom didn't want to move to the Department of Justice. He wasn't certain that he wanted to stay in his current job either. He didn't want to spend his days fighting fires and chafing against bureaucracy. He didn't want to traipse from meeting to function to photo opportunity. He disliked the way everything had become regimented, sterile, formulaic. He couldn't stand how the deference was sucking him in. He'd enjoyed being a constituency TD. But this? Jesus, he hated it. And it was only going to get worse. The more he saw, the more he appreciated his limitations. He was a figurehead. A guy who looked and sounded convincing on the telly. *But what about the power?* people would ask. Tom had no power. If he proposed anything radical, his colleagues and his civil servants would squash him like an ant under a size-twelve boot.

The problem was, he'd left it too late. He'd played the game too well. Dropping out of the cabinet wouldn't be like dropping out of UCD, as tough as that had been. His parents would be upset. Vanessa would be incandescent.

He couldn't back out now.

The kettle clicked off. Tom made his tea and settled into the squeaky leather sofa. From the black suite to the outsize lamps to the chrome and glass table, the furnishings were completely soulless. The pictures – grey and purple abstract prints – looked to have come from a bankrupt hotel. Nothing about the apartment was to his taste, but he was paying only a token rent and couldn't complain.

His whirlwind day – and depleted brainpower – had left him with insufficient time to think through Tess's revelations. It had never occurred to him that Ginny might have been raped. He remembered hearing about Noel O'Grady's death, all of them sitting in that miserable London pub, bickering about home. How little they'd known. Familiar as Tom was with political scams and strokes, he was stunned by the way Flan and Ginny had got their revenge. 'I suppose we'll never know who did kill Father Galvin,' Tess had said. At that point, Tom should have come out with a bland statement of agreement. Instead he'd come close to telling the truth. One more drink and he might have done. It had been years since he'd felt a compulsion to talk about the night of the party. Even with Vanessa, he'd never been tempted to tell the full story. There was something dangerous, though, about getting drunk with an old friend, especially one who'd just revealed a huge secret. The urge to say, 'Me too,' was overwhelming.

Tom hadn't asked his father about the loan from Father Galvin. He hadn't needed to. His father had done nothing wrong. By the sound of things, the priest's lending operation had been harmless, more credit union than Ponzi scheme.

As justice minister, he might be pressed to reopen the Galvin case. If somebody within the gardaí made that decision, he doubted he'd be able to stop them. It was unlikely they'd get anywhere.

Tom leaned back into the leather. He'd go to bed soon. Tomorrow would be hectic, and he could do with a solid night's sleep. He allowed the milky tea to wash down his throat. Smoking all those cigarettes hadn't been wise. He didn't smoke any more. Correction: he didn't smoke in Kilmitten. Or in the presence of Vanessa. In Dublin, he did as he pleased. Tess didn't smoke any more either. 'Except when I'm really desperate,' she'd said. 'Like now. If I get lung cancer, I'll blame the O'Gradys.'

Vanessa hadn't been happy about his extended stay at the funeral. She'd met him at the door. 'The state of you,' she'd said, over and over again. The fact that he'd been with Tess had deflated her anger a little. Vanessa would travel up to Dublin in the morning. She didn't want to miss the big day. The boys had to go to school but they'd been there when he first became a minister, and the occasion had gone over their heads. Tom's parents and Dympna were also making the journey. Eamon would stay at home to mind the garage. 'We could do with a day out,' his dad had said, 'and it'll give the ladies a chance to get my Christmas box.' Tom had considered inviting Conor but decided against. While their friendship hadn't been sundered, it was under strain, and he figured Conor would see through the cynicism. He wouldn't want to become a photo opportunity.

Tom took another slug of tea. A wave of weariness swept over him. He would rest his eyes for ten minutes. Then he'd definitely go to bed.

How long he'd been asleep, he couldn't say. Perhaps an hour. Perhaps a few minutes. Long enough for his neck to go stiff. He'd been woken by the jangling of his phone, which was beside him on the sofa.

'Go away,' he said. He knew it wasn't Vanessa: they'd spoken before he'd left town. His parents rarely called after nine, so it was unlikely to be them. It was probably his press officer. Or a journalist from one of the morning shows. Or someone looking for something. Too many people had his number. He'd have to address that. The phone stopped. No message. That was good.

Almost immediately, the damn thing sprang to life again. Tom remained in a stupor. He ought to get up and go to bed. Eyes gummed together, he squinted at the screen.

'Ah, hell,' he said, before deciding he'd better answer. 'Conor?'

'Uh, howarya? I hope I'm getting you at the right time.'

'It's the middle of the night.'

'It's ten past ten.'

'Oh.' Tom stood up, and in doing so, knocked over his half-full mug of tea. 'Shit.'

'Sorry?' said Conor.

'Ah, nothing,' replied Tom, stepping into the puddle of tea. He asked his default question: 'What can I do for you?'

'I was hoping to have a word.'

'You're having one.'

'I meant a proper word, face to face.'

'When?'

'What about now? I'm downstairs.'

'You're not serious?' Tom resolved that when he did get a new number, he wouldn't give it to Conor. Old friend or not, the guy was becoming a menace. 'For feck's sake, man, I was about to go to bed. I don't know if you've heard, but I'm kind of busy.'

'That's why I wanted to talk to you.'

Tom thought for a moment. The problem was, if he didn't invite Conor in, he'd spend the rest of the night worrying.

Hearing him out would be easier. 'All right,' he said. 'I'll buzz you up. But my bed's calling. Last night was a late one.'

'So I heard.'

A couple of minutes later, Conor was in the apartment. His face was pink from the cold, and there was a sprinkling of sleet on the shoulders of his anorak. With barely a pause for breath, he ran through a string of platitudes about the reshuffle. In return, Tom gave a version of his well-rehearsed speech about the challenges of the job.

You liar, he thought. *Conor's your best friend. Why can't you tell him the truth? Why can't you admit that you want your old life back?*

They touched on the funeral. Tom said he'd spent much of the evening talking to Tess, but didn't say what about. Short of looking at his watch, he did everything possible to make his impatience clear. Finally, Conor took the hint.

'I appreciate you seeing me like this,' he said, 'although I've a feeling that when you hear what it's about, you'll tell me to get lost. What I'd ask—'

'Ah, Christ,' said Tom, 'not again.' Here he was, brain mangled, one sock wringing with cold tea, and Conor wanted to play Columbo. 'Do we really have to do this now?'

'I've learned something new about Father Galvin, something that could explain what happened. Before I take it any further, and I will have to take it further, I want to discuss it with you.'

'Okay. Once you understand that I don't have all night.'

'Hopefully, it won't take long.' Conor rubbed his hands

together. 'First things first, though. Is there any chance of a cup of tea? I've just driven up from home, and it's a foul old night.'

Tom wondered why Conor had been in Kilmitten. He presumed he'd soon find out. 'You know where the kitchen is. Make me one too, would you? I'll be back in a minute. I, ahm, need to change my socks.'

'No bother,' said Conor, his tone almost absurdly breezy. 'While I'm at it, I might put on some toast. I could do with a bite. Will I put on a slice for you?'

'Um, yeah, fine.'

While they ate, an artificial calm descended. They sat across from each other: Tom in his favourite position on the sofa, Conor in one of the enormous armchairs. Tom told himself that he wouldn't be cajoled or coerced. Whatever Conor had to say would be finished by eleven thirty, midnight at the latest. There would still be time for a decent night's sleep. He wouldn't think about politics or Vanessa or his parents or anyone else. What mattered was what happened in this room. How he handled it. How he handled himself. If anyone knew how to say the right thing, it was him.

'So,' said Conor, 'on my way back up, I gave quite a lot of thought to what I wanted to say. I know you don't trust me, and I was thinking, well, I could get all tricksy here. I could play games. Instead, I'm going to tell you about the conversation I had with Hannah Galvin, Leo Galvin's sister-in-law. No embellishments. No flashy stuff.'

'I know who Hannah Galvin is.'

'Sorry. Of course you do. What you probably don't know is that she was very friendly with Father Leo. In fact, upon reflection, I wonder if she wasn't in love with him herself.'

'Come again?' said Tom.

'Ah, don't mind me. I'm getting ahead of myself.'

Tom listened closely while Conor went through what Hannah had told him. There was no denying it: her story rang true. Even so, all she had were isolated conversations. Little parts of a picture. What Tom knew might belong to the same picture. Or it might be part of a different puzzle.

'Obviously,' Conor was saying, 'I was disappointed not to have a name. What I did have, though, was the information about the church flowers. That's one of the reasons I was in Kilmitten today. I had to find out more.'

The rhythm of his words reminded Tom of when they were children. Of how Conor would get a fixation – with Liverpool statistics or building a new den or making the most of ten pence worth of sweets. Then he'd approach his obsession from every angle. He would talk it all through, as if by doing so he was convincing himself.

When Tom tuned back in, Conor had moved on to Peggy McGoldrick: 'Remember Peggy with the limp? God rest her, she wasn't exactly affair material, so I knew I'd have to look elsewhere. Could there have been another woman who did the church flowers?'

Despite his reassurance about not playing games, that was exactly what Conor was doing. He was teasing Tom, telling a tale but drawing back before the punchline. Tom was reminded of the fable about the scorpion and the frog.

The frog is carrying the scorpion across the river when his passenger stings him. 'Why did you do that?' asks the frog. 'Now we'll both drown.' The scorpion says, 'I know, but I couldn't help myself. It's in my nature.' That was Conor. Even though reopening the Father Galvin investigation meant hurting his family and friends, he couldn't help himself. It was in his nature.

Tom folded his arms, told himself to stop thinking about scorpions. 'Listen, I'll be straight with you. I don't know where this is going. What Hannah told you is very sad, but it's no more than a theory. Now the time is ticking on, so maybe you should get to the point.'

Conor nodded. 'I wouldn't blame you for being sceptical. The last time we spoke I got it wrong. I admit that. You deserve an apology. So does your father, come to think of it. What I'm doing here is laying everything out in front of you. I want you to see where I'm coming from.'

Tom went to speak, but Conor was more forceful. A slight flick of the hand, as if dismissing a gnat, and he continued: 'Since last summer, I've been saying to myself, "Tom saw something – or somebody – and decided to keep schtum. Did he see the priest's body, was that it? Or did he see something more? Did he see someone else in the room?" I've been trying to figure out why you'd stayed quiet. Well, to begin with, you must have been confused. Scared too, I'd imagine. You were twelve years old, for God's sake. And twelve-year-olds nowadays are much more grown-up than we were. I mean, we were still reading comics and climbing trees. Then, when you'd had time to consider the repercussions, you must have concluded that saying nothing was the smartest approach. After all, people would question your motives. They'd ask why you hadn't said something before. They might suspect you had a score to settle.'

Tom flinched. He hoped it hadn't been obvious, yet feared it had. 'We've been through this before,' he said, 'so tell me—'

Conor wouldn't give way. 'And in more recent years, you may have thought it was too late. Besides, Noel O'Grady was carrying the can. You knew he wasn't a killer. But, hey, let people believe what they want to believe. Isn't that right?'

'If O'Grady was blamed in the wrong – and I'm not saying he was – it was your own father's doing.' Conor was bobbing and weaving, but Tom had landed a punch. 'Tess told me,' he explained. 'Yesterday.'

'Did she give you the full story?'

'If you mean did she tell me he'd raped her mother, yeah, she did.'

Conor clasped his hands together. 'I spent most of the day talking to Dad and Ginny. When I told Ginny about Hannah, she gave me her blessing to ask more questions. Dad was the same. We might disagree on a lot of things, but whatever the old man did, he did for good reasons. Like you.'

Tom snorted.

'Anyway, let's go back to the church flowers. It turns out that, while she wasn't a regular fixture, Nina's mam used to do the flowers on big occasions. To be blunt about it, she had a lot more style than the likes of Peggy McGoldrick.

She still does. These days, someone like Helen would go to art college or write for a glossy magazine or run one of those style blogs. Back in the seventies and eighties, though, having a husband with a well-paid job was meant to be enough. Women like Helen weren't supposed to have ambitions beyond looking after their family. Only can you imagine being married to Emmet Minogue? Granted, he's got more finesse than Noel O'Grady. And a lot more money. But, Jesus, what a boor. All those years, above in his surgery, looking down on the rest of the village. The way he treated Tess and Ginny was terrible. And he was never mad about you either, was he?'

'That hardly matters,' said Tom, his voice annoyingly feeble. What he was hearing was familiar and strange. Right and wrong.

Conor didn't react, just resumed his monologue. 'Who would blame Helen if she did have an affair with Father Galvin? Actually, that sounds tawdry and, judging by what Hannah told me, there was nothing tawdry about their relationship. They were in love. Nina had been shipped off to that god-awful boarding school, which gave her mother a little more freedom. Leo was on the verge of leaving the priesthood. Perhaps the two were making plans for a life together. So, what happened? Did Helen get careless? Did Emmet find out?'

Increasingly, Tom felt as if he was trapped in a twilight place. He was taking everything in, but didn't know how to react. Twenty-four hours earlier, he'd been ready to talk, but the circumstances had been different. He forced himself to speak. 'With the greatest respect, you haven't a clue whether any of that's true.'

'I can find out, though. I can ask. On my way back to Dublin this evening, events began to connect. I got to thinking about Emmet Minogue and his reaction to Father Galvin's death. Do you remember – of course you do – how we went up to the house the following day? He was adamant that whoever was to blame must have come in from outside. That put the frighteners on us. I was terrified Dad would find out what we'd been up to. And you? There was hardly a peep out of you. You were in a bad way. He's a clever fellow, is Emmet. If he took so much trouble to spin his story to a bunch of kids, presumably he did the same with everyone else. Not, of course, that it worked. Once the guards knew that we were to blame for the footprints, they had no reason to believe the killer came from outdoors.'

'Again,' said Tom, his throat tightening, 'that doesn't mean anything.'

'You're right. Maybe it doesn't. But, like I say, all I can do is ask. And, believe me, I will.'

'Fine, but why are you telling me all of this tonight?' Tom looked at his watch. 'It's nearly twelve o'clock. I've listened to you, but I've got a full day tomorrow. I—'

'Because I still think you saw someone that night. Oh, and by the way, so does Nina.'

'What?'

'That's one of the awkward things about all of this. Up until today, she was the only person to give me any encouragement. She didn't fall for the O'Grady line either.'

Conor leaned forward. 'But if I was running a proper investigation here, I'd be starting to suspect that the person you saw was Emmet Minogue. Was he near the body? Or, more likely, was he walking away? Does that explain why you saw him, but he didn't spot you?'

Tom told himself that the time had come for turning on the theatrics. He ought to be dismissing Conor's statements as fantasy. The deluded ramblings of someone who'd lost all perspective. He ought to say he'd heard enough. But he couldn't. He was paralysed.

'So I have this information and what I need, Tom, is for you to help me out. This time I don't think I've got it wrong. But I'm not infallible either. What I'm looking for is a nudge in the right direction.' Conor paused. 'We didn't get to do Latin in St Ursula's – it wasn't that sort of school – but we all have a few phrases. There's one on the front of the Bridewell, near the Four Courts. You probably know it already but, if not, you're likely to come across it in your new job. *Fiat justitia ruat caelum*: let justice be done though the heavens fall. Now, I'll be honest with you, I've always considered that a wee bit overblown. Despite what some people think, I'm the same as every other cop. I've cut a few dodgy deals in my time. I've ignored skulduggery because my priorities were elsewhere. Sometimes justice isn't clear-cut. My father knew that. That was why he felt free to do what he did. But he was disillusioned. He was convinced the truth would always be out of reach. Thanks to Hannah Galvin, it doesn't have to be.'

Tom was listening, but not listening. The years had fallen

away. His head – no, not just his head, his entire body – had returned to 1982. To a winter's night even colder than this one. He saw the priest's legs, then his head. He saw the person leaving the room. He saw it all as clearly as if it was happening now. It was imprinted on his brain and would never be erased.

'No doubt,' said Conor, 'you've convinced yourself that what happened thirty-five years ago doesn't matter. But it does. I'll have to report what Hannah told me. Emmet and Helen are likely to be questioned. Perhaps Nina, too, for fear she remembers anything. Let's face it, they're bound to suspect Emmet. If his wife was about to leave him, he had more reason than anyone to attack Father Galvin.'

Tom was rocking back and forth. There was a fast flapping high in his chest. 'Stop it,' he heard himself say. 'Stop it.'

'Why?'

'Because you've got it wrong.'

The flapping became quicker.

'What do you mean?' asked Conor.

'That wasn't what happened.'

'Oh, I think it was.'

'No,' said Tom, his voice too high, too thin. 'It wasn't Emmet Minogue I saw leaving the room. It was Helen.'

Chapter 43

Conor took a long, shuddering breath. In front of him, Tom was sobbing, his head bowed, his body trembling. What were they going to do? What was *he* going to do? Of course, he'd known it was possible that Tom had seen Helen. He just hadn't considered it likely. Every part of him had said, 'It must be Emmet. It's got to be Emmet.' Once again, he'd been wrong.

He scrambled for alternative explanations. Suppose the priest had already been on the floor when Helen had reached the back kitchen? Suppose she'd panicked and dashed back to the front room? But if that had been the case why hadn't she raised the alarm? Why had she left the discovery to Cora Crossan? No, whatever had happened, Nina's mother had been to blame. Conor asked himself if Emmet knew. He didn't think it likely.

One lamp didn't give enough light for the entire room. The place was grey, airless. It was quiet too, the only noise coming from Tom's hiccups and whimpers. How strange to see his friend in tears. Even as a child, Tom hadn't cried. Sometimes he'd got angry. Sometimes he'd sulked. But only once before had Conor seen tears in his eyes. He recalled that night in Pilkington's: Tom raw from his break-up with Nina, the O'Gradys taunting him, Seánie falling to the floor.

Although he felt he should do something, Conor was unable to move. His body was rigid, his mouth soldered shut. In a few hours, the man on the other side of the room was due to become the minister for justice. He'd be in charge of the police, the courts, the country's security. It would, Conor reckoned, be a popular appointment. He was a popular man. But what if people knew he'd suppressed information that could have solved a serious crime? That he'd done so for more than thirty years? And that, because of it, a family's suffering had been prolonged?

If the truth emerged, there would be ructions, not just a regular political ding-dong but a genuine scandal.

Conor should have given it all more thought. He'd been so obsessed with proving his theory that other considerations had given way. What he needed now was to hear Tom's explanation. Asking questions wouldn't be easy. Conor wasn't in an interview room with a conscience-free drug dealer or a young scrote who'd pulled a knife during a robbery. He was with someone he'd known since he was six years old.

'*Jesus*,' he said, the force of his own voice taking him by surprise.

It surprised Tom too – and shook him from his daze. He rubbed a palm across his face. 'I'm sure you want to hear more about what I saw,' he said, 'and why I stayed quiet.'

'I'm guessing there's more than one reason.'

Tom pinched the top of his nose. 'It's hard to know where to begin. But the first thing you've got to appreciate is this: I didn't know that Father Galvin was dead. He didn't look good, but I couldn't see his face. I saw Helen's back. That's all. Then I ran. Well, I couldn't run . . . because of the snow. I moved as quickly as I could and hid around the corner. I was scared someone would see me. When I'd calmed down a bit, I went back to the shed. The Lord knows how, but I managed to spin the rest of you a tale about the door being locked.'

'And it was definitely Helen you saw?'

Tom straightened his back. 'Please,' he said, voice crackling with irritation, 'after everything you've done, after the way you wrung her name out of me, don't say you doubt my word.'

'Sorry,' said Conor. 'I didn't mean to doubt you. I'm trying to get everything straight in my head.'

'Well, have no doubt about this: I saw Helen Minogue. I would have known her anywhere. She was different from the other women in the village.'

Conor recalled Tess saying that, while most of the blondes in Kilmitten looked like they dyed their hair with Domestos, Helen's grooming was so perfect she might have been French. He knew what she meant. Even from behind, none of them would have mistaken Helen Minogue for anyone else.

Tom continued: 'Later that night, when your dad told us that Father Galvin was dead, I was terrified. I kept thinking that maybe I could have saved him . . . and that if anyone found out, I'd be sent away. After that, one lie spawned another until I figured it was too late to change my story.' He hesitated. 'I don't expect you to understand this, but I learned to box it all off. What happened, what I'd seen, was in a special compartment.

'Sometimes, though, for no reason, that would change. I remember the feeling: it was like someone banging a stick against a sheet of metal. Like the truth was desperate to get out. I wouldn't be able to think of anything else. Then I'd withdraw. I couldn't describe what was happening, or explain why, so the only option was to say nothing. Nina used to get annoyed with me. "Why won't you tell me what's wrong?" she'd ask. I'd pretend it was no big deal. That I was just a bit down. Then I'd lie there, waiting it out, hoping I'd feel normal again the next day.'

'You were never tempted to talk to her?'

'No. Actually, there was one occasion but . . . What's that phrase the bishops used when they were trying to explain why they hadn't reported child abuse?'

'I'm sorry,' said Conor. 'I'm not with you.'

'"Mental reservations": that's it. I convinced myself that no good would come of telling the truth. That in this case a lie wasn't really a lie. Nina was very close to her mother, not so close to her father. By pointing the finger at Helen, I'd be hurting Nina.'

'The time you came close to telling her, was that when you were splitting up?'

'How did you know?'

'She told me.'

'For truth? Why did she—'

'Obviously, she had no idea it was her mother you'd seen, but she got the impression you knew more than you were saying.'

'Look . . . whatever else you think about what I did . . . you've got to accept that I wanted to protect Nina. I loved her.' Tom was having difficulty with the words, his sentences coming out in fragments. 'Afterwards . . . after we'd broken up, I mean . . . I realised I couldn't speak. People would . . . They'd suspect that I was trying to harm the Minogues because of the way Nina had left me. They'd claim I was settling a score. In other circumstances, that's . . . that's what I would have thought.'

'Did you have any idea why Helen might hurt Leo Galvin?'

'At the start, not a notion in the world. That's one of the reasons I was so confused. Later, it did occur to me that there could have been something between them, that this was the most likely explanation. But, straight up, I thought of other motives too. Like, I wondered if Father Galvin might have interfered with Hugh – or with Nina.'

Tom's words were punctuated by rattling breaths. Conor was surprised by how dirty he felt. Although accustomed to being there on the worst day of people's lives, he was usually at one remove. He interviewed reluctant witnesses, comforted victims, came down hard on suspects. But on those occasions he always maintained some detachment. Strangely, even getting shot had felt less personal than this. In the Avondhu, he'd been an unlucky bystander. An observer who'd got in the way. Here, he was a participant. Tom was his friend. As was Nina. What he decided to do might shape the rest of their lives.

'Don't take this the wrong way,' he said, knowing even

as the words left his mouth that there was no right way to take them, 'but did you ever think your parents deserved to know what you'd seen? That if the crime had been solved it would have made their lives easier?'

'Yes and no.' Tom paused before continuing. 'This is hard to explain, but the more time passed, the more I believed that breaking my silence would make everything worse. Not only would someone my parents admired be in the frame for Father Galvin's death, but they'd also be upset that I hadn't spoken earlier. And then, after the TV documentary was shown and the O'Grady theory caught fire, everything changed. Even though I was thousands of miles away, I could tell they were . . . not happy – happy would be going too far – but they were relieved. They were able to move on.'

He was crying hard now, his face twisted with misery, his body slumped forward. Conor got up to look for tissues. Unable to find any, he went to the bathroom and removed a roll of toilet paper. He placed it beside Tom, who wrapped a substantial wad around one hand and made an attempt to clean himself up. Conor returned to his chair.

'What now?' asked Tom.

'I don't know.' So much of what Conor had said earlier had been bluster. When he'd arrived at the apartment, he hadn't yet made up his mind about where to take this. He still hadn't. What would he advise anyone else to do? Go to the guards. He *was* the guards. And yet . . .

'We can't just sleep on it,' said Tom. 'I'm meeting the taoiseach at nine in the morning.'

'Can you delay the meeting?'

'By half an hour maybe, but that's all. Won't you have to work in the morning?'

'I'm sick.'

Tom tore off another hank of toilet paper and gave him a sceptical look.

'It's a long story,' said Conor, rubbing his shoulder. It always hurt when he got tired. 'Listen, I want you to understand: now that I know what happened, I can't unknow it. I almost wish I could, but I can't.'

Thoughts flew around his head. He pictured Hannah Galvin, waiting for news. He pictured his dad and Ginny. He wondered why Helen had attacked Father Galvin. What had happened to give rise to such fury? He thought of the ways in which they were all bound together. It reminded him of those graphics you saw in the Sunday supplements, the curved lines connecting Europe's royal families or Hollywood's power players. In their small world, everybody was connected.

'Don't think I'm crackers here,' he said. 'Actually, there's every danger that I am, but my head's a mess and yours is worse. I think we need someone else to help us think this through.'

'You're not serious,' said Tom. 'You want to bring in an outsider – and at this hour of the night? What are you going to do – ring one of your garda buddies? Fuck it, why not call a press conference and be done with it?'

'That's not what I said. I'm not talking about an outsider. I'm thinking about Tess. I happen to know she's in Dublin.'

'What time is it?'

'One o'clock. Late for most people, but not for her.'

For the first time, Tom was perfectly still. The two sat, not speaking, hardly breathing. 'Okay,' he said eventually, 'call Tess. You're not going to give her the full rundown on the phone, though, are you?'

'No, no. But if I say we both want to talk to her, she'll get a cab over here. I presume she's staying in a hotel in town.'

Tom rose from the sofa. 'I'll wash my face.'

Conor took out his phone. He didn't know how to explain the situation to Tess. Neither could he say what he expected her to do. He wasn't even sure that she was the best person to contact. What he did know was that he couldn't deal with this on his own.

Chapter 44

Tess was intrigued by Conor's call. Why was he in Tom's apartment? And what was so urgent that he needed to see her at one in the morning?

'You do know it's well past my bedtime?' she said. 'I had a late night at the funeral and I've had an emotional evening. In fact, we were about to turn in.'

'We?' said Conor.

She told him where she was. Given that he'd spent so long encouraging her to contact Nina, she'd expected him to be pleased they were together. Instead he sounded put out. Sometimes he was hard to fathom.

'How did you know I was still in Dublin?' she asked.

'I was in Kilmitten today. Your mam told me.'

Curiouser and curiouser.

'By the way,' he said, 'just so you're clear about this, we want your perspective. Not Nina's.'

'You're not going to tell me what it's about?'

'It's kind of sensitive. When you get here you'll understand, trust me.'

And more curious still.

Tess stretched out her legs. She was tired, and her flight was at ten in the morning. She had planned on bedding down in Nina's spare room. They'd shared the champagne and most of the wine, and she didn't fancy going back to the hotel. She asked herself if she really wanted to head out into the cold on a mystery mission. Then she remembered Tom's kindness. Not only had he rescued her from the horrors of the O'Grady brothers, he'd listened as she meandered through her mother's story. If he needed her help, he deserved to have it.

'All right, then,' she said. 'You say Tom's place is nearby?'

'On a better night, you'd walk it. I'll text you the address. Don't hang about, will you?'

Given what he was asking, Tess didn't think Conor was in the best position to lay down terms and conditions. She was too tired to argue, however, so she assured him that she'd ring a taxi and see them shortly.

What she hadn't counted on was Nina getting stroppy. 'Why can't I come with you?' she asked.

'He didn't say.'

'That means there's no reason. He just didn't expect us to be together.'

'I suppose.'

'I've missed so much,' said Nina. 'Please don't exclude me.'

Tess looked at Nina's red-rimmed eyes and concave cheeks. They'd spent a large part of the evening discussing the most intimate details of their lives: one talking about her biological father being a violent criminal, the other about the ugly disintegration of her marriage. They'd talked about their mothers' lives and their own lives.

'I hate having so many regrets,' Nina had said.

'Only very shallow people regret nothing,' Tess had replied, 'or so I like to think.'

'What's wrong with shallow? I'm all for shallow.'

They'd laughed then, and the tension between them had started to unwind. Tess couldn't shunt these past few hours aside. She couldn't say, 'My other friends have called, so I'm off now. See you in another twenty-five years.'

'You know what, Nina?' she said. 'You're dead right. Let's tidy ourselves up and find out what's going on.'

From the back of the taxi, Tess watched as young people flitted about, the weather no impediment to their revelry. Icy rain tapped against the windows, and the car made a skeetering sound as it splashed through puddles. The sky was a yellowish grey. The girls wore sequined party dresses, their ankles wobbling from the combined effect of strong drink and spike heels. Two or three sported antlers. Tess wondered if they went out every night during December. She hoped so. For many years, she'd done the same. Oh, to have their energy.

'They'll catch their death, those girls,' said Nina, with a smile.

When they got to the apartment block, Tess played it safe. Best not to let Tom and Conor know that Nina was with her.

'It's me,' she said.

'We're on the first floor,' said Conor, as he buzzed her into the building. 'Third door on the left.'

Tess had never been skilled at reading expressions, but when Conor opened the door, even she couldn't miss the alarm on his face.

'Were you not listening?' he said. 'Sorry, Nina, but I asked Tess to come on her own.'

Bravado took over and Tess bustled her way in, yanking Nina by the arm. 'Come on,' she said, quickly followed by, 'It's absolutely freezing in here. Lads, you need to put the heating back on. And would you mind making some coffee? I'm parched.'

If her curiosity had been piqued by the late-night summons, it was now at fever pitch. Why were Conor and Tom so worked up? Did one of them have a problem at home? Had some other family-related issue popped up? Or, and she feared this was the most likely explanation, was the emergency connected to Conor's Father Galvin obsession? Whatever was going on, there was no reason to send Nina back out into the night. If they insisted on being awkward, they would have to cope without Tess's advice.

'If I'm not wanted . . .' said Nina, with a tinkle of nervous laughter.

'Of course you're wanted,' replied Tess. 'You're with me.'

They were in the kitchen now, Conor bending over to fiddle with the coffee machine. 'We'll have a coffee, anyway,' he mumbled, 'but perhaps we should leave it at that. I probably shouldn't have called.'

'Ah, here . . .' started Tess, her words coming to an abrupt halt when Tom entered the room.

His face was swollen – had he been crying? – and his suit looked like he'd stolen it from a scarecrow. Tess had thought Nina looked rough, but compared to Tom, she was ready for the cover of *Vogue*.

'Is there a problem?' she said. 'I thought you had an important day tomorrow.'

'I do.' His gaze darted past her towards Nina. 'Oh, God,' he said, looking at Nina like she was a white-hot coal, a vial of ricin, something not to be touched.

Tess had been in quite a few bizarre situations, but she couldn't think of anything to compare with this. 'What's going on?' she said.

'Nothing,' said Conor, still playing with the coffee machine. 'It can wait.'

'Yeah, yeah, yeah, and the rest. Half an hour ago, you were all urgency. "You've got to get over here," you said. So I do as you ask, only for you to say, "Meh, maybe my problem isn't such a big deal after all. Why don't we have a coffee and forget about it?" Seriously, Conor, this isn't fair. I'm entitled to know what's happening.'

'What did I do?' asked Nina.

'Nothing,' repeated Conor.

Tom made a small noise, a cross between a catch of breath and a moan. 'We'll have to tell them,' he said. 'They're going to find out at some stage.'

Conor looked up. 'This isn't the right time.'

'It's my story, and I want to tell it.'

*

They sat in the half-light, Tom and Conor on the sofa, Nina and Tess across the room in two outsize armchairs. The strange preface, the furtive looks, the off-beam comments had warned Tess to expect trouble. Still, when Conor and Tom began, she had difficulty grasping their words. It was as if they were communicating in Morse code: the sounds were familiar, but she didn't know what they meant.

From time to time, she intervened. When Tom spoke about seeing Helen Minogue, she gasped. When Conor spoke about this not turning out the way he'd expected, she wanted to pick up one of the ugly ornaments and throw it at him. 'Is that a fact?' she snapped. 'It's a bit late for regrets now.'

He didn't reply.

What have I done? she thought. *Why did I bring Nina here?*

Nina was oddly composed. Her lips trembled. She fidgeted with her rings. But there were no histrionics. Her tears were silent, her comments brief. 'The poor man,' she said, and 'I never would have known. Never.'

Tess worried that Nina had gone into shock. Proper shock where your throat closes over, your blood pressure plummets and your limbs lose all feeling. She should be talking about her mother. She should be making noise. Tess turned towards her and reached out a hand.

Nina took it, squeezed and gave a nervous smile. 'I'm okay,' she whispered.

When Tom and Conor had finished, she said simply, 'What happens now?'

Before either had an opportunity to answer, Tess rushed in. 'Does anything have to happen?'

'What do you mean?' asked Conor.

'Why not let it rest? What do you know for sure? Nothing. You think Helen was seeing the priest. But Hannah Galvin is how old? She could have got it wrong. And Tom reckons he saw Helen. So what? He was a child. And he'd been drinking. It's all mights and maybes. I've said from the start that there was nothing to be gained by resurrecting this. We're talking about something that happened half a lifetime ago. Let it stay there.'

Tom's head jerked up, but he said nothing.

'It doesn't make sense,' continued Tess. 'Helen's a good person. You know that. I met her yesterday at the funeral. We were talking about Nina. She asked me about Daisy. I can't believe she'd hurt someone and be able to keep it to herself.'

'People do,' said Conor. 'It happens all the time. If it didn't, every crime would be solved.'

Tess had to accept that this was true. She ran the possibilities around her head. She didn't want to believe that Helen was guilty. Not just for Nina's sake, but for her own. She didn't want to admit that someone she liked had been to blame for Leo Galvin's death. When they were children, Nina's mother had made the best hot chocolate. In the summer, she'd always given them orange juice from a carton. At home, Tess had only ever had juice from a tin and even that had been considered a treat. She remembered how Helen had allowed them to wear her earrings and spray her perfume. To this day, all it took was one whiff of Rive Gauche and Tess was transported back to Nina's house. True, Helen had acquiesced with her husband in banishing Tess from their house, but Emmet was a bully. She'd probably been scared of him. She couldn't be a killer. She didn't look like one. She didn't feel like one. Then again, how many people did? That had been the genius of Noel O'Grady: he'd been such a plausible bad guy. Even though Helen must have gone missing from the party, nobody had noticed. It was like that old line: get a reputation as an early riser and you can sleep until midday. Nina's mother had been beyond reproach.

'Just say it is true,' she said to Conor. 'Just say she did hit Father Galvin or push him or whatever. She can't have meant to kill him. From what Hannah told you, they were in love.'

'So?' he replied.

'So why should what you've told us go any further than this room? It's not as though there's anything official about your investigation. Apart from the Galvins, no one knows. We can leave here tonight and never talk about it again.'

'Do you genuinely believe that?'

'Yes. Yes, I do. You probably aren't aware of this, but Nina and Julian have split up. Her marriage is over. Her life is hard enough. For her sake, for everyone's sake, let this Father Galvin obsession go.'

Tess had long ago concluded that life was rarely lived in absolutes. There were times for blurred edges, for walking away from trouble, for the grey in-between. This was one of those times.

Conor examined his hands.

Tom swayed to and fro.

Noise – a car horn, the rumble of a motorbike, a squeal of laughter – filtered in from outside.

Finally, Nina spoke. 'You can do whatever you like,' she said. 'But I can't pretend this didn't happen. If I do, it's not as if what I know will evaporate. Like Tom said, it will always be there.' Tess went to speak, but Nina continued: 'You should have told me,' she said to Tom. 'I can see why you didn't and I'm . . . I don't have the right word . . . I'm touched that you tried to protect me. But it was too much. Too much to carry around.'

'I'm sorry,' he said.

'I can't understand why my mother would hurt Father Galvin.' Her voice broke, and she paused to compose herself. 'But I have to know why.' For a moment, she pressed her fingers against her eyes. 'If it's true, she has to admit it, and she has to face the consequences.'

'No!' said Tess. 'Please think about what you're saying. She doesn't have to do anything of the sort.'

'Yes, she does. Tess, I know you want to help, and I appreciate it. But this is my decision.'

'You don't have to make up your mind now. Take some time. We've been drinking all evening. You're upset. This isn't the way to deal with it.' Tess sent a pleading look to Conor and Tom. Well, to Conor anyway. Tom appeared to be in a trance.

Once more, it was Nina who spoke. 'One way or another I won't stop thinking about it. Delaying a day or a week won't change that. I'll just replay everything again and again and keep asking myself why.'

Tess was astonished by her lucidity. Her friend was far stronger than she had thought. More courageous too. Whatever was going on beneath the surface, she had somehow acquired a veneer of calm.

'The one thing I would ask,' said Nina, 'is that you allow me to talk to her. I can do it tomorrow. I'll call in sick to work. They'll cope without me for one day. Well, more than that, perhaps. We'll see.'

'Do you want me to come with you?' asked Conor.

'That would be good.'

'I'll come too if it would help,' said Tess, who was starting to accept that Nina wouldn't change her mind. 'I promise I won't interfere, but I'll be there if you need anything.'

'Thanks. I'd like that. Don't you have to go home, though?'

'They'll understand.'

'You're very lucky,' she said.

Tess willed herself not to cry. This wasn't the time. She remembered as a young woman realising that everyone had their own rules and codes and that sometimes these were hard to comprehend. She wouldn't have been capable of reacting like Nina.

Neither would she have been able to keep a secret like Tom. She thought of the days after Father Galvin's death, when the village had been convulsed by what had happened. She thought of the hullabaloo in the papers and on the TV. Tom's head must have been in turmoil, yet he hadn't said a word. And in later years – when Julian Heaney had arrived, when Nina had cheated on him, when the documentary had been shown – he had maintained his silence. How he'd managed it, she would never know.

True, Tess had said little about her mother's rape, but she'd always felt like it wasn't her tale to tell.

For a little while, they sat in the gloom, the four of them together again. Tess's tiredness returned. She longed for her bed, not that she'd be able to sleep. She wanted to be at home in Willowthorpe with Miles. She wanted Daisy in the next room so she could kiss her soft hair and inhale her gorgeous Daisy smell.

Tom sighed. 'You must be wondering what I'm going to do.'

'Yes,' she said. There was nothing to be gained by pretending otherwise. She glanced at Conor and Nina for support. Both were lost in their own worlds.

'I won't claim I don't have a choice,' he said, 'because I do. I could brazen it out. I could turn up in the morning and accept the promotion. I could trot up to the Park, shake hands with the president and pose for the photos. I could do the job, working like crazy so that, when the end did arrive, the pundits would say I wasn't the worst of all time, that I'd done the state some service. Still, they'd insist, I'd committed a grave error and had to go. For a short while, I'd be in disgrace. I'd be on every front page and all over Twitter. But six months later – no, six weeks later – I'd be forgotten. I'd be yesterday's scandal.'

'I'm sorry, Tom,' said Tess, 'I don't follow you.'

'What I'm saying, Tessy, is that I'm going to resign. I'll call my colleagues first thing in the morning. Then I'll go and see the taoiseach. There are other considerations, but I won't worry about them tonight.'

Nina rearranged herself in the leather chair. 'You don't have to step down.'

'I do,' said Tom. 'If I don't, I'll spend every day waiting for the story to emerge. To use that awful phrase, I used to think I'd "come to terms" with what had happened on the night Father Galvin died . . . and what I did afterwards. But it's been in my head for thirty-five years. I don't know that it will ever go away.'

'But—'

'And this may be hard to believe but . . . it's not as if the job means that much to me.'

'Please,' said Nina, 'you don't have to say that.'

'I do because it's true.'

Tess didn't doubt him. She thought back to their conversation in the graveyard and his seemingly flippant comments about promotion. She wondered if this was what he'd wanted to tell her last night. She was tempted to ask about Vanessa, but this wasn't the right time. 'Take care,' she said. It sounded silly. Her thoughts had turned to mush, though, and she wasn't able to come up with anything more appropriate.

Tom patted Conor on his bad shoulder. 'I'm going to try and get some sleep,' he said. 'We can talk again tomorrow.'

Chapter 45

After the rain, the sky had cleared, and the morning had a bright crystalline quality. Had they been travelling west for any other reason, Nina would have enjoyed the journey. Conor was driving. She was beside him. Tess was in the back, wearing large sunglasses, like a visiting movie star.

Nina had surprised herself by getting a couple of hours' sleep. Tess had stayed with her, flapping around like she wasn't sure what to do with herself. Her presence had been a useful distraction. If Nina was on her own, if she stopped to think, who knew where her brain would take her? As it was, her head was heavy and her mouth felt as if it was filled with gravel. The others didn't understand her muted reaction. They expected more fury, more tears.

There would be plenty of time for those.

She'd called her mother to say she was on her way to Kilmitten. 'Something's come up,' she'd said, 'and I want to have a word with you.'

'Aren't you at work?' her mam had replied.

Nina had lied, saying the school had been forced to close for a couple of days because the heating was broken.

Both Conor and Tess had asked again if she was sure about confronting her mother. Conor in particular believed she should take more time. Nina didn't agree. She had encouraged him to pursue the case. Helped him. Running away now would be wrong. She'd been timid about many things, but this was different. She needed to find out what had happened, and delaying wouldn't change that. She'd been relieved to discover that her father was in Cork meeting old medical friends. She'd also told Conor and Tess that, while she appreciated their support, she didn't want an audience. They'd agreed to wait in the car.

As they passed Portlaoise, Conor turned on the radio for the eleven o'clock news. The newsreader told them that plans for a cabinet reshuffle were shrouded in confusion following the sudden resignation of rural and regional affairs minister Tom Crossan.

'Oh,' said Nina.

'Turn it up there,' said Tess.

The reporter's sing-song voice filled the car. '"Shocked and stunned," is how one cabinet member described himself following the confirmation that his colleague Tom Crossan had resigned. Deputy Crossan first broke the news to independent colleagues in a series of early-morning phone calls. He later met the taoiseach. I understand he gave no specific reason for the decision, which has rocked the government and thrown plans for a cabinet reshuffle into disarray. I have been assured, however, that his resignation is not health-related.

'The Clare TD's move is all the more surprising given that he'd been widely tipped for a move to the Department of Justice. Plans for the reshuffle have been put on hold. This has annoyed many here in Leinster House, with sources saying that some in government are livid. One senior source claimed the independent politician could rule out any future participation in government. "If he came crawling back, nobody would touch him," the source said. "He's just poisoned his career."'

'Poor Tom,' said Tess, managing to brush aside what she knew about the reason for his resignation. 'It wouldn't kill them to point out that he was good at his job. They'll miss him. The rest of them are useless.'

'Shush,' said Conor.

'Given the shaky nature of the government's majority, questions have also been raised about the administration's future. It's understand the outgoing minister has informed colleagues that he will stay on the back-benches for now and that he will support the government from there. This has yet to be confirmed, however, and observers aren't ruling out a snap election.'

The bulletin continued with news about a possible bus strike and a kidnapped greyhound. After a brief diversion for sport, the current affairs programme returned to Tom's resignation. Breathless correspondents, deep-voiced analysts and minor-league politicians speculated about the possible reasons. They spoke, too, about the febrile atmosphere in the Dáil. 'No one wants an election,' they said. Plainly this was a lie for each one sounded more excited than the last.

You could practically hear the saliva dripping from their chops.

Nina zoned out. A piercing pain had developed over her eyes and under her cheekbones. There was something absurd about Tom being on the news. This was about her family, his family, their village. Obviously it was also about the Galvins. But listening to the wider repercussions on the radio made her lightheaded. It wasn't as though the ways of the media were unfamiliar to her. She'd met Julian because he'd wanted to put Kilmitten on the television. During the recession, his father had been a regular fixture in the papers. He'd even featured on a TV documentary, squashing designer shopping bags into the boot of his Lexus while his building business collapsed around him, a reporter asking if he had a message for his impoverished investors. Nina had felt detached from all of that. Now, though, the story was personal, and she didn't want any part of it to be feasted on by others.

Unwelcome thoughts were seeping into her head. She thought of Tom, and the blend of cowardice, kindness and misplaced loyalty that had led to his silence. She wondered whether his political career, his relentless desire to campaign and fix and renovate, had been motivated by the secret he'd kept. Had he been trying to compensate for not telling the truth, or was that too simplistic? *Oh, Tom*, she thought, *I didn't deserve your loyalty.* She thought of Bea, Alannah and Julian and what she would tell them. She thought of Tess and Ginny. It was hard to comprehend that, only hours earlier, Tess had told her about Ginny being raped.

Most of all, she thought of her mother. She tried telling herself that Tom had been mistaken or that there was some other explanation. She pictured her mam in her everyday clothes, her soft trousers and cashmere sweater. Her brown eyes would widen with astonishment. She'd laugh her musical laugh and say, 'Oh, Nina, pet, you've got it all wrong. What actually happened was . . .' And Nina would feel foolish and cheap for having doubted her.

She was jolted out of her reverie by Conor. 'If you need anything,' he said, 'just shout. We can stop if you want a coffee or a bottle of water.'

'Or anything at all,' added Tess, a strained brightness to her voice.

Nina assured them that she was fine.

The closer they got to Kilmitten, the more anxious she became. She tried to focus on the landscape. She'd always loved the approach from the east, and the way the village and surrounding fields stretched out like a tapestry in front of her. Today, those fields were sprinkled with a wintry glitter. Every inch of road was familiar, every house and tree. She imagined giving a guided tour: 'You see that boreen?' she'd say. 'That's the shortcut to Toomey's Hill. We used to play there when we were kids. And the bend in the road? That was where Noel O'Grady crashed his car. He was drunk, of course. If you look to your left, that's where the phone box used to be. Not, mind you, that many people used it – it was always broken. Oh, and that house on our right, the grey one with the red creeper? I grew up there.'

*

Nina's mother spoke in a quiet voice. 'You probably won't believe me,' she said, 'but I always thought today would come. Don't get me wrong, I didn't think it would be you approaching me. I reckoned it would be Flan or some other guard, maybe even Conor.'

'Why Conor?' asked Nina

'The other day, at the funeral, Tess said he was asking questions about Leo's death. He's a clever man, and I wondered if he'd be the one to see through the Noel O'Grady story. When you called this morning, I had the feeling that this was what you wanted to talk about. The surprise is Tom. It had never occurred to me that somebody might have seen us.'

Nina straightened her back and, briefly, closed her eyes. She had expected to bargain and haggle. She had expected obfuscation and denials. Once again, what she was hearing was at odds with what she'd anticipated. 'You're telling me that everything I put to you is true? You had an affair with Father Galvin and later, for whatever reason, you killed him?'

'When you phrase it like that, it sounds very harsh. It sounds unforgivable. But, and I can appreciate why you'd be sceptical about this, it was all a lot more complex. I didn't set out to kill him. Of course I didn't.'

'Tell me about it, then. I've got plenty of time.'

Her mother, who was in the middle of the beige sofa, tipped her head towards the sitting-room window. 'Will you not invite Conor and Tess in? They must be very cold out there.'

'They're fine. They don't want to come in. This isn't about them.'

Conor had bought coffee and sandwiches from the Cherry Tree café, and the two were sitting in his car listening to the radio, monitoring the upheaval caused by Tom's resignation. They couldn't risk going home, they said. Not yet. Flan and Ginny would have more questions than they'd be able to answer.

'Okay,' said her mother, her voice faltering slightly, 'nothing I say will be easy for you, but I want you to know that I never meant to kill Leo. The truth is I loved him. And what Hannah said is right: he loved me. Or, at least, I thought he did.'

'I need to know how it started.'

'Quite suddenly, actually. We got talking while I was in the church doing flowers for a wedding. I remember I was in front of the altar, fiddling about with some roses. He was sitting in the front row. We started chatting. Up until that point, I'd viewed him as "the priest": the man who said Mass and heard confessions and visited old people. I think we talked about books or politics. Something non-religious, anyway. The connection was immediate. After that day, we kept on finding excuses to meet until . . . Well, you don't need to hear all the details, do you?'

Nina's eyes locked onto her mother. 'You must have known the relationship couldn't go anywhere.'

'To begin with, I didn't think that far ahead. I was unhappy at home. I'd come to realise that I'd married the wrong man. I'd met someone else, someone whom I believed was the right man. Thinking didn't really come into it. I was in love. Simple as that.'

'Except it wasn't simple. And please don't pin your own bad behaviour on Dad.'

'I'm not. I'm just saying it wasn't a very warm marriage. It wasn't what I'd hoped for.'

Nina rested her face in her palms before speaking again. 'Forgive me for pointing this out, but compared to many people around here, I would have thought your life was pretty good. Dad always looked after you. He looked after all of us. We had nice clothes and meals in restaurants and foreign holidays when most people in the village thought a bag of chips was a big treat. And I'm not just talking about people who didn't have the money for anything else. There were plenty who spent their money in the pub or at the races rather than on their family. Dad was never mean.'

'I didn't say he was. But it's possible to be generous with money and mean with everything else. You must know that. I would have swapped every bloody holiday for a few laughs, for some affection, that sense of being kindred spirits. I wanted to feel like I was with the right person.'

Nina could understand. How she envied people who found, and recognised, the right one. She figured that both Conor and Tess had done this. About Tom, she was starting to have doubts. 'I can appreciate all of that,' she said. 'That sort of connection is what most of us want. But—'

'But compared to many women, my burden was light. Is that what you were going to say?'

'Yes.'

'I agree. Your father was never cruel. Well, not physically, at any rate. He was cold, though. And he was controlling. Do you have any idea what it's like to be trapped with someone you don't love?'

'As it happens, I do. That's beside the point, though.'

'The truth, Nina, is that I loved Leo. He was funny and kind. He had a brain. He was wasted as a priest. He should have had another life with a wife and a family. Over the years, his memory has got distorted. People talk about the card games, but those were for company as much as anything else. He just happened to be a good poker player. And they say he was a moneylender. What of it? He lent money to people who needed it. He didn't charge interest. Where was the harm in that?' She tucked her pale blonde hair behind her ears. 'I wanted to be with Leo. He said he wanted the same. He told me he'd leave the priesthood so we could be together.'

The sitting room felt like it didn't contain enough air. Nina shook her head. 'Seriously, what were you going to do? Abandon me and Hugh so you could run away with the parish priest?'

'No! I couldn't have done that. I would have arranged it so that you could be with us.'

'Oh, come on, Dad wouldn't have allowed you to take us away.'

Her mother stood up and walked towards the window. 'I hadn't got everything figured out, but I was confident that it would happen. We would be together. And then . . .' Her words tapered off.

'And then what?' asked Nina.

'And then, that Christmas, the Christmas of 'eighty-one, he changed his mind. He told me he'd been to see his parents and realised he couldn't abandon the priesthood. One of his brothers had trained to be a priest but had left before being ordained. Leo said his parents were old and that his vocation was what kept them going. "If I left, it would be the death of them," he said.' She paused. 'Christ, that Christmas was grim. I was in shock. Emmet was in bad humour. You were maundering about the place. It was only later that you told us about being bullied at Millmount. The only reason I went to Haulie and Cora's party was because I hoped to talk to Leo. I was convinced I could persuade him that he was wrong. With hindsight, I was far too keyed up. I was too emotional.'

'So what happened?'

Nina's mother turned, ran a hand through her hair. 'He wouldn't see sense. In fact, it was worse than that. He said we should probably cool it for a while. There was a danger, he claimed, that people would gossip about us. I kept on at him. I kept telling him he was making a mistake, that we deserved to be together. My life wouldn't be worth living, I said, if I had to stay with my husband.' Her words were pouring out now, no space between them, no pause for breath. 'I was upset. I was seething. I begged him to think again. It got heated, and he threw his glass against the wall. I pushed him but I didn't mean to hurt him. I swear I didn't. He toppled back and hit his head against a cupboard. I didn't know what to do. There was nothing I could do.

You've got to believe me. The last thing I would have wanted was to hurt him.'

She walked back to the sofa and sat down again, as though all her energy was spent.

Nina gripped the edge of her chair. 'So you just ran away and left him on the floor? Did you not see that he was in trouble?'

'You've got to realise, Nina, I was petrified. I was in a state of panic. I was shaking. Everything had happened so quickly. When I got back to the front room no one seemed to notice. Everyone had been drinking. There was music and chatter and a raucous sort of atmosphere. If it had been quiet, if there had been fewer people, I could never have hidden the state I was in. Plus, and you'll have to take my word on this, I had no idea Leo was so seriously injured.'

'Before long you did.'

'Yes.'

'Did it not occur to you that you could have prevented his death? That if you'd fetched Dad, you might have been able to save him?'

Her mother's face was jaded, washed out. Every one of her seventy-four years was visible. 'How would I have explained what had happened? What would I have said about the shattered glass? Once I'd taken those initial steps back to the front room, once I'd left Leo behind me, I couldn't go back.'

'Yes, you could. You could have found an excuse.'

'No! That's not true.' Her mother's voice wobbled. 'But don't think it hasn't eaten away at me. I've spent every day since thinking, *What if, what if.* My mind goes back and,

I swear to you, the scene is so real it seems like it was only last week.'

Although Nina had already known much of the story, hearing her mother's words made it different. Something shifted within her. Fleetingly, she thought about what would have happened if Tom had come forward at the time. Their lives would have been very different. Hugh had been a small child. His mother would have been taken away. Something else struck her: how few female killers there were. Most were notorious, their faces and nicknames known in every house, their crimes the subject of best-selling books and lurid documentaries. She couldn't picture her mother as part of that grisly gallery.

'What about the days after the party?' she asked. 'There was chaos in the village. Everyone was pointing the finger at everyone else. Knowing what you'd done, how did you keep quiet? How did you go to the funeral and shake hands with his family? It's not . . . normal.'

Her mother blinked several times, as though resurfacing after a long time under water. 'In my head, I went to another place. I won't say I bargained with God. That would be wrong. I bargained with the world. I said, "Let me get over this and I'll be the best wife and mother ever. I'll stay here and never step out of line again." I saw staying with your father, doing everything he wanted, as a sort of penance.'

'Oh, listen to yourself, would you?' said Nina. 'You make it sound like you were a child trying to slither away from a minor offence, like you'd stolen fifty pence from the Mass collection or something. That you hadn't meant to hurt

Father Galvin is neither here nor there. You attacked him – and you killed him.'

'I know that what I'm saying sounds stupid, wrongheaded, but I'm trying to be honest with you. As I saw it, the best thing I could do was to stay here and do what everyone asked. So, in the days after Leo's death, I concentrated on staying out of trouble. I remember when your father found out about you and Tess being in the shed with the boys, he decided he didn't want you palling around with her any more. He'd been chuntering on about the poor girl for ages. She was a bad influence, he said. I'd always disagreed. But after that . . . I decided I'd have to give in.'

'You do know that Ginny was flattened by what you did? Tess said it upset her for years afterwards.'

'I'm very sorry about that. They both deserved better.'

'What I'll never get,' said Nina, 'is how you've managed to keep everything to yourself ever since. You've had endless opportunities to confess. Instead you stayed quiet and got on with your life. I mean, did you not feel guilty? Father Galvin had a family who loved him. According to Conor, they still mourn him.'

Her mother made a gesture with her hands, like she was sweeping this aside. 'I loved him too,' she said. 'Don't forget that.'

Nina slumped forward again and fixed her gaze to the floor. It occurred to her that this would be easier if her mother displayed a sudden flash of evil. If she revealed a cloven hoof. If there was a stench of sulphur. But in her navy trousers and baby-blue sweater, a silver chain at her neck, she looked the same as ever. She sounded the same. Admittedly, there was something impenetrable about her, but that had always been the case.

Although Nina was angry, she didn't have the right phrases, or the energy, to express her rage. She felt drained. Scared. Most of all, she felt a dark, bottomless sadness.

For some time, they sat in silence. The church bell clanged for three o'clock. Before long, the light would be gone.

Finally, her mother spoke. 'What do you want me to do?' she asked.

Chapter 46

Kilmitten, June 2017

A walk, they'd decided, would be best. There was nowhere else the four could talk without drawing an audience. They'd arranged to meet on the boreen near Toomey's Hill. Tom was early. There were other things he should have been doing, but it was Sunday, and everyone was entitled to a day of rest. When he'd told Vanessa about his plans, she'd shrugged; her reflex reaction. He'd grown accustomed to long silences punctuated by tart remarks. He didn't blame her. The truth and everything that followed had been hard for her to accept.

'You're not the person I thought you were,' she'd said. He couldn't argue. Their ambitions had been entwined, and his sudden departure from government had hit her like a bereavement. His less charitable side believed the resignation had caused her more upset than learning the truth about Father Galvin. Their relationship was over. They just hadn't acknowledged it yet. They needed to find the best way to bring their marriage to a close, and that wouldn't be easy. The three boys still looked at Tom with awe, as though he had the answer to every question they would ever ask. That this would change filled him with sadness.

His parents had shown more understanding than he'd deserved. At first, both had erupted. 'What sort of fellow are you?' his father had asked, his voice splintering with rage. His mother had cried. Within hours, their anger had shifted focus. Tom's dad said he'd never thought the day would come when he'd feel sorry for Emmet Minogue.

His mam wanted to tackle Helen. 'Does that woman have any idea what she did to us?' she asked.

Tom urged her not to do anything rash. 'You'll get your chance,' he promised. She did as he asked. As so many times before, his parents displayed an astonishing ability to absorb difficult news and carry on.

Two days before Christmas, Helen Minogue and her solicitor went to the garda station in Templemorris. In early spring, she made her first court appearance. Outside, a barrage of cameras followed her. In the papers, she was described as 'serene' and 'elegant', as if she was a visiting royal rather than a woman accused of killing a man. Among politicos there was suspicion that Tom's resignation was connected to the case. Helen being charged prevented the papers from trying to firm up the connection. Even on social media, people were circumspect. Attacking Tom was one thing; prejudicing a criminal prosecution was an altogether more serious matter. Oh, of course, out on the wilder fringes of the internet there were pages of ill-informed speculation. But railing against those was futile.

In Kilmitten, few knew the full story. That might change, but for now Tom was keeping his head down and getting on with what was left of his job. Many locals were unhappy. They'd liked having a ministerial car about the place and couldn't understand his decision.

He was the first to arrive at their meeting spot. The afternoon was a fine one, sunny with a scattering of thin white cloud. The fields and hedgerows were laden with flowers. On a day like this, all of his gripes about home drifted away.

After he'd stepped down from the cabinet, his alliance of independent politicians had imploded. Unable to agree on his replacement, they'd fought like rats in a sack. For a while, the country seemed to be lurching towards an election. Eventually, a web of deals led to the elevation of a cautious Tipperary man called Roy Comerford. The reshuffle also saw the re-emergence of Cyril Dinan. He was now the junior minister for mental health. Emboldened by his return from the wilderness, Cyril was trying to offend everyone he hadn't already offended. Tom stood back and watched. As promised, he continued to support the government. He would retire at the next general election. Already, a range of possible successors had let it be known that they were willing to serve. Tom wasn't sure what he would do. He didn't know if it would be possible to return to youth work. His father assured him that there'd always be a job in the filling station.

The courts had decided that Helen didn't represent a flight risk. She'd been given bail and was living with Nina in Dublin. Emmet remained in Kilmitten. He was distraught, all his bluster and arrogance blown away. Only the very hard-hearted wouldn't have had sympathy for him. Julian and Nina were getting a legal separation. He was living with his new partner. 'I hope they're very happy,' said Nina, 'because I definitely don't want him back.'

Tom and Nina had met several times. They had a lot to talk about. At their last meeting, a month or so ago, she'd told him that she spent most days picking shrapnel from her wounds. Occasionally, though, she felt like she was recovering the person she'd left behind many years before.

As he thought of her, there she was, sauntering up the track, Tess to one side, Conor a few paces behind. She'd done something to her hair. It was a bit shorter, a lot glossier. She was wearing a blue summer dress. Tom approved. She must have noticed his appraisal for the first thing she said was 'Today might be our summer. I didn't want to leave the poor dress mouldering at the back of the wardrobe.'

'We went shopping yesterday – in Dublin,' said Tess, who was wearing a similar dress in green.

'Well, Tess did most of the shopping,' said Nina.

'Some things never change,' said Conor.

They began rambling up the gentle slope of Toomey's Hill, the sun at their backs. In a couple of months' time, the grass might have withered to a dull yellow. That afternoon it was still a bright tufted green.

'So,' said Tess to Tom, 'did you hear Conor's news?'

'Nope, but I've a feeling you're about to fill me in.'

'I think that's his job.'

'Ah,' said Conor, 'so what it is . . . well, the thing is . . .'

'What he's trying to tell you,' said Tess, with an exaggerated sigh, 'is that he's been promoted. He's going to become a superintendent.'

'I'm kind of surprised,' said Conor. 'A couple of months ago, it was put to me that applying for promotion would do no harm. So, I said to myself, "Ah, sure why not?" I didn't really expect to succeed. But when it comes down to it, it's hard to reject a man with two bullet wounds.'

He was unusually inarticulate, and Tom could only assume that he was embarrassed by their contrasting fortunes.

In the months since Helen Minogue's court appearance, there had been more upheaval for Tess and Conor's family. The O'Gradys had gone on the rampage, telling anyone willing to listen that their father had been framed. One evening in Pilkington's Lounge, tensions had reached boiling point. Seánie, who'd been drinking for a large part of the day, started bellowing at Flan and Ginny. He claimed that Flan had always known about Helen's involvement in Father Galvin's death but had hushed it up because she was the doctor's wife.

'My mother went to the grave with that hanging over her,' he shouted.

Flan attempted to reason with him, as did several others. Seánie had passed the stage of reason. 'My father was the most decent man in Ireland,' he insisted. 'He never did a bad turn to anyone.'

Ginny didn't say anything, but made a noise suggesting she didn't agree with this portrayal of Noel O'Grady.

Seánie reared up in front of her. 'What the fuck would you know about my father?' he roared.

And so she told him.

Although Pilkington's was quiet, it didn't take long for the word to spill out to the wider world. A journalist made a few phone calls. Another reporter turned up in the village. Despite her departure from the spotlight, Tess still sold papers. She decided she'd have to take control of the story, so with the help of some contacts from her former life, she set up an interview with an English Sunday supplement. A pale young journalist called Jemima travelled to Willowthorpe. The pictures were taken by an old photographer friend. The magazine agreed not to name Noel O'Grady. Almost everybody thought the article was tasteful. This didn't stop the tabloids and websites from putting their own spin on it. A torrent of stories appeared with headlines like *Tess: My Mum's Rape Hell* and *Why Famous Beauty Won't Forgive Her Rapist Father.* She also had to try to explain it all to Daisy. 'I want you to understand,' she said, to her solemn-faced daughter, 'what a brave woman your grandmother in Ireland is.' When the initial fuss died down, several charities asked Tess if she'd be interested in working with them. She was now on the board of an organisation that provided counselling to rape victims.

For a while, the four sat at the top of the hill. They kicked off their sandals and savoured the feeling of grass between their toes. Mostly, their conversation was light.

Below them, the woods shimmered in the sun. In the near distance, Kilmitten was a series of white and grey smudges. A horseshoe of yellow houses marked the place where Tom's family home had once stood.

Tom said little. He just wanted to enjoy this sliver of time with his friends, the three people who knew him at his most basic.

Tess was first to move. 'Come on, Detective Superintendent Varley,' she said, with a wink. 'We'd better head home. If we're late, we'll be in serious trouble.' She got to her feet. 'Mam's having a special promotion tea for Conor.'

Conor put on his sandals and rose to join her. 'We've almost a full contingent: Dad, Ginny, Sharon, Miles, Daisy and Lauren.'

They didn't mention Paula. Relations between Conor's sister and the rest of the family were difficult. She'd been more upset than most by the revelations about her late father-in-law. In particular, she'd been annoyed by Tess's interview. 'That's my children's grandfather you're talking about,' she said, glossing over two important facts: she'd never liked Noel O'Grady and her children were almost thirty years old.

It was another reminder of how old crimes continued to mould their lives, the consequences rippling on and on.

After Tess and Conor had left, Nina talked about her mother. 'Some days I wonder if I did the right thing,' she said. 'If I'd just let it go, pretended that I didn't know anything, what would have happened?'

'I'm not sure I'm the man to ask for advice.'

She smiled. 'I hear you.'

'Anyway, Conor wouldn't have let it rest.'

'True. You're obviously still on good terms, though.'

Tom lifted his face towards the sun. 'We are. I'm not saying he did me a favour – that would be overstating it – but I've enough going on without holding a grudge.'

'Wise decision. Take it from the woman who fell out with her best friend for twenty-five years, these things can get out of control.'

As they began their descent of the hill, Tom thought of all the times they'd walked this land and these lanes. Of the stories they'd told. Of what they'd shared and what they'd kept hidden. Here they were, hurtling towards fifty, yet in his head they remained the same as they'd been in 1982. Among all the clichés about life, there was one that resonated with him. When you were young, you couldn't appreciate how quickly time passed. A tough week at school felt like a lengthy prison sentence. When you got older, one year faded into another. An entire decade could disappear.

'Did I tell you I met Hannah Galvin?' said Nina.

'Really? When?'

'Last week. Conor gave her my number. She found an excuse to come to Dublin, and we had a chat. I'd a feeling Mam's solicitor wouldn't approve, so I didn't tell anybody else.'

'What did you say?'

Nina took off her sunglasses and looked at Tom. 'I'd prepared a speech, then forgot it all. It was difficult, you know? But I felt it was something I had to do. In the end, I just said I was sorry and that all of us had liked Father Leo. She didn't say much. She's fairly fragile. She was gracious, though. Not bitter like many people would be.'

'Does she know there was a witness?'

'God, no. She has no idea. She said that while part of her wanted Mam to suffer, she knew this was wrong. "I'm sure Leo would want me to forgive her," she said.'

Nina put her glasses back on, and they continued on their way. A slight breeze fluttered around them, bringing with it the coconut smell of nearby furze bushes.

At the end of the boreen, they stopped. Tom ran a finger along the back of Nina's hand. 'I hope you're okay.'

'Thanks. There are times when I'm overwhelmed by everything that's happened. Living with my mother can be hard. Dad's still in a bad way. Hugh doesn't know what to do. Bea and Alannah are confused. Oh, and Julian doesn't believe in making life easy. But other people have been supportive. Conor and Tess have been amazing.' She took his hand. 'And you, obviously . . . I'm grateful that you've been there for me.'

Tom smiled and squeezed Nina's hand. 'Where else would I be?' he said, as they crossed the road and turned towards home.

Acknowledgements

Thanks to my editor Ciara Considine for her enthusiasm, her encouragement – and for making the book better. Thanks also to Hazel Orme for the fabulous copy-edit.

I'm very grateful to everybody at Hachette Ireland, especially Breda Purdue, Joanna Smyth, Ruth Shern and Jim Binchy. A big thank you to Susie Cronin for all of her publicity work.

Thanks to my agent Robert Kirby and also to Kate Walsh at United Agents.

My colleague, Dr Gavin Jennings, provided medical advice, while Sergeant Damian Hogan of the Garda Press Office gave me some guidance on garda matters. Many thanks to them. Obviously, any mistakes are my own.

Huge gratitude to all of the readers, bloggers and booksellers, especially Gwen Allman in The Company of Books in Ranelagh and Eoin Hoctor in Eason's in Shannon.

I'm incredibly grateful to all of the writers who have been so kind to me, especially the brilliant Patricia Scanlan.

For their support, forbearance and good humour at half five in the morning, thanks to my *Morning Ireland* colleagues and friends.

Massive thanks to my mother and father, Ruth and Tony English.

Finally, thank you to Eamon Quinn, who's just the best.